THE BLACK CABINET

Stories based on True Crimes are in

THE BLACK CABINET

Unlocked by
PETER LOVESEY

Library of Congress Cataloging-in-Publication Data

The Black Cabinet [edited by] Peter Lovesey. – 1st Carroll & Graf ed
    p. cm.

  ISBN 0-88184-513-2: $17.95

  1. Detective and mystery stories. I. Lovesey, Peter.
PN6120.95.045857   1989
808.83'872—dc20

First published by Xanadu Publications Ltd, London
First published in the United States of America by
Carroll & Graf Publishers, Inc. 1989 by arrangement
with Xanadu Publications Ltd.

Carroll & Graf Publishers, Inc.
260 Fifth Avenue,
New York, NY 10001.

Manufactured in Great Britain

Contents

PROLOGUE

PART ONE

INTERVAL

PART TWO

EPILOGUE

PETER LOVESEY
Introduction

A question commonly put to writers is *Where do you get your ideas from?* To a crime writer there can be a disturbing suggestion of suspicion in the enquiry. I've faced it myself and watched a good dinner go cold on my plate as I struggled to give a reassuring answer.

The truth is that the getting of ideas defies analysis. It is intuitive and personal, never quite the same. *The Black Cabinet* presents fourteen stories based on real crimes. To what degree any of the writers regarded real crime as the spark that inspired their stories is open to suggestion. What is certain — and fascinating — is their ingenuity in using and developing the facts of the cases.

Of course, writers sometimes *are* personally involved in crime, though not all, like William Sydney Porter, are so unfortunate as to have served a prison sentence, or would have turned it to such advantage as he. 'A Retrieved Reformation', which derived from an episode he heard from one of his cellmates, laid the foundation of a marvellous career as a short story writer. He also had the happy thought in the penitentiary of borrowing something else, from one of the guards, his pen-name, O. Henry.

Abraham Lincoln's more respectable involvement in crime, as a lawyer, provided him with personal experience of a strange case, 'The Trailor Murder Mystery', that he relates with characteristic lucidity. He is scrupulously objective, though unable finally to suppress his fascination in the mystery. As a straightforward presentation of a case it is, I think, a touchstone for this collection.

Lincoln permits himself one concluding paragraph of speculation. Others in these stories use speculation as the mainspring of their plots. Crime writers from Edgar Allan Poe onwards have enjoyed meeting the challenge of famous unsolved mysteries. In 'J. Habakuk Jephson's Statement', Sir Arthur Conan Doyle, a brave and tireless investigator in real life, offers his own ingenious solution to the mystery of the *Marie Celeste*.

Speculation tips over into the supernatural in Anthony Boucher's gruesomely wry horror story, 'They Bite', which begs the question whether such evil as that committed by the Bender family is ever totally suppressed. It is literally a haunting tale that lingers in the memory.

The range of this collection is becoming clear. Quite another approach is that of the writer who takes a real crime and fits it to a literary convention. Anthony Berkeley repeatedly drew on case histories to bring authenticity to his writing. With his novel, *Malice Aforethought*, written under his *alter ego* of Francis Iles, he became one of the great innovators of crime fiction. In 'The Wrong Jar', he plots in the traditional style, but adapts a real poisoning to the old-fashioned puzzle story so favoured by writers of the inter-war years. With its emphasis on timing and alibis it is a perfect opportunity for his amateur detective, Roger Sheringham, to point out the only logical solution.

Lillian de la Torre works in another convention in her short stories, the elegant pastiches of James Boswell's style which treat us to previously unheralded feats of detection from one of England's men of letters, Dr Johnson. In 'Milady Bigamy', Johnson applies some eighteenth century rationality to a case involving the Duchess of Kingsbury (or dare we say Kingston?). Incidentally, Lillian de la Torre's three novels, *Elizabeth is Missing*, *The Heir of Douglas* and *The Truth about Belle Gunness* are outstanding examples of true mysteries presented and solved in a fictional framework.

If your taste runs to realism, you should experience the heat and the festering hatred in Angela Carter's brilliant account of the hours leading up to the Borden murders in 'The Fall River Axe Murders'. Or the brutality of the lynchings in Miriam Allen de Ford's ironically titled 'Homecoming'. The nature of violence and the mixed feelings of fascination and guilt it arouses are explored to horrifying effect by Harlan Ellison in 'The Whimper of Whipped Dogs', as strong a portrayal of urban violence as I can remember reading.

That stories of such power can sit in a collection with the more amiable work of O. Henry and John Dickson Carr may bring shocks to the unwary. But then anybody who reads crime stories ought to expect shocks.

Ethical objections are sometimes raised over the use of real characters in fiction. It is unacceptable, the purists argue, to mix fact with fiction, as if it is some unfortunate practice invented by modern writers. It is, of course, a practice as old as literature itself. Nearly all novelists use real people in their writing. Not all of them are so reckless as to retain the original names, but some of the Victorians were quite fearless in this respect. The decorous Mrs Gaskell was obliged to write to the relatives of a murdered man to apologise for the distress she caused when she referred openly to the murder in *Mary Barton*. I am sure she was more careful after that, but I have no doubt that she continued to draw on real life for her inspiration. I am reminded of the rejection letter sent by a publisher to a would-be author: 'You say on the first page that all the characters are fictitious and bear no resemblance to any persons living or dead. Well, that's what's wrong with it.'

PROLOGUE

ABRAHAM LINCOLN

The Trailor Murder Mystery

ABRAHAM LINCOLN (1809 – 65) was an early and avid admirer of Poe, and his story 'The Trailor Murder Mystery' — appearing here for the first time in my collection — is based upon a real case in which he was involved as a young lawyer. It offers a fascinating glimpse into the rural life of the period, and any awkwardness of style is outweighed by its historical and sheer curiosity value: a noteworthy prologue to the collection.

In the year 1841, there resided, at different points in the State of Illinois, three brothers by the name of Trailor. Their Christian names were William, Henry and Archibald. Archibald resided at Springfield, then as now the seat of Government of the State. He was a sober, retiring, and industrious man, of about thirty years of age; a carpenter by trade, and a bachelor, boarding with his partner in business — a Mr Myers. Henry, a year or two older, was a man of like retiring and industrious habits; had a family, and resided with it on a farm, at Clary's Grove, about twenty miles distant from Springfield in a north-westerly direction. William, still older, and with similar habits, resided on a farm in Warren county, distant from Springfield something more than a hundred miles in the same north-westerly direction. He was a widower, with several children.

In the neighbourhood of William's residence, there was, and had been for several years, a man by the name of Fisher, who was somewhat above the age of fifty; had no family, and no settled home; but who boarded and lodged a while here and a while there, with persons for whom he did little jobs of work. His habits were remarkably economical, so that an impression got about that he had accumulated a considerable amount of money.

In the latter part of May, in the year mentioned, William formed the purpose of visiting his brothers at Clary's Grove and Springfield; and Fisher, at the time having his temporary residence at his house, resolved to accompany him. They set out together in a buggy with a single horse. On Sunday evening they reached Henry's residence, and stayed over night. On Monday morning, being the first Monday of June, they started on to Springfield, Henry accompanying them on horseback. They reached town about noon, met Archibald, went with him to his boarding house, and there took up their lodgings for the time they should remain.

After dinner, the three Trailors and Fisher left the boarding house in company, for the avowed purpose of spending the evening together in looking about the town. At supper, the Trailors had all returned, but Fisher was missing, and some enquiry was made about him. After supper, the Trailors went out professedly in search of him. One by one they returned, the last coming in after late tea time, and each stating that he had been unable to discover anything of Fisher.

The next day, both before and after breakfast, they went professedly in search again, and returned at noon, still unsuccessful. Dinner again being had, William and Henry expressed a determination to give up the search, and start for their homes. This was demonstrated against by some of the boarders about the house, on the ground that Fisher was somewhere in the vicinity, and would be left without any conveyance, as he and William had come in the same buggy. The remonstrance was disregarded, and they departed for their homes respectively.

Up to this time, the knowledge of Fisher's mysterious disappearance had spread very little beyond the few boarders at Myers', and excited no considerable interest. After the lapse of three or four days, Henry returned to Springfield, for the ostensible purpose of making further search for Fisher. Procuring some of the boarders, he, together with them and Archibald, spent another day in ineffectual search, when it was again abandoned, and he returned home.

No general interest was yet excited.

On the Friday, week after Fisher's disappearance, the Postmaster at Springfield received a letter from the Postmaster near William's residence, in Warren county, stating that William had returned home without Fisher, and was saying, rather boastfully, that Fisher was dead, and had willed him his money, and that he had got about fifteen hundred dollars by it. The letter further stated that William's story and conduct seemed strange, and desired the Postmaster at Springfield to ascertain and write what was the truth in the matter.

The Postmaster at Springfield made the letter public, and at once, excitement became universal and intense. Springfield, at that time, had a population of about 3,500, with a city organisation. The Attorney

General of the State resided there. A purpose was forthwith formed to ferret out the mystery, in putting which into execution, the Mayor of the city and the Attorney General took the lead. To make search for, and, if possible, find the body of the man supposed to be murdered, was resolved on as the first step.

In the pursuance of this, men were formed into large parties, and marched abreast, in all directions, so as to let no inch of ground in the vicinity remain unsearched. Examinations were made of cellars, wells, and pits of all descriptions, where it was thought possible the body might be concealed. All the fresh, or tolerably fresh graves in the graveyard, were pried into, and dead horses and dead dogs were disinterred, where, in some instances, they had been buried by their partial masters.

This search, as has appeared, commenced on Friday. It continued until Saturday afternoon without success, when it was determined to dispatch officers to arrest William and Henry, at their residences, respectively. The officers started on Sunday morning; meanwhile, the search for the body was continued, and rumours got afloat of the Trailors having passed, at different times and places, several gold pieces, which were readily supposed to have belonged to Fisher.

On Monday, the officers sent for Henry, having arrested him, arrived with him. The Mayor and Attorney Gen'l took charge of him, and set their wits to work to elicit a discovery from him. He denied, and persisted in denying. They still plied him in every conceivable way, till Wednesday, when, protesting his own innocence, he stated that his brothers, William and Archibald, had murdered Fisher; that they had killed him, without his (Henry's) knowledge at the time, and made a temporary concealment of his body; that, immediately preceding his and William's departure from Springfield for home, on Tuesday, the day after Fisher's disappearance, William and Archibald communicated the fact to him, and engaged his assistance in making a permanent concealment of the body; that, at the time he and William left professedly for home, they did not take the road directly, but, meandering their way through the streets, entered the woods at the North West of the city, two or three hundred yards to the right of where the road they should have travelled, entered them; that, penetrating the woods some few hundred yards, they halted and Archibald came a somewhat different route, on foot, and joined them; that William and Archibald then stationed him (Henry) on an old and disused road that ran near by, as a sentinel, to give warning of the approach of any intruder; that William and Archibald then removed the buggy to the edge of a dense brush thicket, about forty yards distant from his (Henry's) position, where, leaving the buggy, they entered the thicket, and in a few minutes returned with the body, and placed it in the buggy; that from his station he could and did distinctly see that the object placed in the buggy was a dead man, of the general appearance and size of Fisher; that William and Archibald then moved off with the buggy in the direction of Hickox's mill pond, and after an absence of half an hour, returned, saying they had put him in a safe place; that Archibald then left for town, and he and William found their way to the road, and made for their homes.

At this disclosure, all lingering credulity was broken down, and excitement rose to an almost inconceivable height. Up to this time, the well-known character of Archibald had repelled and put down all suspicions as to him. Till then, those who were ready to swear that a murder had been committed, were almost as confident that Archibald had had no part in it. But now, he was seized and thrown into jail; and indeed, his personal security rendered it by no means objectionable to him.

And now came the search for the brush thicket, and the search of the mill pond. The thicket was found, and the buggy tracks at the point indicated. At one point within the thicket, the signs of a struggle were discovered, and a trail from thence to the buggy track was traced. In attempting to follow the track of the buggy from the thicket, it was found to proceed in the direction of the mill pond, but could not be traced all the way. At the pond, however, it was found that a buggy had been backed down to, and partially into the water's edge.

Search was now to be made in the pond; and it was made in every imaginable way. Hundreds and hundreds were engaged in raking, fishing, and draining. After much fruitless effort in this way, on Thursday morning the mill dam was cut down, and the water of the pond partially drawn off, and the same processes of search again gone through with.

About noon of this day, the officer sent for William, returned having him in custody; and a man calling himself Dr Gilmore, came in company with them. It seems that the officer arrested William at his own house, early in the day on Tuesday, and started to Springfield with him; that after dark awhile, they reached Lewiston, in Fulton county, where they stopped for the night; that late in the night this Dr Gilmore arrived, stating that Fisher was alive at his house, and that he had followed on to give the information, so that William might be released without further trouble; that the officer, distrusting Dr

Gilmore, refused to release William, bur brought him on to
Springfield, and the Dr accompanied them.

On reaching Springfield, the Dr re-asserted that Fisher was alive,
and at his house. At this, the multitude for a time, were utterly
confounded. Gilmore's story was communicated to Henry Trailor,
who without faltering, reaffirmed his own story about Fisher's
murder. Henry's adherence to his own story was communicated to
the crowd, and at once the idea started, and became nearly, if not
quite universal, that Gilmore was a confederate of the Trailors, and
had invented the tale he was telling, to secure their release and escape.

Excitement was again at its zenith.

About three o'clock the same evening, Myers, Archibald's partner,
started with a two-horse carriage, for the purpose of ascertaining
whether Fisher was alive, as stated by Gilmore, and if so, of bringing
him back to Springfield with him.

On Friday a legal examination was gone into before two Justices,
on the charge of murder against William and Archibald. Henry was
introduced as a witness by the prosecution, and on oath re-affirmed
his statements, as heretofore detailed, and at the end of which he bore
a thorough and rigid cross-examination without faltering or exposure.
The prosecution also proved, by a respectable lady, that on the
Monday evening of Fisher's disappearance, she saw Archibald, whom
she well knew, and another man whom she did not then know, but
whom she believed at the time of testifying to be William, (then
present,) and still another, answering the description of Fisher, all
enter the timber at the North West of town, (the point indicated by
Henry,) and after one or two hours, saw William and Archibald return
without Fisher.

Several other witnesses testified, that on Tuesday, at the time
William and Henry professedly gave up the search for Fisher's body,
and started for home, they did not take the road directly, but did
go into the woods, as stated by Henry. By others, also, it was proved,
that since Fisher's disappearance, William and Archibald had passed
rather an unusual number of gold pieces. The statements heretofore
made about the thicket, the signs of a struggle, the buggy tracks, &c.,
were fully proven by numerous witnesses.

At this the prosecution rested.

Dr Gilmore was then introduced by the defendants. He stated that
he resided in Warren county, about seven miles distant from William's
residence; that on the morning of William's arrest, he was out from
the home, and heard of the arrest, and of its being on a charge of

the murder of Fisher; that on returning to his own house, he found Fisher there; that Fisher was in very feeble health, and could give no rational account as to where he had been during his absence; that he (Gilmore) then started in pursuit of the officer, as before stated; and that he should have taken Fisher with him, only that the state of his health did not permit. Gilmore also stated that he had known Fisher for several years, and that he had understood he was subject to temporary derangement of mind, owing to an injury about his head received in early life.

There was about Dr Gilmore so much of the air and manner of truth, that his statement prevailed in the minds of the audience and of the court, and the Trailors were discharged, although they attempted no explanation of the circumstances proven by the other witnesses.

On the next Monday, Myers arrived in Springfield, bringing with him the now famed Fisher, in full life and proper person.

Thus ended this strange affair and while it is readily conceived that a writer of novels could bring a story to a more perfect climax, it may well be doubted whether a stranger affair ever really occurred. Much of the matter remains in mystery to this day. The going into the woods with Fisher, and returning without him, by the Trailors; their going into the woods at the same place the next day, after they professed to have given up the search; the signs of a struggle in the thicket, the buggy tracks at the edge of it; and the location of the thicket, and the signs about it, corresponding precisely with Henry's story, are circumstances that have never been explained. William and Archibald have both died since — William in less than a year, and Archibald in about two years after the supposed murder. Henry is still living, but never speaks of the subject.

It is not the object of the writer of this to enter into the many curious speculations that might be indulged upon the facts of this narrative; yet he can scarcely forbear a remark upon what would, almost certainly, have been the fate of William and Archibald, had Fisher not been found alive. It seems he had wandered away in mental derangement, and, had he died in this condition, and his body been found in the vicinity, it is difficult to conceive what could have saved the Trailors from the consequence of having murdered him. Or, if he had died, and his body never found, the case against them would have been quite as bad, for, although it is a principle of law that conviction for murder shall not be had, unless the body of the deceased be discovered, it is to be remembered, that Henry testified that he saw Fisher's dead body.

PART ONE

SIR ARTHUR CONAN DOYLE

J. Habakuk Jephson's Statement

SIR ARTHUR CONAN DOYLE *(1859–1930) was, of course, the creator of the most celebrated detective of all time, Sherlock Holmes. 'J. Habakuk Jephson's Statement', one of his earliest and rarest published tales, is a fictional explanation of what could have happened aboard the notorious* Marie Celeste.

In the month of December in the year 1873, the British ship *Dei Gratia* steered into Gibraltar, having in tow the derelict brigantine *Marie Celeste*, which had been picked up in latitude 38°40', longitude 17°15' W. There were several circumstances in connection with the condition and appearance of this abandoned vessel which excited considerable comment at the time, and aroused a curiosity which has never been satisfied. What these circumstances were was summed up in an able article which appeared in the *Gibraltar Gazette*. The curious can find it in the issue for January 4, 1874, unless my memory deceives me. For the benefit of those, however, who may be unable to refer to the paper in question, I shall subjoin a few extracts which touch upon the leading features of the case.

'We have ourselves,' says the anonymous writer in the *Gazette*, 'been over the derelict *Marie Celeste*, and have closely questioned the officers of the *Dei Gratia* on every point which might throw light on the affair. They are of the opinion that she had been abandoned several days, or perhaps weeks, before being picked up. The official log, which was found in the cabin, states that the vessel sailed from Boston to Lisbon, starting upon October 16. It is, however, most imperfectly kept, and affords little information. There is no reference to rough weather, and, indeed, the state of the vessel's paint and rigging excludes the idea that she was abandoned for any such reason. She is perfectly watertight. No signs of a struggle or of violence are to be detected, and there is absolutely nothing to account for the disappearance of the crew. There are several indications that a lady was present on board, a sewing-machine being found in the cabin and some articles of female attire. These probably belonged to the captain's wife, who is mentioned in the log as having accompanied her husband. As an instance of the mildness of the weather, it may be remarked that a bobbin of silk was found standing upon the sewing-machine, though the least roll of the vessel would have precipitated it to the floor. The boats were intact and slung upon the davits; and the cargo, consisting of tallow and American clocks, was untouched. An old-fashioned sword of curious workmanship was discovered among some lumber in the fore-castle, and this weapon is said to exhibit a longitudinal striation on the steel, as if it had been recently wiped. It has been placed in the hands of the police, and submitted to Dr Monaghan, the analyst, for inspection. The result of his examination has not yet been published. We may remark, in conclusion, that Captain Dalton, of the *Dei Gratia*, an able and intelligent seaman, is of opinion that the *Marie Celeste* may have been abandoned a considerable distance from the spot at which she was picked up, since a powerful current runs up in that latitude from the African coast. He confesses his inability, however, to advance any hypothesis which can reconcile all the facts of the case. In the utter absence of a clue or grain of evidence, it is to be feared that the fate of the crew of the *Marie Celeste* will be added to those numerous mysteries of the deep which will never be solved until the great day when the sea shall give up its dead. If crime has been committed, as is much to be suspected, there is little hope of bringing the perpetrators to justice.'

I shall supplement this extract from the *Gibraltar Gazette* by quoting a telegram from Boston, which went the round of the English papers, and represented the total amount of information which had been collected about the *Marie Celeste*. 'She was,' it said, 'a brigantine of 170 tons burden, and belonged to White, Russell & White, wine importers, of this city. Captain J. W. Tibbs was an old servant of the firm, and was a man of known ability and tried probity. He was accompanied by his wife, aged thirty-one, and their youngest child, five years old. The crew consisted of seven hands, including two coloured seamen, and a boy. There were three passengers, one of whom was the well-known Brooklyn specialist on consumption, Dr Habakuk Jephson, who was a distinguished advocate for Abolition in the early days of the movement, and whose pamphlet, entitled 'Where is thy Brother?' exercised a strong influence on public opinion before the war. The other passengers were Mr J. Harton, a writer in the employ of the firm, and Mr Septimius Goring, a half-caste gentleman, from New Orleans. All investigations have failed to throw any light upon the fate of these fourteen human beings. The loss of Dr Jephson will be felt both in political and scientific circles.'

I have here epitomised, for the benefit of the public, all that has been hitherto known concerning the *Marie Celeste* and her crew, for the past ten years have not in any way helped to elucidate the mystery. I have now taken up my pen with the intention of telling all that I know of the ill-fated voyage. I consider that it is a duty which I owe to society, for symptoms which I am familiar with in others lead me to believe that before many months my tongue and hand may be alike incapable of conveying information. Let me remark, as a preface to my narrative, that I am Joseph Habakuk Jephson, Doctor of Medicine of the University of Harvard, and ex-Consulting Physician of the Samaritan Hospital of Brooklyn.

Many will doubtless wonder why I have not proclaimed myself before, and why I have suffered so many conjectures and surmises to pass unchallenged. Could the ends of justice have been served in any way by my revealing the facts in my possession I should unhesitatingly have done so. It seemed to me, however, that there was no possibility of such a result; and when I attempted after the occurrence, to state my case to an English official, I was met with such offensive incredulity that I determined never again to expose myself to the chance of such an indignity. I can excuse the discourtesy of the Liverpool magistrate, however, when I reflect upon the treatment which I received at the hands of my own relatives, who, though they knew my unimpeachable character, listened to my statement with an indulgent smile as if humouring the delusion of a monomaniac. This slur upon my veracity led to a quarrel between myself and John Vanburger, the brother of my wife, and confirmed me in my resolution to let the matter sink into oblivion — a determination which I have only altered through my son's solicitations. In order to make my narrative intelligible, I must run lightly over one or two incidents in my former life which throw light upon subsequent events.

My father, William K. Jephson, was a preacher of the sect called Plymouth Brethren, and was one of the most respected citizens of Lowell. Like most of the other Puritans of New England, he was a determined opponent of slavery, and it was from his lips that I received those lessons which tinged every action of my life. While I was studying medicine at Harvard University, I had already made a mark as an Abolitionist; and when, after taking my degree, I bought a third share of the practice of Dr Willis, of Brooklyn, I managed, in spite of my professional duties, to devote a considerable time to the cause which I had at heart, my pamphlet, 'Where is thy Brother?' (Swarburgh, Lister & Co., 1859) attracting considerable attention.

When the war broke out I left Brooklyn and accompanied the 113th New York Regiment through the campaign. I was present at the second battle of Bull's Run and at the battle of Gettysburg. Finally, I was severely wounded at Antietam, and would probably have perished in the field had it not been for the kindness of a gentleman named Murray, who had me carried to his house and provided me with every comfort. Thanks to his charity, and to the nursing which I received from his black domestics, I was soon able to get about the plantation with the help of a stick. It was during this period of convalescence that an incident occurred which is closely connected with my story.

Among the most assiduous of the negresses who had watched my couch during my illness there was one old crone who appeared to exert considerable authority over the others. She was exceedingly attentive to me, and I gathered from the few words that passed between us that she had heard of me, and that she was grateful to me for championing her oppressed race.

One day as I was sitting alone in the verandah, basking in the sun, and debating whether I should rejoin Grant's army, I was surprised to see this old creature hobbling towards me. After looking cautiously around to see that we were alone, she fumbled in the front of her dress, and produced a small chamois leather bag which was hung round her neck by a white cord.

'Massa,' she said, bending down and croaking the words into my ear, 'me die soon. Me very old woman. Not stay long on Massa Murray's plantation.'

'You may live a long time yet, Martha,' I answered. 'You know I am a doctor. If you feel ill let me know about it, and I will try to cure you.'

'No wish to live — wish to die. I'm gwine to join the heavenly host.' Here she relapsed into one of those half-heathenish rhapsodies in which negroes indulge. 'But, massa, me have one thing must leave behind me when I go. No able to take it with me across the Jordan. That one thing very precious, more precious and more holy than all thing else in the world. Me, a poor old black woman, have this because my people, very great people, 'spose they was back in the old country. But you cannot understand this same as black folk could. My fader give it me, and his fader give it him, but now who shall I give it to? Poor Martha hab no child, no relation, nobody. All round I see black man very bad man. Black woman very stupid woman. Nobody worthy of the stone. And so I say, Here is Massa Jephson who write books and fight for coloured folk — he must be a good man, and he shall have it though he is white man, and nebber can know what it mean or where it came from.' Here the old woman fumbled in the chamois leather bag and pulled out a flattish black stone with a hole through the middle of it. 'Here, take it,' she said, pressing it into my hand; 'take it. No harm nebber come from anything good. Keep it safe — nebber lose it!' and with a warning gesture the old crone hobbled away in the same cautious way as she had come, looking from side to side to see if we had been observed. I was more amused than impressed by the old woman's earnestness, and was only prevented from laughing during her oration by the fear of hurting her feelings. When she was gone I took a good look at the stone which she had given me. It was intensely black, of extreme hardness, and oval in shape — just such a flat stone as one would pick up on the seashore if one wished to throw a long way. It was about three inches long, and an inch and half broad at the middle, but rounded off at the extremities. The most curious part about it was several well-marked ridges which ran in semicircles over its surface, and gave it exactly the appearance of a human ear. Altogether I was rather interested in my new possession and determined to submit it, as a geological specimen to my friend Professor Shroeder of the New York Institute upon the earliest opportunity. In the meantime I thrust it into my pocket, and rising from my chair started off for a short stroll in the shrubbery, dismissing the incident from my mind.

As my wound had nearly healed by this time, I took my leave of Mr Murray shortly afterwards. The Union armies were everywhere victorious and converging on Richmond, so that my assistance seemed unnecessary, and I returned to Brooklyn. There I resumed my practice, and married the second daughter of Josiah Vanburger, the well known wood engraver. In the course of a few years I built up a good connection and acquired considerable reputation in the treatment of pulmonary complaints. I still kept the old black stone in my pocket, and frequently told the story of the dramatic way in which I had become possessed of it. I also kept my resolution of showing it to Professor Shroeder, who was much interested both by the anecdote and the specimen. He pronounced it to be a piece of meteoric stone, and drew my attention to the fact that its resemblance to an ear was not accidental, but that it was most carefully worked into that shape. A dozen little anatomical points showed that the worker had been as accurate as he was skilful. 'I should not wonder,' said the Professor, 'if it were broken off from some larger statue, though how such hard material could be so perfectly worked is more than I can understand. If there is a statue to correspond I should like to see it!' So I thought at the time, but I have changed my opinion since.

The next seven or eight years of my life were quiet and uneventful. Summer followed spring, and spring followed winter, without any variation in my duties. As the practice increased I admitted J.S. Jackson as partner, he to have one-fourth of the profits. The continued strain had told upon my constitution, however, and I became at last so unwell that my wife insisted upon my consulting Dr Kavanagh Smith, who was my colleague at the Samaritan hospital. That gentleman examined me, and pronounced the apex of my left lung to be in a state of consolidation, recommending me at the same time to go through a course of medical treatment and to take a long sea-voyage.

My own disposition, which is naturally restless, predisposed me strongly in favour of the latter piece of advice, and the matter was clinched by my meeting young Russell, of the firm of White, Russell & White, who offered me a passage in one of his father's ships, the *Marie Celeste*, which was starting from Boston. 'She is a snug little ship,' he said, 'and Tibbs, the captain, is an excellent fellow. There is nothing like a sailing ship for an invalid.' I was very much of the same opinion myself, so I closed with the offer on the spot.

My original plan was that my wife should accompany me on my travels. She has always been a very poor sailor, however, and there were strong family reasons against her exposing herself to any risk at the time, so we determined that she should remain at home. I am not a religious man or an effusive man; but oh, thank God for that! As to leaving my practice, I was easily reconciled to it, as Jackson, my partner, was a reliable and hard working man.

I arrived in Boston on October 12, 1873, and proceeded immediately to the office of the firm in order to thank them for their courtesy. As I was sitting in the counting-house waiting until they should be at liberty to see me, the words *Marie Celeste* suddenly attracted my attention. I looked round and saw a very tall, gaunt man, who was leaning across the polished mahogany counter asking some questions of the clerk at the other side. His face was turned half towards me, and I could see that he had a strong dash of negro blood in him, being probably a quadroon or even nearer akin to the black. His curved aquiline nose and straight lank hair showed the white strain; but the dark, restless eye, sensuous mouth, and gleaming teeth all told of his African origin. His complexion was of a sickly, unhealthy yellow, and as his face was deeply pitted with small-pox, the general impression was so unfavourable as to be almost revolting. When he spoke, however, it was in a soft, melodious voice, and in well-chosen words, and he was evidently a man of some education.

'I wished to ask a few questions about the *Marie Celeste*,' he repeated, leaning across to the clerk. 'She sails the day after to-morrow, does she not?'

'Yes, sir,' said the young clerk, awed into unusual politeness by the glimmer of a large diamond in the stranger's shirt front.

'Where is she bound for?'

'Lisbon.'

'How many of a crew?'

'Seven, sir.'

'Passengers?'

'Yes, two. One of our young gentlemen, and a doctor from New York.'

'No gentlemen from the South?' asked the stranger eagerly.

'No, none, sir.'

'Is there room for another passenger?'

'Accommodation, for three more,' answered the clerk.

'I'll go,' said the quadroon decisively; 'I'll go, I'll engage my passage at once. Put it down, will you — Mr Septimius Goring, of New Orleans.'

The clerk filled up a form and handed it over to the stranger, pointing to a blank space at the bottom. As Mr Goring stooped over to sign it I was horrified to observe that the fingers of his right hand had been lopped off, and that he was holding the pen between his thumb and the palm. I have seen thousands slain in battle, and assisted at every conceivable surgical operation, but I cannot recall any sight which gave me such a thrill of disgust as that great brown sponge-like hand with the single member protruding from it. He used it skilfully enough, however, for dashing off his signature, he nodded to the clerk and strolled out of the office just as Mr White sent out word that he was ready to receive me.

I went down to the *Marie Celeste* that evening, and looked over my berth, which was extremely comfortable considering the small size of the vessel. Mr Goring, whom I had seen in the morning, was to have the one next to mine. Opposite was the captain's cabin and a small berth for Mr John Harton, a gentleman who was going out in the interests of the firm. These little rooms were arranged on each side of the passage which led from the main-deck to the saloon. The latter was a comfortable room, the panelling tastefully done in oak and mahogany, with a rich Brussels carpet and luxurious settees. I was very much pleased with the accommodation, and also with Tibbs the captain, a bluff, sailor-like fellow, with a loud voice and hearty manner, who welcomed me to the ship with effusion, and insisted upon our splitting a bottle of wine in his cabin. He told me that he intended to take his wife and youngest child with him on the voyage, and that he hoped with good luck to make Lisbon in three weeks. We had a pleasant chat and parted the best of friends, he warning me to make the last of my preparations next morning, as he intended to make a start by the mid-day tide, having now shipped all his cargo. I went back to my hotel, where I found a letter from my wife awaiting me, and, after a refreshing night's sleep returned to the boat in the morning. From this point I am able to quote from the journal which I kept in order to vary the monotony of the long sea-voyage. If it is somewhat bald in places I can at least rely upon its accuracy in details, as it was written conscientiously from day to day.

October 16th. — Cast off our warps at half-past two and were towed out into the bay, where the tug left us, and with all sail set we bowled along at about nine knots an hour. I stood upon the poop watching the low land of America sinking gradually upon the horizon until the evening haze hid it from my sight. A single red light, however, continued to blaze balefully behind us, throwing a long track like a trail of blood upon the water, and it is still visible as I write, though reduced to a mere speck. The captain is in a bad humour, for two of his hands disappointed him at the last moment, and he was compelled to ship a couple of negroes who happened to be on the quay. The missing men were steady, reliable fellows, who had been with him several voyages, and their non-appearance puzzled as well as irritated him. Where a crew of several men have to work a fair-sized ship the loss of two experienced seamen is a serious one, for though the negroes may take a spell at the wheel or swab the decks, they are of little or no use in rough weather. Our cook is also a black man, and Mr Septimius Goring has a little darkie servant, so that we are rather a piebald community. The accountant, John Harton, promises to be an acquisition, for he is a cheery, amusing young fellow.

Strange how little wealth has to do with happiness! He has all the world before him and is seeking his fortune in a far land, yet he is as transparently happy as a man can be. Goring is rich, if I am not mistaken, and so am I; but I know that I have a lung, and Goring has some deeper trouble still, to judge by his features. How poorly do we both contrast with the careless, penniless clerk!

October 17th. — Mrs Tibbs appeared upon the deck for the first time this morning — a cheerful, energetic woman, with a dear little child just able to walk and prattle. Young Harton pounced on it at once, and carried it away to his cabin, where no doubt he will lay the seeds of future dyspepsia in the child's stomach. Thus medicine doth make cynics of us all! The weather is still all that could be desired, with a fine fresh breeze from the west-sou'-west. The vessel goes so steadily that you would hardly know that she was moving were it not for the creaking of the cordage, the bellying of the sails, and the long white furrow in our wake. Walked the quarter-deck all morning with the captain, and I think the keen fresh air has already done my breathing good, for the exercise did not fatigue me in any way. Tibbs is a remarkably intelligent man, and we had an interesting argument about Maury's observations on ocean currents, which we terminated by going down into his cabin to consult the original work. There we found Goring, rather to the captain's surprise, as it is not usual for passengers to enter that sanctum unless specially invited. He apologised for his intrusion, however, pleading his ignorance of the usages of ship life; and the good-natured sailor simply laughed at the incident, begging him to remain and favour us with his company. Goring pointed to the chronometers, the case of which he had opened, and remarked that he had been admiring them. He has evidently some practical knowledge of mathematical instruments, as he told at a glance which was the most trustworthy of the three, and also named their price within a few dollars. He had a discussion with the captain too upon the variation of the compass, and when we came back to the ocean currents he showed a thorough grasp of the subject. Altogether he rather improves upon acquaintance, and is a man of decided culture and refinement. His voice harmonises with his conversation, and both are the very antithesis of his face and figure.

The noonday observation shows that we have run two hundred and twenty miles. Towards evening the breeze freshened up, and the first mate ordered reefs to be taken in the topsails and top-gallant sails in expectation of a windy night. I observe that the barometer has fallen to twenty-nine. I trust our voyage will not be a rough one, as I am a poor sailor, and my health would probably derive more harm than good from a stormy trip, though I have the greatest confidence in the captain's seamanship and in the soundness of the vessel. Played cribbage with Mrs Tibbs after supper, and Harton gave us a couple of tunes on the violin.

October 18th. — The gloomy prognostications of last night were not fulfilled, as the wind died away again and we are lying now in a long greasy swell, ruffled here and there by a fleeting catspaw which is insufficient to fill the sails. The air is colder than it was yesterday, and I have put on one of the thick woollen jerseys which my wife knitted for me. Harton came into my cabin in the morning, and we had a cigar together. He says that he remembers having seen Goring in Cleveland, Ohio, in '69. He was, it appears, a mystery then as now, wandering about without any visible employment, and extremely reticent on his own affairs. The man interests me as a psychological study. At breakfast this morning I suddenly had that vague feeling of uneasiness which comes over some people when closely stared at, and, looking quickly up, I met his eyes bent upon me with an intensity which amounted to ferocity, though their expression instantly softened as he made some conventional remark upon the weather. Curiously enough, Harton says that he had a very similar experience yesterday upon the deck. I observe that Goring frequently talks to the coloured seamen as he strolls about — a trait which I rather admire, as it is common to find half-breeds ignore their dark strain and treat their black kinsfolk with greater intolerance than a white man would do. His little page is devoted to him, apparently, which speaks well for his treatment of him. Altogether, the man is a curious mixture of incongruous qualities, and unless I am deceived in him will give me food for observation during the voyage.

The captain is grumbling about his chronometers, which do not register exactly the same time. He says it is the first time they have ever disagreed. We were unable to get a noonday observation on account of the haze. By dead reckoning, we have done about a hundred and seventy miles in the twenty-four hours. The dark seamen have proved, as the skipper prophesied, to be very inferior hands, but as they can both manage the wheel well they are kept steering, and so leave the more experienced men to work the ship. These details are trivial enough, but a small thing serves as food for gossip aboard ship. The appearance of a whale in the evening caused quite a flutter among us. From its sharp back and forked tail, I should pronounce it to have ben a rorqual, or 'finner,' as they are called by the fishermen.

October 19th. — Wind was cold, so I prudently remained in my cabin all day, only creeping out for dinner. Lying in my cabin bunk I can, without moving, reach my books, pipes, or anything else I may want, which is one advantage of a small apartment. My old wound began to ache a little to-day, probably from the cold. Read *Montaigne's Essays* and nursed myself. Harton came in in the afternoon with Doddy, the captain's child, and the skipper himself followed, so that I held quite a reception.

October 20th and 21st. — *Still cold, with a continual drizzle of rain, and I have not been able to leave the cabin. This confinement makes me feel weak and depressed. Goring came in to see me, but his company did not tend to cheer me up much, as he hardly uttered a word, but contented himself with staring at me in a peculiar and rather irritating manner. He then got up and stole out of the cabin without saying anything. I am beginning to suspect that the man is a lunatic. I think I mentioned that his cabin is next to mine. The two are simply divided by a thin wooden partition which is cracked in many places, some of the cracks being so large that I can hardly avoid, as I lie in my bunk, observing his motions in the adjoining room. Without any wish to play the spy, I see him continually stooping over what appears to be a chart and working with a pencil and compasses. I have remarked the interest he displays in matters connected with navigation, but I am surprised that he should take the trouble to work out the course of the ship. However, it is a harmless amusement enough, and no doubt he verifies his results by those of the captain.*

I wish the man did not run in my thoughts so much. I had a nightmare on the night of the 20th, in which I thought my bunk was a coffin, that I was laid out in it, and that Goring was endeavouring to nail up the lid, which I was frantically pushing away. Even when I woke up, I could hardly persuade myself that I was not in a coffin. As a medical man, I know that a nightmare is simply a vascular derangement of the cerebral hemisphere, and yet in my weak state I cannot shake off the morbid impression which it produces.

October 22nd. — A fine day, with hardly a cloud in the sky, and a fresh breeze from the sou'-west which wafts us gaily on our way. There has evidently been some heavy weather near us, as there is a tremendous swell on, and the ship lurches until the end of the fore-yard nearly touches the water. Had a refreshing walk up and down the quarter-deck, though I have hardly found my sea-legs yet. Several small birds — chaffinches, I think — perched in the rigging.

4.40 P.M. — While I was on the deck this morning I heard a sudden explosion from the direction of my cabin, and, hurrying down, found that I had very nearly met with a serious accident. Goring was cleaning a revolver, it seems, in his cabin, when one of the barrels which he thought was unloaded went off. The ball passed through the side partition and imbedded itself in the bulwarks in the exact place where my head usually rests. I have been under fire too often to magnify trifles, but there is no doubt that if I had been in the bunk it must have killed me. Goring, poor fellow, did not know that I had gone on deck that day, and must therefore have felt terribly frightened. I never saw such emotion in a man's face as when, on rushing out of his cabin with the smoking pistol in his hand, he met me face to face as I came down from the deck. Of course, he was profuse in his apologies, though I simply laughed at the incident.

11 P.M. — A misfortune has occurred so unexpected and so horrible that my little escape of the morning dwindles into insignificance. Mrs Tibbs and her child have disappeared — utterly and entirely disappeared. I can hardly compose myself to write the sad details. About half-past eight Tibbs rushed into my cabin with a very white face and asked me if I had seen his wife. I answered that I had not. He then ran wildly into the saloon and began groping about for any trace of her, while I followed him, endeavouring vainly to persuade him that his fears were ridiculous. We hunted over the ship for an hour and a half without coming on any sign of the missing woman and child. Poor Mr Tibbs lost his voice completely from calling her name. Even the sailors, who are generally stolid enough, were deeply affected by the sight of him as he roamed bareheaded and dishevelled about the deck, searching with feverish anxiety the most impossible places, and returning to them again and again with a piteous pertinacity. The last time she was seen was about seven o'clock, when she took Doddy on to the poop to give him a breath of fresh air before putting him to bed. There was no one there at the time except the black seaman at the wheel, who denies having seen her at all. The whole affair is wrapped in mystery. My own theory is that while Mrs Tibbs was holding the child and standing near the bulwarks it gave a spring and fell overboard, and that in her convulsive attempt to catch or save it, she followed it. I cannot account for the double dissappearance in any other way. It is quite feasible that such a tragedy should be enacted without the knowledge of the man at the wheel, since it was dark at the time, and the peaked skylights of the saloon screen the greater part of the quarter-deck. Whatever the truth may be it is a terrible catastrophe, and has cast the darkest gloom upon the voyage. The mate has put the ship about, but of course there is

not the slightest hope of picking them up. The captain is lying in a state of stupor in his cabin. I gave him a powerful dose of opium in his coffee that for a few hours at least his anguish may be deadened.

October 23rd. — Woke with a vague feeling of heaviness and misfortune, but it was not until a few moments' reflection that I was able to recall our loss of the night before. When I came on deck I saw the poor skipper standing gazing back at the waste of waters behind us which contains everything dear to him upon earth. I attempted to speak to him, but he turned brusquely away, and began pacing the deck with his head sunk upon his breast. Even now, when the truth is so clear, he cannot pass a boat or an unbent sail without peering under it. He looks ten years older than he did yesterday morning. Harton is terribly cut up, for he was fond of little Doddy, and Goring seems sorry too. At least he has shut himself up in his cabin all day, and when I got a casual glance at him his head was resting on his two hands as if in a melancholy reverie. I fear we are about as dismal a crew as ever sailed. How shocked my wife will be to hear of our disaster! The swell has gone down now, and we are doing about eight knots with all sail set and a nice breeze. Hyson is practically in command of the ship, as Tibbs, though he does his best to bear up and keep a brave front, is incapable of applying himself to serious work.

October 24th. — Is the ship accursed? Was there ever a voyage which began so fairly and which changed so disastrously? Tibbs shot himself through the head during the night. I was awakened about three o'clock in the morning by an explosion, and immediately sprang out of the bed and rushed into the captain's cabin to find out the cause, though with a terrible presentiment in my heart. Quickly as I went, Goring went more quickly still, for he was already in the cabin stooping over the dead body of the captain. It was a hideous sight, for the whole front of his face was blown in, and the little room was swimming in blood. The pistol was lying beside him on the floor, just as it had dropped from his hand. He had evidently put it to his mouth before pulling the trigger. Goring and I picked him reverently up and laid him on his bed. The crew had all clustered into his cabin, and the six white men were deeply grieved, for they were old hands who had sailed with him many years. There were dark looks and murmurs among them too, and one of them openly declared that the ship was haunted. Harton helped to lay the poor skipper out, and we did him up in canvas between us. At twelve o'clock the fore-yard was hauled aback, and we committed his body to the deep, Goring reading the

Church of England burial service. The breeze has freshened up, and we have done ten knots all day and sometimes twelve. The sooner we reach Lisbon and get away from this accursed ship the better pleased shall I be. I feel as though we were in a floating coffin. Little wonder that the poor sailors are superstitious when I, an educated man, feel it so strongly.

October 25th. — Made a good run all day. Feel listless and depressed.

October 26th. — Goring, Harton, and I had a chat together on deck in the morning. Harton tried to draw Goring out as to his profession, and his object in going to Europe, but the quadroon parried all his questions and gave us no information. Indeed, he seemed to be slightly offended by Harton's pertinacity, and went down into his cabin. I wonder why we should both take such an interest in this man! I suppose it is his striking appearance, coupled with his apparent wealth, which piques our curiosity. Harton has a theory that he is really a detective, that he is after some criminal who has got away to Portugal, and that he chooses this peculiar way of travelling that he may arrive unnoticed and pounce upon his quarry unawares. I think the supposition is rather a far-fetched one, but Harton bases it upon a book which Goring left on deck, and which he picked up and glanced over. It was a sort of scrap-book, it seems, and contained a large number of newspaper cuttings. All these cuttings related to murders which had been committed at various times in the States during the last twenty years or so. The curious thing which Harton observed about them, however, was that they were invariably murders the authors of which had never been brought to justice. They varied in every detail, he says, as to the manner of execution and the social status of the victim, but they uniformly wound up with the same formula that the murderer was still at large, though, of course, the police had every reason to expect his speedy capture. Certainly the incident seems to support Harton's theory, though it may be a mere whim of Goring's, or, as I suggested to Harton, he may be collecting materials for a book which shall outvie De Quincy. In any case it is no business of ours.

October 27th, 28th. — Wind still fair, and we are making good progress. Strange how easily a human unit may drop out of its place and be forgotten! Tibbs is hardly ever mentioned now; Hyson has take possession of his cabin, and all goes on as before. Were it not for Mrs Tibbs's sewing-machine upon a side-table we might forget that the unfortunate family had ever existed. Another accident occurred on board today, though fortunately not a very serious one.

One of our white hands had gone down the afterhold to fetch up a spare coil of rope, when one of the hatches which he had removed came crashing down on top of him. He saved his life by springing out of the way, but one of his feet was terribly crushed, and he will be of little use for the remainder of the voyage. He attributes the accident to the carelessness of his negro companion, who had helped him to shift the hatches. The latter, however, puts it down to the roll of the ship. Whatever be the cause, it reduces our short-handed crew still further. This run of ill-luck seems to be depressing Harton, for he has lost his usual good spirits and joviality. Goring is the only one who preserves his cheerfulness. I see him still working at his chart in his own cabin. His nautical knowledge would be useful should anything happen to Hyson — which God forbid!

October 29th, 30th. — Still bowling along with a fresh breeze. All quiet and nothing of note to chronicle.

October 31st. — My weak lungs, combined with the exciting episodes of the voyage, have shaken my nervous system so much that the most trivial incident affects me. I can hardly believe that I am the same man who tied the external iliac artery, an operation requiring the nicest precision, under a heavy rifle fire at Antietam. I am as nervous as a child. I was lying half dozing last night about four bells in the middle watch trying in vain to drop into a refreshing sleep. There was no light inside my cabin, but a single ray of moonlight streamed in through the port-hole, throwing a silvery flickering circle upon the floor. As I lay I kept my drowsy eyes upon this circle, and was conscious that it was gradually becoming less well-defined as my senses left me, when I was suddenly recalled to full wakefulness by the appearance of a small dark object in the very centre of the luminous disc. I lay quietly and breathlessly watching it. Gradually it grew larger and plainer, and then I perceived that it was a human hand which had been cautiously inserted through the chink of the half closed door — a hand which, as I observed with a thrill of horror, was not provided with fingers. The door swung cautiously backwards, and Goring's head followed his hand. It appeared in the center of the moonlight, and was framed as it were in a ghastly uncertain halo, against which his features showed out plainly. It seemed to me that I had never seen such an utterly fiendish and merciless expression upon a human face. His eyes were dilated and glaring, his lips drawn back so as to show his white fangs, and his straight black hair appeared to bristle over his low forehead like the hood of a cobra. The sudden and noiseless apparition had such an effect upon me that I sprang up in bed trembling in every limb, and held out my hand towards my revolver. I was heartily ashamed of my hastiness when he explained the object of his intrusion, as he immediately did in the most courteous language. He had been suffering from toothache, poor fellow! and had come in to beg some laudanum, knowing that I possessed a medicine chest. As to a sinister expression he is never a beauty, and what with my state of nervous tension and the effect of the shifting moonlight it was easy to conjure up something horrible. I gave him twenty drops, and he went off again, with many expressions of gratitude. I can hardly say how much this trivial incident affected me. I have felt unstrung all day.

A week's record of our voyage is here omitted, as nothing eventful occurred during the time, and my log consists merely of a few pages of unimportant gossip.

November 7th. — Harton and I sat on the poop all the morning, for the weather is becoming very warm as we come into southern latitudes. We reckon that we have done two-thirds of our voyage. How glad we shall be to see the green banks of the Tagus, and leave this unlucky ship for ever! I was endeavouring to amuse Harton today and to while away the time by telling him some of the experiences of my past life. Among others I related to him how I came into the possession of my black stone, and as a finale I rummaged in the side pocket of my old shooting coat and produced the identical object in question. He and I were bending over it together, I pointing out to him the curious ridges upon its surface, when we were conscious of a shadow falling between us and the sun, and looking round saw Goring standing behind us glaring over our shoulders at the stone. For some reason or other he appeared to be powerfully excited, though he was evidently trying to control himself and to conceal his emotion. He pointed once or twice at my relic with his stubby thumb before he could recover himself sufficiently to ask what it was and how I obtained it — a question put in such a brusque manner that I should have been offended had I not known the man to be an eccentric. I told him the story very much as I had told it to Harton. He listened with the deepest interest and then asked me if I had any idea what the stone was. I said I had not, beyond that it was meteoric. He asked me if I had ever tried its effect upon a negro. I said I had not. 'Come,' said he, 'we'll see what our black friend at the wheel thinks of it.' He took the stone in his hand and went across to the sailor, and the two examined it carefully. I could see the man gesticulating and nodding his head excitedly as if making some assertion, while his face betrayed the utmost astonishment, mixed, I think, with some reverence. Goring came across the deck to us presently, still holding the stone in his hand. 'He says it is a worthless, useless thing,' he said, 'and fit only to be chucked overboard,' with which he raised his hand and would most certainly have made an end of my relic, had the black sailor behind him not rushed forward and seized him by the wrist. Finding himself secured Goring dropped the stone and turned away with a very bad grace to avoid my angry remonstrances at his breach of faith. The black picked up the stone and handed it to me with a low bow and every sign of profound respect. The whole affair is inexplicable. I am rapidly coming to conclusion that Goring is a maniac or something very near one. When I compare the effect produced by the stone upon the sailor, however, with the respect shown to Martha on the plantation, and the surprise of Goring on its production, I cannot but come to the conclusion that I have really got hold of some powerful talisman which appeals to the whole dark race. I must not trust it in Goring's hands again.

November 8th, 9th. — What splendid weather we are having! Beyond one little blow, we have had nothing but fresh breezes the whole voyage. These two days we have made better runs than any hitherto. It is a pretty thing to watch the spray fly up from our prow as it cuts through the waves. The sun shines through it and breaks it up into a number of miniature rainbows — 'sun-dogs', the sailors call them. I stood on the fo'c'sle-head for several hours today watching the effect, and surrounded by a halo of prismatic colours. The steersman has evidently told the other blacks about my wonderful stone, for I am treated by them all with greatest respect. Talking about optical phenomena, we had a curious one yesterday evening which was pointed out to me by Hyson. This was the appearance of a triangular well-defined object high up in the heavens to the north of us. He explained that it was exactly like the Peak of Teneriffe as seen from a great distance — the peak was, however, at that moment at least five hundred miles to the south. It may have been a cloud, or it may have been one of those strange reflections of which one reads. The weather is very warm. The mate says that he never knew it so warm in these latitudes. Played chess with Harton in the evening.

November 10th. — It is getting warmer and warmer. Some land birds came and perched in the rigging today though we are still a considerable way from our destination. The heat is so great that we are too lazy to do anything but lounge about the decks and smoke. Goring came over to me today and asked me some more questions about my stone; but I answered him rather shortly, for I have not quite forgiven him yet for the cool way in which he attempted to deprive me of it.

November 11th, 12th. — Still making good progress. I had no idea Portugal was ever as hot as this, but no doubt it is cooler on land. Hyson himself seemed surprised at it, and so do the men.

November 13th. — A most extraordinary event has happened, so extraordinary as to be almost inexplicable. Either Hyson has blundered wonderfully, or some magnetic influence has disturbed our instruments. Just about daybreak the watch on the fo'c'sle-head shouted out that he heard the sound of the surf ahead, and Hyson thought he saw the loom of land. The ship was put about, and, though no lights were seen, none of us doubted that we had struck the Portuguese coast a little sooner than we had expected. What was our surprise to see the scene which was revealed to us at break of day! As far as we could look on either side was one long line of surf, great, green billows rolling in and breaking into a cloud of foam. But behind the surf what was there! Not the green banks nor the high cliffs of the shores of Portugal, but a great sandy waste which stretched away and away until it blended with the skyline. To right and left, look where you would, there was nothing but yellow sand, heaped in some places into fantastic mounds, some of them several hundred feet high, while in other parts were long stretches as level apparently as a billiard board. Harton and I, who had come on deck together, looked at each other in astonishment, and Harton burst out laughing. Hyson is exceedingly mortified at the occurrence, and protests that the instruments have been tampered with. There is no doubt that this is the mainland of Africa, and that it was really the Peak of Teneriffe which we saw some days ago upon the northern horizon. At the time when we saw the land birds we must have been passing some of the Canary Islands. If we continued on the same course, we are now to the north of Cape Blanco, near the unexplored country which skirts the great Sahara. All we can do is to rectify our instruments as far as possible and start afresh for our destination.

8.30 P.M. — Have been lying in a calm all day. The coast is now about a mile and half from us. Hyson has examined the instruments, but cannot find any reason for their extraordinary deviation.

This is the end of my private journal, and I must make the remainder of my statement from memory. There is little chance of my being mistaken about the facts, which have seared themselves into my recollection. That very night the storm which had been brewing so long burst over us, and I came to learn whither all those little incidents were tending which I had recorded so aimlessly. Blind fool that I was not to have seen it sooner! I shall tell what occurred as precisely as I can.

I had gone into my cabin about half-past eleven, and was preparing to go to bed, when a tap came at my door. On opening it I saw Goring's little black page, who told me that his master would like to have a word with me on the deck. I was rather surprised that he should want me at such a late hour, but I went up without hesitation. I had hardly put my foot on the quarter-deck before I was seized from behind, dragged down upon my back, and a handkerchief slipped round my mouth. I struggled as hard as I could, but a coil of rope was rapidly and firmly wound round me, and I found myself lashed to the davit of one of the boats, utterly powerless to do or say anything, while the point of a knife pressed to my throat warned me to cease my struggles. The night was so dark that I had been unable hitherto to recognise my assailants, but as my eyes became accustomed to the gloom, and the moon broke out through the clouds that obscured it, I made out that I was surrounded by the two negro sailors, the black cook, and my fellow-passenger, Goring. Another man was crouched on the deck at my feet, but he was in the shadow and I could not recognise him.

All this occurred so rapidly that a minute could hardly have elapsed from the time I mounted the companion until I found myself gagged and powerless. It was so sudden that I could scarce bring myself to realise it, or to comprehend what it all meant. I heard the gang round me speaking in short, fierce whispers to each other, and some instinct told me that my life was the question at issue. Goring spoke authoritatively and angrily — the others doggedly and all together, as if disputing his commands. Then they moved away in a body to the opposite side of the deck, where I could still hear them whispering, though they were concealed from my view by the saloon skylights.

All this time the voices of the watch on deck chatting and laughing at the other end of the ship were distinctly audible, and I could see them gathered in a group, little dreaming of the dark doings which were going on within thirty yards of them. Oh! That I could have given them one word of warning, even though I had lost my life in doing it! but it was impossible. The moon was shining fitfully through the scattered clouds, and I could see the silvery gleam of the surge, and beyond it the vast weird desert with its fantastic sand-hills. Glancing down, I saw that the man who had been crouching on the deck was still lying there, and as I gazed upon him a flickering ray of moonlight fell full upon his upturned face. Great heaven! even now, when more than twelve years have elapsed, my hand trembles as I write that, in spite of distorted features and projecting eyes, I recognised the face of Harton, the cheery young clerk who had been my companion during the voyage. It needed no medical eye to see that he was quite dead, while the twisted handkerchief round the neck, and the gag in his mouth, showed the silent way in which the hell-hounds had done their work. The clue which explained every event of our voyage came upon me like a flash of light as I gazed on poor Harton's corpse. Much was dark and unexplained, but I felt a great dim perception of the truth.

I heard the striking of a match at the other side of the skylights, and then I saw the tall, gaunt figure of Goring standing up on the bulwarks and holding in his hands what appeared to be a dark lantern. He lowered this for a moment over the side of the ship, and, to my inexpressible astonishment, I saw it answered instantaneously by a flash among the sand-hills on shore, which came and went so rapidly, that unless I had been following the direction of Goring's gaze, I should never have detected it. Again he lowered the lantern, and again it was answered from the shore. He then stepped down from the bulwarks, and in doing so slipped, making such a noise, that for a moment my heart bounded with the thought that the attention of the watch would be directed to his proceedings. It was a vain hope. The night was calm and the ship motionless, so that no idea of duty kept them vigilant. Hyson, who after the death of Tibbs was in command of both watches, had gone below to snatch a few hours' sleep, and the boatswain, who was left in charge, was standing with the other two men at the foot of the foremast. Powerless, speechless, with the chords cutting into my flesh and the murdered man at my feet, I awaited the next act in the tragedy.

The four ruffians were standing up now at the other side of the deck. The cook was armed with some sort of a cleaver, the others had knives, and Goring had a revolver. They were all leaning against the rail and looking out over the water as if watching for something. I saw one of them grasp another's arm and point as if at some object, and following the direction I made out the loom of a large moving mass making towards the ship. As it emerged from the gloom I saw that it was a great canoe crammed with men and propelled by at least a score of paddles. As it shot under our stern the watch caught sight of it also, and raising a cry hurried aft. They were too late, however.

A swarm of gigantic negroes clambered over the quarter, and led by Goring swept down the deck in an irresistible torrent. All opposition was overpowered in a moment, the unarmed watch were knocked over and bound, and the sleepers dragged out of their bunks and secured in the same manner. Hyson made an attempt to defend the narrow passage leading to his cabin, and I heard a scuffle, and his voice shouting for assistance. There was none to assist, however, and he was brought on to the poop with the blood streaming from a deep cut in his forehead. He was gagged like the others, and a council was held upon our fate by the negroes. I saw our black seamen pointing towards me and making some statement, which was received with murmurs of astonishment and incredulity by the savages. One of them then came over to me, and plunging his hand into my pocket took out my black stone and held it up. He then handed it to a man who appeared to be a chief, who examined it as minutely as the light would permit, and muttering a few words passed it on to the warrior beside him, who also scrutinised it and passed it on until it had gone from hand to hand round the whole circle. The chief then said a few words to Goring in the native tongue, on which the quadroon addressed me in English. At this moment I seem to see the scene. The tall masts of the ship with the moonlight streaming down, silvering the yards and bringing the network of cordage into hard relief; the group of dusky warriors leaning on their spears; the dead man at my feet; the line of white-faced prisoners, and in front of me the loathsome half-breed, looking in his white linen and elegant clothes a strange contrast to his associates.

'You will bear me witness,' he said in his softest accents, 'that I am no party to sparing your life. If it rested with me you would die as these other men are about to do. I have no personal grudge against either you or them, but I have devoted my life to the destruction of the white race, and you are the first that has ever been in my power and has escaped me. You may thank that stone of yours for your life. These poor fellows reverence it, and indeed if it really be what they think it is they have cause. Should it prove when we get ashore that they are mistaken, and that its shape and material is a mere chance, nothing can save your life. In the meantime we wish to treat you well, so if there are any of your possessions which you would like to take with you, you are at liberty to get them.' As he finished he gave a sign, and a couple of the negroes unbound me, though without removing the gag. I was led down into the cabin, where I put a few valuables into my pockets, together with a pocket-compass and my journal of the voyage. They then pushed me over the side into a small canoe, which was lying beside the large one, and my guards followed me, and shoving off began paddling for the shore. We had got about a hundred yards or so from the ship when our steersman held up his hand, and the paddlers paused for a moment and listened. Then on the silence of the night I heard a sort of dull, moaning sound, followed by a succession of splashes in the water. That is all I know of the fate of my poor shipmates. Almost immediately afterwards the large canoe followed us, and the deserted ship was left drifting about — a dreary spectre-like hulk. Nothing was taken from her by the savages. The whole fiendish transaction was carried through as decorously and temperately as though it were a religious rite.

The first grey of daylight was visible in the east as we passed through the surge and reached the shore. Leaving half a dozen men with the canoes, the rest of the negroes set off through the sand-hills, leading me with them, but treating me very gently and respectfully. It was difficult walking, as we sank over our ankles into the loose, shifting sand at every step, and I was nearly dead beat by the time we reached the native village, or town rather, for it was a place of considerable dimensions. The houses were conical structures not unlike bee-hives, and were made of compressed seaweed cemented over with a rude form of mortar, there being neither stick nor stone upon the coast nor anywhere within many hundreds of miles. As we entered the town an enormous crowd of both sexes came swarming out to meet us, beating tom-toms and howling and screaming. On seeing me they redoubled their yells and assuming a threatening attitude, which was instantly quelled by a few words shouted by my escort. A buzz of wonder succeeded the war-cries and yells of the moment before, and the whole dense mass proceeded down the broad central street of the town, having my escort and myself in the centre.

My statement hitherto may seem strange as to excite doubt in the minds of those who do not know me, but it was the fact which I am now about to relate which caused my own brother-in-law to insult me by disbelief. I can but relate the occurrence in the simplest words, and trust to chance and time to prove their truth. In the center of this main street there was a large building, formed in the same primitive way as the others, but towering high above them; a stockade of beautifully polished ebony rails was planted all round it, the framework of the door was formed by two magnificent elephant's tusks sunk in the ground on each side and meeting at the top, and the aperture was closed by a screen of native cloth richly embroidered with gold. We made our way to this imposing-looking structure, but on reaching the opening in the stockade, the multitude stopped and squatted down upon their hams, while I was led through into the enclosure by a few of the chiefs and elders of the tribe, Goring accompanying us, and in fact directing the proceedings. On reaching the screen which closed the temple — for such it evidently was — my hat and my shoes were removed, and I was then led in, a venerable old negro leading the way carrying in his hand my stone, which had been taken from my pocket. The building was only lit up by a few long slits in the roof, through which the tropical sun poured, throwing broad golden bars upon the clay floor, alternating with intervals of the darkness.

The interior was even larger than one would have imagined from the outside appearance. The walls were hung with native mats, shells, and other ornaments, but the remainder of the great space was quite empty, with exception of a single object in the center. This was the figure of a colossal negro, which I at first thought to be some real king or high priest of titanic size, but as I approached it I saw by the way in which the light was reflected from it that it was a statue admirably cut in jet-black stone. I was led up to this idol, for such it seemed to be, and looking at it closer I saw that though it was perfect in every other respect, one of its ears had been broken short off. The grey-haired negro who held my relic mounted upon a small stool, and stretching up his arm fitted Martha's black stone on to the jagged surface on the side of the statue's head. There could be no doubt that the one had been broken off from the other. The parts dovetailed together so accurately that when the old man removed his hand the ear stuck in its place for a few seconds before dropping into his open palm. The group round me prostrated themselves upon the ground at the sight with a cry of reverence, while the crowd outside, to whom the result was communicated, set up a wild whooping and cheering.

In a moment I found myself converted from a prisoner into a demi-god. I was escorted back through the town in triumph, the people pressing forward to touch my clothing and to gather up the dust on which my foot had trod. One of the largest huts was put at my disposal, and a banquet of every native delicacy was served me. I still felt, however, that I was not a free man, as several spearmen were placed as a guard at the entrance of my hut. All day my mind was occupied with plans of escape, but none seemed in any way feasible. On the one side was the great arid desert stretching away to Timbuctoo, on the other was a sea untraversed by vessels. The more I pondered over the problem the more hopeless did it seem. I little dreamed how near I was to its solution.

Night had fallen, and the clamour of the negroes had died gradually away. I was stretched on the couch of skins which had been provided for me, and was still meditating over my future, when Goring walked stealthily into the hut. My first idea was that he had come to complete his murderous holocaust by making away with me, the last survivor, and I sprang up upon my feet, determined to defend myself to the last. He smiled when he saw the action, and motioned me down again while he seated himself upon the other end of the couch.

'What do you think of me?' was the astonishing question with which he commenced our conversation.

'Think of you!' I almost yelled. 'I think you the vilest, most unnatural renegade that ever polluted the earth. If we were away from these black devils of yours I would strangle you with my hands!'

'Don't speak so loud,' he said, without the slightest appearance of irritation. 'I don't want our chat to be cut short. So you would strangle me, would you!' he went on, with an amused smile. 'I suppose I am returning good for evil, for I have come to help you to escape.'

'You!' I gasped incredulously.

'Yes, I,' he continued. 'Oh, there is no credit to me in the matter. I am quite consistent. There is no reason why I should not be perfectly candid with you. I wish to be king over these fellows — not a very high ambition, certainly, but you know what Caesar said about being first in a village in Gaul. Well, this unlucky stone of yours has not only saved your life, but has turned all their heads so that they think you are come down from heaven, and my influence will be gone until you are out of the way. That is why I am going to help you to escape, since I cannot kill you' — this in the most natural and dulcet voice, as if the desire to do so were a matter of course.

'You would give the world to ask me a few questions,' he went on, after a pause; 'but you are too proud to do it. Never mind, I'll tell you one or two things, because I want your fellow white men to know them when you go back — if you are lucky enough to get back. About that cursed stone of yours, for instance. These negroes, or at least so the legend goes, were Mahometans originally. While Mahomet himself was still alive, there was a schism among his followers, and the smaller party moved away from Arabia, and eventually crossed Africa. They took away with them, in their exile, a valuable relic of their old faith in the shape of a large piece of the black stone of Mecca. The stone was a meteoric one, as you may have heard, and in its fall upon the earth it broke into two pieces. One of these pieces is still at Mecca. The larger piece was carried away to Barbary, where a skilful worker modelled it into the fashion which you saw today. These men are the descendants of the original seceders from Mahomet, and they have brought their relic safely through all their wanderings until they settled in this strange place, where the desert protects them from their enemies.'

'And the ear?' I asked, almost involuntarily.

'Oh, that was the same story over again. Some of the tribe wandered away to the south a few hundred years ago, and one of them, wishing to have good luck for the enterprise, got into the temple at night and carried off one of the ears. There has been a tradition among the negroes ever since that the ear would come back some day. The fellow who carried it was caught by some slaver, no doubt, and that was how it got into America, and so into your hands — and you have had the honour of fulfilling the prophecy.'

He paused for a few minutes, resting his head upon his hands, waiting apparently for me to speak. When he looked up again, the whole expression of his face had changed. His features were firm and set, and he changed the air of half-levity with which he had spoken before for one of sternness and almost ferocity.

'I wish you to carry a message back,' he said, 'to the white race, the great dominating race whom I hate and defy. Tell them that I have battened on their blood for twenty years, that I have slain them until even I became tired of what had once been a joy, that I did this unnoticed and unsuspected in the face of every precaution which their civilisation could suggest. There is no satisfaction in revenge when your enemy does not know who has struck him. I am not sorry, therefore, to have you as a messenger. There is no need why I should tell you how this great hate became born in me. See this,' and he held up his mutilated hand; 'that was done by a white man's knife. My father was white, my mother was a slave. When he died she was sold again, and I, a child then, saw her lashed to death to break her of some of the little airs and graces which her late master had encouraged in her. My young wife, too, oh, my young wife!' a shudder ran through his whole frame. 'No matter! I swore my oath, and I kept it. From Maine to Florida, and from Boston to San Francisco, you could track my steps by sudden deaths which baffled the police. I warred against the whole white race as they for centuries had warred against the black one. At last, as I tell you, I sickened of blood. Still, the sight of a white face was abhorrent to me, and I determined to find some bold free black people and to throw in my lot with them, to cultivate their latent powers and to form a nucleus for a great coloured nation. This idea possessed me, and I travelled over the world for two years seeking for what I desired. At last I almost despaired of finding it. There was no hope of regeneration in the slave dealing Soudanese, the debased Fantee, or the Americanised negroes of Liberia. I was returning from my quest when chance brought me in contact with this magnificent tribe of dwellers in the desert, and I threw in my lot with them. Before doing so, however, my old instinct of revenge prompted me to make one last visit to the United States, and I returned from it in the *Marie Celeste*.

'As to the voyage itself, your intelligence will have told you by this time that, thanks to my manipulation, both compasses and chronometers were entirely untrustworthy. I alone worked out the course with correct instruments of my own, while the steering was done by my black friends under my guidance. I pushed Tibb's wife overboard. What! You look surprised and shrink away. Surely you had guessed that by this time. I would have shot you that day through the partition, but unfortunately you were not there. I tried again afterwards, but you were awake. I shot Tibbs. I think the idea of suicide was carried out rather neatly. Of course when once we got on the coast the rest was simple. I had bargained that all on board should die; but that stone of yours upset my plans. I also bargained that there should be no plunder. No one can say we are pirates. We have acted from principle, not from any sordid motive.'

I listened in amazement to the summary of his crimes which this strange man gave me, all in the quietest and most composed of voices, as though detailing incidents of every-day occurrence. I still seem to see him sitting like a hideous nightmare at the end of my couch, with the single rude lamp flickering over his cadaverous features.

'And now,' he continued, 'there is no difficulty about your escape. These stupid adopted children of mine will say that you have gone back to heaven from whence you came. The wind blows off the land. I have a boat all ready for you, well stored with provisions and water. I am anxious to be rid of you, so you may rely that nothing is neglected. Rise up and follow me.'

I did what he commanded, and he led me through the door of the hut. The guards had either been withdrawn, or Goring had arranged matters with them. We passed unchallenged through the town and across the sandy plain. Once more I heard the roar of the sea, and saw the long white line of the surge. Two figures were standing upon the shore arranging the gear of a small boat. They were the two sailors who had been with us on the voyage.

'See him safely through the surf,' said Goring. The two men sprang in and pushed off, pulling me in after them. With mainsail and jib we ran out from the land and passed safely over the bar. Then my two companions without a word of farewell sprang overboard, and I saw their heads like black dots on the white foam as they made their way back to the shore, while I scudded away into the blackness of the night. Looking back I caught a glimpse of Goring. He was standing upon the summit of a sand-hill, and the rising moon behind him threw his gaunt angular figure into hard relief. He was waving his arms frantically to and fro; it may have been to encourage me on my way, but the gestures seemed to me at the time to be threatening ones, and I often thought that it was more likely that his old savage instinct had returned when he realised that I was out of his power. Be that as it may, it was the last that I ever saw or ever shall see of Septimius Goring.

There is no need for me to dwell upon my solitary voyage. I steered as well as I could for the Canaries, but was picked up upon the fifth day by the British and African Steam Navigation Company's boat *Monrovia*. Let me take this opportunity of tendering my sincerest thanks to Captain Stornoway and his officers for the great kindness which they showed me from that time till they landed me in Liverpool, where I was enabled to take one of the Guion boats to New York.

From the day on which I found myself once more in the bosom of my family I have said little of what I have undergone. The subject is still an intensely painful one to me, and the little which I have dropped has been discredited. I now put the facts before the public as they occurred, careless how far they may be believed, and simply writing them down because my lung is growing weaker, and I feel the responsibility of holding my peace no longer. I make no vague statement. Turn to your map of Africa. There above Cape Blanco, where the land trends away north and south from the westernmost point of the continent, there it is that Septimius Goring still reigns over his dark subjects, unless retribution has overtaken him; and there, where the long green ridges run swiftly in to roar and hiss upon the hot yellow sand, it is there that Harton lies with Hyson and the other poor fellows who were done to death in the *Marie Celeste*.

ANGELA CARTER

The Fall River Axe Murders

ANGELA CARTER *(born 1940) is one of the most elegant and powerful modern writers, whose reputation has grown steadily over the last twenty years. Her books range from outrageous fantasies like* The Infernal Desire Machine of Dr Hoffman *to the recently revised* Love, *and she has published a number of updated myths and fairy-tales, including one filmed as* The Company of Wolves; *'The Fall River Axe Murders' follows in close detail the events leading up to Lizzie Borden's murder of both her parents in particularly appalling circumstances.*

Early in the morning of the fourth of August, 1982, in Fall River, Massachusetts.

Hot, hot hot . . . very early in the morning, before the factory whistle, but, even at this hour, everything shimmers and quivers under the attack of white, furious sun already high in the still air.

Its inhabitants have never come to terms with these hot, humid summers - for it is the humidity more than the heat that makes them intolerable; the weather clings like a low fever you cannot shake off. The Indians who lived here first had the sense to take off their buckskins when hot weather came and sit up to their necks in ponds; not so the descendants of the industrious, self-mortifying saints who imported the Protestant ethic wholesale into a country intended for the siesta and are proud proud! of flying in the face of nature. In most latitudes with summers like these, everything slows down, then. You stay all day in penumbra behind drawn blinds and closed shutters; you wear clothes loose enough to make your own breeze to cool yourself when you infrequently move. But the ultimate decade of the last century finds us at the high point of hard work, here; all will soon be bustle, men will go out into the furnace of the morning well wrapped up in flannel underclothes, linen shirts, vests and coats and trousers of sturdy woollen cloth, and they garrotte themselves with neckties, too, they think it is so virtuous to be uncomfortable.

And today it is the middle of a heat wave; so early in the morning and the mercury has touched the middle eighties, already, and shows no sign of slowing down its headlong ascent.

As far as clothes were concerned, women only appeared to get off more lightly. On this morning, when after breakfast and the performance of a few household duties, Lizzie Borden will murder her parents, she will, on rising, don a simple cotton frock — but, under that, went a long, starched cotton petticoat; another short, starched cotton petticoat; long drawers; woollen stockings; a chemise, and a whalebone corset that took her viscera in a stern hand and squeezed them very tightly. She also strapped a heavy linen napkin between her legs because she was menstruating.

In all these clothes, out of sorts and nauseous as she was, in this dementing heat, her belly in a vice, she will heat up a flat-iron on a stove and press handkerchiefs with the heated iron until it is time for her to go down to the cellar woodpile to collect the hatchet with which our imagination — 'Lizzie Borden with an axe' — always equips her, just as we always visualise St Catherine rolling along her wheel, the emblem of her passion.

Soon, in just as many clothes as Miss Lizzie wears, if less fine, Bridget, the servant girl, will slop kerosene on a sheet of last night's newspaper crumpled with a stick or two of kindling. When the fire settles down, she will cook breakfast; the fire will keep her suffocating company as she washes up afterwards.

In a serge suit, one look at which would be enough to bring you out in prickly heat, Old Borden will perambulate the perspiring town, truffling for money like a pig until he will return home mid-morning to keep a pressing appointment with destiny.

But nobody here is up and about, yet; it is still early morning, before the factory whistle, the perfect stillness of hot weather, a sky already white, the shadowless light of New England like blows from the eye of God, and the sea, white, and the river white.

If we have largely forgotten the physical discomforts of the itching, oppressive garments of the past and the corrosive effects of perpetual physical discomfort on the nerves, then we have mercifully forgotten, too, the smells of the past, the domestic odours — ill-washed flesh; infrequently changed underwear; chamber-pots; slop-pails; inadequately plumbed privies; rotting food; unattended teeth; and the streets are no fresher than indoors, the omnipresent acridity of horse piss and dung, drains, sudden stench of old death from butchers' shops, the amniotic horror of the fishmonger.

You would drench your handkerchief with cologne, and press it to your nose. You would splash yourself with parma violet so that the reek of fleshly decay you always carried with you was overlaid by that of the embalming parlour. You would abhor the air you breathed.

Five living creatures are asleep in a house on Second Street, Fall River. They comprise two old men and three women. The first old man owns all the women by either marriage, birth or contract. His house is narrow as a coffin and that was how he made his fortune — he used to be an undertaker but he has recently branched out in several directions and all his branches bear fruit of the most fiscally gratifying kind.

But you would never think, to look at his house, that he is a successful and a prosperous man. His house is cramped, comfortless, small and mean — 'unpretentious', you might say, if you were his sycophant — while Second Street itself saw better days some time ago. The Borden house — see 'Andrew J. Borden' in flowing script on the brass plate next to the door — stands by itself with a few scant feet of yard on either side. On the left is a stable, out of use since he sold the horse. In the back lot grow a few pear trees, laden at this season.

On this particular morning, as luck would have it, only one of the two Borden girls sleeps in their father's house. Emma Lenora, his oldest daughter, has taken herself off to nearby New Bradford for a few days, to catch the ocean breeze, and so she will escape the slaughter.

Few of their social class stay in Fall River in the sweating months of June, July and August but, then, few of their social class live on Second Street, in the low part of the town where heat gathers like fog. Lizzie was invited away, too, to a summer house by the sea to join a merry band of girls but, as if on purpose to mortify her flesh, as if important business kept her in the exhausted town, as if a wicked fairy spelled her in Second Street, she did not go.

The other old man is some kind of kin of Borden's. He doesn't belong here; he is visiting, passing through, he is a chance bystander, he is irrelevant.

Write him out of the script.

Even though his presence in the doomed house is historically unimpeachable, the colouring of his domestic apocalypse must be crude and the design profoundly simplified for the maximum emblematic effect.

Write John Vinnicum Morse out of the script.

One old man and two of his women sleep in the house on Second Street.

The City Hall clock whirrs and sputters the prolegomena to the first stroke of six and Bridget's alarm clock gives a sympathetic skip and click as the minute-hand stutters on the hour; back to the little hammer jerks, about to hit the bell on top of her clock, but Bridget's damp eyelids do not shudder with premonition as she lies in her sticking flannel nightgown under one thin sheet on an iron bedstead, lies on her back, as the good nuns taught her in her Irish girlhood, in case she dies during the night, to make less trouble for the undertaker.

She is a good girl, on the whole, although her temper is sometimes uncertain and then she will talk back to the missus, sometimes, and will be forced to confess the sin of impatience to the priest. Overcome by heat and nausea — for everyone in the house is going to wake up sick today — she will return to this little bed later in the morning. While she snatches a few moments rest, upstairs, all hell will be let loose, downstairs.

A rosary of brown glass beads, a cardboard-backed colour print of the Virgin bought from a Portuguese shop, a flyblown photograph of her solemn mother in Donegal — these lie or are propped on the mantelpiece that, however sharp the Massachusetts winter, has never seen a lit stick. A banged tin trunk at the foot of the bed holds all Bridget's worldly goods.

There is a stiff chair beside the bed with, upon it, a candlestick, matches, the alarm clock that resounds the room with a dyadic, metallic clang, for it is a joke between Bridget and her mistress that the girl could sleep through anything, *anything*, and so she needs the alarm as well as all the factory whistles that are about to blast off, just this very second about to blast off . . .

A splintered deal washstand holds the jug and bowl she never uses; she isn't going to lug water up to the third floor just to wipe herself down, is she? Not when there's water enough in the kitchen sink.

Old Borden sees no necessity for baths. He does not believe in total immersion. To lose his natural oils would be to rob his body.

A frameless square mirror reflects in corrugated waves a cracked, dusty soap dish containing a quantity of black metal hairpins.

On bright rectangles of paper blinds move the beautiful shadows of the pear trees.

Although Bridget left the door open a crack in forlorn hopes of coaxing a draught into the room, all the spent heat of the previous day has packed itself tightly into her attic. A dandruff of spent whitewash flakes from the ceiling where a fly drearily whines.

The house is thickly redolent of sleep, that sweetish, clinging smell. Still, all still; in all the house nothing moves except the droning fly. Stillness on the staircase. Stillness pressing against the blinds. Stillness, mortal stillness in the room below, where Master and Mistress share the matrimonial bed.

Were the drapes open or the lamp lit, one could better observe the differences between this room and the austerity of the maid's room. Here is a carpet splashed with vigorous flowers, even if the carpet is of the cheap and cheerful variety; there are mauve, ochre and harsh cerise flowers on the wallpaper, even though the wallpaper was old when the Bordens arrived in the house. A dresser with another distorting mirror; no mirror in this house does not take your face and twist it. On the dresser, a runner embroidered with forget-me-nots; on the runner, a bone comb missing three teeth and lightly threaded with grey hairs, a hairbrush backed with ebonised wood, and a number of lace mats underneath small china boxes holding safety-pins, hairnets etc. The little hairpiece that Mrs Borden attaches to her balding scalp for daytime wear is curled up like a dead squirrel. But of Borden's male occupation of this room there is no trace because he has a dressing-room of his own, through *that* door, on the left . . .

What about the other door, the one next to it?

It leads to the back stairs.

And that yet other door, partially concealed behind the head of the heavy, mahogany bed?

If it were not kept securely locked, it would take you into Miss Lizzie's room.

One peculiarity of this house is the number of doors the rooms contain and, a further peculiarity, how all these doors are always locked. A house full of locked doors that open only into other rooms with other locked doors, for, upstairs and downstairs, all the rooms lead in and out of one another like a maze in a bad dream. It is a house without passages. There is no part of the house that has not been marked as some inmate's personal territory; it is a house with no shared, no common spaces between one room and the next. It is a house of privacies sealed as close as if they had been sealed with wax on a legal document.

The only way to Emma's room is through Lizzie's. There is no way out of Emma's room. It is a dead end.

The Borden's custom of locking all the doors, inside and outside, dates from a time, a few years ago, shortly before Bridget came to work for them, when the house was burgled. A person unknown came through the side door while Borden and his wife had taken one of their trips out together; he had loaded her into a trap and set out for the farm they owned at Swansea to ensure his tenant was not bilking him. The girls stayed at home in their rooms, napping on their beds or repairing ripped hems or sewing loose buttons more securely or writing letters or contemplating acts of charity among the deserving poor or staring vacantly into space.

I can't imagine what else they might do.

What the girls do when they are on their own is unimaginable to me.

Emma is more mysterious by far than Lizzie, for we know much less about her. She is a blank space. She has no life. The door from her room leads only into the room of her sister.

'Girls' is, of course, a courtesy term. Emma is well into her forties, Lizzie in her thirties, but they did not marry and so live in their father's house, where they remain in a fictive, protracted childhood.

While the master and the mistress were away and the girls asleep or otherwise occupied, some person or persons unknown tiptoed up the back stairs to the matrimonial bedroom and pocketed Mrs Borden's gold watch and chain, the coral necklace and silver bangle of her remote childhood, and a roll of dollar bills Old Borden kept under clean union suits in the third drawer of the bureau on the left. The intruder attempted to force the lock of the safe, that featureless block of black iron like a slaughtering block or an altar sitting squarely next to the bed on Old Borden's side, but it would have taken a crowbar to penetrate adequately the safe and the intruder tackled it with a pair of nail scissors that were lying handy on the dresser so *that* didn't come off.

Then the intruder pissed and shat on the cover of the Bordens' bed, knocked the clutter of this and that on the dresser to the floor, smashing everything, swept into Old Borden's dressing-room there to maliciously assault his funeral coat as it hung in the moth-balled dark of his closet with the self-same nail scissors that had been used on the safe (the nail scissors now split in two and were abandoned on the closet floor), retired to the kitchen, smashed the flour crock and the treacle crock, and then scrawled an obscenity or two on the parlour window with the cake of soap that lived beside the scullery sink.

What a mess! Lizzie stared with vague surprise at the parlour window; she heard the soft bang of the open screen door, swinging idly, although there was no breeze. What was she doing, standing clad only in her corset in the middle of the sitting room? How had she got there? Had she crept down when she heard the screen door rattle? She did not know. She could not remember.

All that happened was: all at once here she is, in the parlour, with a cake of soap in her hand.

She experienced a clearing of the senses and only then began to scream and shout.

'Help! We have been burgled! Help!'

Emma came down and comforted her, as the big sister had comforted the little one since babyhood. Emma it was who cleared from the sitting-room carpet the flour and treacle Lizzie had heedlessly tracked in from the kitchen on her bare feet in her somnambulist trance. But of the missing jewellery and dollar bills no trace could be found.

I cannot tell you what effect the burglary had on Borden. It utterly disconcerted him; he was a man stunned. It violated him, even. He was a man raped. It took away his hitherto unshakeable confidence in the integrity inherent in things.

The burglary so moved them that the family broke its habitual silence with one another in order to discuss it. They blamed it on the Portuguese, obviously, but sometimes on the Canucks. If their outrage remained constant and did not diminish with time, the focus of it varied according to their moods, although they always pointed the finger of suspicion at the strangers and newcomers who lived in the gruesome ramparts of the company housing a few squalid blocks away. They did not always suspect the dark strangers exclusively; sometimes they thought the culprit might very well have been one of the mill-hands fresh from saucy Lancashire across the ocean who committed the crime, for a slum landlord has few friends among the criminal classes.

However, the possibility of a poltergeist occurs to Mrs Borden, although she does not know the word; she knows, however, that her young stepdaughter is a strange one and could make the plates jump out of sheer spite, if she wanted to. But the old man adores his daughter. Perhaps it is then, after the shock of the burglary, that he decides she needs a change of scene, a dose of sea air, a long voyage, for it was after the burglary he sent her on the grand tour.

After the burglary, the front door and the side door were always locked three times if one of the inhabitants of the house left it for just so much as to go into the yard and pick up a basket of fallen pears when the pears were in season or if the maid went out to hang a bit of washing or Old Borden, after supper, took a piss under a tree.

From this time dated the custom of locking all the bedroom doors on the inside when one was on the inside oneself or on the outside when one was on the outside. Old Borden locked his bedroom door in the morning, when he left it, and put the key in sight of all on the kitchen shelf.

The burglary awakened Old Borden to the evanescent nature of private property. He thereafter undertook an orgy of investment. He would forthwith invest his surplus in good brick and mortar, for who can make away with an office block?

A number of leases fell in simultaneously at just this time on a certain street in the downtown area of the city and Borden snapped them up. He owned the block. He pulled it down. He planned the Borden building, an edifice of shops and offices, dark-red brick, deep-tan stone, with cast-iron detail, from whence, in perpetuity, he might reap a fine harvest of unsaleable rents, and this monument, like that of Ozymandias, would long survive him — and, indeed, stands still, foursquare and handsome, the Andrew Borden Building, on South Main Street.

Not bad for a fish peddler's son, eh?

For, although 'Borden' is an ancient name in New England and the Borden clan between them owned the better part of Fall River, our Borden, Old Borden, these Bordens, did not spring from a wealthy branch of the family. There were Bordens and Bordens and he was the son of a man who sold fresh fish in a wicker basket from house to house to house. Old Borden's parsimony was bred of poverty but learned to thrive best on prosperity, for thrift has a different meaning for the poor; they get no joy of it, it is stark necessity to them. Whoever heard of a penniless miser?

Morose and gaunt, this self-made man is one of few pleasures. His vocation is capital accumulation.

What is his hobby?

Why, grinding the faces of the poor.

First, Andrew Borden was an undertaker, and death, recognising an accomplice, did well by him. In the city of spindles, few made old bones; the little children who laboured in the mills died with especial frequency. When he was an undertaker, no! — it was not true he cut the feet off corpses to fit into a job lot of coffins bought cheap as Civil War surplus! That was a rumour put about by his enemies!

With the profits from his coffins, he bought up a tenement or two and made fresh profit off the living. He bought shares in the mills. Then he invested in a bank or two, so that now he makes a profit on money itself, which is the purest form of profit of all.

Foreclosures and evictions are meat and drink to him. He loves nothing better than a little usury. He is halfway on the road to his first million.

At night, to save the kerosene, he sits lampless dark. He waters the pear trees with his urine; waste not, want not. As soon as the daily newspapers are done with, he rips them up in geometric squares and stores them in the cellar privy so that they all can wipe their arses with them. He mourns the loss of the good organic waste that flushes down the WC. He would like to charge the very cockroaches in the kitchen rent. And yet he has not grown fat on all this; the pure flame of his passion has melted off his flesh, his skin sticks to his bones out of sheer parsimony. Perhaps it is from his first profession that he has acquired his bearing, for he walks with the stately dignity of a hearse.

To watch Old Borden bearing down the street towards you was to be filled with an instinctual respect for mortality, whose gaunt ambassador he seemed to be. And it made you think, too, what a triumph over nature it was when we rose up to walk on two legs instead of four, in the first place! For he held himself upright with such ponderous assertion it was a perpetual reminder to all who witnessed his progress how it is not *natural* to be upright, that it is a triumph of will over gravity, in itself a transcendence of the spirit over matter.

His spine is like an iron rod, forged, not born, impossible to imagine that spine of Old Borden's curled up in the womb in the big C of the foetus; he walks as if his legs had joints at neither knee nor ankles so that his feet hit the trembling earth like a bailiff pounding a door.

He has a white, chin-strap beard, old-fashioned already in those days. He looks as if he'd gnawed his lips off. He is at peace with his god for he has used his talents as the Good Book says he should.

Yet do not think he has no soft spot. Like Old Lear, his heart — and, more than that, his cheque-book — is putty in his youngest daughter's hands. On his pinky — you cannot see it, it lies under the covers — he wears a gold ring, not a wedding ring but a high-school ring, a singular trinket for a fabulously misanthropic miser. His youngest daughter gave it to him when she left school and asked him to wear it, always, and so he always does, and will wear it to the grave to which she is going to send him later in the morning of this combustible day.

He sleeps fully dressed in a flannel nightshirt over his long-sleeved underwear, and a flannel nightcap, and his back is turned towards his wife of thirty years, as is hers to his.

They are Mr and Mrs Jack Spratt in person, he tall and gaunt as a hanging judge and she, such a spreading, round little doughball. He is a miser, while she, she is a glutton, a solitary eater, most innocent of vices and yet the shadow of parodic vice of his, for he would like to eat up all the world, or, failing that, since fate has not spread him a sufficiently large table for his ambition, he is a mute, inglorious Napoleon, he does not know what he might have done because he never had the opportunity — since he has not access to the entire world, he would like to gobble up the city of Fall River. But she, well, she just gently, continuously stuffs herself, doesn't she; she's always nibbling away at something, at the cud, perhaps.

Not that she gets much pleasure from it, either; no gourmet, she forever meditating the exquisite difference between a mayonnaise sharpened with a few drops of Orleans vinegar or one pointed up with a squeeze of fresh lemon juice. No. Abby never aspired so high, nor would she ever think to do so even if she had the option; she is satisfied to stick to simple gluttony and she eschews all overtones of the sensuality of indulgence. Since she relishes not one single mouthful of the food she eats, she knows her ceaseless gluttony is no transgression.

Here they lie in bed together, living embodiments of two of the Seven Deadly Sins, but he knows his avarice is no offence because he never spends any money and she knows she is not greedy because the grub she shovels down gives her dyspepsia.

She employs an Irish cook and Bridget's rough-and-ready hand in the kitchen fulfils Abby's every criterion. Bread, meat, cabbage, potatoes — Abby was made for the heavy food that made her. Bridget merrily slaps on the table boiled dinners, boiled fish, cornmeal mush, Indian pudding, johnnycakes, cookies.

But those cookies . . . ah! there you touch on Abby's little weakness. Molasses cookies, oatmeal cookies, raisin cookies. But when she tackles a sticky brownie, oozing chocolate, then she feels a queasy sense of having gone almost too far, that sin might be just around the corner if her stomach did not immediately palpitate like a guilty conscience.

Her flannel nightdress is cut on the same lines as his nightshirt except for the limp flannel frill round the neck. She weighs two hundred pounds. She is five feet nothing tall. The bed sags on her side. It is the bed in which his first wife died.

Last night, they dosed themselves with castor oil, due to the indisposition that kept them both awake and vomiting the whole night before that; the copious results of their purges brim the chamber-pots beneath the bed. It is fit to make a sewer faint.

Back to back they lie. You could rest a sword in the space between the old man and his wife, between the old man's backbone, the only rigid thing he ever offered her, and her soft, warm, enormous bum. Their purges flailed them. Their faces show up decomposing green in the gloom of the curtained room, in which the air is too thick for flies to move.

The youngest daughter dreams behind the locked door.

Look at the sleeping beauty!

She threw back the top sheet and her window is wide open but there is no breeze, outside, this morning, to shiver deliciously the screen. Bright sun floods the blinds so that the linen-coloured light shows us how Lizzie has gone to bed as for a levée in a pretty, ruffled nightdress of starched white muslin with ribbons of pastel pink satin threaded through the eyelets of the lace, for is it not the naughty Nineties, everywhere but dour Fall River? Don't the gilded steamships of the Fall River Line signify all the squandered luxury of the Gilded Age within their mahogany and chandeliered interiors? But don't they sail *away* from Fall River, to where, elsewhere, it is the Belle Epoque? In New York, Paris, London, champagne corks pop, in Monte Carlo the bank is broken, women fall backwards in a crisp meringue of petticoats for fun and profit, but not in Fall River. Oh, no. So, in the immutable privacy of her bedroom, for her own delight, Lizzie puts on a rich girl's pretty nightdress, although she lives in a mean house, because she is a rich girl, too.

But she is plain.

The hem of her nightdress is rucked up above her knees because she is a restless sleeper. Her light, dry, reddish hair, crackling with static, slipping loose from the night-time plait, crisps and stutters over the square pillow at which she clutches as she sprawls on her stomach, having rested her cheek on the starched pillowcase for coolness' sake at some earlier hour.

Lizzie was not an affectionate diminutive but the name with which she had been christened. Since she would always be known as 'Lizzie', so her father reasoned, why burden her with the effete and fancy prolongation of 'Elizabeth'? A miser in everything, he even cropped off half her name before he gave it to her. So 'Lizzie' it was, stark and unadorned, and she is a motherless child, orphaned at two years old, poor thing.

Now she is two-and-thirty and yet the memory of that mother she cannot remember remains an abiding source of grief: 'If mother had lived, everything would have been different.'

How? Why? Different in what way? She wouldn't have been able to answer that, lost in a nostalgia for unknown love. Yet how could she have been loved better than by her sister, Emma, who lavished the pent-up treasures of a New England spinster's heart upon the little thing? Different, perhaps, because her natural mother, the first Mrs Borden, subject as she was to fits of sudden, wild, inexplicable rage, might have taken the hatchet to Old Borden on her own account? But Lizzie *loves* her father. All are agreed on that. Lizzie adores the adoring father who, after her mother died, took to himself another wife.

Her bare feet twitch a little, like those of a dog dreaming of rabbits. Her sleep is thin and unsatisfying, full of vague terrors and indeterminate menaces to which she cannot put a name or form once she is awake. Sleep opens within her a disorderly house. But all she knows is, she sleeps badly, and this last, stifling night has been troubled, too, by vague nausea and the gripes of her female pain; her room is harsh with the metallic smell of menstrual blood.

Yesterday evening she slipped out of the house to visit a woman friend. Lizzie was agitated; she kept picking nervously at the shirring on the front of her dress.

'I am afraid . . . that somebody . . . will *do* something,' said Lizzie.

'Mrs Borden . . .' and here Lizzie lowered her voice and her eyes looked everywhere in the room except at Miss Russell . . . 'Mrs Borden — oh! will you ever believe? Mrs Borden thinks somebody is trying to *poison* us!'

She used to call her stepmother 'mother', as duty bade, but after a quarrel about money after her father deeded half a slum property to her stepmother five years before, Lizzie always, with cool scrupulosity, spoke of 'Mrs Borden' when she was forced to speak of her, and called her 'Mrs Borden' to her face, too.

'Last night, Mrs Borden and poor father were so sick! I heard them, through the wall. And, as for me, I haven't felt myself all day, I have felt so strange. So very . . . strange.'

For there were those somnambulist fits. Since a child, she endured occasional 'peculiar spells', as the idiom of the place and time called odd lapses of behaviour, unexpected, involuntary trances, moments of disconnection. Those times when the mind misses a beat. Miss Russell hastened to discover an explanation within reason; she was embarrassed to mention the 'peculiar spells'. Everyone knew there was nothing odd about the Borden girls.

'Something you ate? It must have been something you have eaten. What was yesterday's supper?' solicitously queried kind Miss Russell.

'Warmed-over swordfish. We had it hot for dinner though I could not take much. Then Bridget heated up the leftovers for supper but, again, for myself, I could only get down a forkfull. Mrs Borden ate up the remains and scoured her plate with her bread. She smacked her lips but then was sick all night.' (Note of smugness, here.)

'Oh, Lizzie! In all this heat, this dreadful heat! Twice-cooked fish! You know how quickly fish goes off in this heat! Bridget should have known better than to give you twice-cooked fish!'

It was Lizzie's difficult time of the month, too; her friend could tell by a certain haggard, glazed look on Lizzie's face. Yet her gentility forbade her to mention that. But how could Lizzie have got it into her head that the entire household was under siege from malign forces without?

'There have been threats,' Lizzie pursued remorselessly, keeping her eyes on her nervous fingertips. 'So many people, you understand, dislike father.'

This cannot be denied. Miss Russell politely remained mute.

'Mrs Borden was so very sick she called the doctor in and Father was abusive towards the doctor and shouted at him and told him he would not pay a doctor's bills whilst we had our own good castor oil in the house. He shouted at the doctor and all the neighbours heard and I was so ashamed. There is a man, you see . . .' and here she ducked her head, while her short, pale eyelashes beat on her cheek bones . . . 'such a man, a *dark* man, with aspect, yes, of death upon his face, Miss Russell, a dark man I've seen outside the house at odd, at unexpected hours, early in the morning, late at night, whenever I cannot sleep in this dreadful shade if I raise the blind and peep out, there I see him in the shadows of the pear trees, in the yard, a dark man . . . perhaps he puts poison in the milk, in the mornings, after the milkman fills his can. Perhaps he poisons the ice, when the iceman comes.'

'How long has he been haunting you?' asked Miss Russell, properly dismayed.

'Since . . . the burglary,' said Lizzie and suddenly looked Miss Russell full in the face with a kind of triumph. How large her eyes were; prominent, yet veiled. And her well-manicured fingers went on pecking away at the front of her dress as if she were trying to unpick the shirring.

Miss Russell knew, she just *knew*, this dark man was a figment of Lizzie's imagination. All in a rush, she lost patience with the girl; dark men standing outside her bedroom window, indeed! Yet she was kind and cast about for ways to reassure.

'But Bridget is up and about when the milkman, the iceman call and the whole street is busy and bustling, too; who would dare to put poison in either milk or ice-bucket while half of Second Street looks on? Oh, Lizzie, it is the dreadful summer, the heat, the intolerable heat that's put us all out of sorts, makes us fractious and nervous, makes us sick. So easy to imagine things in this terrible weather, that taints the food and sows worms in the mind . . . I thought you'd planned to go away, Lizzie, to the ocean. Didn't you plan to take a little holiday, by the sea? Oh, do go! Sea air would blow away these silly fancies!'

Lizzie neither nods nor shakes her head but continues to worry at her shirring. For does she not have important business in Fall River? Only that morning, had she not been down to the drug-store to try to buy some prussic acid herself? But how can she tell kind Miss Russell she is gripped by an imperious need to stay in Fall River and murder her parents?

She went to the drug-store on the corner of Main Street in order to buy prussic acid but nobody would sell it to her, so she came home empty-handed. Had all that talk of poison in the vomiting house put her in mind of poison? The autopsy will reveal no trace of poison in the stomachs of either parent. She did not try to poison them; she only had it in mind to poison them. But she had been unable to buy poison. The use of poison had been denied her; so what can she be planning, now?

'And this dark man,' she pursued to the unwilling Miss Russell, 'oh! I have seen the moon glint upon an *axe*!

When she wakes up, she can never remember her dreams; she only remembers she slept badly.

Hers is a pleasant room of not ungenerous dimensions, seeing the house is so very small. Besides the bed and dresser, there is a sofa and a desk; it is her bedroom and also her sitting-room and her office, too, for the desk is stacked with account books of the various charitable organisations with which she occupies her ample spare time. The Fruit and Flower Mission, under whose auspices she visits the indigent old in hospital with gifts; the Women's Christian Temperance Union, for whom she extracts signatures for petitions against the Demon Drink; Christian Endeavour, whatever that is — this is the golden age of good works and she flings herself into committees with a vengeance. What would the daughters of the rich do with themselves if the poor ceased to exist?

There is the Newsboys' Thanksgiving Dinner Fund; and the Horsetrough Association; and the Chinese Conversion Association — no class nor kind is safe from her merciless charity.

Bureau; dressing-table; closet; bed; sofa. She spends her days in this room, moving between each of these dull items of furniture in a circumscribed, undeviating, planetary round. She loves her privacy, she loves her room, she locks herself up in it all day. A shelf contains a book or two: *Heroes of the Mission Field*, *The Romance of Trade*, *What Katy Did*. On the walls, framed photographs of high-school friends, sentimentally inscribed, with, tucked inside one frame, picture postcard showing a black kitten peeking through a horseshoe. A watercolour of a Cape Cod seascape executed with poignant amateur incompetence. A monochrome photograph or two of works of art, a Della Robbia madonna and the Mona Lisa; these she bought in the Uffizi and the Louvre respectively when she went to Europe.

Europe!

For don't you remember what Katy did next? The story-book heroine took the steamship to smoky old London, to elegant, fascinating Paris, to sunny, antique Rome and Florence, the story-book heroine sees Europe reveal itself before her like an interesting series of magic-lantern slides on a gigantic screen. All is present and all unreal. The Tower of London; click. Notre Dame; click. The Sistine Chapel; click. Then the lights go out and she is in the dark again.

Of this journey she retained only the most circumspect of souvenirs, that madonna, that Mona Lisa, reproductions of objects of art consecrated by a universal approval of taste. If she came back with a bag full of memories stamped 'Never to be Forgotten', she put the bag away under the bed on which she had dreamed of the world before she set out to see it and on which, at home again, she continued to dream, the dream, the dream having been transformed not into lived experience but into memory, which is only another kind of dreaming.

Wistfully: 'When I was in Florence . . .'

But then, with pleasure, she corrects herself: 'When *we* were in Florence . . .'

Because a good deal, in fact most, of the gratification the trip gave her came from having set out from Fall River with a select group of the daughters of respectable and affluent mill-owners. Once away from Second Street, she was able to move comfortably in the segment of Fall River society to which she belonged by right of old name and new money but from which, when she went home, her father's plentiful personal eccentricities excluded her. Sharing bedrooms, sharing staterooms, sharing berths, the girls travelled together in a genteel gaggle that bore its doom already upon it, for they were the girls who would not marry, now, and any pleasure they might have obtained from the variety and excitement of the trip was spoiled in advance by the knowledge they were eating up what might have been their own wedding-cake, using up what should have been, if they'd had any luck, their marriage settlements.

All girls pushing thirty, privileged to go out and look at the world before they resigned themselves to the thin condition of New England spinsterhood; but it was a case of look, don't touch. They knew they must not get their hands dirtied or their dresses crushed by the world, while their affectionate companionship en route had a certain steadfast, determined quality about it as they bravely made the best of the second-best.

It was a sour trip, in some ways, sour; and it was a round trip, ended at the sour place from where it had set out. Home, again; the narrow house, the rooms all locked like those in Bluebeard's castle, and the fat, white stepmother whom nobody loves sitting in the middle of the spider web, she has not budged a single inch while Lizzie was away but she has grown fatter.

This stepmother oppressed her like a spell.

The days open their cramped spaces into other cramped spaces and old furniture and never anything to look forward to, nothing.

When Old Borden dug in his pocket to shell out for Lizzie's trip to Europe, the eye of God on the pyramid blinked to see daylight, but no extravagance is too excessive for the miser's younger daughter who is the wild card in this house and, it seems, can have anything she wants, play ducks and drakes with her father's silver dollars if it so pleases her. He pays all her dressmakers' bill on the dot and how she loves to dress up fine! She is addicted to dandyism. He gives her each week in pin-money the same as the cook gets for wages and Lizzie gives that which she does not spend on personal adornment to the deserving poor.

He would give his Lizzie anything, anything in the world that lives under the green sign of the dollar.

She would like a pet, a kitten or a puppy, she loves small animals and birds, too, poor, helpless things. She piles high the bird-table all winter. She used to keep some white pouter pigeons in the disused stable, the kind that look like shuttlecocks and go 'vroo croo', soft as a cloud.

Surviving photographs of Lizzie Borden show a face it is difficult to look at as if you knew nothing about her; coming events cast their shadow across her face, or else you see the shadows these events have cast — something terrible, something ominous in this face with its jutting, rectangular jaw and those mad eyes of the New England saints, eyes that belong to a person who does not listen to you . . . fanatic's eyes, you might say, if you knew nothing about her. If you were sorting through a box of old photographs in a junk shop and came across this particular, sepia, faded face above the choked collars of the 1890s, you might murmur when you saw her: 'Oh, what big eyes you have!' as Red Riding Hood said to the wolf, but then you might not even pause to pick her out and look at her more closely, for hers is not, in itself, a striking face.

But as soon as the face has a name, once you recognise her, when you know who she is and what it was she did, the face becomes as if of one possessed, and now it haunts you, you look at it again and again, it secretes mystery.

This woman, with her jaw of a concentration-camp attendant, and such eyes . . .

In her old age, she wore pince-nez, and truly with the years the mad light has departed from those eyes or else is deflected by her glasses — if, indeed, it *was* a mad light, in the first place, for don't we all conceal somewhere photographs of ourselves that make us look like crazed assassins? And, in those early photographs of her young womanhood, she herself does not look so much like a crazed assassin as somebody in extreme solitude, oblivious of that camera in whose direction she obscurely smiles, so that it would not surprise you to learn that she is blind.

There is a mirror on the dresser in which she sometimes looks at those times when time snaps in two and then she sees herself with blind, clairvoyant eyes, as though she were another person.

'Lizzie is not herself, today.'

At those times, those irremediable times, she could have raised her muzzle to some aching moon and howled.

At other times, she watches herself doing her hair and trying her clothes on. The distorting mirror reflects her with the queasy fidelity of water. She puts on dresses and then she takes them off. She looks at herself in her corset. She pats her hair. She measures herself with the tape-measure. She pulls the measure tight. She pats her hair. She tries on a hat, a little hat, a chic little straw toque. She punctures it with a hatpin. She pulls the veil down. She pulls it up. She takes the hat off. She drives the hatpin into it with a strength she did not know she possessed.

Time goes by and nothing happens.

She traces the outlines of her face with an uncertain hand as if she were thinking of unfastening the bandages on her soul but it isn't time to do that, yet: she isn't ready to be seen, yet.

She is a girl of Sargasso calm.

She used to keep her pigeons in the loft above the disused stable and feed them grain out of the palms of her cupped hands. She liked to feel the soft scratch of their beaks. They murmured 'vroo croo' with infinite tenderness. She changed their water every day and cleaned up their leprous messes but Old Borden took a dislike to their cooing, it got on his nerves, who'd have thought he *had* any nerves but he invented some, they got on them, one afternoon he took out the hatchet from the woodpile in the cellar and chopped those pigeons' heads right off, he did.

Abby fancied the slaughtered pigeons for a pie but Bridget the servant girl put her foot down, at that: what?!? Make a pie out of Miss Lizzie's beloved turtledoves? JesusMaryandJoseph!!! she exclaimed with characteristic impetuousness, what can they be thinking of! Miss Lizzie so nervy with her funny turns and all! (The maid is the only one in the house with any sense and that's the truth of it.) Lizzie came home from the Fruit and Flower Mission for whom she had been reading a tract to an old woman in a poorhouse: 'God bless you, Miss Lizzie.' At home was all blood and feathers.

She doesn't weep, this one, it isn't her nature, she is still waters, but, when moved, she changes colour, her face flushes, it goes dark, angry, mottled red. The old man loves his daughter this side of idolatry and pays for everything she wants, but all the same he killed her pigeons when his wife wanted to gobble them up.

That is how she sees it. That is how she understands it. She cannot bear to watch her stepmother eat, now. Each bite the woman takes seems to go: 'Vroo croo.'

Old Borden cleaned off the hatchet and put it back in the cellar, next to the woodpile. The red receding from her face, Lizzie went down to inspect the instrument of destruction. She picked it up and weighed it in her hand.

That was a few weeks before, at the beginning of the spring.

Her hands and feet twitch in her sleep; the nerves and muscles of this complicated mechanism won't relax, just won't relax, she is all twang, all tension, she is taut as the strings of a wind-harp from which random currents of the air pluck out tunes that are not our tunes.

At the first stroke of the City Hall clock, the first factory hooter blares, and then, on another note, another, and another, the Metacomet Mill, the American Mill, the Mechanics Mill . . . until every mill in the entire town sings out loud in a common anthem of summoning and the hot alleys where the factory folk live blacken with the hurrying throng: hurry! scurry! to loom, to bobbin, to spindle, to dye-shop as to places of worship, men, and women, too, and children, the street blacken, the sky darkens as the chimneys now belch forth, the clang, bang, clatter of the mills commences.

Bridget's clock leaps and shudders on its chair, about to sound its own alarm. Their day, the Bordens' fatal day, trembles on the brink of beginning.

Outside, above, in the already burning air, see! the angel of death roosts on the roof-tree.

O. HENRY

A Retrieved Information

O. HENRY *(real name William S. Porter, 1862 – 1910), one of America's most notable short-story writers, led an eventful and troubled life. Charged with embezzling bank funds when he was a teller, he fled to South America and led an outlaw existence until his wife fell ill; when he returned to Texas he was arrested and spent five years in jail, where he met the character on whom Jimmy Valentine in 'A Retrieved Information' is based. On his release he supported himself by his writing but drank a quart of whisky a day, and died of consumption in New York.*

A guard came to the prison shoe-shop, where Jimmy Valentine was assiduously stitching uppers, and escorted him to the front office. There the warden handed Jimmy his pardon, which had been signed that morning by the governor. Jimmy took it in a tired kind of way. He had served nearly ten months of a four-year sentence. He had expected to stay only about three months, at the longest. When a man with as many friends on the outside as Jimmy Valentine had is received in the 'stir' it is hardly worth while to cut his hair.

'Now, Valentine,' said the warden, 'you'll go out in the morning. Brace up, and make a man of yourself. You're not a bad fellow at heart. Stop cracking safes, and live straight.'

'Me?' said Jimmy, in surprise. 'Why, I never cracked a safe in my life.'

'Oh, no,' laughed the warden. 'Of course not. Let's see, now. How was it you happened to get sent up on that Springfield job? Was it because you wouldn't prove an alibi for fear of compromising somebody in extremely high-toned society? Or was it simply a case of a mean old jury that had it in for you? It's always one or the other with you innocent victims.'

'Me?' said Jimmy, still blankly virtuous. 'Why, warden, I never was in Springfield in my life!'

'Take him back, Cronin,' smiled the warden, 'and fix him up with outgoing clothes. Unlock him at seven in the morning, and let him come to the bull-pen. Better think over my advice, Valentine.'

At a quarter past seven on the next morning Jimmy stood in the warden's outer office. He had on a suit of the villainously fitting, ready-made clothes and a pair of stiff, squeaky shoes that the state furnishes to its discharged compulsory guests.

The clerk handed him a railroad ticket and the five-dollar bill with which the law expected him to rehabilitate himself into good citizenship and prosperity. The warden gave him a cigar and shook hands. Valentine, 9762, was chronicled on the books 'Pardoned by Governor,' and Mr James Valentine walked out into the sunshine.

Disregarding the song of the birds, the waving green trees, and the smell of the flowers, Jimmy headed straight for a restaurant. There he tasted the first sweet joys of liberty in the shape of a broiled chicken and a bottle of white wine — followed by a cigar a grade better than the one the warden had given him. From there he proceeded leisurely to the depot. He tossed a quarter into the hat of a blind man sitting by the door, and boarded his train. Three hours set him down in a little town near the state line. He went to the café of one Mike Dolan and shook hands with Mike, who was alone behind the bar.

'Sorry we couldn't make it sooner, Jimmy, me boy,' said Mike. 'But we had that protest from Springfield to buck against, and the governor nearly balked. Feeling all right?'

'Fine,' said Jimmy. 'Got my key?'

He got his key and went upstairs, unlocking the door of a room at the rear. Everything was just as he had left it. There on the floor was still Ben Price's collar-button that had been torn from that eminent detective's shirt-band when they had overpowered Jimmy to arrest him.

Pulling out from the wall a folding-bed, Jimmy slid back a panel in the wall and dragged out a dust-covered suitcase. He opened this and gazed fondly at the finest set of burglar's tools in the East. It was a complete set, made of specially tempered steel, the latest designs in drills, punches, braces and bits, jimmies, clamps and augers, with two or three novelties invented by Jimmy himself, in which he took pride. Over nine hundred dollars they had cost him to have made at—, a place where they make such things for the profession.

In half an hour Jimmy went downstairs and through the café. He was now dressed in tasteful and well-fitting clothes, and carried his dusted and cleaned suitcase in his hand.

'Got anything on?' asked Mike Dolan, genially.

'Me?' said Jimmy, in a puzzled tone. 'I don't understand. I'm representing the New York Amalgamated Short Snap Biscuit Cracker and Frazzled Wheat Company.'

This statement delighted Mike to such an extent that Jimmy had to take a seltzer-and-milk on the spot. He never touched 'hard' drinks.

A week after the release of Valentine, 9762, there was a neat job of safe-burglary done in Richmond, Indiana, with no clue to the author. A scant eight hundred dollars was all that was secured. Two weeks after that a patented, improved, burglar-proof safe in Logansport was opened like a cheese to the tune of fifteen hundred dollars, currency; securities and silver untouched. That began to interest the rogue-catchers. Then an old-fashioned bank-safe in Jefferson City became active and threw out of its crater an eruption of bank-notes amounting to five thousand dollars. The losses were now high enough to bring the matter up into Ben Price's class of work. By comparing notes, a remarkable similarity in the methods of the burglaries was noticed. Ben Price investigated the scenes of the robberies, and was heard to remark:

'That's Dandy Jim Valentine's autograph. He's resumed business. Look at that combination knob — jerked out as easy as pulling up a radish in wet weather. He's got the only clamps that can do it. And look how clean those tumblers were punched out! Jimmy never has to drill but one hole. Yes, I guess I want Mr Valentine. He'll do his bit next time without any short-time or clemency foolishness.'

Ben Price knew Jimmy's habits. He had learned them while working up the Springfield case. Long jumps, quick get-aways, no confederates, and a taste for good society — these ways had helped Mr Valentine to become noted as a successful dodger of retribution. It was given out that Ben Price had taken up the trail of the elusive cracksman, and other people with burglar-proof safes felt more at ease.

One afternoon Jimmy Valentine and his suitcase climbed out of the mail-hack in Elmore, a little town five miles off the railroad down in the black-jack country of Arkansas. Jimmy, looking like an athletic young senior just home from college, went down the board sidewalk towards the hotel.

A young lady crossed the street, passed him at the corner and entered a door over which was the sign 'The Elmore Bank.' Jimmy Valentine looked into her eyes, forgot what he was, and became another man. She lowered her eyes and coloured slightly. Young men of Jimmy's style and looks were scarce in Elmore.

Jimmy collared a boy that was loafing on the steps of the bank as if he were one of the stock-holders, and began to ask him questions about the town, feeding him dimes at intervals. By and by the young lady came out, looking royally unconscious of the young man with the suitcase, and went her way.

'Isn't that young lady Miss Polly Simpson?' asked Jimmy, with specious guile.

'Naw,' said the boy. 'She's Annabel Adams. Her pa owns this bank. What'd you come to Elmore for? Is that a gold watch-chain? I'm going to get a bulldog. Got any more dimes?'

Jimmy went to the Planter's Hotel, registered as Ralph D. Spencer, and engaged a room. He leaned on the desk and declared his platform to the clerk. He said he had come to Elmore to look for a location to go into business. How was the shoe business now in the town? He had thought of the shoe business. Was there an opening?

The clerk was impressed by the clothes and manner of Jimmy. He, himself, was something of a pattern of fashion to the thinly gilded youth of Elmore, but he now perceived his shortcomings. While trying to figure out Jimmy's manner of tying his four-in-hand he cordially gave information.

Yes, there ought to be a good opening in the shoe line. There wasn't an exclusive shoe-store in the place. The dry goods and general stores handled them. Business in all lines was fairly good. Hoped Mr Spencer would decide to locate in Elmore. He would find it a pleasant town to live in, and the people very sociable.

Mr Spencer thought he would stop over in the town a few days and look over the situation. No, the clerk needn't call the boy. He would carry up his suitcase, himself; it was rather heavy.

Mr Ralph Spencer, the Phoenix that arose from Jimmy Valentine's ashes — ashes left by the flame of a sudden and alternative attack of love — remained in Elmore, and prospered. He opened a shoe-store and secured a good run of trade.

Socially he was also a success, and made many friends. And he accomplished the wish of his heart. He met Miss Annabel Adams, and became more and more captivated by her charms.

At the end of a year the situation of Mr Ralph Spencer was this: he had won the respect of the community, his shoe-store was flourishing, and he and Annabel were engaged to be married in two weeks. Mr Adams, the typical, plodding, country banker, approved of Spencer. Annabel's pride in him almost equalled her affection. He was as much at home in the family of Mr Adams and that of Annabel's married sister as if he were already a member.

One day Jimmy sat down in his room and wrote this letter, which he mailed to the safe address of one of his old friends in St Louis:

Dear Old Pal:

I want you to be at Sullivan's place, in Little Rock, next Wednesday night at nine o'clock. I want you to wind up some little matters for me. And, also, I want to make you a present of my kit of tools. I know you'll be glad to get them — you couldn't duplicate the lot for a thousand dollars. Say, Billy, I've quit the old business — a year ago. I've got a nice store. I'm making an honest living, and I'm going to marry the finest girl on earth two weeks from now. It's the only life, Billy — the straight one. I wouldn't touch a dollar of another man's money now for a million. After I get married I'm going to sell out and go West, where there won't be so much danger of having old scores brought up against me. I tell you, Billy, she's an angel. She believes in me; and I wouldn't do another crooked thing for the whole world. Be sure to be at Sully's, for I must see you. I'll bring along the tools with me.

Your old friend,
Jimmy

On the Monday night after Jimmy wrote this letter, Ben Price jogged unobtrusively into Elmore in a livery buggy. He lounged about town in his quiet way until he found out what he wanted to know. From the drug-store across the street from Spencer's shoe-store he got a good look at Ralph D. Spencer.

'Going to marry the banker's daughter are you, Jimmy?' said Ben to himself, softly. 'Well, I don't know!'

The next morning Jimmy took breakfast at the Adamses. He was going to Little Rock that day to order his wedding-suit and buy something nice for Annabel. That would be the first time he had left town since he came to Elmore. It had been more than a year now since those last professional 'jobs,' and he thought he could safely venture out.

After breakfast quite a family party went down town together — Mr Adams, Annabel, Jimmy, and Annabel's married sister with her two little girls, aged five and nine. They came by the hotel where Jimmy still boarded, and he ran up to his room and brought along his suitcase. Then they went on to the bank. There stood Jimmy's horse and buggy and Dolph Gibson, who was going to drive him over to the railroad station.

All went inside the high, carved oak railings into the banking-room — Jimmy included, for Mr Adams's future son-in-law was welcome anywhere. The clerks were pleased to be greeted by the good-looking, agreeable young man who was going to marry Miss Annabel. Jimmy set his suitcase down. Annabel, whose heart was bubbling with happiness and lively youth, put on Jimmy's hat and picked up the suitcase. 'Wouldn't I make a nice drummer?' said Annabel. 'My! Ralph, how heavy it is. Feels like it was full of gold bricks.'

'Lot of nickel-plated shoe-horns in there,' said Jimmy, coolly, 'that I'm going to return. Thought I'd save express charges by taking them up. I'm getting awfully economical.'

The Elmore Bank had just put in a new safe and vault. Mr Adams was very proud of it, and insisted on an inspection by every one. The vault was a small one, but it had a new patented door. It fastened with three solid steel bolts thrown simultaneously with a single handle, and had a time-lock. Mr Adams beamingly explained its workings to Mr Spencer, who showed a courteous but not too intelligent interest. The two children, May and Agatha, were delighted by the shining metal and funny clock and knobs. While they were thus engaged Ben Price sauntered in and leaned on his elbow, looking casually inside between the railings. He told the teller that he didn't want anything; he was just waiting for a man he knew. Suddenly there was a scream or two from the women, and a commotion. Unperceived by the elders, May, the nine-year-old girl, in a spirit of play, had shut Agatha in the vault. She had then shot the bolts and turned the knob of the combination as she had seen Mr Adams do.

The old banker sprang to the handle and tugged at it for a moment. 'The door can't be opened,' he groaned. 'The clock hasn't been wound nor the combination set.'

Agatha's mother screamed again, hysterically.

'Hush!' said Mr Adams, raising his trembling hand. 'All be quiet for a moment, Agatha!' he called as loudly as he could: 'Listen to me.' During the following silence they could just hear the faint sound of the child wildly shrieking in the dark vault in a panic of terror.

'My precious darling!' wailed the mother. 'She will die of fright! Open the door! Oh, break it open! Can't you men do something?'

'There isn't a man nearer than Little Rock who can open that door,' said Mr Adams, in a shaky voice. 'My God! Spencer, what shall we do? That child — she can't stand it long in there. There isn't enough air, and, besides, she'll go into convulsions from fright.'

Agatha's mother, frantic now, beat the door of the vault with her hands. Somebody wildly suggested dynamite. Annabel turned to Jimmy, her large eyes full of anguish, but not yet despairing. To a woman nothing seems quite impossible to the powers of the man she worships.

'Can't you do something, Ralph – *try*, won't you?'

He looked at her with a queer, soft smile on his lips and in his keen eyes.

'Annabel,' he said, 'give me that rose you are wearing, will you?'

Hardly believing that she heard him aright, she unpinned the bud from the bosom of her dress, and placed it in his right hand. Jimmy stuffed it into his vest-pocket, threw off his coat and pulled up his shirt-sleeves. With that act Ralph D. Spencer passed away and Jimmy Valentine took his place.

'Get away from the door, all of you,' he commanded, shortly.

He set his suitcase on the table, and opened it out flat. From that time on he seemed to be unconscious of the presence of any one else. He laid out the shining, queer implements swiftly and orderly, whistling softly to himself as he always did when at work. In a deep silence and immovable, the others watched him as if under a spell.

In a minute Jimmy's pet drill was biting smoothly into the steel door. In ten minutes — breaking his own burglarious record — he threw back the bolts and opened the door.

Agatha, almost collapsed, but safe, was gathered into her mother's arms. Jimmy Valentine put on his coat, and walked outside the railings towards the front door. As he went he thought he heard a far-away voice that he once knew call 'Ralph!' but he never hesitated.

At the door a big man stood somewhat in his way.

'Hello, Ben!' said Jimmy, still with his strange smile. 'Got around at last, have you? Well, let's go. I don't know that it makes much difference, now.'

And then Ben Price acted rather strangely.

'Guess you're mistaken, Mr Spencer,' he said. 'Don't believe I recognise you. Your buggy's waiting for you, ain't it?'

And Ben Price turned and strolled down the street.

ALDOUS HUXLEY

The Gioconda Smile

ALDOUS HUXLEY *(1894 – 1963), author of brilliant sceptical novels such as* Crome Yellow, Antic Hay *and* Brave New World, *also wrote a number of short stories which are largely (and unjustly) neglected today. 'The Gioconda Smile' is one of the most notable, and while it has occasionally been anthologised as a tale of terror, it is not widely known that it was inspired by a real case — though precisely which one is not certain. The Greenwood poisoning case was the one that Huxley himself acknowledged, although Ellery Queen has argued strongly that the infamous Major Armstrong provided the spark. Both cases are treated in detail in the* Notable British Trials *series, for readers who might wish to pursue the question.*

I

'Miss Spence will be down directly, sir.'

'Thank you,' said Mr Hutton, without turning round. Janet Spence's parlourmaid was so ugly — ugly on purpose, it always seemed to him, malignantly, criminally ugly — that he could not bear to look at her more than was necessary. The door closed. Left to himself, Mr Hutton got up and began to wander round the room, looking with meditative eyes at the familiar objects it contained.

Photographs of Greek statuary, photographs of the Roman Forum, coloured prints of Italian masterpieces, all very safe and well known. Poor, dear Janet, what a prig — what an intellectual snob! Her real taste was illustrated in that water-colour by the pavement artist, the one she had paid half a crown for (and thirty-five shillings for the frame). How often he had heard her tell the story, how often expatiate on the beauties of that skilful imitation of an oleograph! 'A real artist in the streets,' and you could hear the capital A in Artist as she spoke the words. She made you feel that part of his glory had entered into Janet Spence when she tendered him that half-crown for the copy of the oleograph. She was implying a compliment to her own taste and penetration. A genuine Old Master for half a crown. Poor, dear Janet!

Mr Hutton came to a pause in front of a small mirror. Stooping a little to get a full view of his face, he passed a white, well-manicured finger over his moustache. It was as curly, as freshly auburn as it had been twenty years ago. His hair still retained its colour, and there was no sign of baldness yet — only a certain elevation of the brow. 'Shakespeare,' thought Mr Hutton, with a smile, as he surveyed the smooth and polished expanse of his forehead.

Others abide our question, thou art free . . . Footsteps in the sea . . . Majesty . . . Shakespeare, thou shouldst be living at this hour. No, that was Milton, wasn't it? Milton, the Lady of Christ's. There was no lady about him. He was what the women would call a manly man. That was why they liked him — for the curly auburn moustache and the discreet redolence of tobacco. Mr Hutton smiled again; he enjoyed making fun of himself. Lady of Christ's? No, no. He was the Christ of Ladies. Very pretty, very pretty. The Christ of Ladies. Mr Hutton wished there were somebody he could tell the joke to. Poor, dear Janet wouldn't appreciate it, alas!

He straightened himself up, patted his hair, and resumed his peregrination. Damn the Roman Forum; he hated those dreary photographs.

Suddenly he became aware that Janet Spence was in the room, standing near the door. Mr Hutton started, as though he had been taken in some felonious act. To make these silent and spectral appearances was one of Janet Spence's peculiar talents. Perhaps she had been there all the time, and seen him looking at himself in the mirror. Impossible! But, still, it was disquieting.

'Oh, you gave me such a surprise,' said Mr Hutton, recovering his smile and advancing with outstretched hand to meet her.

Miss Spence was smiling too: her Gioconda smile, he had once called it in a moment of half-ironical flattery. Miss Spence had taken the compliment seriously, and always tried to live up to the Leonardo standard. She smiled on in silence while Mr Hutton shook hands; that was part of the Gioconda business.

'I hope you're well,' said Mr Hutton. 'You look it.'

What a queer face she had! That small mouth pursed forward by the Gioconda expression into a little snout with a round hole in the middle as though for whistling — it was like a penholder seen from the front. Above the mouth a well-shaped nose, finely aquiline. Eyes large, lustrous, and dark, with the largeness, lustre, and darkness that seems to invite sties and an occasional bloodshot suffusion. They were fine eyes, but unchangingly grave. The pen-holder might do its Gioconda trick, but the eyes never altered in their earnestness. Above them, a pair of boldly arched, heavily pencilled black eyebrows lent a surprising air of power, as of a Roman matron, to the upper portion of the face. Her hair was dark and equally Roman; Agrippina from the brows upward.

'I thought I'd just look in on my way home,' Mr Hutton went on. 'Ah, it's good to be back here' — he indicated with a wave of his hand the flowers in the vases, the sunshine and greenery beyond the windows – 'it's good to be back in the country after a stuffy day of business in town.'

Miss Spence, who had sat down, pointed to a chair at her side.

'No, really, I can't sit down,' Mr Hutton protested. 'I must get back to see how poor Emily is. She was rather seedy this morning.' He sat down, nevertheless. 'It's these wretched liver chills. She's always getting them. Women –' He broke off and coughed, so as to hide the fact that he had uttered. He was about to say that women with weak digestions ought not to marry; but the remark was too cruel, and he didn't really believe it. Janet Spence, moreover, was a believer in eternal flames and spiritual attachments. 'She hopes to be well enough,' he added, 'to see you at luncheon tomorrow. Can you come? Do!' He smiled persuasively. 'It's my invitation too, you know.'

She dropped her eyes, and Mr Hutton almost thought that he detected a certain reddening of the cheek. It was a tribute; he stroked his moustache.

'I should like to come if you think Emily's really well enough to have a visitor.'

'Of course. You'll do her good. You'll do us both good. In married life three is often better company than two.'

'Oh, you're cynical.'

Mr Hutton had a desire to say 'Bow-wow-wow' whenever that last word was spoken. It irritated him more than any other word in the language. But instead of barking he made haste to protest.

'No, no. I'm only speaking a melancholy truth. Reality doesn't always come up to the ideal, you know. But that doesn't make me believe any the less in the ideal. Indeed, I believe in it passionately — the ideal of a matrimony between two people in perfect accord. I think it's realisable. I'm sure it is.'

He paused significantly and looked at her with an arch expression. A virgin of thirty-six, but still unwithered; she had her charms. And there was something really rather enigmatic about her. Miss Spence made no reply, but continued to smile. There were times when Mr Hutton got rather bored with the Gioconda. He stood up.

'I must really be going now. Farewell, mysterious Gioconda.' The smile grew intenser, focused itself, as it were, in a narrower snout. Mr Hutton made a Cinquecento gesture, and kissed her extended hand. It was the first time he had done such a thing; the action seemed not to be resented. 'I look forward to tomorrow.'

'Do you?'

For answer Mr Hutton once more kissed her hand, then turned to go. Miss Spence accompanied him to the porch.

'Where's your car?' she asked.

'I left it at the gate of the drive.'

'I'll come and see you off.'

'No, no.' Mr Hutton was playful, but determined. 'You must do no such thing. I simply forbid you.'

'But I should like to come,' Miss Spence protested, throwing a rapid Gioconda at him.

Mr Hutton held up his hand. 'No,' he repeated, and then, with a gesture that was almost the blowing of a kiss, he started to run down the drive, lightly, on his toes, with long, bounding strides like a boy's. He was proud of that run; it was quite marvellously youthful. Still, he was glad the drive was no longer. At the last bend, before passing out of sight of the house, he halted and turned round. Miss Spence was still standing on the steps, smiling her smile. He waved his hand, and this time quite definitely and overtly wafted a kiss in her direction. Then, breaking once more into his magnificent canter, he rounded the last dark promontory of trees. Once out of sight of the house he let his high paces decline to a trot, and finally to a walk. He took out his handkerchief and began wiping his neck inside his collar. What fools, what fools! Had there ever been such an ass as poor, dear Janet Spence? Never, unless it was himself. Decidedly he was the more malignant fool, since he, at least, was aware of his folly and still persisted in it. Why did he persist? Ah, the problem that was himself, the problem that was other people . . .

He had reached the gate. A large, prosperous-looking motor was standing at the side of the road.

'Home, M'Nab.' The chauffeur touched his cap. 'And stop at the cross-roads on the way as usual,' Mr Hutton added, as he opened the door of the car. 'Well?' he said, speaking into the obscurity that lurked within.

'Oh, Teddy Bear, what an age you've been!' It was a fresh and childish voice that spoke the words. There was the faintest hint of Cockney impurity about the vowel sounds.

Mr Hutton bent his large form and darted into the car with the agility of an animal regaining his burrow.

'Have I?' he said, as he shut the door. The machine began to move. 'You must have missed me a lot if you found the time so long.' He sat back in the low seat; a cherishing warmth enveloped him.

'Teddy Bear . . .' and with a sigh of contentment a charming little head declined on to Mr Hutton's shoulder. Ravished, he looked down sideways at the round, babyish face.

'Do you know, Doris, you look like the pictures of Louise de Kerouaille.' He passed his fingers through a mass of curly hair.

'Who's Louise de Kera-whatever-it-is?' Doris spoke from remote distances.

'She was, alas! *Fuit*. We shall all be "was" one of these days. Meanwhile . . .'

Mr Hutton covered the babyish face with kisses. The car rushed smoothly along. M'Nab's back, through the front window, was stonily impassive, the back of a statue.

'Your hands,' Doris whispered. 'Oh, you mustn't touch me. They give me electric shocks.'

Mr Hutton adored her for the virgin imbecility of the words. How late in one's existence one makes the discovery of one's body!

'The electricity isn't in me, it's in you.' He kissed her again, whispering her name several times: Doris, Doris, Doris. The scientific appellation of the sea-mouse, he was thinking as he kissed the throat she offered him, white and extended like the throat of a victim awaiting the sacrificial knife. The sea-mouse was a sausage with iridescent fur: very peculiar. Or was Doris the sea-cucumber, which turns itself inside out in moments of alarm? He would really have to go to Naples again, just to see the aquarium. These sea creatures were fabulous, unbelievably fantastic.

'Oh, Teddy Bear!' (More zoology; but he was only a land animal. His poor little jokes!) 'Teddy Bear, I'm so happy.'

'So am I,' said Mr Hutton. Was it true?

'But I wish I knew if it were right. Tell me, Teddy Bear, is it right or wrong?'

'Ah, my dear, that's just what I've been wondering for the last thirty years.'

'Be serious, Teddy Bear. I want to know if this is right; if it's right that I should be here with you and that we should love one another, and that it should give me electric shocks when you touch me.'

'Right? Well, it's certainly good that you should have electric shocks rather than sexual repressions. Read Freud; repressions are the devil.'

'Oh, you don't help me. Why aren't you ever serious? If only you knew how miserable I am sometimes, thinking it's not right. Perhaps, you know, there is a hell, and all that. I don't know what to do. Sometimes I think I ought to stop loving you.'

'But could you?' asked Mr Hutton, confident in the powers of his seduction and his moustache.

'No, Teddy Bear, you know I couldn't. But I could run away, I could hide from you, I could lock myself up and force myself not to come to you.'

'Silly little thing!' He tightened his embrace.

'Oh, dear. I hope it isn't wrong. And there are times when I don't care if it is.'

Mr Hutton was touched. He had a certain protective affection for this little creature. He laid his cheek against her hair and so, interlaced, they sat in silence, while the car, swaying and pitching a little as it hastened along, seemed to draw in the white road and the dusty hedges towards it devouringly.

'Good-bye, good-bye.'

The car moved on, gathered speed, vanished round a curve, and Doris was left standing by the sign-post at the cross-roads, still dizzy and weak with the languor born of those kisses and the electrical touch of those gentle hands. She had to take a deep breath, to draw herself up deliberately, before she was strong enough to start her homeward walk. She had half a mile in which to invent the necessary lies.

II

Mrs Hutton was lying on the sofa in her boudoir, playing Patience. In spite of the warmth of the July evening a wood fire was burning on the hearth. A black Pomeranian, extenuated by the heat and the fatigues of digestion, slept before the blaze.

'Phew! Isn't it rather hot in here?' Mr Hutton asked as he entered the room.

'You know I have to keep warm, dear.' The voice seemed breaking on the verge of tears. 'I get so shivery.'

'I hope you're better this evening.'

'Not much, I'm afraid.'

The conversation stagnated. Mr Hutton stood leaning his back against the mantelpiece. He looked down at the Pomeranian lying at his feet, and with the toe of his right boot he rolled the little dog over and rubbed its white-flecked chest and belly. The creature lay in an inert ecstasy. Mrs Hutton continued to play Patience. Arrived at an *impasse*, she altered the position of one card, took back another, and went on playing. Her Patiences always came out.

'Dr Libbard thinks I ought to go to Llandrindod Wells this summer.'

'Well, go, my dear — go, most certainly.'

Mr Hutton was thinking of the events of the afternoon: how they had driven, Doris and he, up to the hanging wood, had left the car to wait for them under the shade of the trees, and walked together out into the windless sunshine of the chalk down.

'I'm to drink the waters for my liver, and he thinks I ought to have massage and electric treatment, too.'

Hat in hand, Doris had stalked four blue butterflies that were dancing together round a scabious flower with a motion that was like the flickering of blue fire. The blue fire burst and scattered into whirling sparks; she had given chase, laughing and shouting like a child.

'I'm sure it will do you good, my dear.'

'I was wondering if you'd come with me, dear.'

'But you know I'm going to Scotland at the end of the month.'

Mrs Hutton looked up at him entreatingly. 'It's the journey,' she said. 'The thought of it is such a nightmare. I don't know if I can manage it. And you know I can't sleep in hotels. And then there's the luggage and all the worries. I can't go alone.'

'But you won't be alone. You'll have your maid with you.' He spoke impatiently. The sick woman was usurping the place of the healthy one. He was being dragged back from the memory of the sunlit down and the quick, laughing girl, back to this unhealthy, overheated room and its complaining occupant.

'I don't think I shall be able to go.'

'But you must, dear, if the doctor tells you to. And, besides, a change will do you good.'

'I don't think so.'

'But Libbard thinks so, and he knows what he's talking about.'

'No, I can't face it. I'm too weak. I can't go alone.' Mrs Hutton pulled a handkerchief out of her black silk bag, and put it to her eyes.

'Nonsense, my dear, you must make the effort.'

'I had rather be left in peace to die here.' She was crying in earnest now.

'O Lord! Now do be reasonable. Listen now, please.' Mrs Hutton only sobbed more violently. 'Oh, what is one to do?' He shrugged his shoulders and walked out of the room.

Mr Hutton was aware that he had not behaved with proper patience; but he could not help it. Very early in his manhood he had discovered that not only did he not feel sympathy for the poor, the weak, the diseased, and deformed; he actually hated them. Once, as an undergraduate, he spent three days at a mission in the East End. He had returned, filled with a profound and ineradicable disgust. Instead of pitying, he loathed the unfortunate. It was not, he knew, a very comely emotion, and he had been ashamed of it at first. In the end he had decided that it was temperamental, inevitable, and he felt no further qualms. Emily had been healthy and beautiful when he married her. He had loved her then. But now — was it his fault that she was like this?

Mr Hutton dined alone. Food and drink left him more benevolent than he had been before dinner. To make amends for his show of exasperation he went up to his wife's room and offered to read to her. She was touched, gratefully accepted the offer, and Mr Hutton, who was particularly proud of his accent, suggested a little light reading in French.

'French? I am so fond of French.' Mrs Hutton spoke of the language of Racine as though it were a dish of green peas.

Mr Hutton ran down to the library and returned with a yellow volume. He began reading. The effort of pronouncing perfectly absorbed his whole attention. But how good his accent was! The fact of its goodness seemed to improve the quality of the novel he was reading.

At the end of fifteen pages an unmistakable sound aroused him. He looked up; Mrs Hutton had gone to sleep. He sat still for a little while, looking with a dispassionate curiosity at the sleeping face. Once it had been beautiful; once, long ago, the sight of it, the recollection of it, had moved him with an emotion profounder, perhaps, than any he had felt before or since. Now it was lined and cadaverous. The skin was stretched tightly over the cheekbones, across the bridge of the sharp, bird-like nose. The closed eyes were set in profound bone-rimmed sockets. The lamplight striking on the face from the side emphasised with light and shade its cavities and projections. It was the face of a dead Christ by Morales.

> *Le squelette était invisible*
> *Au temps heureux de l'art paien.*

He shivered a little, and tiptoed out of the room.

On the following day Mrs Hutton came down to luncheon. She had had some unpleasant palpitations during the night, but she was feeling better now. Besides, she wanted to do honour to her guest. Miss Spence listened to her complaints about Llandrindod Wells, and was loud in sympathy, lavish with advice. Whatever she said was always said with intensity. She leaned forward, aimed, so to speak, like a gun, and fired her words. Bang! the charge in her soul was ignited, the words whizzed forth at the narrow barrel of her mouth. She was a machine-gun riddling her hostess with sympathy. Mr Hutton had undergone similar bombardments, mostly of a literary or philosophic character — bombardments of Maeterlinck, of Mrs Besant, of Bergson, of William James. Today the missiles were medical. She talked about insomnia, she expatiated on the virtues of harmless drugs and beneficent specialists. Under the bombardment Mrs Hutton opened out, like a flower in the sun.

Mr Hutton looked on in silence. The spectacle of Janet Spence evoked in him an unfailing curiosity. He was not romantic enough to imagine that every face masked an interior physiognomy of beauty or strangeness, that every woman's small talk was like a vapour hanging over mysterious gulfs. His wife, for example, and Doris; they were nothing more than what they seemed to be. But with Janet Spence it was somehow different. Here one could be sure that there was some kind of a queer face behind the Gioconda smile and the Roman eyebrows. The only question was: What exactly was there? Mr Hutton could never quite make out.

'But perhaps you won't have to go to Llandrindod after all,' Miss Spence was saying. 'If you get well quickly Dr Libbard will let you off.'

'I only hope so. Indeed, I do really feel rather better today.'

Mr Hutton felt ashamed. How much was it his own lack of sympathy that prevented her from feeling well every day? But he comforted himself by reflecting that it was only a case of feeling, not of being better. Sympathy does not mend a diseased liver or a weak heart.

'My dear, I wouldn't eat those red currants if I were you,' he said suddenly solicitous. 'You know that Libbard has banned everything with skins and pips.'

'But I am so fond of them,' Mrs Hutton protested, 'and I feel so well today.'

'Don't be a tyrant,' said Miss Spence, looking first at him and then at his wife. 'Let the poor invalid have what she fancies; it will do her good.' She laid her hand on Mrs Hutton's arm and patted it affectionately two or three times.

'Thank you, my dear.' Mrs Hutton helped herself to the stewed currants.

'Well, don't blame me if they make you ill again.'

'Do I ever blame you, dear?'

'You have nothing to blame me for,' Mr Hutton answered playfully. 'I am the perfect husband.'

They sat in the garden after luncheon. From the island of shade under the old cypress trees they looked out across a flat expanse of lawn, in which the parterres of flowers shone with a metallic brilliance.

Mr Hutton took a deep breath of the warm and fragrant air. 'I's good to be alive,' he said.

'Just to be alive,' his wife echoed, stretching one pale, knot-jointed hand into the sunlight.

A maid brought the coffee; the silver pots and the little blue cups were set on a folding table near the group of chairs.

'Oh, my medicine!' exclaimed Mrs Hutton. 'Run in and fetch it, Clara, will you? The white bottle on the sideboard.'

'I'll go,' said Mr Hutton. 'I've got to go and fetch a cigar in any case.'

He ran towards the house. On the threshold he turned round for an instant. The maid was walking back across the lawn. His wife was sitting up in her deck-chair, engaged in opening her white parasol. Miss Spence was bending over the table, pouring out the coffee. He passed into the cool obscurity of the house.

'Do you like sugar in your coffee?' Miss Spence inquired.

'Yes, please. Give me rather a lot. I'll drink it after my medicine to take the taste away.'

Mrs Hutton leaned back in her chair, lowering the sunshade over her eyes, so as to shut out from her vision the burning sky.

Behind her, Miss Spence was making a delicate clinking among the coffee-cups.

'I've given you three large spoonfuls. That ought to take the taste away. And here comes the medicine.'

Mr Hutton had reappeared, carrying a wine-glass, half full of a pale liquid.

'It smells delicious,' he said, as he handed it to his wife.

'That's only the flavouring.' She drank it off at a gulp, shuddered, and made a grimace. 'Ugh, it's so nasty. Give me my coffee.'

Miss Spence gave her the cup; she sipped at it. 'You've made it like syrup. But it's very nice, after that atrocious medicine.'

At half-past three Mrs Hutton complained that she did not feel as well as she had done, and went indoors to lie down. Her husband would have said something about the red currants, but checked himself; the triumph of an 'I told you so' was too cheaply won. Instead, he was sympathetic, and gave her his arm to the house.

'A rest will do you good,' he said. 'By the way, I shan't be back till after dinner.'

'But why? Where are you going?'

'I promised to go to Johnson's this evening. We have to discuss the war memorial, you know.'

'Oh, I wish you weren't going.' Mrs Hutton was almost in tears. 'Can't you stay? I don't like being alone in the house.'

'But, my dear, I promised — weeks ago.' It was a bother having to lie like this. 'And now I must get back and look after Miss Spence.'

He kissed her on the forehead and went out again into the garden. Miss Spence received him aimed and intense.

'Your wife is dreadfully ill,' she fired off at him.

'I thought she cheered up so much when you came.'

'That was purely nervous, purely nervous. I was watching her closely. With a heart in that condition and her digestion wrecked — yes, wrecked — anything might happen.'

'Libbard doesn't take so gloomy a view of poor Emily's health.' Mr Hutton held open the gate that led from the garden into the drive; Miss Spence's car was standing by the front door.

'Libbard is only a country doctor. You ought to see a specialist.'

He could not refrain from laughing. 'You have a macabre passion for specialists.'

Miss Spence held up her hand in protest. 'I am serious. I think poor Emily is in a very bad state. Anything might happen — at any moment.'

He handed her into the car and shut the door. The chauffeur started the engine and climbed into his place, ready to drive off.

'Shall I tell him to start?' He had no desire to continue the conversation.

Miss Spence leaned forward and shot a Gioconda in his direction.

'Remember, I expect you to come and see me again soon.'

Mechanically he grinned, made a polite noise, and, as the car moved forward, waved his hand. He was happy to be alone.

A few minutes afterwards Mr Hutton himself drove away. Doris was waiting at the cross-roads. They dined together twenty miles from home, at a roadside hotel. It was one of those bad, expensive meals which are only cooked in country hotels frequented by motorists. It revolted Mr Hutton, but Doris enjoyed it. She always enjoyed things. Mr Hutton ordered a not very good brand of champagne. He was wishing he had spent the evening in his library.

When they started homewards Doris was a little tipsy and extremely affectionate. It was very dark inside the car, but looking forward, past the motionless form of M'Nab, they could see a bright and narrow universe of forms and colours scooped out of the night by the electric head-lamps.

It was after eleven when Mr Hutton reached home. Dr Libbard met him in the hall. He was a small man with delicate hands and well-formed features that were almost feminine. His brown eyes were large and melancholy. He used to waste a great deal of time sitting at the bedside of his patients, looking sadness through those eyes and talking in a sad, low voice about nothing in particular. His person exhaled a pleasing odour, decidedly antiseptic but at the same time suave and discreetly delicious.

'Libbard?' said Mr Hutton in surprise. 'You here? Is my wife ill?'

'We tried to fetch you earlier,' the soft, melancholy voice replied. 'It was thought you were at Mr Johnson's, but they had no news of you there.'

'No, I was detained. I had a breakdown,' Mr Hutton answered irritably. It was tiresome to be caught out in a lie.

'Your wife wanted to see you urgently.'

'Well, I can go now.' Mr Hutton moved towards the stairs.

Dr Libbard laid a hand on his arm. 'I am afraid it's too late.'

'Too late?' He began fumbling with his watch; it wouldn't come out of the pocket.

'Mrs Hutton passed away half an hour ago.'

The voice remained even in its softness, the melancholy of the eyes did not deepen. Dr Libbard spoke of death as he would speak of a local cricket match. All things were equally vain and equally deplorable.

Mr Hutton found himself thinking of Janet Spence's words. At any moment — at any moment. She had been extraordinarily right.

'What happened?' he asked. 'What was the cause?'

Dr Libbard explained. It was heart failure brought on by a violent attack of nausea, caused in turn by the eating of something of an irritant. Red currants? Mr Hutton suggested. Very likely. It had been too much for the heart. There was chronic valvular disease: something had collapsed under the strain. It was all over; she could not have suffered much.

III

'It's a pity they should have chosen the day of the Eton and Harrow match for the funeral,' old General Grego was saying as he stood, his top hat in his hand, under the shadow of the lych gate, wiping his face with his handkerchief.

Mr Hutton overheard the remark and with difficulty restrained a desire to inflict grievous bodily pain on the General. He would have liked to hit the old brute in the middle of his big red face. Monstrous great mulberry, spotted with meal! Was there no respect for the dead? Did nobody care? In theory he didn't much care; let the dead bury their dead. But here, at the graveside, he had found himself actually sobbing. Poor Emily, they had been pretty happy once. Now she was lying at the bottom of a seven-foot hole. And here was Grego complaining that he couldn't go to the Eton and Harrow match.

Mr Hutton looked round at the groups of black figures that were drifting slowly out of the churchyard towards the fleet of cabs and motors assembled in the road outside. Against the brilliant background of the July grass and flowers and foliage, they had a horribly alien and unnatural appearance. It pleased him to think that all these people would soon be dead too.

That evening Mr Hutton sat up late in his library reading the life of Milton. There was no particular reason why he should have chosen Milton; it was the book that first came to hand, that was all. It was after midnight when he had finished. He got up from his armchair, unbolted the French windows, and stepped out on to the little paved terrace. The night was quiet and clear. Mr Hutton looked at the stars and at the holes between them, dropped his eyes to the dim lawns and hueless flowers of the garden, and let them wander over the farther landscape, black and grey under the moon.

He began to think with a kind of confused violence. There were the stars, there was Milton. A man can be somehow the peer of stars and night. Greatness, nobility. But is there seriously a difference between the noble and the ignoble? Milton, the stars, death, and himself — himself. The soul, the body; the higher and the lower nature. Perhaps there was something in it, after all. Milton had a god on his side and righteousness. What had he? Nothing, nothing whatever. There were only Doris's little breasts. What was the point of it all? Milton, the stars, death, and Emily in her grave, Doris and himself — always himself . . .

Oh, he was a futile and disgusting being. Everything convinced him of it. It was a solemn moment. He spoke aloud: 'I will, I will.' The sound of his own voice in the darkness was appalling; it seemed to him that he had sworn that infernal oath which binds even the gods: 'I will, I will.' There had been New Year's days and solemn anniversaries in the past, when he had felt the same contritions and recorded similar resolutions. They had all thinned away, these resolutions, like smoke, into nothingness. But this was a greater moment and he had pronounced a more fearful oath. In the future it was to be different. Yes, he would live by reason, he would be industrious, he would curb his appetites, he would devote his life to some good purpose. It was resolved and it would be so.

In practice he saw himself spending his mornings in agricultural pursuits, riding round with the bailiff, seeing that his land was farmed in the best modern way — silos and artificial manures and continuous cropping, and all that. The remainder of the day should be devoted to serious study. There was that book he had been intending to write for so long — *The Effect of Diseases on Civilisation*.

Mr Hutton went to bed humble and contrite, but with a sense that grace had entered into him. He slept for seven and a half hours, and woke to find the sun brilliantly shining. The emotions of the evening before had been transformed by a good night's rest into his customary cheerfulness. It was not until a good many seconds after his return to conscious life that he remembered his resolution, his Stygian oath. Milton and death seemed somehow different in the sunlight. As for the stars, they were not there. But the resolutions were good; even in the day time he could see that. He had his horse saddled after breakfast, and rode round the farm with the bailiff. After luncheon he read Thucydides on the plague at Athens. In the evening he made a few notes on malaria in Southern Italy. While he was undressing he remembered that there was a good anecdote in Skelton's jest-book about the Sweating Sickness. He would have made a note of it if only he could have found a pencil.

On the sixth morning of his new life Mr Hutton found among his correspondence an envelope addressed in that peculiarly vulgar handwriting which he knew to be Doris's. He opened it, and began to read. She didn't know what to say; words were so inadequate. His wife dying like that, and so suddenly — it was too terrible. Mr Hutton sighed, but his interest revived somewhat as he read on:

> Death is so frightening, I never think of it when I can help it. But when something like this happens, or when I am feeling ill or depressed, then I can't help remembering it is there so close, and I think about all the wicked things I have done and about you and me, and I wonder what will happen, and I am so frightened. I am so lonely, Teddy Bear, and so unhappy, and I don't know what to do. I can't get rid of the idea of dying, I am so wretched and helpless without you. I didn't mean to write to you; I meant to wait till you were out of mourning and could come and see me again, but I was so lonely and miserable, Teddy Bear, I had to write. I couldn't help it. Forgive me, I want you so much; I have nobody in the world but you. You are so good and gentle and understanding; there is nobody like you. I shall never forget how good and kind you have been to me, and you are so clever and know so much, I can't understand how you ever came to pay any attention to me, I am so dull and stupid, much less like me and love me, because you do love me a little, don't you, Teddy Bear?

Mr Hutton was touched with shame and remorse. To be thanked like this, worshipped for having seduced the girl — it was too much. It had just been a piece of imbecile wantonness. Imbecile, idiotic: there was no other way to describe it. For, when all was said, he had derived very little pleasure from it. Taking all things together, he had probably been more bored than amused. Once upon a time he had believed himself to be a hedonist. But to be a hedonist implies a certain process of reasoning, a deliberate choice of known pleasures, a rejection of known pains. This had been done without reason, against it. For he knew beforehand — so well, so well — that there was no interest in the pleasure to be derived from these wretched affairs. And yet each time the vague itch came upon him he succumbed, involving himself once more in the old stupidity. There had been Maggie, his wife's maid, and Edith, the girl on the farm, and Mrs Pringle, and the waitress in London, and others — there seemed to be dozens of them. It had all been so stale and boring. He knew it would be; he always knew. And yet, and yet . . . Experience doesn't teach.

Poor little Doris! He would write to her kindly, comfortingly, but he wouldn't see her again. A servant came to tell him that his horse was saddled and waiting. He mounted and rode off. That morning the old bailiff was more irritating than usual.

Five days later Doris and Mr Hutton were sitting together on the pier at Southend; Doris, in white muslin with pink garnishings, radiated happiness; Mr Hutton, legs outstretched and chair tilted, had pushed the panama back from his forehead, and was trying to feel like a tripper. That night, when Doris was asleep, breathing and warm by his side, he recaptured, in this moment of darkness and physical fatigue, the rather cosmic emotion which had possessed him that evening, not a fortnight ago, when he had made his great resolution. And so his solemn oath had already gone the way of so many other resolutions. Unreason had triumphed; at the first itch of desire he had given way. He was hopeless, hopeless.

For a long time he lay with closed eyes, ruminating his humiliation. The girl stirred in her sleep. Mr Hutton turned over and looked in her direction. Enough faint light crept in between the half-drawn curtains to show her bare arm and shoulders, her neck, and the dark tangle of hair on the pillow. She was beautiful, desirable. Why did he lie there moaning over his sins? What did it matter? If he were hopeless, then so be it; he would make the best of his hopelessness. A glorious sense of irresponsibility suddenly filled him. He was free, magnificently free. In a kind of exaltation he drew the girl towards him. She woke, bewildered, almost frightened under his rough kisses.

The storm of his desire subsided into a kind of serene merriment. The whole atmosphere seemed to be quivering with enormous silent laughter.

'Could anyone love you as much as I do, Teddy Bear?' The question came faintly from distant worlds of love.

'I think I know somebody who does,' Mr Hutton replied. The submarine laughter was swelling, rising, ready to break the surface of silence and resound.

'Who? Tell me. What do you mean?' The voice had come very close; charged with suspicion, anguish, indignation, it belonged to this immediate world.

'Ah – ah!'

'Who?'

'You'll never guess.' Mr Hutton kept up the joke until it began to grow tedious, and then pronounced the name: 'Janet Spence.'

Doris was incredulous. 'Miss Spence of the Manor? That old woman?' It was too ridiculous. Mr Hutton laughed too.

'But it's quite true,' he said. 'She adores me.' Oh, the vast joke! He would go and see her as soon as he returned — see and conquer. 'I believe she wants to marry me,' he added.

'But you wouldn't . . . you don't intend . . .'

The air was fairly crepitating with humour. Mr Hutton laughed aloud. 'I intend to marry you,' he said. It seemed to him the best joke he had ever made in his life.

When Mr Hutton left Southend he was once more a married man. It was agreed that, for the time being, the fact should be kept secret. In the autumn they would go abroad together, and the world would be informed. Meanwhile he was to go back to his own house and Doris to hers.

The day after his return he walked over in the afternoon to see Miss Spence. She received him with the old Gioconda.

'I was expecting you to come.'

'I couldn't keep away,' Mr Hutton gallantly replied.

They sat in the summer-house. It was a pleasant place — a little old stucco temple bowered among dense bushes of evergreen. Miss Spence had left her mark on it by hanging up over the seat a blue-and-white Della Robbia plaque.

'I am thinking of going to Italy this autumn,' said Mr Hutton. He felt like a ginger-beer bottle, ready to pop with bubbling humorous excitement.

'Italy . . .' Miss Spence closed her eyes ecstatically. 'I feel drawn there too.'

'Why not let yourself be drawn?'

'I don't know. One somehow hasn't the energy and initiative to set out alone.'

'Alone . . .' Ah, sounds of guitars and throaty singing! 'Yes, travelling alone isn't much fun.'

Miss Spence lay back in her chair without speaking. Her eyes were still closed. Mr Hutton stroked his moustache. The silence prolonged itself for what seemed a very long time.

Pressed to stay to dinner, Mr Hutton did not refuse. The fun had hardly started. The table was laid in the loggia. Through its arches they looked out on to the sloping garden to the valley below and the farther hills. Light ebbed away; the heat and silence were oppressive. A huge cloud was mounting up the sky, and there were distant breathings of thunder. The thunder drew nearer, a wind began to blow, and the first drops of rain fell. The table was cleared. Miss Spence and Mr Hutton sat on in the growing darkness.

Miss Spence broke a long silence by saying meditatively:

'I think everyone has a right to a certain amount of happiness, don't you?'

'Most certainly.' But what was she leading up to? Nobody makes generalisations about life unless they mean to talk about themselves. Happiness: he looked back on his own life, and saw a cheerful, placid existence disturbed by no great griefs or discomforts or alarms. He had always had money and freedom; he had been able to do very much as he wanted. Yes, he supposed he had been happy — happier than most men. And now he was not merely happy; he had discovered in irresponsibility the secret of gaiety. He was about to say something about his happiness when Miss Spence went on speaking.

'People like you and me have a right to be happy some time in our lives.'

'Me?' said Mr Hutton, surprised.

'Poor Henry! Fate hasn't treated either of us very well.'

'Oh, well, it might have treated me worse.'

'You're being cheerful. That's brave of you. But don't think I can't see behind the mask.'

Miss Spence spoke louder and louder as the rain came down more and more heavily. Periodically the thunder cut across her utterances. She talked on, shouting against the noise.

'I have understood you so well and for so long.'

A flash revealed her, aimed and intent, leaning towards him. Her eyes were two profound and menacing gun-barrels. The darkness re-engulfed her.

'You were a lonely soul seeking a companion soul. I could sympathise with you in your solitude. Your marriage . . .'

Thunder cut short the sentence. Miss Spence's voice became audible once more with the words:

'. . . could offer no companionship to a man of your stamp. You needed a soul mate.'

A soul mate — he! a soul mate. It was incredibly fantastic. 'Georgette Leblanc, the ex-soul mate of Maurice Maeterlinck.' He had seen that in the paper a few days ago. So it was thus that Janet Spence had painted him in her imagination — as a soul-mate. And for Doris he was a picture of goodness and the cleverest man in the world. And actually, really, he was what? — Who knows?

'My heart went out to you. I could understand; I was lonely, too.' Miss Spence laid her hand on his knee. 'You were so patient.' Another flash. She was still aimed, dangerously. 'You never complained. But I could guess — I could guess.'

'How wonderful of you!' So he was an *âme incomprise*. 'Only a woman's intuition . . .'

The thunder crashed and rumbled, died away, and only the sound of the rain was left. The thunder was his laughter, magnified, externalised. Flash and crash, there it was again, right on top of them.

'Don't you feel that you have within you something that is akin to this storm?' He could imagine her leaning forward as she uttered the words. 'Passion makes one the equal of the elements.'

What was his gambit now? Why, obviously, he should have said, 'Yes,' and ventured on some unequivocal gesture. But Mr Hutton suddenly took fright. The ginger beer in him had gone flat. The woman was serious — terribly serious. He was appalled.

Passion? 'No,' he desperately answered. 'I am without passion.'

But his remark was either unheard or unheeded, for Miss Spence went on with a growing exaltation, speaking so rapidly, however, and in such a burningly intimate whisper that Mr Hutton found it very difficult to distinguish what she was saying. She was telling him, as far as he could make out the story of her life. The lightning was less frequent now, and there were long intervals of darkness. But at each flash he saw her still aiming towards him, still yearning forward with a terrifying intensity. Darkness, the rain, and then flash! her face was there, close at hand. A pale mask, greenish white; the large eyes, the narrow barrel of the mouth, the heavy eyebrows. Agrippina, or wasn't it rather — yes, wasn't it rather George Robey?

He began devising absurd plans for escaping. He might suddenly jump up, pretending he had seen a burglar — Stop thief! stop thief! — and dash off into the night in pursuit. Or should he say that he felt faint, a heart attack? or that he had seen a ghost — Emily's ghost — in the garden? Absorbed in his childish plotting, he had ceased to pay any attention to Miss Spence's words. The spasmodic clutching of her hand recalled his thoughts.

'I honoured you for that, Henry,' she was saying.

Honoured him for what?

'Marriage is a sacred tie, and your respect for it, even when the marriage was, as it was in your case, an unhappy one, made me respect you and admire you, and — shall I dare say the word? —'

Oh, the burglar, the ghost in the garden! But it was too late.

'. . . yes, love you, Henry, all the more. But we're free now, Henry.'

Free? There was a movement in the dark, and she was kneeling on the floor by his chair.

'Oh, Henry, Henry, I have been unhappy too.'

Her arms embraced him, and by the shaking of her body he could feel that she was sobbing. She might have been a suppliant crying for mercy.

'You musn't, Janet,' he protested. Those tears were terrible, terrible, terrible. 'Not now, not now! You must be calm; you must go to bed.' He patted her shoulder, then got up, disengaging himself from her embrace. He left her still crouching on the floor beside the chair on which he had been sitting.

Groping his way into the hall, and without waiting to look for his hat, he went out of the house, taking infinite pains to close the front door noiselessly behind him. The clouds had blown over, and the moon was shining from a clear sky. The were puddles all along the road, and a noise of running water rose from the gutters and ditches. Mr Hutton splashed along, not caring if he got wet.

How heartrendingly she had sobbed! With the emotions of pity and remorse that the recollection evoked in him there was a certain resentment: why couldn't she have played the game that he was playing — the heartless, amusing game? Yes, but he had known all the time that she wouldn't, she couldn't, play that game; he had known and persisted.

What had she said about passion and the elements? Something absurdly stale, but true, true. There she was, a cloud black-bosomed and charged with thunder, and he, like some absurd little Benjamin Franklin, had sent up a kite into the heart of the menace. Now she was complaining that his toy had drawn the lightning.

She was probably still kneeling by that chair in the loggia, crying.

But why hadn't he been able to keep up the game? Why had his irresponsibility deserted him, leaving him suddenly sober in a cold world? There were no answers to any of his questions. One idea burned steady and luminous in his mind — the idea of flight. He must get away at once.

IV

'What are you thinking about, Teddy Bear?'

'Nothing.'

There was a silence. Mr Hutton remained motionless, his elbows on the parapet of the terrace, his chin in his hands, looking down over Florence. He had taken a villa on one of the hilltops to the south of the city. From a little raised terrace at the end of the garden one looked down a long fertile valley on to the town and beyond it to the bleak mass of Monte Morello and, eastward of it, to the peopled hill of Fiesole, dotted with white houses. Everything was clear and luminous in the September sunshine.

'Are you worried about anything?'

'No, thank you.'

'Tell me, Teddy Bear.'

'But, my dear, there's nothing to tell.' Mr Hutton turned round, smiled, and patted the girl's hand. 'I think you'd better go in and have your siesta. It's too hot for you here.'

'Very well, Teddy Bear. Are you coming too?'

'When I've finished my cigar.'

'All right. But do hurry up and finish it, Teddy Bear.' Slowly, reluctantly, she descended the steps of the terrace and walked towards the house.

Mr Hutton continued his contemplation of Florence. He had need to be alone. It was good sometimes to escape from Doris and the restless solicitude of her passion. He had never known the pains of loving hopelessly, but he was experiencing now the pains of being loved. These last weeks had been a period of growing discomfort. Doris was always with him, like an obsession, like a guilty conscience. Yes, it was good to be alone.

He pulled an envelope out of his pocket and opened it, not without reluctance. He hated letters; they always contained something unpleasant — nowadays, since his second marriage. This was from his sister. He began skimming through the insulting home-truths of which it was composed. The words 'indecent haste', 'social suicide', 'scarcely cold in her grave', 'person of the lower classes' all occurred. They were inevitable now in any communication from a well-meaning and right-thinking relative. Impatient, he was about to tear the stupid letter to pieces when his eye fell on a sentence at the bottom of the third page. His heart beat with uncomfortable violence as he read it. It was too monstrous! Janet Spence was going about telling everyone that he had poisoned his wife in order to marry Doris. What damnable malice! Ordinarily a man of the suavest temper, Mr Hutton found himself trembling with rage. He took the childish satisfaction of calling names — he cursed the woman.

Then suddenly he saw the ridiculous side of the situation. The notion that he should have murdered anyone in order to marry Doris! If they only knew how miserably bored he was. Poor, dear Janet! She had tried to be malicious; she had only succeeded in being stupid.

A sound of footsteps aroused him; he looked round. In the garden below the little terrace the servant girl of the house was picking fruit. A Neapolitan, strayed somehow as far north as Florence, she was a specimen of the classical type — a little debased. Her profile might have been taken from a Sicilian coin of a bad period. Her features, carved floridly in the grand tradition, expressed an almost perfect stupidity. Her mouth was the most beautiful thing about her; the calligraphic hand of nature had richly curved it into an expression of mulish bad temper . . . Under her hideous black clothes, Mr Hutton divined a powerful body, firm and massive. He had looked at her before with a vague interest and curiosity. Today the curiosity defined and focused itself into a desire. An idyll of Theocritus. Here was the woman; he, alas, was not precisely like a goatherd on the volcanic hills. He called to her.

'Armida!'

The smile with which she answered him was so provocative, attested so easy a virtue, that Mr Hutton took fright. He was on the brink once more — on the brink. He must draw back, oh! quickly, quickly, before it was too late. The girl continued to look up at him.

'*Ha chiamato?*' she asked at last.

Stupidity or reason? Oh, there was no choice now. It was imbecility every time.

'*Scendo,*' he called back to her. Twelve steps led from the garden to the terrace. Mr Hutton counted them. Down, down, down, down . . . He saw a vision of himself descending from one circle of the inferno to the next — from a darkness full of wind and hail to an abyss of stinking mud.

V

For a good many days the Hutton case had a place on the front page of every newspaper. There had been no more popular murder trial since George Smith had temporarily eclipsed the European War by drowning in a warm bath his seventh bride. The public imagination was stirred by this tale of a murder brought to light months after the date of the crime. Here, it was felt, was one of those incidents in human life, so notable because they are so rare, which do definitely justify the ways of God to man. A wicked man had been moved by an illicit passion to kill his wife. For months he had lived in sin and fancied security — only to be dashed at last more horribly into the pit he had prepared for himself. 'Murder will out,' and here was a case of it. The readers of the newspapers were in a position to follow every moment of the hand of God. There had been vague, but persistent, rumours in the neighbourhood; the police had taken action at last. Then came the exhumation order, the post-mortem examination, the inquest, the evidence of the experts, the verdict of the coroner's jury, the trial, the condemnation. For once Providence had done its duty, obviously, grossly, didactically, as in a melodrama. The newspapers were right in making of the case the staple intellectual food of a whole season.

Mr Hutton's first emotion when he was summoned from Italy to give evidence at the inquest was one of indignation. It was a monstrous, a scandalous thing that the police should take such idle, malicious gossip seriously. When the inquest was over he would bring an action for malicious prosecution against the Chief Constable; he would sue the Spence woman for slander.

The inquest was opened; the astonishing evidence unrolled itself. The experts had examined the body, and had found traces of arsenic; they were of the opinion that the late Mrs Hutton had died of arsenic poisoning.

Arsenic poisoning . . . Emily had died of arsenic poisoning? After that, Mr Hutton learned with surprise that there was enough arsenicated insecticide in his greenhouse to poison an army.

It was now, quite suddenly, that he saw it: there was a case against him. Fascinated, he watched it growing, growing, like some monstrous tropical plant. It was enveloping him, surrounding him; he was lost in a tangled forest.

When was the poison administered? The experts agreed that it must have been swallowed eight or nine hours before death. About lunchtime? Yes, about lunch-time. Clara, the parlourmaid, was called. Mrs Hutton, she remembered, had asked her to go and fetch her medicine. Mr Hutton had volunteered to go instead; he had gone alone. Miss Spence — ah, the memory of the storm, the white aimed face! the horror of it all! — Miss Spence confirmed Clara's statement, and added that Mr Hutton had come back with the medicine already poured out in a wineglass, not in the bottle.

Mr Hutton's indignation evaporated. He was dismayed, frightened.

It was all too fantastic to be taken seriously, and yet this nightmare was a fact — it was actually happening.

M'Nab had seen them kissing, often. He had taken them for a drive on the day of Mrs Hutton's death. He could see them reflected in the wind-screen, sometimes out of the tail of his eye.

The inquest was adjourned. That evening Doris went to bed with a headache. When he went to her room after dinner, Mr Hutton found her crying.

'What's the matter?' He sat down on the edge of her bed and began to stroke her hair. For a long time she did not answer, and he went on stroking her hair mechanically, almost unconsciously; sometimes, even, he bent down and kissed her bare shoulder. He had his own affairs, however, to think about. What had happened? Emily had died of arsenic poisoning. It was absurd, impossible. The order of things had been broken, and he was at the mercy of an irresponsibility. What had happened, what was going to happen? He was interrupted in the midst of his thoughts.

'It's my fault — it's my fault!' Doris suddenly sobbed out. 'I shouldn't have loved you; I oughtn't to have let you love me. Why was I ever born?'

Mr Hutton didn't say anything, but looked down in silence at the abject figure of misery lying on the bed.

'If they do anything to you I shall kill myself.'

She sat up, held him for a moment at arm's length, and looked at him with a kind of violence, as though she were never to see him again.

'I love you, I love you, I love you.' She drew him, inert and passive towards her, clasped him, pressed herself against him. 'I didn't know you loved me as much as that, Teddy Bear. But why did you do it — why did you do it?'

Mr Hutton undid her clasping arms and got up. His face became very red. 'You seem to take it for granted that I murdered my wife,' he said. 'It's really too grotesque. What do you all take me for? A cinema hero?' He had begun to lose his temper. All the exasperation, all the fear and bewilderment of the day, was transformed into a violent anger against her. 'It's all such damned stupidity. Haven't you any conception of a civilised man's mentality? Do I look the sort of man who'd go about slaughtering people? I suppose you imagined I was so insanely in love with you that I could commit any folly. When will you women understand that one isn't insanely in love? All one asks for is a quiet life, which you won't allow one to have. I don't know what the devil ever induced me to marry you. It was all a damned stupid, practical joke. And now you go about saying I'm a murderer. I won't stand it.'

Mr Hutton stamped towards the door. He had said horrible things, he knew — odious things that he ought speedily to unsay. But he wouldn't. He closed the door behind him.

'Teddy Bear!' He turned the handle; the latch clicked into place. 'Teddy Bear!' The voice that came to him through the closed door was agonised. Should he go back? He ought to go back. He touched the handle, then withdrew his fingers and quickly walked away. When he was half-way down the stairs he halted. She might try to do something silly — throw herself out of the window or Gods knows what! He listened attentively; there was no sound. But he pictured her very clearly, tiptoeing across the room, lifting the sash as high as it would go, leaning out into the cold night air. It was raining a little. Under the window lay the paved terrace. How far below? Twenty-five or thirty feet? Once, when he was walking along Piccadilly, a dog had jumped out of a third-storey window of the Ritz. He had seen it fall; he had heard it strike the pavement. Should he go back? He was damned if he would; he hated her.

He sat for a long time in the library. What had happened? What was happening? He turned the question over and over in his mind and could find no answer. Suppose the nightmare dreamed itself out to its horrible conclusion. Death was waiting for him. His eyes filled with tears; he wanted so passionately to live. 'Just to be alive.' Poor Emily had wished it too, he remembered: 'Just to be alive.' There were still so many places in this astonishing world unvisited, so many queer delightful people still unknown, so many lovely women never so much as seen. The huge white oxen would still be dragging their wains along the Tuscan roads, the cypresses would still go up, straight as pillars, to the blue heaven; but he would not be there to see them. And the sweet southern wines — Tear of Christ and Blood of Judas — others would drink them, not he. Others would walk down the obscure and narrow lanes between the bookshelves in the London Library, sniffing the dusty perfume of good literature, peering at strange titles, discovering unknown names, exploring the fringes of vast domains of knowledge. He would be lying in a hole in the ground. And why, why? Confusedly he felt that some extraordinary kind of justice was being done. In the past he had been wanton and imbecile and irresponsible. Now Fate was playing as wantonly, as irresponsibly, with him. It was tit for tat, and God existed after all.

He felt that he would like to pray. Forty years ago he used to kneel by his bed every evening. The nightly formula of his childhood came to him almost unsought from some long unopened chamber of the memory. 'God bless Father and Mother, Tom and Cissie and the Baby, Mademoiselle and Nurse, and everyone that I love, and make me a good boy. Amen.' They were all dead now — all except Cissie.

His mind seemed to soften and dissolve; a great calm descended upon his spirit. He went upstairs to ask Doris's forgiveness. He found her lying on the couch at the foot of the bed. On the floor beside her stood a blue bottle of liniment, marked 'Not to be taken'; she seemed to have drunk about half of it.

'You didn't love me,' was all she said when she opened her eyes to find her bending over her.

Dr Libbard arrived in time to prevent any very serious consequences. 'You mustn't do this again,' he said while Mr Hutton was out of the room.

'What's to prevent me?' she asked defiantly.

Dr Libbard looked at her with his large, sad eyes. 'There's nothing to prevent you,' he said. 'Only yourself and your baby. Isn't it rather bad luck on your baby, not allowing it to come into the world because you want to go out of it?'

Doris was silent for a time. 'All right,' she whispered. 'I won't.'

Mr Hutton sat by her bedside for the rest of the night. He felt himself now to be indeed a murderer. For a time he persuaded himself that he loved this pitiable child. Dozing in his chair, he woke up, stiff and cold, to find himself drained dry, as it were, of every emotion. He had nothing but a tired and suffering carcase. At six o'clock he undressed and went to bed for a couple of hours' sleep. In the course of the same afternoon the coroner's jury brought in a verdict of 'Wilful Murder,' and Mr Hutton was committed for trial.

VI

Miss Spence was not at all well. She had found her public appearances in the witness-box very trying, and when it was all over she had something that was very nearly a breakdown. She slept badly, and suffered from nervous indigestion. Dr Libbard used to call every other day. She talked to him a great deal — mostly about the Hutton case . . . Her moral indignation was always on the boil. Wasn't it appalling to think that one had had a murderer in one's house? Wasn't it extraordinary that one could have been for so long mistaken about the man's character? (But she had had an inkling from the first.) And then the girl he had gone off with — so low class, so little better than a prostitute. The news that the second Mrs Hutton was expecting a baby — the posthumous child of a condemned and executed criminal — revolted her; the thing was shocking — an obscenity. Dr Libbard answered her gently and vaguely, and prescribed bromide.

One morning he interrupted her in the midst of her customary tirade. 'By the way,' he said in his soft, melancholy voice, 'I suppose it was really you who poisoned Mrs Hutton.'

Miss Spence stared at him for two or three seconds with enormous eyes, and then quietly said, 'Yes.' After that she started to cry.

'In the coffee, I suppose.'

She seemed to nod in assent. Dr Libbard took out his fountain-pen, and in his neat, meticulous calligraphy wrote out a prescription for a sleeping-draught.

ANTHONY BOUCHER

They Bite

ANTHONY BOUCHER *(1911 – 68) with 'They Bite' takes a frightening leap into the unknown, as perhaps only this accomplished writer could: he wrote fantasy and science fiction in addition to his classical detective stories, edited* The Magazine of Fantasy and Science Fiction, *was a polished critic in both genres, and edited fine true-crime collections such as* The Quality of Murder. *The present story was based, he said, upon an idle speculation as to what might have happened to the Benders after death; they, you may recall, were the bloody family who murdered lonely travellers under the pretence of offering them hospitality (especially from daughter Kate).*

There was no path, only the almost vertical ascent. Crumbled rock for a few yards, with the roots of sage finding their scanty life in the dry soil. Then jagged outcroppings of crude crags, sometimes with accidental footholds, sometimes with overhanging and untrustworthy branches of grease-wood, sometimes with no aid to climbing but the leverage of your muscles and the ingenuity of your balance.

The sage was as drably green as the rock was drably brown. The only colour was the occasional rosy spikes of barrel cactus.

Hugh Tallant swung himself up onto the last pinnacle. It had a deliberate, shaped look about it — a petrified fortress of Lilliputians, a Gibraltar of pygmies. Tallant perched on its battlements and unslung his field glasses.

The desert valley spread below him. The tiny cluster of buildings that was Oasis, the exiguous cluster of palms that gave name to the town and shelter of his own tent and to the shack he was building, the dead-end highway leading straightforwardly to nothing, the oiled roads diagraming the vacant blocks of an optimistic subdivision.

Tallant saw none of these. His glasses were fixed beyond the oasis and the town of Oasis on the dry lake. The gliders were clear and vivid to him, and the uniformed men busy with them were as sharply and minutely visible as a nest of ants under glass. The training school was more than usually active. One glider in particular, strange to Tallant, seemed the focus of attention. Men would come and examine it and glance back at the older models in comparison.

Only the corner of Tallant's left eye was not preoccupied with the new glider. In that corner something moved, something little and thin and brown as the earth. Too large for a rabbit, much too small for a man. It darted across that corner of vision, and Tallant found gliders oddly hard to concentrate on.

He set down the bifocals and deliberately looked about him. His pinnacle surveyed the narrow, flat area of the crest. Nothing stirred. Nothing stood out against the sage and rock but one barrel of rosy spikes. He took up the glasses again and resumed his observations. When he was done, he methodically entered the results in the little black notebook.

His hand was still white. The desert is cold and often sunless in winter. But it was a firm hand, and as well trained as his eyes, fully capable of recording faithfully the designs and dimensions which they had registered so accurately.

Once his hand slipped, and he had to erase and redraw, leaving a smudge that displeased him. The lean, brown thing had slipped across the edge of his vision again. Going towards the east edge, he would swear, where that set of rocks jutted like the spines on the back of a stegosaur.

Only when his notes were completed did he yield to curiosity, and even then with cynical self-reproach. He was physically tired, for him an unusual state, from this daily climbing and from clearing the ground for his shack-to-be. The eye muscles play odd nervous tricks. There could be nothing behind the stegosaur's armour.

There was nothing. Nothing alive and moving. Only the torn and half-plucked carcass of a bird, which looked as though it had been gnawed by some small animal.

It was halfway down the hill — hill in Western terminology, though anywhere east of the Rockies it would have been considered a sizable mountain — that Tallant again had a glimpse of a moving figure.

But this was no trick of a nervous eye. It was not little nor thin nor brown. It was tall and broad and wore a loud red-and-black lumberjacket. It bellowed, 'Tallant!' in a cheerful and lusty voice.

Tallant drew near the man and said, 'Hello.' He paused and added, 'Your advantage, I think.'

The man grinned broadly. 'Don't know me? Well, I daresay ten years is a long time and the California desert ain't exactly the Chinese rice fields. How's stuff? Still loaded down with Secrets for Sale?'

Tallant tried desperately not to react to that shot, but he stiffened a little. 'Sorry. The prospector getup had me fooled. Good to see you again, Morgan.'

The man's eyes narrowed. 'Just having my little joke,' he smiled. 'Of course you wouldn't have no serious reason for mountain climbing around a glider school, now, would you? And you'd kind of need field glasses to keep an eye on the pretty birdies.'

'I'm out here for my health.' Tallant's voice sounded unnatural even to himself.

'Sure, sure. You were always in it for your health. And come to think of it, my own health ain't been none too good lately. I've got me a little cabin way to hell-and-gone around here, and I do me a little prospecting now and then. And somehow it just strikes me, Tallant, like maybe I hit a pretty good lode today.'

'Nonsense, old man. You can see – '

'I'd sure hate to tell any of them Army men out at the field some of the stories I know about China and the kind of men I used to know there. Wouldn't cotton to them stories a bit, the Army wouldn't. But if I was to have a drink too many and get talkative-like – '

'Tell you what,' Tallant suggested brusquely. 'It's getting near sunset now, and my tent's chilly for evening visits. But drop around in the morning and we'll talk over old times. Is rum still your tipple?'

'Sure is. Kind of expensive now, you understand – '

'I'll lay some in. You can find the place easily — over by the oasis. And we . . . we might be able to talk about your prospecting, too.'

Tallant's thin lips were set firm as he walked away.

The bartender opened a bottle of beer and plunked it on the damp-circled counter. 'That'll be twenty cents,' he said, then added as an afterthought, 'Want a glass? Sometimes tourists do.'

Tallant looked at the others sitting at the counter — the red-eyed and unshaven old man, the flight sergeant unhappily drinking Coke — it was after Army hours for beer — the young man with the long, dirty trench coat and the pipe and the new-looking beard — and saw no glasses. 'I guess I won't be a tourist,' he decided.

This was the first time Tallant had had a chance to visit the Desert Sport Spot. It was as well to be seen around in a community. Otherwise people begin to wonder and say, 'Who is that man out by the oasis? Why don't you ever see him anyplace?'

The Sport Spot was quiet that night. The four of them at the counter, two Army boys shooting pool, and a half-dozen of the local men gathered about a round poker table, soberly and wordlessly cleaning a construction worker whose mind seemed more on his beer than on his cards.

'You just passing through?' the bartender asked sociably.

Tallant shook his head. 'I'm moving in. When the Army turned me down for my lungs, I decided I better do something about it. Heard so much about your climate here I thought I might as well try it.'

'Sure thing,' the bartender nodded. 'You take up until they started this glider school, just about every other guy you meet in the desert is here for his health. Me, I had sinus, and look at me now. It's the air.'

Tallant breathed the atmosphere of smoke and beer suds, but did not smile. 'I'm looking forward to miracles.'

'You'll get 'em. Whereabouts you staying?'

'Over that way a bit. The agent called it "the old Carker place".'

Tallant felt the curious listening silence and frowned. The bartender had started to speak and then thought better of it. The young man with the beard looked at him oddly. The old man fixed him with red and watery eyes that had a faded glint of pity in them. For a moment, Tallant felt a chill that had nothing to do with the night air of the desert.

The old man drank his beer in quick gulps and frowned as though trying to formulate a sentence. At last he wiped beer from his bristly lips and said, 'You wasn't aiming to stay in the adobe, was you?'

'No. It's pretty much gone to pieces. Easier to rig me up a little shack than try to make the adobe livable. Meanwhile, I've got a tent.'

'That's all right, then, mebbe. But mind you don't go poking around that there adobe.'

'I don't think I'm apt to. But why not? Want another beer?'

The old man shook his head reluctantly and slid from his stool to the ground. 'No thanks. I don't rightly know as I –'

'Yes?'

'Nothing. Thanks all the same.' He turned and shuffled to the door.

Tallant smiled. 'But why should I stay clear of the adobe?' he called after him.

The old man mumbled.

'What?'

'They bite,' said the old man, and went shivering into the night.

The bartender was back at his post. 'I'm glad he didn't take that beer you offered him,' he said. 'Along about this time in the evening I have to stop serving him. For once he had the sense to quit.'

Tallant pushed his own empty bottle forward. 'I hope I didn't frighten him away.'

'Frighten? Well, mister, I think maybe that's just what you did do. He didn't want beer that sort of came, like you might say, from the old Carker place. Some of the old-timers here, they're funny that way.'

Tallant grinned. 'Is it haunted?'

'Not what you'd call haunted, no. No ghosts there that I ever heard of.' He wiped the counter with a cloth and seemed to wipe the subject away with it.

The flight sergeant pushed his Coke bottle away, hunted in his pocket for nickels, and went over to the pinball machine. The young man with the beard slid onto his vacant stool. 'Hope old Jake didn't worry you,' he said.

Tallant laughed. 'I suppose every town has its deserted homestead with a grisly tradition. But this sounds a little different. No ghosts, and they bite. Do you know anything about it?'

'A little,' the young man said seriously. 'A little. Just enough to –'

Tallant was curious. 'Have one on me and tell me about it.'

The flight sergeant swore bitterly at the machine.

Beer gurgled through the beard. 'You see,' the young man began, 'the desert's so big you can't be alone in it. Ever notice that? It's all empty and there's nothing in sight, but there's always something moving over there where you can't quite see it. It's something very dry and thin and brown, only when you look around it isn't there. Ever see it?'

'Optical fatigue –' Tallant began.

'Sure. I know. Every man to his own legend. There isn't a tribe of Indians hasn't got some way of accounting for it. You've heard of the Watchers? And the twentieth-century white man comes along, and it's optical fatigue. Only in the nineteenth century things weren't quite the same, and there were the Carkers.'

'You've got a special localised legend?'

'Call it that. You glimpse things out of the corner of your mind, same like you glimpse lean, dry things out of the corner of your eye. You encase 'em in solid circumstances and they're not so bad. That is known as the Growth of Legend. The Folk Mind in Action. You take the Carkers and the things you don't quite see and you put 'em together. And they bite.'

Tallant wondered how long that beard had been absorbing beer. 'And what were the Carkers?' he prompted politely.

'Ever hear of Sawney Bean? Scotland — reign of James First, or may be the Sixth, though I think Roughhead's wrong on that for once. Or let's be more modern — ever hear of the Benders? Kansas in the 1870s? No? Ever hear of Procrustes? Or Polyphemus? Or Fee fi-fo-fum?

'There are ogres, you know. They're no legend. They're fact, they are. The inn where nine guests left for every ten that arrived, the mountain cabin that sheltered travellers from the snow, sheltered them all winter till the melting spring uncovered their bones, the lonely stretches of road that so many passengers travelled halfway — you'll find 'em everywhere. All over Europe and pretty much in this country too before communications became what they are. Profitable business. And it wasn't just the profit. The Benders made money, sure; but that wasn't why they killed all their victims as carefully as a kosher butcher. Sawney Bean got so he didn't give a damn about the profit; he just needed to lay in more meat for the winter.

'And think of the chances you'd have at an oasis.'

'So these Carkers of yours were, as you call them ogres?'

'Carkers, ogres — maybe they were Benders. The Benders were never seen alive, you know, after the townspeople found those curiously butchered bones. There's a rumour they got this far west. And the time checks pretty well. There wasn't any town here in the eighties. Just a couple of Indian families, last of a dying tribe living on at the oasis. They vanished after the Carkers moved in. That's not so surprising. The white race is a sort of super-ogre, anyway. Nobody worried about them. But they used to worry about why so many travellers never got across this stretch of desert. The travellers used to stop over at the Carkers', you see, and somehow they often never got any farther. Their wagons'd be found maybe fifteen miles beyond in the desert. Sometimes they found the bones, too, parched and white. Gnawed-looking, they said sometimes.'

'And nobody ever did anything about these Carkers?'

'Oh, sure. We didn't have King James Sixth — only I still think it was the First — to ride up on a great white horse for a gesture, but twice Army detachments came here and wiped them all out.'

'Twice? One wiping-out would do for most families.' Tallant smiled.

'Uh-uh. That was no slip. They wiped out the Carkers twice because, you see, once didn't do any good. They wiped 'em out and still travellers vanished and still there were gnawed bones. So they wiped 'em out again. After that they gave up, and people detoured the oasis. It made a longer harder trip, but after all – '

Tallant laughed. 'You mean to say these Carkers were immortal?'

'I don't know about immortal. They somehow just didn't die very easy. Maybe, if they were the Benders — and I sort of like to think they were — they learned a little more about what they were doing out here on the desert. Maybe they put together what the Indians knew and what they knew, and it worked. Maybe whatever they made their sacrifices to understood them better out here than in Kansas.'

'And what's become of them — aside from seeing them out of the corner of the eye?'

'There's forty years between the last of the Carker history and this new settlement at the oasis. And people won't talk much about what they learned here in the first year or so. Only that they stay away from that old Carker adobe. They tell some stories — The priest says he was sitting in the confessional one hot Saturday afternoon and thought he heard a penitent come in. He waited a long time and finally lifted the gauze to see was anybody there. Something was there, and it bit. He's got three fingers on his right hand now, which looks funny as hell when he gives a benediction.'

Tallant pushed their two bottles towards the bartender. 'That yarn, my young friend, has earned another beer. How about it, bartender? Is he always cheerful like this, or is this just something he's improvised for my benefit?'

The bartender set out the fresh bottles with great solemnity. 'Me, I wouldn't've told you all that myself, but then, he's a stranger too and maybe don't feel the same way we do here. For him it's just a story.'

'It's more comfortable that way,' said the young man with the beard, and he took a firm hold on his beer bottle.

'But as long as you've heard that much,' said the bartender, 'you might as well — It was last winter, when we had that cold spell. You heard funny stories that winter. Wolves coming into prospectors' cabins just to warm up. Well, business wasn't so good. We don't have a license for hard liquor, and the boys don't drink much beer when it's that cold. But they used to come in anyway because we've got that big oil burner.

'So one night there's a bunch of 'em in here — old Jake was here, that you was talking to, and his dog Jigger — and I think I hear somebody else come in. The door creaks a little. But I don't see nobody, and the poker game's going, and we're talking just like we're talking now, and all of a sudden I hear a kind of noise like crack! over there in that corner behind the juke box near the burner.

'I go over to see what goes and it gets away before I can see it very good. But it was little and thin and it didn't have no clothes on. It must've been damned cold that winter.'

'And what was the cracking noise?' Tallant asked dutifully.

'That? That was a bone. It must've strangled Jigger without any noise. He was a little dog. It ate most of the flesh, and if it hadn't cracked the bone for the marrow it could've finished. You can still see the spots over there. The blood never did come out.'

There had been silence all through the story. Now suddenly all hell broke loose. The flight sergeant let out a splendid yell and began pointing excitedly at the pinball machine and yelling for his payoff. The construction worker dramatically deserted the poker game, knocking his chair over in the process, and announced lugubriously that these guys here had their own rules, see?

Any atmosphere of Carker-inspired horror was dissipated. Tallant whistled as he walked over to put a nickel in the jukebox. He glanced casually at the floor. Yes, there was a stain, for what that was worth.

He smiled cheerfully and felt rather grateful to the Carkers. They were going to solve his blackmail problem very neatly.

Tallant dreamed of power that night. It was a common dream with him. He was a ruler of the new American Corporate State that would follow the war; and he said to this man, 'Come!' and he came, and to that man, 'Go!' and he went, and to his servants, 'Do this!' and they did it.

Then the young man with the beard was standing before him, and the dirty trench coat was like the robes of an ancient prophet. And the young man said, 'You see yourself riding high, don't you? Riding the crest of the wave — the Wave of the Future, you call it. But there's a deep, dark undertow that you don't see, and that's a part of the Past. And the Present and even your Future. There is evil in mankind that is blacker even than your evil, and infinitely more ancient.'

And there was something in the shadows behind the young man, something little and lean and brown.

Tallant's dream did not disturb him the following morning. Nor did the thought of the approaching interview with Morgan. He fried his bacon and eggs devoured them cheerfully. The wind had died down for a change, and the sun was warm enough so that he could strip to the waist while he cleared land for his shack. His machete glinted brilliantly as it swung through the air and struck at the roots of the brush.

When Morgan arrived his full face was red and sweating.

'It's cool over there in the shade of the adobe,' Tallant suggested. 'We'll be more comfortable.' And in the comfortable shade of the adobe he swung the machete once and clove Morgan's full, red, sweating face in two.

It was so simple. It took less effort than uprooting a clump of sage. And it was so safe. Morgan lived in a cabin way to hell-and-gone and was often away on prospecting trips. No one would notice his absence for months, if then. No one had any reason to connect him with Tallant. And no one in Oasis would hunt for him in the Carker-haunted adobe.

The body was heavy, and the blood dripped warm on Tallant's bare skin. With relief he dumped what had been Morgan on the floor of the adobe. There were no boards, no flooring. Just earth. Hard, but not too hard to dig a grave in. And no one was likely to come poking around in this taboo territory to notice the grave. Let a year or so go by, and the grave and bones it contained would be attributed to the Carkers.

The corner of Tallant's eye bothered him again. Deliberately he looked about the interior of the adobe.

The little furniture was crude and heavy, with no attempt to smooth down the stokes of the axe. It was held together with wooden pegs or half-rotted thongs. There were age-old cinders in the fireplace, and the dusty shards of a cooking jar among them.

And there was a deeply hollowed stone, covered with stains that might have been rust, if stone rusted. Behind it was a tiny figure, clumsily fashioned of clay and sticks. It was something like a man and something like a lizard, and something like the things that flit across the corner of the eye.

Curious now, Tallant peered about further. He penetrated to the corner that the one unglassed window lighted but dimly. And there he let out a little choking gasp. For a moment he was rigid with horror. Then he smiled and all but laughed aloud.

This explained everything. Some curious individual had seen this, and from his accounts had burgeoned the whole legend. The Carkers had indeed learned something from the Indians, but that secret was the art of embalming.

It was a perfect mummy. Either the Indian art had shrunk bodies, or this was that of a ten-year-old boy. There was no flesh. Only skin and bone and taut, dry stretches of tendon between. The eyelids were closed; the sockets looked hollow under them. The nose was sunken and almost lost. The scant lips were tightly curled back from the long and very white teeth, which stood forth all the more brilliantly against the deep-brown skin.

It was a curious little trove, this mummy. Tallant was already calculating the chances for raising a decent sum of money from an interested anthropologist — murder can produce such delightfully profitable chance by-products — when he noticed the infinitesimal rise and fall of the chest.

The Carker was not dead. It was sleeping.

Tallant did not dare stop to think beyond the instant. This was no time to pause to consider if such things were possible in a well-ordered world. It was no time to reflect on the disposal of the body of Morgan. It was time to snatch up your machete and get out of there.

But in the doorway he halted. There, coming across the desert, heading for the adobe, clearly seen this time, was another — a female.

He made an involuntary gesture of indecision. The blade of the machete clanged ringingly against the adobe wall. He heard the dry shuffling of a roused sleeper behind him.

He turned fully now, the machete raised. Dispose of this nearer one first, then face the female. There was no room even for terror in his thoughts, only for action.

The lean brown shape darted at him avidly. He moved lightly away and stood poised for its second charge. It shot forward again. He took one step back, machete arm raised, and fell headlong over the corpse of Morgan. Before he could rise, the thin thing was upon him. Its sharp teeth had met through the palm of his left hand.

The machete moved swiftly. The thin dry body fell headless to the floor. There was no blood.

The grip of the teeth did not relax. Pain coursed up Tallant's left arm — a sharper more bitter pain than you would expect from the bite. Almost as though venom — .

He dropped the machete, and his strong white hand plucked and twisted at the dry brown lips. The teeth clenched, unrelaxing. He sat bracing his back against the wall and gripped the head between his knees. He pulled. His flesh ripped, and blood formed dusty clots on the dirt floor. But the bite was firm.

His world had become reduced now to that hand and that head. Nothing outside mattered. He must free himself. He raised his aching arm to his face, and with his own teeth he tore at the unrelenting grip. The dry flesh crumbled away in desert dust, but the teeth were locked fast. He tore his lip against their white keenness, and tasted in his mouth the sweetness of blood and something else.

He staggered to his feet again. He knew what he must do. Later he could use cautery, a tourniquet, see a doctor with a story about a Gila monster — their heads grip too, don't they? — but he knew what he must do know.

He raised the machete and struck again.

His white hand lay on the brown floor, gripped by the white teeth in the brown face. He propped himself against the adobe wall, momentarily unable to move. His open wrist hung over the deeply hollowed stone. His blood and his strength and his life poured out before the little figure of sticks and clay.

The female stood in the doorway now, the sun bright on her thin brownness. She did not move. He knew that she was waiting for the hollow stone to fill.

SIR OSBERT SITWELL

The Greeting

SIR OSBERT SITWELL *(1892 – 1969), brother of Edith and Sachererell, was a vastly entertaining writer in many fields, notably his autobiographical series* Left Hand, Right Hand. *Conrad Aiken, reviewing his* Triple Fugue, *remarked that one story therein, 'The Greeting,' was 'based on a well-known case'. Sir Osbert replied tartly, 'Mr Conrad Aiken, of course, knows nothing of the work of my mind — and too much about the working of his own. I cannot recall that the story . . . was based on any precise murder.' It was, though, as students of the Luard case will immediately recognise.*

From outside the long, large windows fires could be seen flickering in many wide grates, while comforting sense, more than smell, of warm food oozed out of the whole house, subduing the sharper scent of frosty air. The dining-room table, she noticed as she passed by, was laid for three persons, and decorated with four small silver vases, from which a few very rigid flowers drew themselves up into the light of the windows. The sideboard showed beyond, bearing various drab meats and some pieces of plate, its cold glitter tempered by the flames with patches of warm orange.

As soon as Nurse Gooch was shown into the drawing-room, almost, indeed, before she had shaken hands or remarked how nice it was to see a fire, they went into luncheon. But seated before this white expanse, these three people could not succeed in materialising any conversation, that, as talk should, drawing its strength from the group but stronger than any individual member of it, would continue almost automatically, reproducing itself or taking on a fresh form from time to time. In the same way in which spiritualists claim that the presence of one sceptic at a séance is sufficient to prevent any manifestation, however hoped for and credited by the majority, here it was difficult for the talk to glow or prosper, when one of this small party was continually exerting her will to the utmost in order to produce a lasting and uncomfortable silence. The stagnant quiet room was seldom broken, then, except by the rather horse-like stepping of the footmen, or by the thin, stringy voice of the invalid projected through the mute air in querulous inquiry. And, in the very act of speaking herself, both by the purpose and calculated tone of her question, she enforced a silence on the others. Colonel Tonge tried to make conversation to the newcomer, placed between him and his sick wife, but his abrupt, pompous little sentences soon withered, frozen on the air by his wife's disapproval. Mrs Tonge, however, as we have said, permitted herself to ask a question occasionally — a question which, though it appeared innocent, was designed to convey to her new nurse the impression that she was an injured, ill-used woman. 'When, Humphrey,' she would ask, 'do you intend to put electric light into the house? I have asked you to do it for so many years now. I am sure I should not be such a worry to you or to nurse,' or 'What about that summer-house, Humphrey? Will it be ready for me in the spring? If I am still with you, I intend going there every day when the weather is warmer. Perhaps I shall find a little peace there in the woods. But I fear it hasn't been touched yet.' To these questions the Colonel returned smooth, soothing answers, but ones which did not commit him in any way; but these, rather than conciliating the invalid, seemed only to vex her the more. But at this early period, before she understood her nurse, before she knew that anything she said would soon be pardoned, she did not actually as yet accuse her husband of doing all in his power to make and to keep her ill, but was content to let this accusation remain implicate in her questions, and in the sound of her voice. Still, Nurse Gooch felt instinctively that Mrs Tonge did not want to hurt her, that she was not in reality ill-natured, but that this calculated putting-out of the social fire was the outcome of a thousand little injuries inflicted by an imagination warped by constant illness and want of sleep. But whether it was due to the atmosphere created by this friction between husband and wife, or to something in the surroundings — in the house itself — she did most certainly, at this first moment of her arrival, experience an uneasy feeling, a slight repulsion from the Grove, which passed as soon as she became better acquainted.

Tonge's Grove, a square house, lies like a box thrown down among hanging woods and open commons — a charming residence in many ways. Like a doll's house it seems, each room giving the correct proportion to the rather under-life-size figures it displays. A curiously inappropriate setting, certainly, for any drama, the protagonists of which must find themselves cramped in their action by the wealth of detail imposed. The very comfort and well-being of the place would give a grotesque air to any but an accustomed or trivial event. For here, long habit appears so much more important then the occasion or fact it originally enshrined, inanimate objects so much more actual, more active, than human beings, that it is upon the house, and not upon its owners, that our attention is first focused. It is this superfluity of things, combined with a rigorous pruning of reality, that gives a certain significance to any fact of life should it be strong enough to enter these gates, yet remain quick. For reality, which is usually unpleasant, seldom touches lives such as these except at birth, of which, fortunately, we are all ignorant, or at death, a latent, lurking fear (an ogre at the end of every passage), but one which it is our very human convention to ignore.

The Grove is not really a small house; the rooms in it are large and numerous; but, like square toy thrown in among garden beds and stables, crinoline-shaped lime-trees and red-walled angular orchards, among, in fact, all the long-settled paraphernalia annexed to a prosperous, well – ordered way-of-life, it was endowed with a perfection such as at first to make it seem miniature, like some exquisite model seen through a glass-case.

Certainly there is beauty about an estate of this kind: that tamed country sentiment, so English in quality, clings to it, even the bird-song that trickles down through the dripping blue shadows thrown by the tall trees seems arranged, punctual, and correct as the mechanical chirping of one of those clock-work birds that lifts enamelled wings out of a square black box; and even the cuckoo, who makes so ominous a sound from the cool green fortification of wood or hedgerow, here changes his note till it rings hollow and pure as a church bell. No sense of mystery broods in the green and open spaces bathed in yellow summer sunlight; here are no caves, grottos, or tumbling torrents: everything is neat, shallow as the clear, slightly running streams that border the wood; yet surely such beauty is, in a way, more fantastic than any of Leonardo's piled-up rocks or those worlds of ogres and giants to which we are carried off by some of the primitive painters.

In the winter it is, that all these country places are seen in their best, their most typical, phase. Stout built for cold weather, these houses take on a new quality, upstanding among hoar-frost, glowing warmly through the crisp, grey air. The first impression of the Grove would be, we think, a childlike memory of potting-shed smells, full of the hidden growth; an odour of bulbs, stoves, rich fibrous mould, and bass, mingles with the sharp aromatic smell of the bonfire that crackles outside. On the walls of the shed the bass is hung up like so many beards of old men — ritual beards; like those of Pharaoh or Egyptian priest, which, perhaps, the gardener will don for the great occasions of his year. This one he would put on for the opening of the first spring flower, coming up glazed and shrill, its petals folded as if in prayer, out of the cold brown earth, beneath the laced shadows woven by the bare branches of the trees; this he will wear for the brazen trumpet-like blowing of the tulip-tree; while that one he reserves for the virginal unfolding of the magnolia, or the gathering up of petals let drop by the last rose. But the gardener himself soon dispels these tender imaginings, as you see his burly form bent over various cruel tasks — the trapping of the soft mole, or in aiming at the fawn-coloured fluffy arcs of the rabbits, as they crouch in their green cradles, their ears well back, nibbling the tender white shoots that he had so carefully nurtured.

Outside the shed in many glass frames large violets, ranging in tone from a deep purple through magenta to an almost brick-red, their petals scintillating damply, glisten like crystallised fruit seen through a glass window, sweet but unapproachable. The ground of the kitchen garden is hard and shiny, starched with frost; trees, shrubs, and the very grass are stiff and brittle, sweeping down under the slight wind with a shrill, steely sound. But the orchard walls still glow as if stained with the juice of the ripe fruits that press against them in the summer and autumn, red, purple, and bloomy, while the house beyond shows warmly through the tree whose topmost twigs pattern themselves about it, like cobwebs against the sky; soft it is, as if cut from red velvet. Out of doors and windows sounds the monotonous, dry-throated rattle of pet dogs, setting up a comfortable yet irritating competition with the noises of stable and farmyard, where rosy-faced men bustle about, lumbering in heavy boots; or, leaning to one side, the right arm lifted and at an angle, blow loudly and whistle, as they polish still more the varnished horses, their breathing lingering on after them in the sharp air like dragon's breath. Through the windows of the house each fireplace shows up, while the red flowers blaze in it, or die down to a yellow flicker, fighting ineffectually against the thin silver rapiers of the winter sun. But more than all these things would you notice here the bitter cackle of a green parrot, falling through the drawn-out air with a horrid clatter, tumbling all lesser sounds down like a pack of cards. Certainly that menacing silly sound of a parrot's laughter would be your most abiding memory.

On such a noon as this it was that Nurse Gooch had first driven up to the Grove; so that, even if her first impression was a rather uneasy one, she had at any rate seen it wearing its most pleasant, most comfortable, aspect; for at night the character of every house changes — and this one alters more than most. The smiling comfort of the surroundings is lost, fades out into utter blackness, and a curious sub-flavour, unnoticed in the day, manifests itself. There are places and moments when the assumptions, the lean conventions on which our lives are based, become transparent, while, for an instant, the world we have made rocks with them. It is, for example, usually assumed that there are no such creatures as sea-serpents, yet there are certain places in Europe, on our own placid coasts even, of such marvellous formation that we feel, suddenly, that the existence of these monsters is a certainty — that it would surprise us less to see a vast beast, such as those painted by Piero di Cosimo, with flame-forked tongue, gigantic head, and long writhing body, coming up out of the fathomless green depths, than to see a passing country cart, a clergyman, or anything to which our experience has accustomed us. There are moments, too, when death, which, as we have said, it is usually our custom to hide away in a dusty corner of our minds, peeps round at us, grimacing — and we realise it as one of the universal and most awful conditions upon which we are permitted to take up life. So it was with the Grove, when darkness coffined it round. The dwarf perfection, which we have attempted to describe, would gradually disappear; for the very dimensions of the house seemed to alter as the rooms became swollen with darkness, full of inexplicable sound. Dead people walk here with more certain step than the living, their existence seems more substantial, their breathing more audible. The boarding of the floor yields under an invisible step, as if some strange memory stirs in it, and the panelling of the walls, the very furniture, make themselves heard with a hard, wooden creaking, which is magnified in these rooms now grown to the new proportions with which night endows them. And, in the darkness outside, everything moves, stirs, rustles.

It was therefore not to be wondered at that the Grove should have acquired the reputation of being haunted, though, really, the unhappy restless air that pervaded it at night may have been due more to its long association with a family of sad, unfortunate temperament — amounting in certain cases to something worse — than to the actual walking presence of any ghost. For ever since the present house was

built, late in the seventeenth century, it had been in the possession
of the Tonges and, until recently, until in fact the present owner had
inherited the estate, there had been a long history connected with
it of brooding melancholy, that must have been nearly allied to
madness.

But Colonel Tonge, as we have seen, presented an ordinary enough
character, with nerves unaffected, betraying no sign of hereditary
disorder. Among the properties we have described — house, lawn,
garden, farm, and stable — this not altogether unattractive figure
emerges, strutting like a bantam. A proud little man, with a fairly
distinguished military career, fond of hunting and shooting, he was
much engaged in the business of an estate, the extent and importance
of which he was apt to magnify in his own mind. In addition to these
interests, he was involved in the affairs of every district committee,
and, as became him in his dual capacity of squire and military man,
was much to the fore in all those local philanthropic schemes which
had for their object the welfare of the ex-soldier, or the helping of
widow and children.

Yet in spite of this inherited make-up of country gentleman and
the acquired one of soldier, there was about the Colonel on closer
acquaintance some quality that removed him ever so little from the
usual specimen of his class, just as there was something about the
Grove that differentiated it from the run of English country houses.
In what, then, did this difference consist? Partly, perhaps, in the stress
that he laid upon the importance of his belongings, and therefore of
himself; but more, surely, in the extraordinary calm that marked his
demeanour — a quiet unruffled calm, not quite in accord with his
bristling appearance and apparent character. One never saw him lose
his temper, never even about trivialities, such as is the way of most
military commanders; yet this restraint did not seem to arise so much
from good nature as from the fear of losing his self-control even for
a moment — suggesting that he was suppressing some instinct or
emotion which must be very strong within him, if it was necessary
continually to exert such an iron self-discipline. This contrast between
nature and manner showed itself, too, in the difference between his
uneasy, wandering eyes and the tightly drawn mouth. But if Nurse
Gooch had, with more than her normal sensitiveness, felt at first that
there was a rather queer atmosphere about the house, she had at any
rate detected nothing unusual in the look or manner of this amiable,
rather pompous, little man, and, indeed, the only person who
appreciated thoroughly these various subtle distinctions was Mrs

Tonge. This poor lady had married her first cousin, and appeared to have inherited or acquired his, as well as her own, share of the peculiarly nervous temperament of this family. Thin, tall, and of that ash-grey colour which betokens constant sleeplessness, her rather sweet expression, while it was in direct contradiction to her restless, irritable soul, was the only remnant of a former prettiness. For, when first she married, she had been a good-looking, high-spirited girl, but had suddenly, swiftly, sunk into this state of perpetual and somewhat nagging melancholy. She was in reality a stupid woman, but her frayed nerves bestowed upon her an understanding of, and insight into, the unpleasant side of life that were alarming in the sureness of their judgement, and must have made of her a trying companion. She added to these heightened perceptions a sense of grievance, aggravated by an absolute lack of interest or occupation, and by the fact that she was childless. She complained constantly, her chief lament being that there were only three creatures in the world that cared for her, two dogs — a Pomeranian and a Pekinese — and her beloved green parrot! Often she would add a remark to the effect that her husband would like — was, in fact, only waiting for — Polly to die. His triumph would then, apparently, be complete. And it must truthfully be said that the only thing which ever seemed to disturb the Colonel's calm was the idiot-laughter which the parrot would let fall through the darkened air of the sick woman's room. But though the slightest noise at any other time would strain Mrs Tonge's taut nerves almost to breaking-point, she appeared actually to enjoy her bird's head-splitting mirth; while the parrot, in return, seemed to acknowledge some bond of affection between his mistress and himself, for, were she more than usually ill, he would be ever so quiet, not venturing to exercise his marked mimetic gifts, even repressing his habitual laughter.

This love for her parrot and her pet dogs, together with a certain trust in, more than affection for, her young nurse — a trust which developed as the months passed — were all the assets of which Mrs Tonge was conscious in this life. For the rest she was lonely and frightened . . . very frightened. Her whole existence was spent in a continual state of fear — one of the worst symptoms, though quite a common one, of neurasthenia; she was afraid of her neighbours, her husband, her house, terrified by everything and everybody alike. But, while frightened of everything, she was as consistently opposed to any plan for the alleviation of these imagined terrors.

Afraid, though seemingly without reason, of her husband, she was yet never able to refrain from making the fullest use of any opportunity to irritate, hurt, or annoy him. But he was very patient with her. She would taunt him with things big and little; she would attack him about his self-importance, or goad him before the nurse about his fondness for giving good advice to others, in a manner that must have made him feel the sting of truth. She would even accuse him of wishing to be rid of her — a poor invalid and one who was in his way — an accusation which, however, she could never really have believed for a moment. She would tell him that he had a cruel soul, and in her sick mind seemed to have fashioned a grotesque, caricatured little image of her husband, which, to her, had at last come to be the reality — an image, unlike yet in a way recognisable, of a queer, patient, cruel, rather wolf-like creature, hiding his true self beneath the usual qualities attached to the various very ordinary interests and pursuits in which his life was spent.

In spite of this extraordinary conception of him, Mrs Tonge was always calling for her husband. Her plaintive voice echoing through the square, lofty rooms would be answered by his gruff, military tones so often that one of the parrot's most ingenious tricks was a perfect rendering of 'Humphrey, come here a minute!' and the answering call 'Yes, Mary, I'm coming,' followed by the sound of hurrying footsteps. Thus, though frightened of him, though almost hating him, the invalid would hardly allow her husband to leave her, if only for a day.

Still more was Mrs Tonge frightened of her house — that home which she knew so intimately. But, in the same perverse manner, she would never quit it, even for a night. While suffering terrible insomnia, and from that fear of darkness which, though it usually leaves us when our childhood is past, had never wholly left her, she was steadfast in her refusal to allow Nurse Gooch to sleep in the same room, thus lessening these nocturnal terrors by human companionship. On the contrary, that sick woman not only insisted on being alone, but was resolute in locking both the doors of her room, one of which led into her husband's bedroom, the other into the passage outside, so that had she been seized with sudden illness, which was not altogether unlikely, no help could have reached her. Thus, bolted securely within those four walls, she would indulge her broken spirit in an orgy of sleepless terror. The dogs slept downstairs: her only companion was Polly, noiseless now, but faithful as ever, sitting hunched up on his perch, his dome-like cage enveloped in a pall of grey felt; and, even had he sounded his bitter, head-splitting laughter, it would have seemed more sweet than the music of any southern nightingales to the poor invalid, tossing about in her bed. For the parrot, alone of the animal-world, could give his mistress some feeling of momentary security.

Day would come at last, to bring with it an hour or two of grey, unrefreshing sleep. The afternoon she would spend knitting, seated in a large arm-chair in front of the fire, in her overheated boudoir, crowded with strong-smelling flowers. Photographs of friends — friends whom she had not seen for years and had perhaps never really cared for — littered all the furniture, and clambered up the walls, over the fire-place, in an endless formation, imbuing the room with that peculiar morbid tone of old photographs, yellow and glazed as death itself. Bustles, bonnets, then straw hats and leg-of-mutton sleeves, showed grotesquely in these little squares of faded, polished cardboard, set off by a palm tree in an art-pot, a balustraded terrace, a mountainous yet flat back-ground, or one of those other queer properties of the old photographic world. The wistful smiles on these pretty faces were now gone like her own, the smoothness of the skin was now replaced by hundreds of ever so small wrinkles, the fruit of care, sorrow, or some seed of ill-nature or bad temper that, undreamt of then, had now blossomed. The rest of open space on table, piano, or writing desk was taken up by diminutive unconnected vases of violets, freesias or jonquils, their heavy breath weighing on the air like a cloud, seeming among these photographs so many floral tributes to dead friendship, each one marking the grave of some pretended or genuine affection. The room was overloaded with these vases; the flowers lent no grace to the room, no sweetness to the over-burdened air. The Pomeranian yapped at Mrs Tonge's feet, the Pekinese lay curled up in a basket, while at her elbow the parrot picked at a large, white grape, the stale odour of the bird's cage mingling with the already stifling atmosphere of the room, till it became almost intolerable. Here the invalid would sit for hours enjoying one of the thousand little grievances from which she was able to choose, turning it over and pecking at it like the parrot at his grape; or, perhaps, she would be gripped by one of the manifold terrors of her life. Then that supreme horror, the fear of death (which, as she grew older, claimed an ever-greater part of her attention), grimaced at her from the scented shadows, till it seemed to her as if she sat there knitting endlessly her own shroud, and the vases of flowers transformed their shapes, rearranging themselves till they became wreaths and crosses, and the hot smell they exhaled became the very odour of death. Then she would ring again, calling for Nurse Gooch, but even that familiar footfall would make her shudder for an instant.

Her only pleasures now consisted in the tormenting of her even-tempered husband, or, in a lesser degree, of the poor young nurse – to whom she had now become attached in the same sense that a dog is attached to any object, such as a doll or an indiarubber ball, which it can worry. But Gooch, good and amiable, clean-looking rather than pretty, her face fully expressing that patience and kindness which were her two great qualities, won the affections not only of the invalid but of Colonel Tonge, and even of the servants — this latter no mean conquest when it is remembered that there is a traditional feud between servants and trained nurse, almost rivalling the other hereditary vendetta between nursery and schoolroom. Nurse Gooch was really fond of her patient, in spite of the maddening irritation of her ways: nor had she been unhappy during these eighteen months that had followed her luncheon at the Grove on that first winter day. For after the hardships of her own childhood, she appreciated this solid, very comfortable, home, while it presented to her a full scope for the exercise of those protective instincts which were particularly deep-rooted in her nature. Often, in a way, she envied Mrs Tonge her kind husband and charming house, thinking how happy the invalid might have been had only her disposition been a different one. For in Colonel Tonge the young nurse could see nothing but consideration for his ill wife, and kindness indeed to everyone, till, slowly, she formed in her own mind an image of him very different from that fashioned by his wife. To Nurse Gooch he was a model of suffering chivalry; to her his stature and heart seemed great, his importance equal to his own estimate of it. In fact, he became that very appealing combination — one which always fascinates the English people — a hero in public, a martyr in private life. And it was a source of great comfort for her to reflect that by keeping Mrs Tonge in as good a mood as possible, or, to borrow a military phrase, by intentionally drawing the fire on to herself, she was able to some small extent to alleviate the trials of the husband. Then she could feel, in some mysterious manner, that he was grateful for it, that he began to take pleasure in her society, in the knowledge that she understood his difficulties, applauded his moderation. Often they used to sit together, consulting with Dr Maynard, a clever doctor, but one who lacked courage, and was in the habit of giving way to his patients. Gradually, therefore, if any new symptoms showed itself, if any new problem arose regarding the invalid, it was with the nurse and not with the doctor that Colonel Tonge would first come to talk it over.

Existence at the Grove, though each day appeared to her

encompassed in the span of an hour, so that she was continually finding herself landed, as if by some magic carpet of the fourth dimension, at the corresponding time of the next day, yet seemed eternal; even the state of the sick woman, though her nerves became even more affected, appeared to be stationary. Outside there was the fat, placid life of the countryside, to be watched, the punctual revolution of the seasons. First came the ice-green glitter of the snowdrops, frosting the grass of the park with their crystal constellations; then these faded, withered, turned yellow, deepened to the butter-colour of the daffodils that ousted them, flowers swaying their large heads under the spring winds, transparent, full of the very colour of the sun; and, almost before you had time to observe it, they would flush to a deep purple, would be transformed into anemones, the centre of their dusky blossoms powdered with pollen, black like charcoal dust, or would adopt the velvet softness of texture which distinguishes the rose from other flowers: and summer would be in its full flame. Then, inside the Grove, you found good food, punctual hours, a calm routine broken only by the outbursts of Mrs Tonge, or by the bitter cackle of the parrot, its feathers green with the depth of a tropical forest, its eyes wary and knowing. It looked cunning, as if in possession of some queer secret — some secret such as that of the parrot encountered in Mexico by the traveller Humboldt — a bird which alone in all the world possessed a tongue of its own, since it spoke a language now extinct. For the tribe who talked it had been killed to a man in the course of America becoming a Christian continent, while the bird had lived on for a century.

The summer was a particularly hot one, and as it burnt to its climax, Mrs Tonge's irritable nerves inflicted an increasing punishment on those around her. The Colonel, who was drawn away on various long-promised visits to old friends and taken to London several times on the business of his estate, left the Grove more than usual this July, so that the full brunt of any trouble in the house fell upon Nurse Gooch, who would often have to shut herself up in her room, and, strong-minded, well-trained woman though she was, cry like a hurt child, so intolerable was the strain imposed upon her by the invalid. The latter soon realised when she had made the tactical error of being too disagreeable — or, perhaps, one should say of concentrating a day's temper in one short hour, instead of spreading it thinly, evenly, over the whole of the sun's passage, so that, looked back upon, it should tinge the day with some unpleasant colour in the minds of her companions or servants. And being possessed of a certain charm or

a false kindliness which she could exert whenever it was necessary
to her, she was soon able again to engage the nurse's pity and affection
'Poor thing,' Gooch would think to herself. 'One can't blame her
for it. Look how she suffers.' But however true was this reflection,
it was the sick woman who was still the chief opponent of any plan
for the mitigation of her sufferings. Though her sleeplessness became
worse, though the prospect of those long, dark hours threw a shadow
blacker than the night itself over each day, yet she still refused to
allow Nurse Gooch to rest in the room with her; while Dr Maynard,
who should have insisted on it, was, as usual, completely overborne
by his patient.

It is difficult to describe, though, how much Mrs Tonge suffered,
locked in her room during those sultry nights, for their darkness
appeared to cover a period easily surpassing the length of any winter
night. As she lay there, her limbs twitching, memories dormant in
her mind for forty years would rise up to torment her. Her parents,
her old nurse (all dead how many summers past!) would return to
her here in the silence. All the disappointments of her life would revive
their former aching. Once more she would see the gas-lit ballrooms
in which she had danced as a girl, and the faces of men she had
forgotten half a lifetime ago. Then, again, she would see her wedding.
All these memories would link up, and coalesce in feverish waking
dreams of but a moment's duration, but which would yet seem to
hold all eternity in their contorted perspectives. Wide awake now,
she would recall her longing for children, or ponder upon one of her
thousand little grievances, which took on new and greater dimensions
in these hours. Here she was . . . with a parrot as her only friend
. . . in this everlasting blackness. The thought of death would return
to her, death that was at the end of each turning, making every life
into a blind hopeless cul-de-sac. Long and hard she would fight this
spectre of finality, against which no religion had the power to fortify
her spirit. Then, after midnight, new terrors began, as the Grove woke
up to its strange nocturnal life. Footsteps would sound outside,
treading stealthily, stealthily on the black, hollow air; the furniture
in the room, cumbersome old cupboards and chests of drawers, would
suddenly tattoo a series of little but very definite hard sounds upon
the silence, as if rapping out some unknown code. But when
everything was swathed in quiet once more, this new absence of noise
would be worse, more frightening than were the sounds themselves.
It would smother everything with its blackness; everything would be
still . . . waiting . . . listening! The silence, from having been merely

a form of muffled sound, or perhaps a negation of it, became itself positive, active — could be felt and tested by the senses. There it was again, that creaking — as if someone was listening . . . someone certainly . . . someone standing on a loose board, crouching down in the darkness outside, afraid to tread for fear of waking one. Then would follow a distraction. A new code would be rapped out as something tapped on the window-pane . . . tap — tap — tap, like a mad thing. Only the wind with that branch of ivy, she supposed. There it was again . . . tap — tap . . . like a mad thing trying to get into her room . . . tap — tap . . . into her very head, it seemed! Outside the house a dog would bark once, menacingly, and then its rough voice would die suddenly, as if silenced. Footsteps would tread again down the long passages, footsteps more distinct than ever this time. And once or twice they lingered stealthily at the bolted door; the handle would creak, grasped very carefully, turned by an invisible hand; and was there not the sound of a smothered, animal-like breathing? The wolf-at-the-door, the wolf-at-the-door, she says to herself in that fevered mind, where it seems as if two people, two strangers, were carrying on a whispered conversation of interminable length. Then silence comes once more; an unequalled stillness pours into the room, and into the corridors outside, so that the tapping, when it returns, takes on a new quality, rippling this quiet blackness with enlarging circles of sound, as when a stone is cast into a small pool. Tap — tap — tap . . . again tap. Perhaps she is only dead, being fastened into her coffin. Tap — tap . . . they are nailing it down, tap — tap; and she lies dead in the silence for ever. Then far away the taps sound out again and the coffin is unnailed. But this time it is the parrot rapping upon the bars of his dome-like cage with his hard beak; and she is reassured. Grey light clutches again at the swathed windows, and the furniture of the room grows slowly into its accustomed shape; the things round her fall back again into their familiar contours, and are recognisable as themselves, for in the night they had assumed new positions, new shapes, strange attitudes . . . and the poor nervous creature lying on the rumpled bed falls asleep for an hour or two.

But as the light drips stealthily in, filling the black hollows of room and corridor, the housemaids, warned by Nurse Gooch to be more than usually quiet, scratch gently in the passage outside like so many mice, scratch with a gentle feeble sound that must inevitably rouse anyone — even a person who sleeps well by habit and is at that moment deeprooted in slumber. For this timid, rodent-like noise is more irritating to the strongest nerves, will awaken more surly, than any of that loud, sudden music to which we are accustomed — that music of blows rained accidentally but with great force upon the fragile legs and corners of old furniture or brittle carving of ancient gilded frames — blows delivered with the back of an ever so light feathery brush. Thus Mrs Tonge would open her eyes upon one more hot and calm morning.

As she lay there, in the semi-darkness, she could hear faint voices sounding in the passage. Soon after she has rung her bell, Nurse Gooch comes in with the letters, as clean and kind as is possible for a human being to be, bright as are all trained nurses in the early morning; too bright, perhaps, too wide awake, and already making the best of it. Her hair has a dark golden colour in it under the light, and gleams very brightly under the cap she is wearing, while she talks in an even, soothing voice. As she goes down the corridor towards the invalid's room the housemaids take her passing presence for a signal that they may resume that noisy bustle of cleanliness with which they salute each day. Suddenly motes of dust whirl up into the air beneath their brushes, turning under the already searching rays of the sun to columns and twisted pillars of sparkling glass that support this heavy firmament, pillars prism-like in the radiant array of their colour. As the housemaids, bent nearly double in their long white print dresses, move slowly over the carpet, brush in one hand, dustpan in the other, their movements break up these columns, so that the atoms that compose them fall through the air like so many sequins, and are violently agitated; then these take on new shapes, and from pillars are converted into obelisks, pyramids, rectangles, and all the variety of glittering forms that, bound by the angles of straight lines, can be imposed upon this dull air and earth by the lance-like rays of the morning sun.

In the room she still lies in bed, turning over the unopened envelopes of her letters. Gooch goes to the window and talks to the parrot. As she uncovers the cage the bird breaks into its metallic laughter, that rattles down through the open window into the shrubbery, like so many brassy rings thrown down by a juggler, for they curve in again at the pantry-window, where John the footman is standing in an apron, cleaning the silver with a dirty-looking piece of old yellow leather and some gritty rose-pink paste. As he polishes the convex mirror formed by the flanks of the silver bowl, while his face reflected in one side assumes a grotesque appearance, the contorted trees and twisted perspective of lawn and garden show in the other. The second housemaid peeps in. 'Oh, you do look a sight!' she cries, bridling with laughter, pointing to the bowl in his hand. 'I may be a sight,' he says, 'or I may not, but I'm not a blarsted slave, am I?' 'Well, you needn't answer so nasty,' she said. 'It's not that, it's that parrot – 'ark at it now. I shall be glad when 'e comes back; one can't do no right in this place. Everything is wrong. First it's one dam thing, then another. Nurse sticks it like a soldier,' he says, 'but I stand up for my rights! I'm not a slave, I'm not, that I should stand there letting that blarsted parrot screech at me like a sergeant-major on a parade ground, and her talking a lot of nonsense. I'd like to wring its bloody neck, I would — they're a pair of them, they are!'

And certainly — Nurse Gooch herself had to admit it — the invalid was this summer more than ever exacting. For many months past she had worried her husband about a summer-house, for which she had formed one of those queer, urgent longings that sick people consider themselves free to indulge. The hut had stood there in the woods, year after year, unnoticed, falling to damp decay, when, as if given new eyes, Mrs Tonge saw it for the first time, and determined to make it her own. Here, she felt, it would be possible to sit quietly, rest peacefully, in an atmosphere different from that of the Grove, and perhaps find that sleep denied her in any other place. As the summer-house was in a very dilapidated condition, she asked her husband to have it repaired for her, but met with a very unexpected opposition. The Colonel, used as he was to furthering every plan of his sick wife, absolutely ignored this new entreaty. Which fact, unfortunately, only strengthened her determination, and made her persist in her caprice.

There was, in reality, some danger in letting Mrs Tonge remain alone for a long period in a spot so remote from the house — she refused, again, to allow anyone to wait with her in this solitude — for though, as in the habit of permanent invalids, she might live for many years, yet she was a nervous, delicate woman, very liable to a sudden attack of illness, and here no help could reach her. But Dr Maynard, with his customary inability to say 'No' to a patient — or, perhaps, because he felt that the rest she hoped to obtain here would be more valuable to her than any unexpected attack of illness would be dangerous — gave his sanction to the new scheme. Colonel Tonge, however, still urged the doctor to forbid it, making a strong protest against what he considered this folly, and himself steadfastly refused to have the place touched up in any way, or even swept out. The invalid changed her tactics: from anger she passed to a mood of plaintive injury. 'I know, Humphrey,' she moaned at him, 'that you only go on like that because you hate to think that I am having a peaceful moment. What harm *can* there be in going to the summer-house? It doesn't hurt you, does it?'

The Colonel, patient as ever, would show no sign of ill-temper, putting the case as reasonably as he could. 'Mary, my dear, it is really very unwise and foolish of you. I know how much unemployment there is, how unsettled is the countryside. You should see some of the tramps that are brought up before me on the Bench. That summer-house may seem deep in the woods, but it is very near the high-road. You can never tell who will come into the park. Anyone can get in. There's no lodge near the gate, I tell you, my dear, it isn't safe. I can't think how you can be so silly. It's folly, sheer folly!'

Mrs Tonge cried a little: 'I'm not afraid of tramps or motor-cars, or of anything on a road. But I know you'd do anything to prevent me getting any rest, Humphrey. I believe you'd like me to go without any sleep at all, as long as it didn't worry you. I know you're only waiting for me to die.' . . . And the poor little man, discomfited, walked away. He was always so patient . . . like that . . . and kind, it made Nurse Gooch feel a great pity for him. But she thought he was wrong in this particular instance — wrong ever to oppose the invalid's wishes, however seldom he did so; and knowing her influence with him, she persuaded the Colonel to say no more about it, though he still seemed a little uneasy. Yet so great had become his reliance on the young nurse's judgement, that she easily induced him to pretend to his wife that he now thought his opposition had been a mistake.

But Mrs Tonge could not be deceived. She knew perfectly well that he did not really approve, and it therefore gave her an increased pleasure to rest in the summer-house. Getting up later than ever in these hot months of the year, she would go there every afternoon. She forbade her two pets to be with her, so that a piteous, plaintive yapping filled the Grove each day after luncheon; only Polly, devoted Polly, was privileged to share this new solitude. Curiously enough, she did not feel frightened here. The rather ominous silence of the woods held no menace for her, she was happier among these dank shadows than in her own bedroom or placid flowering garden; and, whether from perversity or from some form of auto-suggestion, it was a fact that when the nurse walked out to the hut to bring the sick woman back to the house for tea, she often found her in a slumber more peaceful than any she had enjoyed for years.

Between two and three o'clock each fine afternoon a queer

procession could be seen walking over the lawn between the beds of flowers that lay like embossed embroidery among the sleek grass. First of all came Mrs Tonge, never glancing aside at flower or tree, her upright carriage and slow-moving walk bestowing an almost ritual air on the proceedings; then followed the uniform-clad figure of the nurse, holding the newspapers and a small cluster of three or four grapes for the parrot in one hand, while from the other dangled the sacred dome. The grapes transparent, jewel-like, catching the prevailing colour, which was that of the penetrating glow of sunlight through green leaves, focused the eye as they moved along, till they seemed like some mystic regalia, even drawing the eye away from the more metallic colouring of the parrot, who, as he was borne along, shrieked continually, taking an obvious pleasure in scaring the poor timid birds of the English countryside by a display of flaming plumage and alien, rather acrid, laughter. Slowly they passed over the shrill, water-smooth lawns, where single high trees stood up fleecy against the sky, or, over-burdened by the full weight of summer, trailed their branches right down upon the fragrant ground, into the dark woods cloudy with foliage and rank with the smell of tall nettles, elder-trees, bracken, and all those things that grow in unkept places. No birdsong sounded now in this ultimate unfolding of the seasons, and the little path that led winding through this wilderness lay like a curling green ribbon, of a brighter hue than the surrounding shrubs and velvety with moss, from which weeds sprouted up at the corners like small tufts of feathers. This untidy ribbon, lying without purpose across the woodland ground, led to the rustic hut which the caprice of some former mistress of the Grove had caused to be built here, rather pointlessly, some ninety years ago. Under a round roof, sloping down from its centre, and covered with the rough bark of trees, it lay mouldering beneath the structure of branches which hung motionless, as if cut from cardboard, on the heavy air. Sponge-like, it seemed, in its dampness, like some fungus lying about at the foot of a tree. Great knots of ivy clung to the upper part of the door, while, where the peeling bark had fallen away, were revealed arrangements of rusty nails, geometrical, but growing like thorns out of the wood. No view was framed in the pointed spaces of the two windows, except the light which trellised itself with the shadow of green leaves along the ground, or, flooding a stretch of bracken, played first on one leaf, then on another, bringing out unexpected patterns, making each bent-back leaf, as it was touched, the centre of some shifting arabesque design such as is woven in Eastern carpets.

The parrot would be placed on the dingy, bark-covered table; a grape would be half-peeled, and pressed, like a melting jewel, between the bars of the cage. The wire dome would then be draped ceremoniously with grey felt; the invalid would lie back in her long chair, a rug over her knees, the countless newspapers which it was her habit to read placed at her side; and Nurse Gooch would walk back briskly through the dark stillness of the wood out again into the droning odorous languor of the garden.

As Mrs Tonge rested in her long chair, she found, certainly, a peace otherwise denied to her in the grim world of a sick woman's fancy. No argument, she determined, should ever persuade her to give up this siesta. Day followed day, each warm and bright-coloured as the other; only the leaves became a little ranker in their scent, the woods yet more silent. But sometimes, as she was on the border of sleep, already seeing the queer avenues of that land which she could so seldom reach, while through its landscape she could still distinguish the more rational, familiar features of her real surroundings, a sound like a rushing wind, or as if gigantic wings were beating on the taut drum-like fabric of the air, would startle her for a moment, and, looking round, she would see the tall stiff trees lift up their canvas branches, caught by a false breeze, as a motor-car passed between the two high hedges that concealed the road. Above this hidden white scar a high whirling column of dust would dance for a few seconds, as if it were some jinn of the air made visible for the moment; or, again, she would she would be lulled by the kindly, cooing voices of the country people, which floated over to her, for, as her husband had pointed out, the road was in reality very near the summer-house. But these things did not appear unpleasant to her; and, in any case, how much better were these explicable sounds than that state of suspended animation, alternating with a sudden show of life, which she had grown to dread so much at night in her own room!

The hot weather continued, and with it the life of the Grove. Colonel Tonge, as we have remarked, was away this summer more than was his wont, but the routine of the invalid, the nurse, and the servants repeated itself almost automatically. Every afternoon Nurse Gooch would walk out with the patient to the hut and would leave her there, only returning in time to fetch her back to the house for tea. One afternoon, when the Colonel was expected home from a short visit to Major Morley, an old friend and brother-officer whom, though a near neighbour, he saw very seldom, Mrs Tonge suddenly made up her mind to stay out in the summer-house for tea, telling the nurse to bring it out to her at five o'clock. Now, though there was nothing very original or startling in this idea, Gooch, who in matters relating to an invalid did not lack a certain subtlety, at once expostulated — not, indeed, from any feeling of disapproval, but because she well knew that the sick woman would in reality be deeply disappointed if her nurse seemed pleased, or even satisfied, with this new break away from the normal programme. The nurse, therefore, succeeded in putting up a show of anxiety, saying such things as that the patient ought not to be too long alone, or that the Colonel would be hurt and annoyed at finding his wife absent on his return. Finally, pretending to be persuaded against her better judgement, she agreed to bring tea out to the summer-house at five o'clock; then, placing the parrot's cage on the table, she covered it up, completed her ritual, and walked back to the house through the hot, strangely sultry, afternoon.

Mrs Tonge felt an unaccustomed luxurious ease steal over her as she lay stretched out on her couch reading her papers, though perhaps perusing them less carefully today than was her custom. As a rule, she read them from cover to cover — births, deaths, marriages, sales, advertisements of all kinds; and, while these journals represented every shade of political opinion, she was quite unmoved by their varying propaganda. She regarded them, in fact, as her one form of relaxation. This afternoon, however, she could not fix her attention on them. She peeled an amber, honey-scented grape for Polly, who mumbled back lovingly but softly. What a difference even an hour's sleep makes! She wondered when Humphrey was coming back, feeling that she had been rather hard with him lately — in fact, for some time past. With a sudden impulse of affection the image she had formed of him in her own mind was broken, and he became to her again the young man whom she had loved. She determined that she would be nicer to him; and certainly she felt a little better today. The afternoon in the summer-house seemed just warm enough . . . and quiet . . . nicely quiet she thought. Slowly, almost contentedly, and for the first time for many years without any fear, any nervous feeling, she stretched her limbs until every nerve in her body became quiet, and sighing gently, let sleep wash over her tired limbs, her worn-out mind, in soft delicious little waves.

But, though the dampness of the hut may have tempered that afternoon heat for Mrs Tonge, it seemed very breathless outside. Even Nurse Gooch, as she sat sewing in her usually cool room, felt rather overcome. Oh, how hot it was! And the house was very still. As a rule you heard the servants chattering, moving through the passages;

the jingling of silver or the rattling of plates would reach you from pantry or kitchen. But today there was no noise — not a sound, except the hot insect-like droning of the sewing-machine, as she bent over it, running the needle along the white edge of the new linen, which filled the room with a rather stifling scent. But directly she stopped, even for an instant, silence flooded the room. Well, one can't look after a case like this for eighteen months without feeling odd oneself sometimes, she supposed! Yet there was something queer about the stillness. There must be going to be a storm, she thought.

No sound came in from farm or stable at this high-up, open window, on a level with the motionless green cradles of the birds; but down below on the lawn a single leaf would suddenly burst out into a mad fluttering, as if trying to indicate the secret of this general alarm, and then be still, as if it feared to be caught in an act of rebellion . . .In the flower beds, then, a single violent coloured blossom would wave out wildly, flicker for an instant like a tongue of flame, then float once more stiffly upon the glazed heat. She was quite glad to finish her sewing, get the tea ready, and leave the house. But the air outside was even hotter than within — suffocating — so that one could not breathe, and as she passed out into the furtive silence of the woods she seemed separated from the world she knew. If I go on like this, she said to herself, I shall soon be the next invalid! Yet the walk seemed longer than it ought to be, so that she was continually being confronted with little twistings in it which she did not remember, though she had trodden this path at least four times a day for several months past. Still she knew, of course, that it must be the right one. But somehow or other, she was startled this afternoon by things that usually she would not notice — the ordinary, rather inexplicable rustlings of the woodlands, for instance. Doubtless these were audible yesterday as today, but as a rule she did not heed them; and once or twice, certainly, it seemed to her that she heard a peculiar scampering, as of a hurrying through thickets, or the dragging crackle of twigs and brambles as they released their clinging hold on invisible garments. It was with a distinct feeling of relief, then, that after quite a long walk, she caught sight of the summer-house round the next turning. It had a very human, friendly look to her this afternoon; yet it belonged so much to these woods, this soil, that it was like a large mushroom growing out of a taller green tangle. The invalid did not call out to her, even the parrot was silent — an indication, usually, that its mistress was asleep. (How queer it is the way she can sleep here, and nowhere else!) Nurse Gooch cried out cheerfully, 'Wake up, wake up! I've brought you your tea!' Still there was no answer, and, skirting the blind corner of the hut, carrying the tray in front of her, she was already standing in the low doorway before she had even cast a glance at its dark interior. Thrown suddenly into the quiet smallness of the summer-house, where she was at such close quarters with everything, almost within an arm's span of each wall, she was unable to breathe for a moment. An overwhelming sensation of nausea took possession of her, so that she felt that she, too, would fall upon that terrible floor. Yet, though the whole universe swung round, her trained eye observed the slaughter-house details. There lay the murdered woman, her head on one side, her skull crushed by some ferocious blow, her face twisted to a mask of terror — that queer unreasoning terror which had never left her. Dumb, blinking in its overturned cage, the parrot was hunched up, its feathers clotted together with blood. Clutching the bird's cage as if to save it from some fresh disaster, Nurse Gooch rushed wildly out of the summer-house into the motionless woods.

As she approached the Grove, her own sense of discipline asserted itself, forcing her to slow down her pace, to set her mind a little more in order. But now it was, actually, that the full shock came to her, for in that sudden blind moment of fear, when her limbs had melted one into the other, when her heart had bounded to her very lips, she had been unable to think, had experienced no feeling except an endless surprise, pity and disgust. Afterwards curiosity, as well, intervened, and she began to wonder who had done this thing, and why such a brutal fate had engulfed the poor, timid, elderly woman. And then she was forced to steel her soul for the next ordeal: she would have need of every particle of strength in mind and body, since it devolved upon her to break the news. Through the library window she could see Colonel Tonge standing by the empty fireplace, and even while she was still labouring under the blow that had befallen her, she dreaded telling him of it as the not least awful incident in this terrible adventure — nearly as overwhelming, indeed, as had been the actual moment of discovery. Her respect, and fondness, even, for him, her knowledge that his had not been a happy marriage, only made the task a more difficult one to face and endure.

With an unexpected nervous susceptibility the Colonel seemed to feel the burning, panting breath of tragedy almost before she had spoken. Perhaps something out of her control manifested itself in her face, in the air; but as she entered, he looked at her with eyes as fearful as her own, and it seemed as if he, too, were mastering his emotions

to confront something that he dreaded. 'Go on, go on,' he said, 'what
is it?'

Month followed month, and he still shut himself up in his room, till
he became so changed in looks, in manner, as hardly to appear the
same man. All pride, all self-importance had left him. The spring had
gone out of his walk, the jauntiness out of his dress and carriage. Every
hour of the day he loaded himself with reproaches — for not having
been firmer, for not having absolutely refused to allow his wife to
stay out there alone — for having been away at the time of the tragedy.
Gooch would hear him, unable to sleep at night, walking about the
passages, pacing up and down, up and down, till the first grey light
crept in at the corners of blind and curtain. It was as if the spirit of
sleepless terror that had haunted his wife had now transferred its
temple to his body. Incapable of attending to the business of his estate,
to which formerly he had devoted so much consideration, he now
seldom left the house in the daytime, and, if he did, in whatever
direction he might set out, his feet always led him sooner or later to
the same place, and he would be startled, aghast to find himself in
the woods again.

Anything that reminded him of his dead wife had to be hidden away.
The two poor little dogs were removed by his married sister when
she went home, after a quite unsuccessful attempt to cheer her brother
and give him comfort. The parrot, now never laughing, never
speaking, languished in an attic, attended only by Emily, the
housemaid. The other servants, too, were kind to the bird since it
had for them a fatal attraction: not only was it connected with death,
having about it the very odour of the cemetery, but was in itself the
witness and only relic of a brutal crime, so that it possessed the charm
popularly associated with a portion of hangman's rope, and, in
addition, was a living thing possessed of a dreadful secret. But the
parrot would never utter, and downstairs — where the conversation,
however wide the circle of its origin, always in the end drew in on
to one topic — they had to admit that Polly had never been the-same-
like-since. Occasionally Emily would leave the door of the cage open,
hoping that he would walk out or fly round as he used to do. But
nothing could tempt him out of his battered dome. As for Colonel
Tonge, he had never liked the bird, hating its harsh laughter, and
this solitary, now silent, witness of his wife's end filled him at present
with an unconquerable aversion.

Great sympathy was evinced everywhere for the poor widower,

crushed under a catastrophe so unexpected and mysterious. But the public sympathy could do little to help him; and though some solution of the mystery might temporarily have distracted his mind, even if it could not have rallied his spirits, none was forthcoming. He went through all the sordid business associated with murder — inquest and interview; the crime remained odd as ever in its total absence of warning, intention, or clue. Who, indeed, could have plotted to murder this invalid lady, possessed of few friends and no enemies? And what purpose was served by this intolerable brutality? It is true that, after a time, the police found a stained, blunt-headed club, obviously the weapon with which that fatal wound had been inflicted, buried deep in the bracken; but, in a sense, this discovery only removed the murder further from the public experience, in that the possible motive of theft was at the same time disposed of — for with this weapon were found the few rings, the gold watch, and small amount of money that the dead woman had about her, as she had lain asleep in the summer-house on that sultry August afternoon. The police, thinking it possible that these articles had been hidden from an impulse of fear, that the original motive had indeed been the ordinary one, arrested a tramp found wandering in the district, hiding himself at night under hedges and in the shelter of empty barns; but though he could not give a very detailed or convincing account of his doings on the day of the 'Hut Murder' — as it was called — the evidence that connected him with the crime was not enough to secure his conviction. It remained, however, the impression of many people, among them of both Dr Maynard and Nurse Gooch, that he was in reality guilty of the foul act of which he had been suspected. Colonel Tonge, though he followed every detail of the trial with a painful interest, could never be induced to discuss the possible guilt of the tramp, but it was noticeable that after the man's release his nervous condition became more than ever marked, which led them to conclude that, in his opinion too, the person accused should never have been acquitted.

The bereaved husband's insomnia troubled him sorely; he had no peace, no rest by day or night. The only person able to bring him relief, to lighten his burden even for a moment, was Nurse Gooch; so that Dr Maynard felt it his duty, for once, to insist on her remaining at the Grove until the Colonel should display some sign of returning health and a reviving spirit. The nurse, for her part, had always liked, pitied, and admired him, while, by one of those curious human instincts, all the compassion, all the affection even, which she had given so freely to the dead woman, was now made over to her new patient. And then she, too, felt remorse, had things on her mind with which to reproach herself. How well she could understand and sympathise with his self-accusation! Why, conscious as she had been of her influence over him, had she not supported the Colonel's wise protest against his wife's use of the summer-house, instead of urging, as she had done, that it was a reasonable plan, and finally persuading him to withdraw his objection to it? Terribly she felt now the responsibility so foolishly incurred, that perhaps she was in part to blame for the tragedy, even in the matter of allowing that invalid to wait out in the summer-house for tea on that dreadful afternoon; and in the months that followed the murder it was one of the few pleasant things in her life to reflect that she could, by her presence and sympathetic understanding, lessen his misery ever so little, giving him for a little while a passing sense of comfort.

When, after many long, lonely months, he made her an offer of marriage, saying that life without her support would be to him an intolerable burden, she accepted his proposal, realising that the interest she felt in him, the overwhelming pity that sometimes clutched at her heart, was but a disguise for love. Regardless of any difference in age or outlook, she hoped, by becoming his wife, to help and ease the remainder of a life, the unhappy tenor of which had now deepened into a more dreadful tone.

The honeymoon was spent in France, in order to make for them both a complete break from the background of their lives. But even among the lush meadows and rich trees of Normandy, away from ant sting of association, Humphrey did not recover at once, as she had hoped, his old buoyancy. Listless, uneasy, restless, he would for hours be silent, wrapped in a melancholy that did not ordinarily belong to his temperament, while, in his broken slumber and sudden awakenings, his wife could detect the existence of a great well of sorrow that even her anxious affection could not plumb, a grief her love could not solace. The discovery of the extent of his affliction caused her further worry, made her dread their return to the scene of his past life. But as time passed it was obvious that his spirits were returning; and when he told her that during their absence the Grove had been entirely repainted and redecorated, she began to feel happier, hoping that it would seem to him like the beginning of a new life.

Almost two years to a day after the crime, they returned from their honeymoon, but Colonel Tonge did not seem conscious of any sense of anniversary, while she, naturally, would not mention it to him. But it made her feel a little uneasy.

As they drove back from the station, the new chauffeur quite by chance, by one of those dreadful inspirations which are only given to stupid people, drove the newly-married couple down the concealed road near the summer-house, instead of taking them in by the near lodge. Colonel Tonge obviously experienced no emotion, but his wife felt for the moment as if she would be stifled between these two high hedges. How like was this afternoon to that other one! No leaf moved on any tree, no bird let its song trickle through the cloudy, too-dark leafage; the air was hot, motionless and still, though through it ran those same secret tremors, inexplicable tremblings. For the new Mrs Tonge the whole atmosphere was stained with memories.

Yet she soon forgot the uneasy promptings of her heart and mind in the pleasure she felt at the reception which awaited them. She had always been a favourite with the servants, and the latter could never forget the poor Colonel's sufferings, so that they had taken an especial care to give the newly wedded pair an inspiriting welcome. The Colonel stopped to talk to them, while Mrs Tonge, eager to see what alterations had been made, stepped into the house alone. It looked charming, she thought, with the new smooth paint on the old walls; and, unable to repress a slight thrill of pleasure, which she felt to be wrong, though she could not quite exorcise it, at being for the first time mistress of a house — and such a lovely house — she walked on through the empty, gleaming rooms that led one into the other. The last room was the boudoir. She entered it softly, closing the door behind her, wishing to explore its impression to the full, for she wondered whether it would make her feel an usurper, a stranger in someone else's place. But no! it was a new room to her: gone was the feverish atmosphere of the sick-room, with its dead air, over-heated and scented with innumerable flowers: gone was that dead look imparted by the yellow glaze of countless old photographs and by the spreading litter of trivial little objects. And while she bore towards the dead woman no feelings but those of pity and affection, yet, being of a practical nature, she was glad that nothing remained of the old mistress — nothing that could call up painful memories. The room was quiet and restful; the long windows stood wide open on to the pleasant water cool spaces of the lawn, that unfolded up to the borders of the wood where stood tall fleecy green trees, while under their blue shadows ran the murmur of shallow streams. The healthy scents of trees and grass, the peaceful watery sounds, and honey-gathering, contented drone of the bees as they hung over the flowers, drifted into the house, diffusing an air of ease and comfort. This was *her* house, *her* garden, *her* home, and she now had a husband to whom she was devoted. Why, then, should she ever allow her mind to dwell on the tragedies of the past? Was it not better to forget utterly, to obliterate the memory in her husband, by offering him all her love, till gradually these possessions to which he had been so attached became dear to him again? . . . but just then, behind her, she heard the thin voice of the dead woman crying out — a voice grey with fear and breaking. 'Humphrey,' it sighed, 'what is it? Oh, my God!' . . .And then the sound of a heavy dumb blow and low moaning, followed by burst after burst of idiot laughter, as with a fluttering whirl of flaming green feathers the parrot flew up again to its empty attic.

INTERVAL

LILLIAN DE LA TORRE

Milady Bigamy

LILLIAN DE LA TORRE *(born 1902) has delighted us for many years with her scholarly and hugely entertaining stories presenting Dr Johnson as the world's first great detective, with Boswell as the perfect Watson. 'Milady Bigamy' is one of these, and is loosely based upon the lively career of the Duchess of Kingston: an imaginative* tour-de-force *which provides an engaging break before we move on to the modern era of murder, with all its horrors.*

'I have often thought,' remarked Dr Sam: Johnson, one spring morning in the year 1778, 'that if I kept a seraglio –'

He had often thought! — Dr Sam: Johnson, moral philosopher, defender of right and justice, *detector* of crime and chicane, had often thought of keeping a seraglio! I looked at his square bulk, clad in his old-fashioned full-skirted coat of plain mulberry broadcloth, his strong rugged countenance with his little brown scratch-wig clapped on askew above it, and suppressed a smile.

'I say sir, if I kept a seraglio, the houris should be clad in cotton and linen, and not at all in wool and silk, for the animal fibres are nasty, but the vegetable fibres are cleanly.'

'Why, sir,' I replied seriously, 'I too have long meditated on keeping a seraglio, and wondered whether it may not be lawful to a man to have plurality of wives, say one for comfort and another for shew.'

'What, sir, you talk like a heathen Turk!' growled the great Cham, rounding on me. 'If this cozy arrangement be permitted a man, what is to hinder the ladies from a like indulgence? — one husband, say, for support, and t'other for sport? 'Twill be a wise father then that knows his own heir. You are a lawyer, sir, you know the problems of filiation. Would you multiply them? No, sir, bigamy is a crime, and there's an end on't!'

At this I hastily turned the topick, and of bigamy we spoke no more. Little did we then guess that a question of bigamy was soon to engage my friend's attention in the affair of the Duchess of Kingsford — if Duchess in truth she was.

I had first beheld this lady some seven years before, when she was Miss Bellona Chamleigh, the notorious Maid of Honour. At Mrs Cornelys's Venetian ridotto she flashed upon my sight, and took my breath away.

Rumour had not exaggerated her flawless beauty. She had a complection like strawberries and cream, a swelling rosy lip, a nose and firmset chin sculptured in marble. Even the small-pox had spared her, for the one mark it had left her touched the edge of her pouting mouth like a tiny dimple. In stature she was low, a pocket Venus, with a bosom of snow tipped with fire. A single beauty-spot shaped like a new moon adorned her perfect navel –

I go too far. Suffice it to say that for costume she wore a girdle of silken fig-leaves, and personated Eve — Eve after the fall, from the glances she was giving her gallants. One at either rosy elbow, they pressed her close, and she smiled upon them impartially. I recognised them both.

The tall, thin, swarthy, cadaverous apparition in a dark domino was Philip Piercy, Duke of Kingsford, once the handsomest Peer in the Kingdom, but now honed to an edge by a long life of dissipation. If he was no longer the handsomest, he was still the richest. Rumour had it that he was quite far gone in infatuation, and would lay those riches, with his hand and heart, at Miss Bellona's feet.

Would she accept them? Only one obstacle intervened. That obstacle stood at her other elbow: Captain Aurelius Hart, of HMS *Dangerous*, a third-rate of fifty guns, which now lay fitting at Portsmouth, leaving the gallant Captain free to press his suit.

In person, the Captain was the lady's match, not tall, but broad of shoulder, and justly proportioned in every limb. He had far-seeing light blue eyes in a sun-burned face, and his expression was cool, with a look of incipient mirth. The patches of Harlequin set off his muscular masculinity.

With his name too Dame Rumour had been busy. He had won the lady's heart, it was averred; but he was not likely to win her hand, being an impecunious younger son, tho' of an Earl.

So she passed on in her nakedness, giving no sign of which lover — if either — should possess her.

A black-avised young fellow garbed like the Devil watched them go. He scowled upon them with a look so lowering I looked again, and recognised him for Mr Eadwin Maynton, Kingsford's nephew, heir-presumptive to his pelf (tho' not his Dukedom), being the son of the Duke's sister. If Bellona married his Uncle, it would cost Mr Eadwin dear.

The audacity of the Maid of Honour at the masquerade had been too blatant. She was forthwith banished from the Court. Unrepentant, she had rusticated herself. Accompanied only by her confidential woman, one Ann Crannock, she slipped off to her Aunt Hammer's country house at Linton, near Portsmouth.

Near Portsmouth! Where lay the Captain's ship! No more was needed to inflate the tale.

'The Captain calls daily to press his suit.'

'The Captain has taken her into keeping.'

'There you are out, the Captain has wedded her secretly.'

'You are all misled. The *Dangerous* has gone to sea — the Captain has deserted her.'

'And serve her right, the hussy!'

The hussy Maid of Honour was not one to be rusticated for long. Soon she was under their noses again, on the arm of the still infatuated Duke of Kingsford. Mr Eadwin Maynton moved Heaven and earth to forestall a marriage, but only succeeded in mortally offending his wealthy Uncle. Within a year of that scandalous masquerade, Miss Bellona Chumleigh was Duchess of Kingsford.

Appearing at Court on the occasion, she flaunted herself in white sattin encrusted with Brussels point and embroidered with a Duke's ransom in pearls. She would give the world something to talk about!

They talked with a will. They talked of Captain Hart, jilted on the Jamaica station. They talked of Mr Eadwin Maynton, sulking at home. They were still talking several years later when the old Duke suddenly died — of his Duchess's obstreperous behaviour, said some with a frown, of her amorous charms, said others with a snigger.

It was at this juncture that one morning in the year '78 a crested coach drew rain in Bolt Court and a lady descended. From an upper window I looked down on her modish tall powdered head and her furbelowed polonaise of royal purple brocade.

I turned from the window with a smile. 'What, sir, you have an assignation with a fine lady? Am I *de trop*?'

'You are never *de trop*, Bozzy. Pray remain, and let us see what this visitation portends.'

The Duchess of Kingsford swept in without ceremony.

'Pray forgive me, Dr Johnson, my errand is to Mr Boswell. I was directed hither to find him — I *must* have Mr Boswell!'

'And you *shall* have Mr Boswell,' I cried warmly, 'tho' it were for wager of battle!'

'You have hit it, sir! For my honour, perhaps my life is at stake! You shall defend me, sir, in my need — and Dr Johnson,' she added with a sudden flashing smile, 'shall be our counsellor.'

'If I am to counsel you, Madam, you must tell me clearly what is the matter.'

'Know then, gentlemen, that in the winter last past, my dear husband the Duke of Kingsford died, and left me inconsolable — inconsolable, yet not bare, for in token of our undying devotion, he left me all that was his. In so doing, he cut off his nephew Eadwin with a few guineas, and therein lies the difficulty. Mr Eadwin is no friend to me. He has never spared to vilify me for a scheaming adventuress. And now he has hit upon a plan — he thinks — in one motion to disgrace me and deprive me of my inheritance. He goes about to nullify my marriage to the Duke.'

'How can this be done, your Grace?'

'He has resurrected the old gossip about Captain Hart, that we were secretly married at Linton long ago. The whole town buzzes with the tale, and the comedians lampoon me on the stage as Milady Bigamy.'

'What the comedians play,' observed Dr Johnson drily, 'is not evidence. Gossip cannot harm you, your Grace — unless it is true.'

'It is false. There was no such marriage. There might have been, it is true (looking pensive) had he not abandoned me, as Aeneas abandoned Dido, and put to sea in the *Dangerous* — leaving me,' she added frankly, 'to make a better match.'

'Then where is the difficulty?'

'False testimony is the difficulty. Aunt Hammer is dead, and the clergyman is dead. But his widow is alive, and Eadwin has bought her. Worst of all, he has suborned Ann Crannock, my confidential woman that was and she will swear to the wedding.'

'Are there marriage lines?'

'Of course not. No marriage, no marriage lines.'

'And the Captain? Where is he?'

'At sea. He now commands a first-rate, the *Challenger*, and wins great fame, and much prize money, against the French. I am well assured I am safe in that quarter.'

'Then,' said I, 'this accusation of bigamy is soon answered. But I am not accustomed to appear at the Old Bailey.'

'The Old Bailey!' cried she with scorn. 'Who speaks of the Old

Bailey? Shall a Duchess be tried like a greasy bawd at the Old Bailey? I am the Duchess of Kingsford! I shall be tried by my Peers!'

'If you are Mrs Aurelius Hart?'

'I am not Mrs Aurelius Hart! But if I were — Aurelius's brothers are dead in the American war, his father the Earl is no more, and Aurelius is Earl of Westerfell. As Duchess or as Countess, I shall be tried by my Peers!'

Flushed and with flashing eyes, the ci-devant Maid of Honour looked every inch a Peeress as she uttered these words.

''Tis for this I must have Mr Boswell. From the gallery in the House of Lords I recently heard him plead the cause of the heir of Douglas: in such terms of melting eloquence did he defend the good name of Lady Jane Douglas, I will have no other to defend mine!'

My new role as the Duchess's champion entailed many duties that I had hardly expected. There were of course long consults with herself and her solicitor, a dry, prosy old solicitor named Pettigree. But I had not counted on attending her strolls in the park, or carrying her bandboxes from the milliner's.

'And tomorrow, Mr Boswell, you shall squire me to the ridotto.'

'The masquerade! Your Grace jests!'

'Far from it, sir. Eadwin Maynton seeks to drive me under ground, but he shall not succees. No, sir; my heart is set on it, and to the ridotto I will go!'

To the ridotto we went. The Duchess was regal in a domino of Roman purple over a gown of lavender lutestring, and wore a half-mask with a valance of provocative black lace to the chin. I personated a wizard, with my black gown strewn with cabbalistick symbols, and a conical hat to make me tall.

It was a ridotto *al fresco*, in the groves of Vauxhall. In the soft May evening, we listened to the band of musick in the pavilion; we took a syllabub; we walked in the allées to hear the nightingale sing.

It was pleasant strolling beneath the young green of the trees by the light of a thousand lamps, watching the masquers pass: a Boadicea in armour, a Hamlet all in black, an Indian Sultana, a muscular Harlequin with a long-nosed Venetian mask, a cowled monk –

'So, Milady Bigamy!' The voice was loud and harsh. 'You hide your face, as is fit; but we know you for what you are!'

Passing masquers paused to listen. Pulling the mask from her face, the Duchess whirled on the speaker. A thin swarthy countenance glowered at her under the monk's cowl.

'Eadwin Maynton!' she said quietly. 'Why do you pursue me? How have I harmed you? 'Twas your own folly that alienated your kind Uncle.'

''Twas your machinations!' He was perhaps inebriated, and intent on making a scene. More listeners arrived to enjoy it.

'I have irrefutable evidences of your double dealing,' he bawled, 'and when it comes to the proof, I'll un-duchess you, Milady Bigamy!'

'This fellow is drunk. Come, Mr Boswell.'

The Duchess turned away contemptuously. Mr Eadwin seized her arm and swung her back. The next minute he was flat on the ground, and a menacing figure in Harlequin's patches stood over him.

'What is your pleasure, Madam?' asked the Harlequin calmly. 'Shall he beg pardon?'

'Let him lie,' said the Duchess. 'He's a liar, let him lie.'

'Then be off!'

Maynton made off, muttering.

'And you, ladies and gentlemen, the comedy is over.'

Behind the beak-nosed mask, light eyes of ice-blue raked the gapers, and they began to melt away.

'I thank you, my friend. And now, as you say, the comedy is over,' smiled the Duchess.

'There is yet a farce to play,' said the Harlequin. '*The Fatal Marriage*.' He lifted his mask by its snout, and smiled at her. 'Who, unless a husband, shall protect his lady wife?'

The Duchess's face stiffened.

'I do not know you.'

'What, forgot so soon?' His glance laughed at her. 'Such is the fate of the sailor!'

'Do not mock me, Aurelius. You know we are nothing to one another.'

'Speak for yourself, Bellona.'

'I will speak one word, then: Good-bye.'

She reached me her hand, and I led her away. Captain Hart watched us go, his light eyes intent, and a small half-smile upon his lips.

That was the end of Milady Duchess's ridotto. What would come of it?

Nothing good, I feared. My fears were soon doubled. Returning from the river one day in the Duchess's carriage, we found ourselves passing by Mr Eadwin Maynton's lodging. As we approached, a man issued from the door, an erect figure in nautical blue, whose ruddy countenance wore a satisfied smile. He turned away without a glance in our direction.

'Aurelius calling upon Eadwin!' cried the Duchess, staring after him. 'What are they plotting against me?'

To this I had no answer.

Time was running out. The trial was looming close. In Westminster Hall, carpenters were knocking together scaffolding to prepare for the shew. At Kingston House, Dr Johnson was quoting Livy, I was polishing my oration, and old Pettigree was digging up learned instances.

'Keep up your heart, your Grace,' said the solicitor earnestly in his rusty voice, 'for should the worst befall, I have instances to shew that the penalty is no longer death at the stake –'

'At the stake!' gasped the Duchess.

'No, your Grace, certainly not, not death by burning. I shall prove it, but meerly branding on the hand –'

'Branding!' shrieked the Duchess. Her white fingers clutched mine.

'No *alibi*,' fretted old Pettigree, 'no testimony from Linton on your behalf, Captain Hart in the adverse camp — no, no, your Grace must put your hope in me!'

At such Job's comfort Dr Johnson could scarce repress a smile.

'Hope rather,' he suggested, 'in Mr Boswell, for if these women lie, it must be manifest in cross-examination. I shall be on hand to note what they say, as I once noted the Parliamentary debates from the gallery; and it will go hard but we shall catch them out in their lies.'

Bellona Chumleigh lifted her head in a characteristick wilful gesture. 'I trust in Mr Boswell, and I am not afraid.'

Rising early on the morning of the fateful day, I donned my voluminous black advocate's gown, and a lawyer's powdered wig that I had rented from Tibbs the perruquier for a guinea. I thought that the latter well set off my dark countenance, with its long nose and attentive look. Thus attired, I posted myself betimes outside Westminster Hall to see the procession pass.

At ten o'clock it began. First came the factotums and the functionaries, the yeoman-usher robed, heralds in tabards, serjeants-at-arms with maces in their hands. Then the Peers paced into view, walking two and two, splendid in their crimson velvet mantles and snowy capes of ermine powdered with black tail-tips. Last came the Lord High Steward, his long crimson train borne up behind him, and so they passed into Westminster Hall.

When I entered at last, in my turn as a lowly lawyer, the sight struck me with something like awe. The noble hall, with its soaring roof, was packed to the vault with persons of quality seated upon tier after tier of scaffolding. Silks rustled, laces fluttered, brocades glowed, high powdered foretops rose over all. Around three sides of the level floor gathered the Peers in their splendid robes.

All stood uncovered as the King's Commission was read aloud and the white staff of office was ceremoniously handed up to the Lord High Steward where he sat under a crimson canopy. With a sibilant rustle, the packed hall sat, and the trial began.

'Oyez, oyez, oyez! Bellona, duchess-dowager of Kingsford, come into court!'

She came in a little procession of her own, her ladies of honour, her chaplain, her physician and her apothecary attending; but every staring eye saw only her. Old Pettigree had argued in vain that deep mourning was the only wear; she would have none of it. She walked in proudly in white sattin embroidered with pearls, that very court-dress she had flaunted as old Kingsford's bride: 'In token of my innocence,' she told old Pettigree.

With a deep triple reverence she took her place on the elevated platform that served for a dock, and stood with lifted head to listen to the indictment.

'Bellona, duchess-dowager of Kingsford, you stand indicted by the name of Bellona, wife of Aurelius Hart, now Earl of Westerfell, for that you, in the eleventh year of our sovereign lord King George the Third, being then married and the wife of the said Aurelius Hart did marry and take to husband Philip Piercy, Duke of Kingsford, feloniously and with force and arms −'

Though it was the usual verbiage to recite that every felony was committed 'with force and arms,' the picture conjured up of little Bellona, like a highwayman, clapping a pistol to the old Duke's head and marching him to the altar, was too much for the Lords. Laughter swept the benches, and the lady at the bar frankly joined in.

'How say you? Are you guilty of the felony whereof you stand indicted, or not guilty?'

Silence fell. Bellona sobered, lifted her head, and pronounced in her rich voice: 'Not guilty!'

'Culprit, how will you be tried?'

'By God and my Peers.'

'Oyez, oyez, oyez! All manner of persons that will give evidence on behalf of our sovereign lord the King, against Bellona, duchess-dowager of Kingsford, let them come forth, and they shall be heard, for now she stands at the bar upon her deliverance.'

Thereupon Edward Thurlow, Attorney General, came forth, formidable with his bristling hairy eyebrows and his growling voice like distant thunder.

He began with an eloquent denunciation of the crime of bigamy, its malignant complection, its pernitious example, *et caetera, et caetera*. That duty performed, he drily recited the story of the alleged marriage at Linton as, he said, his witnesses would prove it.

'And now, my Lords, we will proceed to call our witnesses. Call Margery Amys.'

Mrs Amys, the clergyman's widow, was a tall stick of a woman well on in years, wearing rusty bombazine and an old-fashioned lawn cap tied under her nutcracker chin. She put a gnarled hand on the Bible clerk held out to her.

'Hearken to your oath. The evidence you shall give on behalf of our sovereign lord the King's majesty, against Bellona duchess-dowager of Kingsford, shall be the truth, the whole truth, and nothing but the truth, so help you God.'

The old dame mumbled something and kissed the book. But when the questions began, she spoke up in a rusty screech, and graphically portrayed a clandestine marriage at Linton church in the year '71.

'They came by night, nigh upon midnight, to the church at Linton, and desired of the late Mr Amys that he should join them two in matrimony.'

Q. Which two?

A. Them two, Captain Hart and Miss Bellona Chamleigh.

Q. And did he so unite them?

A. He did so, and I stood by and saw it done.

Q. Who was the bride?

A. Miss Bellona Chamleigh.

Q. Say if you see her now present?

A. (pointing) That's her, her in the white.

The Duchess stared her down contemptuously.

As I rose to cross-examine, I sent a glance to the upper tier, where sat Dr Jonson. He was writing, and frowning as he wrote; but no guidance came my way. Making up with a portentuous scowl for what I lacked in matter, I began:

Q. It was dark at midnight?

A. Yes, sir, mirk dark.

Q. Then Mrs Amys, how did you see the bride to know her again?

A. Captain Hart lighted a wax taper, and put it in his hat, and by that light they were married, and so I know her again.

Q. (probing) You know a great deal, Madam. What has Mr Eadwin Maynton given you to appear on his behalf?

A. Nothing, sir.

Q. What has he promised you?

A. Nothing neither.

Q. Then why are you here?

A. (piously) I come for the sake of truth and justice, sir.

And on that sanctimonious note, I had to let her go.

'Call Ann Crannock!'

Ann Crannock approached in a flurry of curtseys, scattering smiles like sweetmeats. The erstwhile confidential woman was a plump, round, rosy little thing, of a certain age, but still pleasing, carefully got up like a stage milkmaid in snowy kerchief and pinner. She mounted the platform with a bounce and favoured the Attorney General with a beaming smile. The Duchess hissed something between her teeth. It sounded like 'Judas!'

The clerk with his Bible hastily stepped between. Ann Crannock took the oath, smiling broadly, and Thurlow commenced his interrogation:

Q. You were the prisoner's woman?

A. Yes, sir, and I loved her like my own child.

Q. You saw her married to Captain Hart?

A. Yes, sir, the pretty dears, they could not wait for very lovesickness.

Q. That was at Linton in July of the year 1771?

A. Yes, sir, the third of July, for the Captain sailed with the Jamaica squadron on the fourth. Ah, the sweet poppets, they were loath to part!

Q. Who married them?

A. Mr Amys, sir, the vicar of Linton. We walked to the church together, the lady's Aunt Mrs Hammer, and I myself, and the sweet lovebirds. The clock was going towards midnight, that the servants might not know.

Q. Why must not the servants know?

A. Sir, nobody was to know, lest the Captain's father the Earl cut him off for marrying a lady without any fortune.

Q. Well, and they were married by Mr Amys. Did he give a certificate of the marriage?

A. Yes, sir, he did, he wrote it out with his own hand, and I signed for a witness. I was happy for my lady from my heart.

Q. You say the vicar gave a certificate. (Thurlow sharply raised his voice as he whipped out a paper.) Is this it?

A. (clasping her hands and beaming with pleasure) O sir, that is it. See, there is my handwriting. Well I mind how the Captain kissed it and put it in his bosom to keep!

''Tis false!'

The Duchess was on her feet in a rage. For a breath she stood so in her white sattin and pearls; then she sank down in a swoon. Her attendants instantly raised her and bore her out among them. I saw the little apothecary hopping like a grasshopper on the fringes, flourishing his hartshorn bottle.

The Peers were glad enough of an excuse for a recess, and so was I. I pushed my way to the lobby in search of Dr Johnson. I was furious.

'The jade has lied to us!' I cried as I beheld him. 'I'll throw up my brief!'

'You will do well to do so,' murmured the Attorney General at my elbow. He still held the fatal marriage lines.

'Pray, Mr Thurlow, give me a sight of that paper,' requested Dr Johnson.

'Dr Johnson's wish is my command,' said Thurlow with a bow: he had a particular regard for the burly philosopher.

Dr Johnson held the paper to the light, peering so close with his near-sighted eyes that his lashes almost brushed the surface.

'Aye, sir, look close,' smiled Thurlow. ''Tis authentick, I assure you. I have particular reason to know.'

'Then there's no more to be said.'

Thurlow took the paper, bowed, and withdrew.

All along I had been conscious of another legal figure hovering near. Now I looked at him directly. He was hunched into a voluminous advocate's gown, and topped by one of Mr Tibbs's largest wigs; but there was no missing those ice-blue eyes.

'Captain Hart! You here?'

'I had a mind to see the last of my widow,' he said sardonically. 'I see she is in good hands.'

'But to come here! Will you not be recognised, and detained, and put on the stand?'

'What Peers detain a Peer? No, sir. While the House sits, I cannot be summoned: and when it rises, all is over. Bellona may be easy; I shan't peach. Adieu.'

'Stay, sir – ' But he was gone.

After an hour, the Duchess of Kingsford returned to the hall with her head held high, and inquiry resumed. There was not much more harm Mistress Crannock could do. She was led once more to repeat: she saw them wedded, the sweet dears, and she signed the marriage lines, and that was the very paper now in Mr Thurlow's hand.

'You say this is the paper? That is conclusive, I think. (smiling) You may cross-examine, Mr Boswell.'

Ann Crannock smiled at me, and I smiled back, as I began:

Q. You say, Mistress Crannock, that you witnessed this marriage?

A. Yes, sir.

Q. And then and there you signed the marriage lines?

A. Yes, sir.

Q. On July 3, 1771?

A. Yes, sir.

Q. Think well, did you not set your hand to it at some subsequent date?

A. No, sir.

Q. Perhaps to oblige Mr Eadwin Maynton?

A. No, sir, certainly not. I saw them wedded, and signed forthwith.

Q. Then I put it to you: *How did you on July 3, 1771, set your hand to a piece of paper that was not made at the manufactory until the year 1774?*

Ann Crannock turned red, then pale, opened her mouth, but no sound came. 'Can you make that good, Mr Boswell?' demanded Thurlow.

'Yes, sir, if I may a call a witness, tho' out of order.'

'Aye, call him — let's hear him –' the answer swept the Peers' benches. Their Lordships cared nothing for order.

'I call Dr Samuel Johnson.'

Dr Johnson advanced and executed one of his stately obeisances.

'You must know, my Lords and gentlemen,' he began, 'that I have dealt with paper for half a century, and I have friends among the paper-makers. Paper, my Lords, is made by grinding up rag, and wetting it, and laying it to dry upon a grid of wires. Now he who has a mind to sign his work, twists his mark in wire and lays it in, for every wire leaves its impression, which is called a watermark. With such a mark, in the shape of an S, did my friend Sully the paper-maker sign the papers he made before the year '74.

'But in that year, my Lords, he took his son into partnership, and from thenceforth marked his papers with a double S. I took occasion this afternoon to confirm the date, 1774, from his own mouth. Now, my Lords, if you take this supposed document of 1771 (taking it in his hand) and hold it thus to the light, you may see in it the double

S watermark: which my Lords, proves this so-called conclusive evidence to be a forgery, and Ann Crannock a liar!'

The paper passed from hand to hand, and the Lords began to seethe.

'The Question! The Question!' was the cry. The clamour persisted, and did not cease until perforce the Lord High Steward arose, bared his head, and put the question:

'Is the prisoner guilty of the felony whereof she stands indicted, or not guilty?'

In a breathless hush, the first of the barons rose in his ermine. Bellona lifted her chin. The young nobleman put his right hand upon his heart and pronounced clearly:

'Not guilty, upon my honour!'

So said each and every Peer:

'Not guilty, upon my honour!'

My client was aquitted!

At her Grace's desire, I had provided means whereby, at the trial's end, come good fortune or ill, the Duchess might escape the press of the populace. A plain coach waited at a postern door, and thither, her white satin and pearls muffled in a capuchin, my friend and I hurried her.

Quickly she mounted the step and slipped inside. Suddenly she screamed. Inside the coach a man awaited us. Captain Aurelius Hart in his blue coat lounged there at his ease.

'Nay, sweet wife, my wife no more,' he murmured softly, 'do not shun me, for now that you are decreed to be another man's widow, I mean to woo you anew. I have prepared a small victory feast at my lodgings, and I hope your friends will do us the honour of partaking of it with us.'

'Victory!' breathed Bellona as the coach moved us off. 'How could you be so sure of victory?'

'Because,' said Dr Johnson, 'he brought it about. Am I not right, sir?'

'Why, sir, as to that —'

'As to that, sir, there is no need to prevaricate. I learned this afternoon from Sully the paper-maker that a seafaring man resembling Captain Hart had been at him last week to learn about papers, and had carried away a sheet of the double S kind. It is clear that, being exposed, defeated him.'

All this while the coach was carrying us onward. In the shadowy interior, Captain Hart frankly grinned.

''Twas easy, sir. Mr Eadwin was eager, and quite without scruple, and why should he doubt a paper that came from the hands of the wronged husband? How could he guess that I had carefully contrived it to ruin his cause?'

'It was a bad cause,' said Dr Johnson, 'and he is well paid for his lack of scruple.'

'But, Captain Hart,' I put in, 'how could you be sure that we would detect the forgery and proclaim it?'

'To make sure, I muffled up and ventured into the lobby. I was prepared to slip a billet into Mr Boswell's pocket; but when I saw Dr Johnson studying the watermark, I knew that I need not interfere further.'

We were at the door. Captain Hart lifted down the lady, and with his arm around her guided her up the stair. She yielded mutely, as in a daze.

In the withdrawing room a pleasing cold regale awaited us, but Dr Johnson was in no hurry to go to table. There was still something on his mind.

'Then, sir, before we break bread, satisfy me of one more thing. How came Ann Crannock to say the handwriting was hers?'

'Because, sir,' said Captain Hart with a self-satisfied look, 'it was so like her own. I find I have a pretty turn for forgery.'

'That I can believe, sir. But where did you find an exemplar to fashion your forgery after?'

'Why, sir, I – ' The Captain darted a glance from face to face. 'You are keen, sir. There could only be one document to forge after — and here it is (producing a folded paper from his pocket). Behold the true charter of my happiness!'

I regarded it thunderstruck. A little faded as to ink, a little frayed at the edges, there lay before us a marriage certificate in due form, between Miss Bellona Chamleigh, spinster, and Captain Aurelius Hart, bachelor, drawn up in the Reverend Mr Amys wavering hand, and attested by Sophie Hammer and Ann Crannock, July 3, 1771!

'So, Madam,' growled Dr Johnson, 'you were guilty after all!'

'Oh, no, sir! 'Twas no marriage, for the Captain was recalled to his ship, and sailed for the Jamaica station, without — without –'

'Without making you in deed and in truth my own,' smiled Captain Hart.

At this specimen of legal reasoning, Dr Johnson shook his head in bafflement, the bigamous Duchess looked as innocent as possible, and Captain Hart laughed aloud.

''Twas an unfortunate omission,' he said, 'whence flow all our uneasinesses, and I shall rectify it this night, my Countess consenting. What do you say, my dear?'

For the first time the Duchess looked directly at him. In spite of herself she blushed, and the tiny pox mark beside her lip deepened in a smile.

'Why, Aurelius, since you have saved me from branding or worse, what can I say but yes?'

'Then at last,' cried the Captain, embracing her, 'you shall be well and truly bedded, and so farewell to the Duchess of Kingsford!'

It seemed the moment to withdraw. As we descended, we heard them laughing together.

'Never look so put about, Bozzy,' murmured Dr Johnson on the stair. 'You have won your case; justice, tho' irregularly, is done; the malignancy of Eadwin Maynton has been defeated; and as to the two above — they deserve each other.'

PART TWO

PETER LOVESEY

The Bathroom

PETER LOVESEY *(born 1936) is best known as a writer of crime stories in period settings, notably his series on television featuring the Victorian detective Sergeant Cribb. His award-winning novel* The False Inspector Dew, *set in 1921, is a reworking, with twists, of the murder by Dr Crippen of his wife; and he uses another real mystery, the death of the jockey Fred Archer, in* Bertie and the Tinman. *'The Bathroom' is taken from his short-story collection* Butchers & Other Stories of Crime.

'Sorry, darling. I mean to have my bath and that's the end of it!' With a giggle and a swift movement of her right hand, Melanie Lloyd closed the sliding door of her bathroom. The catch fastened automatically with a reassuring click. Her husband, William, frustrated on the other side, had installed the gadget himself. 'None of your old-fashioned bolts or keys for us,' he had announced, demonstrating it a week before the wedding. 'The door secures itself when you slide it across from the inside. You can move it with one finger, you see, but once it's closed, it's as safe as your money in the bank.'

She felt between her shoulders for the tab of her zip. William could wait for her. Sit on the bed and wait whilst she had a leisurely bath. What was the purpose of a luxurious modern bathroom if not to enjoy a bath at one's leisure? William, after all, had spent *weeks* before the wedding modernising it. 'Everything but asses' milk,' he had joked. 'Mixer taps, spray attachment, separate shower, bidet, heated towel-rails and built-in cupboards. You shall bathe like a queen, my love. Like a queen.'

Queenly she had felt when she first stepped through the sliding door and saw what he had prepared for her. It was all there exactly as he had promised, in white and gold. All that he had promised and more. Ceramic mosaic tiles. Concealed lighting. Steam-proof mirrors. And the floor — wantonly impractical! — carpeted in white, with a white fur rug beside the bath. There was also a chair, an elegant antique chair, over which he had draped a full-length lace négligé. 'Shameless Victoriana,' he had whispered. 'Quite out of keeping with contemporary design, but I'm incurably sentimental.' Then he had kissed her.

In that meeting of the lips she had shed her last doubts about William, those small nagging uncertainties that would probably never have troubled her if Daddy had not kept on so. 'I'm old-fashioned, I know, Melanie, but it seems to me an extraordinarily short engagement. *You* feel that you know him, I've no doubt, but he's met your mother and me only once — and that was by accident. The fellow seemed downright evasive when I questioned him about his background. It's an awkward thing to do, asking a man things like that when he's damned near as old as you are, but, hang it, it's a father's right to know the circumstances of the man who proposes marrying his daughter, even if he is past fifty. Oh, I've nothing against his age; there are plenty of successful marriages on record between young women and older men. Nothing we could do to stop you, or would. You're over twenty-one and old enough to decide such things for yourself. The point is that he knew why I was making my enquiries. I wasn't probing his affairs from idle curiosity. I had your interests at heart, damn it. If the fellow hasn't much behind him, I'd be obliged if he'd say so, so that I can make a decent contribution. Set you both up properly. I would, you know. I've never kept you short, have I? Wouldn't see you come upon hard times for anything in the world. If only the fellow would make an honest statement . . .'

One didn't argue with Daddy. It was no use trying to talk to him about self-respect. Every argument was always swept aside by that familiar outpouring of middle-class propriety. God, if anything drove her into William Lloyd's arms, Daddy did!

She stepped out of the dress and hung it on one of the hooks provided on the wall of the shower compartment. Before removing her slip, she closed the Venetian blind; not that she was excessively modest, nor, for that matter, that she imagined her new neighbours in Bismarck Road were the sort who looked up at bathroom windows. The plain fact was that she was used to frosted glass. When she and William had first looked over the house — it seemed years ago, but it could only have been last April — the windows, more than anything else had given her that feeling of unease. There were several in the house — they had been common enough in Victorian times when the place was built — small oblong frames of glass with frostwork designs and narrow stained-glass borders in deep red and blue. They would have to come out, she decided at once, if William insisted on living there. They seemed so out of keeping, vaguely ecclesiastical, splendid in a chapel or an undertaker's office, but not in *her* new home. William agreed at once to take them out — he seemed so determined to buy that one house. 'You won't recognise the place when I've done it up. I'll put a picture window in the bathroom. The old frames need to come out anyway. The wood's half-rotten outside.' So the old windows went and the picture window, a large single sheet of glass, replaced them. Don't worry about ventilation,' William assured her. 'There's an extractor fan built in above the cabinet there.' He had thought of everything.

Except frosted glass. She *would* have felt more comfortable behind frosted glass. But it wasn't *contemporary*, she supposed. William hadn't consulted her, anyway. He seemed to know about these things. And there *were* the Venetian blinds, pretty plastic things, so much more attractive than the old brown pelmet they replaced.

She fitted the plug and ran the water. Hot and cold came together from a lion's-head tap; you blended the water by operating a lever. Once you were in the bath you could control the intake of water with your foot, using a push-button mechanism. What would the first occupants of 9 Bismarck Road, eighty years ago, have thought of that?

Melanie reviewed the array of ornamental bottles on the shelf above the taps. Salts, oils, crystals and foam baths were prodigally provided. She selected an expensive bath oil and upended the bottle, watching the green liquid dispersed by the cascading water. Its musky fragrance was borne up on spirals of steam. How odd that William should provide all this and seem unwilling for her to use it! Each evening since Monday, when they had returned from the honeymoon, she had suggested she might take a bath and he had found some pretext for discouraging her. It didn't matter *that* much to her, of course. At the hotel in Herne Bay she had taken a daily bath, so she didn't feel desperately in need of one immediately they got back. It was altogether too trivial to make an issue of, she was quite sure. If William and she *had* to have words some time, it wasn't going to be about bath nights, at any rate. So she played the part of the complaisant wife and fallen in with whatever distractions he provided.

Tonight, though, she had deliberately taken him by surprise. She had hidden nightie and book in the towel chest earlier in the day, so when she hesitated at the head of the stairs as they came to bed he was quite unprepared. You don't go for a late-night bath empty-handed, even when your bathroom has every convenience known to the modern home designer. She was sliding the bathroom door across before he realised what had happened. 'Sorry, darling! I mean to have my bath and that's the end of it!'

The door slid gently across on its runners and clicked, the whole movement perfectly timed, without a suspicion of haste, as neatly executed as a pass in the bull ring. That was the way to handle an obstructive husband. Never mind persuasion and pleading; intelligent action was much more dignified, and infinitely more satisfying. Besides, she *had* waited till Friday.

She tested the water with her hand, removed her slip, took her book and plastic shower-cap from the towel chest, shook her mass of flaxen hair, and then imprisoned it in the cap. She turned, saw herself unexpectedly in a mirror, and pulled a comical face. If she had remembered, she would have brought a face pack — the one thing William had overlooked when he stocked the cosmetic shelf. She wasn't going into the bedroom to collect one now, anyway. She took off the last of her underclothes and stepped into the bath.

It was longer than the bath at home or the one in the hotel. Silly really: neither William nor she was tall, but they had installed a six foot, six inch bath — 'Two metres, you see,' the salesman had pointed out, as though that had some bearing on their requirements. Over the years it would probably use gallons more hot water, but it was a beautiful shape, made for luxuriating in, with the back at the angle of a deckchair on the lowest notch, quite unlike the utility five-footer at home, with its chipped sides and overhanging geyser that allowed you enough hot water to cover your knees and no more. William had even insisted on a sunken bath. 'It will sink to four inches below floor level, but that's the limit, I'm afraid, or we'll see the bottom of it through the kitchen ceiling.'

Accustomed to the temperature now, she pressed the button with her toe for more hot water. There was no hurry to rise from this bath. It wouldn't do Mr William Lloyd any harm to wait. Not simply from pique, of course; she felt no malice towards him at all. No, there was just a certain deliciousness — a man wouldn't understand it even if you tried to explain — in taking one's time. Besides, it was a change, a relief if she was honest, to enjoy an hour of solitude, a break from the new experience of being someone's partner, accountable for every action in the day from cooking a dinner to clipping one's toenails.

She reached for the book — one she had found on William's bookshelf with an intriguing title, *Murder is Methodical*. Where better to read a thriller than in a warm bath behind locked doors? There hadn't been much opportunity for reading in the last three weeks. Or before, for that matter, with curtains to make and bridesmaids to dress.

She turned to the first page. Disappointing. It was not a detective fiction at all. Just a dreary old manual on criminology. *William Palmer: the Rugeley Poisoner* was the first chapter. She thumbed the pages absently. *Dr Crippen: a Crime in Camden Town.* How was it that these monsters continued to exert such a fascination on people, years after their trials and executions? The pages fell open at a more whimsical title — from her present position, anyway — *George Joseph Smith: the Brides in the Bath.* Melanie smiled. That chapter ought to have a certain piquancy, particularly as one of the first placenames to catch her eye was Herne Bay. Strange how very often one comes across a reference to a place soon after visiting there. With some slight stirring of interest, she propped the book in the chromium soap-holder that bridged the sides of the bath, dipped her arms under the water, leaned back and began to read.

George Joseph Smith had stayed in Herne Bay, but not at the New Excelsior. Wise man! If the food in 1912 was anything like the apologies for cuisine they dished up these days, he and his wife were far better off at the house they took in the High Street. But it wasn't really a honeymoon the Smiths — or the Williamses, as they called themselves — spent at Herne Bay, because they had been married two years before and he had deserted her soon after, only to meet her again in 1912 on the prom at Weston-super-Mare. In May they had come to Herne Bay and on July 8th they made mutual wills. On July 9th, Smith purchased a new five-foot bath. Bessie, it seemed, decided to take a bath on the 12th, a Friday. At 8 a.m. next morning a local doctor received a note: *Can you come at once? I am afraid my wife is dead.* On July 16th, she was buried in a common grave, and Smith returned the bath to the suppliers, saying he did not require it after all. He inherited £2,500.

£2,500. That must have been worth a lot in 1912. More, almost certainly, than the £5,000 policy William had taken out on her life. Really, when she considered it, the value of money declined so steadily that she doubted whether £5,000 would seem very much when they got it in 1995, or when – ever it was. They might do better to spend the premiums now on decorating some of the rooms downstairs. *Super* to have a luxury bathroom, but they would have to spend a lot to bring the other rooms up to standard. 'Insurance policies are security,' William had said. 'You never know when we might need it.' Well, security seemed important to him, and she could understand why. When you'd spent your childhood in an orphanage, with not a member of your family in the least interested in you, security was not such a remarkable thing to strive for. So he should have his insurance — it was rather flattering, anyway, to be worth £5,000 — and the rest of the house would get decorated in due course.

There was another reason for insurance which she did not much like to think about. For all his energy and good looks William was fifty-six. When the policy matured he would be over eighty, she fifty-two. No good trying to insure him; the premiums would be exorbitant.

For distraction she returned to the book, and read of the death of Alice Burnham in Blackpool in 1913. Miss Burnham's personal fortune had amounted to £140, but the resourceful George Smith had insured her life for a further £500. She had drowned in her bath a month after her wedding, on a Friday night in December. Strange, that Friday night again! Really, it was exquisitely spine-chilling to be sitting in one's bath on a Friday night reading such things, even if they had happened half a century ago. The Friday bath night, in fact, she learned as she read on, was an important part of Smith's infamous system. Inquest and funeral were arranged before there was time to contact the relatives, even when he wrote to them on the Saturday. Alice Burnham, like Bessie Mundy, was buried in a common grave early the following week. 'When they're dead, they're dead,' Smith had explained to his landlord.

Melanie shuddered slightly and looked up from the book. The appalling callousness of the murderer was conveyed with extraordinary vividness in that remark of his. For nearly twenty years he had exploited impressionable girls for profit, using a variety of names, marrying them, if necessary, as unconcernedly as he seduced them, and disappearing with their savings. In the early encounters, those who escaped being burdened with a child could consider themselves fortunate; his later brides were lucky if they escaped with their lives.

It was reassuring for a moment to set her eyes on her modern bathroom, its white carpet and ceramic tiles. Modern, luxurious and *civilised*. Smith and his pathetic brides inhabited a different world. What kind of bathroom had those poor creatures met their fates in? She had a vision of a cheap tin bath set on cold linoleum and filled from water jugs, illuminated by windows with coloured-glass panels. Not so different, she mused, from the shabby room William had converted — transformed rather — for her into this dream of a modern bathroom. Lying back in the water, she caught sight of the cornice

William had repainted, highlighting the moulding with gold paint. So like him to preserve what he admired from the past and reconcile it with the strictly contemporary.

Friday night! She cupped some water in her hands and wetted her face. George Joseph Smith and his crimes had already receded enough for her to amuse herself with the thought that his system would probably work just as well today as it did in 1914. The postal service hadn't improved much in all those years. If, like Daddy, you insisted on living without a telephone, you couldn't get a letter in Bristol before Monday to say that your daughter had drowned in London on Friday evening.

How dreadfully morbid! More hot water with the right toe and back to the murders, quite remote now. When had Smith been tried and executed? 1915 — well, her own William had been alive then, if only a baby. Perhaps it wasn't so long. Poor William, patiently waiting for her to come to bed. It wouldn't be fair to delay much longer. How many pages to go?

She turned to the end to see, and her eye was drawn at once to a paragraph describing the medical evidence at Smith's trial. *The great pathologist, Sir Bernard Spilsbury, stated unequivocally that a person who fainted whilst taking a bath sitting in the ordinary position would fall against the sloping back of the bath. If the water were then taken in through the mouth or nose it would have a marked stimulating effect and probably recover the person. There was no position, he contended, in which a person could easily become submerged in fainting. A person standing or kneeling might fall forward on the face and then might easily be drowned. Then, however, the body would be lying face downwards in the water. The jury already knew that all three women had been found lying on their backs, for Smith's claim that Miss Lofty was lying on her side was nonsense in view of the size of the bath in Bismarck Road.*

Bismarck Road. Melanie jerked up in the water and read the words again. Extraordinary. God, how horrible! It couldn't possibly be so. She snatched up the book and turned back the pages, careless of her wet hands. There it was again! *Margaret made her will and bequeathed everything, nineteen pounds (but he had insured her life for £700) to her husband. Back at Bismarck Road, Highgate, a bath was installed in her kitchen, heard splashes from upstairs, and a sound which might have been wet hands being drawn down the side of the bath. Then there was a sigh. Shortly after, she was jolted by the sound of her own harmonium in the sitting-room. Mr John Lloyd, alias George Joseph Smith, was playing 'Nearer, my God to Thee'.*

Mr John Lloyd. Mr John *Lloyd*. That name. Was it possible? William said he knew nothing of his parents. He had grown up in the orphanage. A foundling, he said, with nothing but a scrap of paper bearing his name; abandoned, apparently, by his mother in the summer of 1915. The summer, she now realised, of the trial of George Joseph Smith, alias John Lloyd, the deceiver and murderer of women. It was too fantastic to contemplate. Too awful . . . An unhappy coincidence. She refused to believe it.

But William — what if he believed it? Rightly or wrongly believed himself the son of a murderer. Might that belief have affected his mind, become a fixation, a dreadful, morbid urge to relive George Joseph Smith's crimes? It would explain all those coincidences: the honeymoon in Herne Bay; the insurance policy; the house in Bismarck Road; the new bath. Yet he had tried to keep her from having a bath, barred the way, as if unable to face the last stage of the ritual. And tonight she had tricked him and she was there, a bride in the bath. And it was Friday.

Melanie's book fell in the water and she sank against the back of the bath and fainted. An hour later, her husband having repeatedly called her name from outside the bathroom, broke through the sliding door and found her. That, at any rate, was the account William Lloyd gave of it at the inquest. She had fainted. Accidental death. A pity Sir Bernard Spilsbury could not have been in court to demonstrate that it was impossible. Even in a two-metre bath.

ROY VICKERS

The Crocodile Dressing-Case

ROY VICKERS (1989 – 1965) pioneered the technique of the 'inverted' detective-story, abandoning the clichéd Great Detective in favour of more naturalistic tales that paved the way for the modern crime novel. Neglected in England, one of his stories was discovered by Ellery Queen, who commissioned more; they were collected in The Department of Dead Ends, *a key book in the history of crime writing, and many of the stories take as their springboard real murders, including the present one, 'The Crocodile Dressing-Case'.*

I

Whenever a husband is murdered by a lover with the connivance of the wife, Englishmen bring up the Thomson-Bywaters case of 1922, and discuss all over again whether Edith Thomson ought to have been hanged. The case has become a modern prototype of a very old crime.

The Chaundry-Lambert case of 1936 ran it very close in essentials. Phyllis Chaundry-who was only ten in 1922, and had probably never heard of the prototype — resembled Edith Thomson in character. Unlike the latter, she was never brought to trial. Indeed, she finally married James Lambert, held the wedding reception at her father's house, with the friends and relatives of both sides present, with two photographers, a write-up in the local paper, and all the trappings of middle-class respectability — and all made possible by the elimination of Arthur Chaundry.

Like Edith Thomson, she wrote and talked a great deal of high-falutin' to her lover. Her letters are so extravagantly sentimental that to quote them directly would be embarrassing to present-day taste. A recurrent theme was that she now felt that it was 'blaspheming against nature' to endure the affection of her forty-seven-year-old husband (who had been forty-five when she had married him, with no little eagerness and pride in his position). The poor fellow, she wrote, was so afflicted with the infirmities of age, so unable to tear his young victim-wife out of his imagination, that she sometimes wished she possessed the courage to help him end his misery. Such an act would be purely and simply a mercy-murder.

Purely and simply! To Phyllis it all had a sincerity of its own. The sincerity of the man in the club who says: 'If I were the Prime Minister, I would soon settle this trouble' — without any intention of embracing a political career.

At first James Lambert thought it rather tall talk. At twenty-six he was as intelligent and mentally healthy as the next man. A lean, attractive man of middle height with a strong talent for mechanics, he was a car agent in the suburb of Rubington, with a growing repair shop. As his service after purchase was known to be patient and efficient, he automatically mopped up most of the new car business of that populous district.

His passion for Phyllis overwhelmed him, to his own vast astonishment. She had large dark eyes, whose stupidity he mistook for unearthly kindness, thick, dark hair, and a sinuous, expressive body. No greedier than an amiable, well-fed cat. Not unduly conceited, but so egocentric that she regarded her own happiness as a moral ideal to be striven for by others.

Gradually in the brain of James Lambert the mercy-murder idea began to take root. After all, if he himself were — well — call it fifty, and prematurely senile ('owing to a life of debauchery which he confessed after we were married') he might well find a bullet a happy solution.

'But you mustn't do anything about it on your own,' he warned her. 'You'd get caught. You do just what I tell you and nothing else, then everything will be all right.'

'Tell me now!' she begged in an ecstasy of obedience.

'On Thursday night at eight he's due at the meeting of the Greenfellows at Warthame. He's treasurer, isn't he? Right! Tell him you'll be lonesome and you're going to the Palais with your sister.'

'But he thinks the Palais is vulgar, and he hates me to dance with other men.'

'Then you'll have to kid him it's all for the best. He'll be using the Chrysler — straight from the office without coming home. You ring up and hire from me, saying you want Albert to drive, as he's so reliable. You will pick up Aileen. Instead of Albert, I shall turn up and come with you to the Palais. I'll tell you the rest on Thursday night.'

On the night — which was that of 6th March — Phyllis rang her husband at nine-forty. The telephone on the committee-room table of the Greenfellows' Club had one of those earpieces which are audible at several feet. So the secretary and the chairman both heard the essentials.

'Arthur, I'm so sorry to interrupt, but I feel you would wish me to. You know I hired a car from Lambert's? Well, James Lambert himself turned up, instead of his man Albert. Lambert is in evening dress and came in with us. I danced twice with him, out of politeness, and I've told him I shan't dance any more. There are some people here who know us, and I thought perhaps it would be better if you were to come here and collect me when your meeting is over — we don't want *talk*, do we, Arthur?'

Arthur Chaundry, a plodding architect, successful in a small way, was inclined to be sensitive in the matter of younger men dancing with his young wife — not in itself a proof of senility.

'You have behaved very properly in ringing me, dear.' He was just old enough to have inherited a Victorian pomposity from his father. 'I will be there about ten-thirty.'

'It closes then, and I shall be left all alone. Try to be here at twenty-past, please, Arthur. If you come by the new road, it's much shorter — it was thrown open on Monday. Turn left as you leave the Greenfellows.'

Crudity such as this characterised the crime throughout. The only part that was not crude and obvious was James Lambert's timing. He left the Palais earlier, met Chaundry on the new road, enticed him to stop the Chrysler and get out, battered him to death with a monkey-wrench, and returned to the Palais within eleven minutes.

Chaundry had been carrying a hundred and nine pounds in currency notes and thirty shillings in silver belonging to the Greenfellows. Lambert subsequently burned the notes and pocketed the silver. No one had seen him leave or re-enter the Palais.

His alibi was not watertight, but he knew that he was not required to prove that he did not kill Chaundry. There was nothing of a positive nature to connect him with the crime — except, of course, Phyllis.

II

At about ten-fifteen the two girls reclaimed their cloaks. When James joined them in the hall, he was pleasurably surprised at Phyllis's coolness.

'If you're both ready I'll bring the car round,' he said.

'Be quick and you'll dodge the rush,' said Phyllis.

That was all wrong. Phyllis ought to have announced that her husband was coming to take her home. Aileen was standing very close to Phyllis.

'You did say you were going to telephone Arthur,' prompted Lambert. 'Did you think better of it?'

'Oh — I forgot! I did telephone him. And he said he would be here about ten-twenty.'

To his astonishment he saw that she really had forgotten.

'It's past ten-twenty,' said Lambert. 'I'll leave word that we've gone on.'

When he brought the car round he tipped the commissionaire.

'If a Mr Chaundry inquires for Mrs Chaundry, tell him that she left with Mr Lambert and her sister.'

As arranged, he took Aileen home first, then drove to Chaundry's house. He went into the house with Phyllis — into Arthur's study, which Phyllis had ably converted into a general living-room, reserving the drawing-room for formal occasions.

'Well, that's that!' said Lambert. 'I'll wait up to half an hour for the police. Better if I'm here when they call. Get me a drink, dear, to make it look natural.'

'The po-*lice*!' echoed Phyllis. And then, with consummate fatuousness: '*What* police?'

'Steady, girlie! You've been wonderful all night. Don't break now. Everything's all right, same as I promised you. I ran the car on to that bit of waste ground and put the lights off. They're sure to spot it almost at once. We want 'em to.'

'Jim!' Her eyes were wide with terror and she was panting. 'Have you killed Arthur?'

'Keep your head, Phyl! I've told you everything's all right. Arthur never felt anything.'

'It's horrible!' she gasped. 'I can't believe it! I shall go mad.'

'It isn't that horrible! It's a mercy-murder. That's what you told me yourself. You meant it, didn't you?'

'What's the good of saying that now!' she sobbed. I never supposed for a moment you would be mad enough to do it!'

Lambert blinked. Phyllis had blurted out a truth about herself that was beyond his comprehension. To him, thought existed solely as a prelude to action. If you didn't intend to do something there was no

sense in thinking about it. He let it go at 'nerves'. There remained
the urgent necessity of calming her before the police arrived.

A fresh wave of horror broke over her.

'Jim! Oh, Jim, you will be hanged! I can't bear it.'

'If you don't stop these tantrums, we'll *both* be hanged!' That
secured her full attention. 'If I'm put in the dock, nothing I can say
or do can save you from coming with me. I did everything, and all
you did was telephone. Admitted. But that telephoning will be
enough.' He expounded the law, but with slight exaggeration.

'I've fixed everything. All you've got to do is tell the truth. Don't
tell one single little lie about anything. Tell 'em you telephoned Arthur
tonight. Tell 'em you forgot you had, when I said I'd fetch the car.
Just as you did forget. Mention everything and admit everything —
except that you know I killed Arthur, and that I told you to telephone.
You said you always wanted to obey me in everything — now's your
chance.'

She gulped in the aftermath of crying. She was steadying.

'Poor Jim!' She smiled wanly. 'I know you wish now that you had
thought of me.' Already she saw him as one who had been so
unfortunate as to cause her distress. 'You mustn't worry. I shall be
all right.'

'That's the stuff, girlie!' He patted her shoulder. She leaned towards
him and wanted to be kissed, but he couldn't manage it, just then.
'Let me mop you up. Don't want 'em to see you've been crying.'

'You'll make it worse,' she warned as he dabbled her face with a
cambric handkerchief. With considerable skill she went quickly to
work with her compact and succeeded beyond his hopes. It had helped
the steadying process, too.

'Was my crocodile dressing-case in the car?' she asked. 'He said
he would bring it back from Lorota's for me.'

'Yes. And that purple scarf of yours. I had a look round —
afterwards. Don't think about details — they're all provided for.'

She accepted the information in silence.

'Anything worrying you?' he asked.

'Is — is Arthur — in the car?'

'No. Keep your mind off all that.'

'I was thinking — I wish you had brought the case away. If there's
no one in the car it might be stolen.'

Poor kid! She had no sense of proportion. Bring the dressing-case
along — and make everything easy for the police!

'It didn't occur to me at the time,' he said to humour her.

'It's a lovely case,' she sighed. 'I felt *wicked* when I tore a gash in it. But Arthur says there's a sort of invisible mending process and that it won't show.'

If he had understood anything of her emotional sequences, he would never have been taken in by her 'mercy-murder' vapourings. With the murder barely an hour old — at this moment when her own life and his depended on the reasonableness of her behaviour — it was inconceivable to him that she could be genuinely anxious about an item of luggage. He assumed that it was a device to stave off what she would call 'the horrors'.

'Arthur paid a hundred and twenty pounds for it — real gold fittings!'

'There now! I didn't know you could spend as much as that for a case.'

She rambled on, giving him details to which he did not listen, though he encouraged her to keep her mind on so safe a subject, while he watched the clock. He could reasonably dally half an hour over a drink to pay his respects to her husband. To stay longer, he had calculated, would be risky. He stretched it ten minutes — then another five minutes in the hall in his overcoat, hoping to be found in the act of departure.

'Directly I've gone, go upstairs and get some of your clothes off. See them in your dressing-gown. Tell them I came in for a drink. Tell them everything truthfully except the one thing — you know!'

'I shall be brave,' she promised, 'for your sake.'

There was no need to argue about that. Self-preservation inspired the most effective response:

'You couldn't be anything but brave! I shall be even more proud of you tomorrow than I am tonight — when I know you've kept your head with the police. Some women would lose their nerve.'

He left her at ten minutes to midnight. She went obediently upstairs. Some fifteen minutes later, wearing an *ensemble-de-nuit* in pale violet, she opened the door to the local superintendent and a sergeant.

He was a good sergeant who knew the gossip of the neighbourhood and had distilled it for his superior. They arrived not unprepared to discover a Thomson-Bywaters set-up — an assumption which was soon to be strengthened by Phyllis Chaundry's demeanour.

She received them with the right degree of dismay. At their own suggestion they entered the house. She had the prudence, at this stage, to remain silent. A call from the police at midnight is certain to mean bad news — the police themselves expect slightly abnormal behaviour from the innocent. In the study she stood facing them, waiting for them, as if nerving herself for the unknown.

The superintendent made the little set speech, breaking to her the news that her husband had been killed.

'*Ah!*' She gave a little gasp, put one hand to her head and with the other plied a tiny wisp of handkerchief to her eyes. 'Forgive me!' Brokenly, she begged them to sit down.

She herself dropped, with some elegance, on to the leather settee, whose cushions happened to make a good background for the violet *ensemble*. The wisp of handkerchief canvasses, as the dramatic critics say, the attention of the audience.

Both the superintendent and the sergeant had seen a great many women cry. They were, in a sense, experts at watching women cry. That wisp of a handkerchief, they could have told you, would have been no earthly use for the real thing. Yet they were asked to believe that it was amply holding its own. The Thomson-Bywaters theory loomed larger. They let the act run for a little and then the sergeant began the routine questioning regarding the known movements of the deceased. Phyllis answered clearly and truthfully.

'As I understand it, Mrs Chaundry,' interposed the superintendent 'your husband told you before he left for the office in the morning that he would pick you up at the dance hall after his Greenfellows meeting?'

'No. I was to hire a car from Lambert's Garage and pick up my sister. I did so. But in the course of the evening I telephoned my husband and asked him to call for me after his meeting.'

'Why?'

'Because Mr Lambert came personally with the car instead of one of his staff. We know him socially and he came in with us and danced with us. And my husband is — was — rather jealous sometimes, so I thought I would telephone him.'

'I have to ask you, Mrs Chaundry, whether he had any reason for his jealousy?'

'Well, I don't know –' She faltered. 'Of course, he hadn't any *reason*, if that's what you really mean, but he may have thought he had. He used to think things and say afterwards he was sorry. And anyhow it seemed better to ring him up and save bother.'

That was an unexpectedly frank admission, but it might have been made in the knowledge that the fact would be certain to emerge. Further questions elicited that she had forgotten that she had telephoned until Lambert had reminded her — that Lambert had come back with her and had waited for her husband until close upon midnight.

The superintendent saw that he would need new facts and a check-up on those given. The sergeant resumed the routine.

'Can you furnish a list of any valuables known or believed to have been carried by the deceased at the time when he met his death?'

'My husband was treasurer of the Greenfellows and he may have been carrying a lot of their cash, and I should think that was why he was killed, if the cash was missing.'

That was the sort of thing they were expecting. She had suggested robbery as the motive. The robber — in the old set-up — would of course be a blind.

'Any other valuables carried by the deceased at the time of –'

'Well, he was carrying my crocodile dressing-case which he was bringing back from Lorota's in Regent Street, where it had gone to be mended, and which cost a hundred and twenty pounds. And a purple scarf of mine which I left behind yesterday. They'd both be on the back seat.' She paused while the sergeant made his note, then added:

'The dressing-case was in the car, wasn't it? — on the back seat?'

'What makes you sure it was in the car, Mrs Chaundry, and on the back seat?'

Phyllis realised dimly that she had made a slip, but her main concern was the fate of her dressing-case.

'He moves — moved — his feet a lot, and I didn't want him to kick it, so he promised me he'd put it on the back seat out of the way.' With growing anxiety she pressed her question: 'It *is* there, isn't it?'

'The scarf was there, but there was no dressing-case.'

'D'you mean to tell me it's *gone* — *stolen?*'

'I only mean to tell you,' answered the superintendent 'that it was not in your husband's car when we made our examination.'

'You must get it back for me!' she shrilled. 'You *must!*'

This time the police were able to add one to the total of women they had seen cry. Indeed, an amateur could have made no mistake. Real tears were smudging her make-up, spoiling her attractive appearance. The wisp of handkerchief only aggravated the damage. She seemed oblivious of the errand of the police. As one who is broken-hearted, she sobbed out details.

'I shall never forgive myself! I ought to have taken it and brought it back myself. That wretched accident! I squeezed it against the door handle of the car and gashed it in the middle — on the side that shows when you carry it.'

The police were bewildered but very patient, even to the point of giving a polite answer when she urged them to move heaven and earth in recovering the dressing-case.

Asked for a description, she restrained her grief and became almost excessively helpful. She described the size, the pattern, the sheen, the triple row of fittings, including manicure set, contents of the bottles, which had not been removed when the case was returned to the dealer's for repair.

The superintendent was somewhat dispirited. The story of the hundred-and-twenty-pound dressing-case menaced the theory of the robbery being a blind — if the story was true.

The police checked on the dealer who had mended the dressing-case — on the attendant at the garage near the Greenfellows' Hall, where Mr Chaundry had deposited a dressing-case of crocodile in the office, declaring it to be specially valuable. The attendant had himself placed it on the back seat of the car when Mr Chaundry drove away to his death.

No dressing-case had been deposited at the Palais — none found by the roadside. If the robbery had been a blind, it would have been just as effective without the addition of the case, so very difficult to dispose of — virtually impossible to dispose of in the very short time between the murder and Lambert's rejoining Mrs Chaundry and her sister in the hall of the Palais.

That was to say, if the robbery was a blind there must have been a real theft of the dressing-case by somebody other than James Lambert while the car was standing on the waste ground.

Suspicion of Lambert rested on evidence of a distressingly negative nature, though there were plenty of clues pointing in his direction. The deceased, though carrying cash and goods of a value exceeding two hundred pounds, had stopped his car in a new by-road at a point near waste ground, which suggested that he had been hailed by someone whose face he knew. Why not Lambert?

Chaundry had got out of the car, whether of his own will or otherwise could not be determined. The body had been found in the ditch a few yards away, together with the canvas bag, stamped with the insignia of the Greenfellows, which had contained the money. Further, Lambert admitted that Mrs Chaundry had admitted that she had asked her husband to call for her and had advised using that route. Brother officials of the Greenfellows had confirmed the statement about the telephone conversation. No one was able to state positively that Lambert was in the Palais between ten and ten-fifteen.

These various facts would have had great cumulative force if there had been one single item of proof that Lambert had in fact been on the scene of the crime at an essential time. A single slip on his part would have brought him to the gallows.

When the coroner's jury returned murder by person or persons unknown, the local police believed them and called in Scotland Yard. The Yard kept an open mind but were unable to establish a *prima facie* case against Lambert.

III

Even if James Lambert had partly accepted the mercy-murder angle, his motive had been that of attaining the woman he desired in conditions of respectability. She had made it clear to him that Chaundry would not consider divorce. She lacked the courage to attack Lambert's fastidious objection to a furtive *affaire* of indefinite duration.

Now, if you murder a man in order to attain respectability, it is uneconomical to throw respectability away immediately after the murder. Respectability, for instance, required Phyllis to impose on herself a period of mourning — a truth she had overlooked when dreaming of the advantages of a mercy-murder to the survivors. She was hurt when James left the coroner's court without offering to see her home. She rang him up to ask if she had offended him.

'If I had taken you home it would have caused a scandal,' he explained. 'You'll see I'm right, if you think about it. And anyway, I don't suppose you would care to discuss such a matter over the telephone.'

'I quite understand, Jim. I'm so upset that I hardly know what I'm doing. That means that you can't come to the house. Where shall we meet?'

'It will cause talk if we meet anywhere — for a bit. Couldn't you go away and stay at a boarding-house for a month or so? What about South Devon? It'll be warm there, and the rest will do you good.'

'A month! Jim, I think that's horrible of you! At least we could meet in Town if you really wanted to see me.'

'We can't just at present. There's your position to be considered.' He heard a disapproving sound and added: 'And it isn't a good idea to ring me up.'

She cut off. It was the first time she had shown temper. Poor kid! he thought. She had every excuse for being nervy. She just hadn't understood what she was letting herself in for.

His knowledge of mechanics had enabled him to know that the telephone had not been tapped. But it might be tapped at any time. And if she were to blurt out her inmost thoughts before he could stop her –

He would have to find some way of dodging her calls. In that moment began an elaborate system of subterfuge, which disturbed his sense of order, wasted his time and became, in short, an infernal nuisance.

But it averted a quarrel. Through her sister Aileen he arranged a meeting at a teashop in London. Aileen left them alone for half an hour, during which Phyllis consented to go not to a boarding-house but to the best hotel in Torquay.

'The solicitor told me that Arthur had left me more than enough to live on, so it would be false economy for me to go to a place I might not like, wouldn't it?'

Jim had not envisaged the possibility of a mercy-murder paying a dividend in cash, and could not figure out quite how he stood.

'That's your affair, girlie. When we set up house-keeping, anything that comes to you from Chaundry will be just pocket money.'

'That'll be lovely! How soon can we get married?'

'That's what I've been wondering. People generally wait a year.'

She was horrified.

'I couldn't be alone for a year! I should be *ill*. And you can't ask me to live with the family. I may be doing them an injustice, but I don't think they really want me to.'

'Well, maybe we can cut it down to six months. See how things go. We can meet here again after you come back from Torquay.'

She was unhappy about it and inclined to be weepish, but she accepted his decision.

'You'll write to me every day, won't you Jim!'

'I'm not going to write to you at all. And you're not going to write to me. You can tell me your news through Aileen, and I'll do the same. You don't want to spoil everything, Phyl. Here's Aileen coming back.' He added, without much conviction: 'Go on being a brave kid. The time will pass soon enough, and we'll have the rest of our lives together.'

She braced up as Aileen returned. It had been arranged that the girls should leave first. Jim was thanking Aileen when Phyllis cut in:

'Oh, Jim, I forgot to tell you about the police!'

He knew a spasm of physical fear — of something approaching momentary hatred of her for the rashness that constantly risked his life.

'That superintendent! I had — well, almost "words" with him! I don't believe he's doing a single thing to help find my dressing-case and I told him he was spoiling his chances by telling the newspapers all about it. I said I was going to ask my solicitor to write to him.'

After she had gone, he tried to come to terms with himself about her. She was putting the murder of Chaundry out of her mind — had already done so. She was kidding herself that she had played no part in the murder. Believing it, too — in the same sense in which she had kidded herself into believing that she wanted to murder him out of mercy.

It was certain that she did not realise that she herself was in peril. She had not supposed he was lying when he had told her that her danger was equal to his. It was 'purely' and 'simply' that her mentality was unable to retain the idea that to telephone a man and ask him to drive you home might be the same, in law, as killing him.

There followed a very shattering corollary. As she was incapable of caring about anybody but herself, it was not at all unreasonable that the loss of a favourite dressing-case should interest her more than her lover's peril. 'Which means that she's not such an almighty fool as I am.'

IV

At his wedding in the following October, James Lambert was unable to shake off a feeling of surprise that they were both at large at the end of six months of separation — on any day of which she might have chattered them into prison.

The sense of triumph, of at last possessing the object of his desire, was altogether lacking. The grand passion, which had suffused his personality, had wilted under the subterfuges and banalities of shoring up their respectability.

He had again come to terms with himself — slightly different terms. His original attitude to her now seemed as absurd as his bitterness at her triviality. Her potent physical attractiveness remained. Though a silly little woman, she was docile when humoured, and had small, pleasing characteristics. At worst, she always purred prettily when he stroked her. Make the best of her as she was, he thought to himself.

At her suggestion they went for their honeymoon to the hotel in Torquay where she had passed the first few weeks of widowhood. She was thinking more about the hotel than about their reunion. She was but dimly aware that the period of separation had reduced James Lambert (*'dream lover, put your arms around me'*) to the stature of a presentable man who asked nothing of life but the right to be kind to her.

James was indulging himself with four weeks' absence from business and, on the whole, enjoyed himself. The strain of the preceding months had made itself felt and he was able to find her prattle restful. He noted without resentment that she had many male acquaintances among the regular patrons. During their last week he felt a pang of animal jealousy in respect of a young man, monied and much more socially gifted than himself, whom he knew only as 'Wilfy'.

He had refused to live in Chaundry's house, which had been left to her. So she sold it and increased her already enormous wardrobe. They moved into his house, conveniently near the garage.

He found her to be a reasonably competent housewife, unexpectedly quick and methodical, so that she had much time on her hands. His business continued to expand and to eat up more of his leisure.

Phyllis had a simple theory of business. If you were your own master, you could obviously take time off whenever you wanted to — a theory which began to produce domestic jars before the first year had been completed. Their squabbles, if frequent, were brief. She was always genuinely sorry for anyone who had the misfortune to displease her, so bore no malice. It was after a small tiff which she had forgotten and he had not, that she happened to remark:

'Oh, did I ever tell you that I went to Scotland Yard about my dressing-case and they didn't do anything either!'

'For God's sake forget that foolery!' he snarled and went out banging the door.

If she was obsessed with dressing-cases, he reasoned, why the devil didn't she buy herself one! She had as much pin money — Chaundry's money — as the wife of a wealthy man. He had not realised that to such a woman as Phyllis a luxury had to be a gift expressive of admiration. But he did realise that his outburst had been a backslide — a failure on his part to accept her as she was and make the best of it.

He made a trip to Regent Street — to Lorota's. He asked for a fitted crocodile dressing-case to cost one hundred and twenty pounds.

Mr Lorota regretted that he had not, just then, a case at exactly that price. The nearest was one at one hundred and fifty or, at a lower figure, a really excellent article at ninety guineas. With, of course, real gold fittings.

Lambert hesitated, then decided on the ninety-guinea one. It was a mistake he would not have made in business. But ninety guineas did seem a pretty substantial apology for a piece of petulant rudeness.

He arrived home at four instead of seven, to find her chatting on the telephone to 'Wilfy'. He waited until she had finished, then displayed the dressing-case.

'Jim you darling!' She gave him a hug. 'You know how I adore crocodile! Why, it's just like mine! She turned it in the light and crooned over it. ' And I'm *sure* it's got a triple row of fittings and its very own manicure set!'

She snapped open the catches.

'Oh!' No more able to conceal her feelings than child, she had given a little moan of disappointment. 'Perhaps the manicure set is on this side.'

It was patent to Lambert that the case had but a double row of fittings and that no manicure set was supplied with the ninety-guinea model. The case lay at her feet, open. He felt that Lorota had cheated him.

He found her looking up at him with large, moist eyes.

'Jim, darling, you mustn't mind! You mustn't be disappointed — really you mustn't!'

Lambert stared at his wife, then stared at the case, with the same expression. He took a flying kick at the case, which sent it hurtling across the room into a Japanese urn, which had been one of her few contributions to the household.

The urn was smashed — so, more or less, was the ninety-guinea dressing-case. Alone in the room, he picked it up and carried it to the hot-water furnace into which he thrust it, gold fittings and all. Then he went back to the garage and worked the whole evening.

Phyllis told herself that Jim no longer loved her — a correct conclusion reached, however, by faulty reasoning. She left him for 'Wilfy' — without any of the tiresome waiting about through fear of what people would say. People said all they could, which was not very much, because neither Lambert nor any of the neighbours knew Wilfy's correct name or whereabouts.

V

Phyllis Chaundry's appeal to Scotland Yard had been made during the period of active investigation. With her assertion that it was 'of the utmost importance to recover the dressing case', Chief Inspector Karslake had agreed though for different reasons. It was obvious that James Lambert had not taken it: he could not have disposed of it.

On the other hand, the man who had stolen the dressing-case was almost certainly the murderer. His very existence, if it could be proved, would destroy the substantial, if negative, evidence suggesting Lambert's guilt.

In the first few days they had picked up a clue of great promise. A casual labourer of no fixed abode, known as Conrad the Tinker, though he was not a tinker, had spent three weeks in a lodging house at Rubington, and had moved on to another lodging house in Warthame a week before the crime. He was given a month's employment as assistant gardener in the municipal park but had disappeared the night Chaundry was murdered. There was a sum of two pounds nine shillings due to him in wages which he had never claimed.

The dragnet had been spread throughout the country without result. Once the hue and cry had been taken up by the newspapers, Karslake thought that they might find the man but they would not find the dressing-case, which could be easily destroyed by fire. Without the dressing-case the man might have little interest for them. They did not find even the man until the Chaundry case had been filed in the Department of Dead Ends for nearly two years.

Not that things had been wholly quiescent. No fewer than five crocodile dressing-cases, three with real gold fittings, had been foisted on Detective-Inspector Rason. Two of them had never been reclaimed. And then, seventeen months after the murder of Chaundry, a sixth crocodile dressing-case arrived with every appearance of being the right one.

With it came the kind of tale which was commonplace in the Department. A six-ton truck had backed into a cottage in Wiltshire, partly destroying it. Among the debris was a wooden chest, six feet by three, padlocked but opened by the Salvage Corps, which contained a number of articles listed as 'missing believed stolen', including a crocodile dressing-case with real gold fittings and the initials 'P.C.'

The cottage had been tenanted by an elderly woman named Mence, living alone in meagre circumstances. The chest, she said, was not hers but her son's. He was the roving sort, but would come to stay with her sometimes. It was now nearly two years since she had seen him. Further questioning left little doubt that her son was Conrad the Tinker. She admitted that he had been to sea, though he was not a seaman, and finally admitted that he was serving a sentence of three years in Scotland, with two years to run.

It looked remarkably like a cinch. All the same, Rason reminded himself that 'P.C.' might stand for 'Polly Crisp,' or any one of the large number of names that begin with 'C'. So he checked on the Chaundry file, concentrating on Phyllis Chaundry's exhaustive description of the dressing-case. Then he checked with Lorota, the dealer, after which he went in search of Phyllis, to invite her to the Yard to make formal identification of her property.

He arrived at Lambert's house before the latter left for the garage. The daily help did not directly answer his request to see Mrs Lambert.

'You'd better see Mr Lambert. He can tell you what's going on a lot better than I can!' Which, from a detective's point of view, was a good beginning.

James Lambert told him quite frankly what was going on, the essential point being that he did not even know whether his wife was in the country or abroad. While he was speaking he was wondering uneasily what would happen if Phyllis was again subjected to police questioning.

'If it would help you for me to identify the dressing case – '

'Thank you, Mr Lambert. Rason always accepted an offer of help, whether he wanted it or not. ''Smatter o' fact, we need you on another angle too. The Tinker — Mence, his name is — says he was employed by you about that time as a temporary washer. We need an identification on that point.'

'It may be true, yet I may never have seen him. I spend most of my time in the office.'

'Other way up, I mean, Mr Lambert. He says he knows you by sight. We want him to pick you out. If I may use your phone they'll have the parade ready by the time we arrive.'

Lambert didn't like the look of it. But refusal would be very dangerous.

'Theft of goods — that's only a trifle,' explained Rason, as they drove to the Yard. 'It's the goods as evidence that counts. Why, come now, Mr Lambert, between you and me, this Chaundry affair must have been something of a nuisance to you? I bet it has! I'm not supposed to say it, but when we've buttoned up this bit about the dressing-case — well, I guess it'll be a relief to you if it turns out he murdered Chaundry?'

'Oh, I see!' Lambert had not seen it before that moment. Now he faced a new kind of horror. He had never envisaged the chances of an innocent man being convicted of the murder. To let another man be hanged for his crime ranked in his mind as mean and undignified — like cheating a man over a car. Something to be avoided if avoidance were possible without going to extremes.

'The tale he offers,' continued Rason, 'is that he found the car all by itself on the waste ground, didn't see the body and thought he'd help himself while he could.' Rason chuckled. 'With his record he ought to know that the D.P.P. won't wear *that*!'

At Scotland Yard Lambert was met by Chief Inspector Karslake as an old acquaintance. Presently a detective sergeant conducted Lambert to a courtyard, where he fell in line with a round dozen men, most of whom were his own physical type.

Conrad the Tinker, in plain dress but without a collar, was told to walk down the line. Lambert risked a glance at the man, which told him nothing. The Tinker stopped for a moment in front of Lambert, in evident recognition, then passed on without speaking. The parade broke up.

'That didn't take long, did it!' chirped Rason. 'We'll get the report on it presently.' Karslake joined them on the way to Rason's office.

'Mr Lambert,' Rason explained to Karslake, 'has promised to help us find Mrs Lambert. You said we must get her, sir, to identify the dressing-case.'

Rason's room was in its normally disgraceful state. A picnic basket and Thermos crowned one of the filing cabinets; a wall map, with flagged pins, was propped up on the floor. On his desk, dumped on an open directory, stood a crocodile dressing-case, which instantly absorbed Lambert's attention.

Lambert picked up the case, turned it and put it down again. He grinned broadly at the two detectives. For he had seen a way of escape for the Tinker — and end of the whole inconvenient inquiry.

'That's not the right dressing-case!' he announced. As Rason gaped at him, he supplemented: 'It's like the one my wife had, but it's not hers.'

'Good lord!' Rason glanced apologetically at the unsympathetic countenance of Chief Inspector Karslake. 'I don't know what's gone wrong sir.' He turned to Lambert. 'I say, Mr Lambert, are you quite sure!'

'Quite sure!' answered Lambert. 'Her case had her initials "P.C." cut on the side. This case has never been cut for initials.'

'Now look here, Mr Lambert!' Rason was laboriously patient. 'Your wife — Mrs Chaundry, as she was then — gave us two hundred and thirty words close description of her dressing-case. All about the bottle and Gawd-knows-what! Not a word about her initials.'

'She forgot — she often does forget the main thing. The initials were there, all right. ''P.C.'' Done curly, instead of straight.'

'Like this?' asked Rason.

From under the wall map sprawling on the floor Rason produced a crocodile dressing-case, looking now a little dingy. It bore the initials 'P.C.' — slightly curly.

Lambert regarded it with profound distaste. Another crocodile dressing-case was a bad break. The Tinker would have to be hanged. He himself would have to make the best of that mean feeling — like that of cheating a man over a car.

'Yes,' he admitted. 'That's her dressing-case.'

'My fault from first to last!' groaned Rason. 'My trouble is, I haven't enough room here. All sorts of articles are sent to me –'

He broke off as a messenger entered and handed a slip to Karslake.

'Report on the Tink — on the convict, Mence, sir.'

Karslake glanced at the slip, then passed it to Rason. Rason read it, then characteristically stowed it in his waistcoat pocket.

'Well, we mustn't talk about my troubles, Mr Lambert. We must talk about yours. I'm sorry, but I have to arrest you and charge you with the murder of Arthur Chaundry.'

While Rason was reciting the routine warning, Lambert reminded himself that there had been no one on the road when he had killed Chaundry and that there was no nearby place of concealment for anyone. There could have been no onlooker.

'That's a bit of a knock, Mr Rason,' he said coolly. 'You know your job. But if you're betting on the unsupported statement of that convict –'

'The Tinker doesn't connect you with the murder!' exclaimed Rason. 'He only says you were the owner of the garage. You can read the report yourself.' He produced it for inspection.

'Then what's it all about?' demanded Lambert.

'Your arrest, d'you mean? Oh, your wife's evidence has dished you.' Noting the other's incredulous expression, he went on:

'Come back to Mrs Chaundry — as she was then, Lambert. She didn't *forget* those initials on her dressing-case. How come? Because she'd never seen those initials on her dressing-case. Lorota tried to mend a gash in the dressing-case, but the invisible mending stunt didn't come off. So he covered the gash by cutting those initials over it — which you don't generally do in crocodile. *She didn't know the initials were there!* But you did! How? Only if you saw them in the car. How could you see them in the car? Only if you killed Chaundry. Your own statements prove that it was not possible for you to have seen those initials *at any other place* or *at any other time*!'

Lambert blinked, groping for an answer.

'You've had a raw deal, Lambert. We'd never have got you if she hadn't bleated about that dressing-case. We know she put Chaundry on the spot for you. What about giving us the dope?'

He had thrown away his life for a doll. To assert that she had conspired with him would be a flattery, which he grudged her.

'The dope is that she hadn't the guts for a job like that. I listened outside the box at the dance hall while she was telephoning. I saw my chance. She didn't know that I intended to kill Chaundry.'

ANTHONY BERKELEY

The Wrong Jar

'ANTHONY BERKELEY' *was one of the pseudonyms of A. B. Cox (1893–1970), whose character Roger Sheringham is the only Great Detective in these pages (fictional Sherlock Holmes was made to tackle real Jack the Ripper by Ellery Queen, but that was a whole novel and won't fit in here). The case that Sheringham tackles in 'The Wrong Jar' was a real, though rather obscure, one; another story, 'The Avenging Chance', was based upon the famous Molineux case, but has been frequently reprinted. Later, Cox abandoned the detective form and as Francis Iles wrote crime novels that became classics of their kind.*

'Eh?' said Roger Sheringham sharply. 'What's that, Moresby? — Have some more beer,' he added perfunctorily.

'Well, thank you, Mr Sheringham. I don't mind if I do. — That Marston poisoning case, I was saying,' resumed the Chief Inspector, when his tankard had been satisfactorily refilled. 'You've read about it, I suppose. Well, can you see that man Bracey poisoning his wife? I'm not sure that I can. Smashing her over the head with a hammer, yes; that's his type. But putting arsenic in her medicine? No, I shouldn't be surprised to hear that the local police have made a bit of a bloomer there. Not a bit I wouldn't, though that's strictly between ourselves. Anyhow, they didn't call us in so it's none of my business. But if I were *you* . . .'

'Yes?' said Roger eagerly.

'You like poking about in that sort of thing, don't you? Well, if you were to go down to Marston and get in touch with this man's solicitors, and offer to do a bit of unofficial nosing around, I shouldn't wonder if you mightn't find something to interest you.'

'Look here, give me the facts. I've hardly looked at a paper for the last fortnight. I thought the coroner's jury brought in a verdict of accidental death?'

'They did. But now the local people have arrested the husband.

So far as I can make out, it's like this.'

A certain Mrs Bracey (said Moresby), living in the small market-town of Marston, in Buckinghamshire, found herself suffering from gastric trouble, and called in her doctor. It was apparently a straightforward case, and the doctor treated her on normal lines. The treatment undoubtedly did her good, but she was still confined to her bed.

The Braceys were people of some consequence in Marston. Bracey himself was a builder. He had been trained as an engineer, but finding no opening in that line had bought up a local building firm soon after the war and set out to specialise in steel-concrete work. He had done very well, and the two had become as comfortably off as anyone in the neighbourhood. So far as could be made out from the newspaper reports Bracey was very popular, a big, hearty, jovial man, with a greeting for everyone, whose workmen never went on strike. Mrs Bracey had been a cut or two above him socially; her father was a regular army officer who had risen to the rank of major-general during the war; but she had never appeared to think that she had married beneath her. She was a particularly charming woman, and her husband, as everyone thought, worshipped her, while she was hardly less in love with him. A phenomenally happy couple, was the opinion of Marston. There were two children.

Mrs Bracey's illness had seemed to be running its normal course, when one evening her doctor had received an urgent telephone call from Bracey to come at once to Silverdene (as the house was called) as his wife had suddenly been taken very much worse. The doctor, whose name was Reid, was surprised, as he had anticipated no developments of such a nature. He found Bracey apparently in a state of great agitation, and Mrs Bracey very bad indeed. He did what he could, but she died in the small hours of the next morning.

Dr Reid was no fool. A less conscientious man might have said: 'Ah, well; gastro-enteritis; never quite know where you are with it.' No so Dr Reid. He refused a certificate. The coroner ordered a post-mortem, and the cause of death at once became plain. Dr Reid had been justified. Mrs Bracey's body contained at least three grains of arsenic. A great deal more must of course have been administered.

The local police at once took the matter in hand with energy. The only possible vehicle of administration which could be discovered was a bottle of medicine, which on analysis was found to be liberally laced with arsenic. By exhaustive enquiry the police were able to account for every minute of the bottle's existence.

It was a new one. Dr Reid had made it up himself after his morning surgery, an ordinary sedative compound of sod. bicarb., bismuth oxicarb., mag. carb. pond., with aqua. menth. pip., or in other words peppermint water. With his own hands he had corked it, wrapped it, sealed the wrapping, and given it to the boy to take round. When it arrived at Silverdene ten minutes later the seal was still intact. There was no possibility of the bottle having been tampered with on the way.

The bottle arrived at Silverdene at twenty-five minutes past ten. Bracey had gone to his office an hour before. The seal was broken and the bottle opened by the professional nurse whom Bracey had insisted upon engaging for his wife, although in such a mild case her services were hardly necessary. The directions on the label stated that a tablespoonful was to be administered every four hours. The nurse at once gave her patient a dose, and subsequent doses were given punctually at half-past two that afternoon and at half-past six. The bottle remained in the sick-room all day and under the nurse's eye the whole time except for one hour in the afternoon when she was off duty from three to four. During that time, it was established, Mrs Bracey had been asleep and no one had gone into the room.

At about twelve o'clock Mrs Bracey had complained of a feeling of nausea and just before her lunch had been sick, which seemed to relieve her. This was such an ordinary symptom of her illness that the nurse had taken it for granted; and as Mrs Bracey retained her lunch and seemed better for it, the nurse had felt no scruples about taking her usual hour off duty in the afternoon. Mrs Bracey was just waking up when she came back, and complained again of nausea, accompanied by a burning pain in her stomach. She took her tea, but was unable to retain it. This too, however, had been a common symptom with her during her illness, and the nurse had no cause to attach particular importance to this manifestation of it.

Bracey got home about five o'clock, and at once went in to see his wife, who was again feeling better but still had some pain, though she concealed the fact from her husband. The nurse left them alone together, and Bracey stayed in the bedroom for about an hour, at the end of which he went down to the garden to get some exercise by mowing the tennis court. He stayed out till dinner-time.

It was not until after the third dose of medicine, at half-past six, that Mrs Bracey became appreciably worse. She and the nurse both attributed it to a normal development of her illness, and Mrs Bracey insisted that her husband should not be informed as it would only make him worry unnecessarily. When he went up to see his wife before dinner he was kept out of the sick-room therefore by the pretext that Mrs Bracey was asleep. By nine o'clock, however, her condition had become so pronounced that the nurse was alarmed, sent for Bracey, and asked him to telephone for the doctor.

No more of the medicine was administered after the dose at half-past six.

At the inquest of course the main question was, how the arsenic could have found its way into the medicine. A number of facts, already discovered by the police, were brought out by the coroner from Dr Reid. Contrary to the usual practice, he kept white arsenic in his surgery, in a jar on the shelves, not in a poison-cupboard. Why? Because he used to carry out chemical experiments, and as he and his partner did all their own dispensing he had not considered the habit a dangerous one; as for poison-cupboards, nobody used them outside the hospitals. And there was no question of outside interference here because he had made up the medicine with his own hands and was ready to take full responsibility. Was the arsenic jar kept on the top shelf in the surgery, almost exactly above the jar containing the carbonate of magnesia? Certainly it was, why not? Dr Reid, a middle-aged man, showed signs of approaching irascibility. Somewhat curtly the coroner told him to stand down.

The surgery used by both partners was a ground-floor room in the house occupied by the other, a younger man of the name of Berry. Dr Berry confirmed Dr Reid's evidence. No, he had never considered it a dangerous thing to keep white arsenic in the surgery in the circumstances. Yes, they did all their own dispensing. Yes, his sister was learning to dispense, but she had not yet taken it over. No, she had never made up a bottle of medicine for a patient. Yes, Dr Berry had seen her in the surgery that morning.

Miss Berry, rather frightened, was called. She was a fluttery woman, several years older than her brother. Yes, she was learning to dispense. Yes, she had been in the surgery that morning. But not when that particular bottle was being made up. She was helping the housemaid make the beds at about that time.

Dr Reid was recalled. Yes, Miss Berry had looked into the surgery that morning. No, she had not been there when he was making up this particular medicine. No, there was no possibility that she had inadvertently handed him the wrong jar, because she had handed him no jars at all, because she was not there; he had taken down the jars he needed himself. No, there was no possibility of a muddle in the prescription. The prescription showed that this had been the only bottle of medicine to be made up that morning.

Was there a chance that he himself had taken down the wrong jar? There was not. Dr Reid had been in practice long enough not to make fool mistakes like that. Besides, all this talk about the jars was beside the point. Evidence had already been given by the official analyst that the medicine did in fact contain all the ingredients which Dr Reid had put into it; if it were a case of accidental substitution of arsenic for one of them, that one would be missing. Did Dr Reid then stake his professional reputation on the fact that when that bottle of medicine left his surgery it contained no arsenic? With a full realisation of what his answer must imply, Dr Reid agreed that he did.

The jury, however, did not agree with Dr Reid. They found that Mrs Bracey had died through an overdose of arsenic contained in the medicine made up by Dr Reid owing to his having taken down the wrong jar from the shelf.

This verdict, imputing to the doctor what amounted to culpable negligence, was tantamount to a verdict of manslaughter against him; but the police made no arrest. It was felt that Dr Reid's point could not be gainsaid. If arsenic had been accidentally substituted for another ingredient, that ingredient would be lacking; and it was not. The verdict was ignored. Dr Reid was held to be right in his assertion that when the bottle of medicine left his surgery it contained no arsenic.

The next step in the case was the arrest of Bracey. The reasons for this had not yet been made public, but Moresby had information that it had followed immediately on the acquisition by the local authorities of the information that at the time of his wife's death Bracey had arsenic in his possession. His own explanation was that he had bought it months earlier, in quantity through the ordinary trade channels for use in some experiments he was making in wood-preservation. In support of this, there was clear evidence both that Bracey had been making such experiments and that he had recently obtained excellent results with certain arsenic compounds. Nevertheless it was equally indisputable that arsenic was in his possession.

As for opportunity, he had been alone with his wife and the medicine bottle for an hour. Only on the question of motive were the police at a loss. If they had been French they would have shrugged their shoulders and said: 'Cherchez la femme.' Not being French they shrugged their shoulder only, but the shrug carried the cynical implications that marriage itself is a motive for murder.

'I see,' Roger nodded, when the Chief Inspector had finished. 'After all, they've got logic behind them. We can certainly eliminate an accident on the doctor's part; and so far as opportunity goes, and if nobody else really did enter the bedroom, that narrows it down to Bracey and the nurse. And why the nurse? Anyhow, we must see what we can see. But one thing seems clear enough it was done from the inside.

'An inside job,' Moresby amended, more professionally.

'I think I'll look into it,' said Roger.

There was no difficulty with Bracey's solicitors. Their welcome was almost eager, and they undertook to put every possible resource at the disposal of their new ally. In a discussion on the case, however, they were unable to offer any helpful ideas or even to bring forward any new facts of the least importance, though agreeing that the case was narrowed down to those having access to the bedroom between the times of the opening of the bottle and Mrs Bracey's first serious symptoms at about seven o'clock.

'But of course we mustn't overlook the possibility of some kind of accident on the doctor's part,' said Roger thoughtfully, 'even if not the particular one suggested at the inquest. Mrs Bracey was bad earlier in the day, I understand.'

That was so, but only in the same way as she had been on previous days. It was impossible to say that these two slight attacks were due to the action of arsenic; not until seven o'clock could arsenic be definitely diagnosed. And there was no possibility of previous administrations; the post-mortem had proved conclusively that the poisoning was acute, and not chronic. Owing to the eliminations it was not possible to state with any accuracy the size of the dose, though the analyst estimated it at about five grains. A test of the medicine showed nine grains of arsenic to the fluid ounce. The dose having been one tablespoon, or half a fluid ounce, this agreed quite well with the theory of a single fatal dose.

'Very well indeed,' nodded Roger. 'Well, now, what about the inmates of the house. The nurse, for instance. Nurses have been known to murder their patients just for the fun of the thing. Marie Jeanneret, for instance.'

'No doubt, no doubt,' agreed the other. 'But there is not the slightest evidence of that here. Naturally we have gone closely into her history. She has the reputation of a very respectable woman with a good record; there are no curious incidents connected with her at all.'

'A pity,' Roger murmured. 'It would have been so simple. Well, the servants?'

The servants similarly had been the subjects of close investigation. Not one of them had been in the house for less than five years; they all bore excellent characters; from the butler downwards they were all exceedingly upset at the death of a much-loved mistress, and hardly less so at the predicament of a very popular master; not one of them but was not ready to stake everything on the fact of Bracey's innocence.

It was clear too that the solicitor held the same opinion, which Roger thought an excellent sign.

'Well,' he said at last, 'all I can do is to look round. I think I'd like to see Bracey first of all. That can be arranged, I suppose?'

It could be and was, on the spot. Within half-an-hour Roger found himself facing the engineer across a table in the county gaol.

Bracey was a large man, with one of those simple red faces which delight publicans and prospective wives. At present his blue eyes wore an expression of pathetic bewilderment, like a dog that has been punished for something it did not do.

'Of course I'll help you all I can, Mr Sheringham,' he said, when he had read the note from the solicitor that Roger had brought with him. 'And remarkably good it is of you to lend us a hand. I only hope you won't be wasting your time.'

'It won't be a waste of my time if I can get you out of here.'

'That's what I meant. They can't keep me here long in any case. They only arrested me because they didn't know what to do. I mean, it's too ridiculous. Me poison Cynthia? Why . . . why . . .'

He was so obviously on the point of breaking down, that Roger hurriedly interposed with a question. 'What is your own opinion, Mr Bracey, then?'

'Why, it was an accident. Must have been. Who'd have poisoned her deliberately? She hasn't an enemy in the world. Everyone loved her. It was that fool of a doctor. Made some ghastly mistake, and now he's trying to save his face. Oh, I know they say there couldn't be any mistake, because everything was in the medicine that should have been; but how else can it have happened?'

'We must examine every possibility, nevertheless,' Roger said, and went on to ask about the servants.

Bracey was stout in their defence. It was utterly out of the question that any of them could have done such a thing.

Nor was there any other person with a conceivable motive for murder. 'I believe the police are nosing round, trying to find out if

I haven't been mixed up with some other woman,' Bracey said
scornfully. 'I could have saved them the trouble if they'd asked me.
I haven't even looked at another woman since I first met Cynthia.'

'No.' Roger stroked his chin. This did not seem to be leading
anywhere. 'Look here, who was your wife's best friend in Marston?'

A wife's best friend knows far more about her than a husband.

'Well, I don't know. She wasn't particularly intimate with anyone.
Plenty of friends, but few intimates. I should think she knew Angela
Berry as well as anyone.'

'That's Dr Berry's sister, who was called at the inquest?'

'Yes. She used to help Cynthia with the children when they were
smaller, before we could afford a nurse. Wouldn't take a penny for
it, either. Said she wanted something to do. She and Cynthia got very
thick. They haven't seen so much of each other lately perhaps, not
since Angela took up helping with the practice; but yes, I should think
you might say she was Cynthia's closest friend in Marston.'

'I see.' Roger mentally noted Angela Berry as a person to whom
he could put certain questions about the dead woman which he could
not very well put to her husband.

That interview, however, would turn upon motive; opportunity was
the more urgent matter for investigation. On leaving the prison Roger
headed his car for Marston again with the intention of making direct
for Silverdene.

The trained nurse was still in residence at the house, in case the
police wished to question her further, and Roger, having handed the
butler a note from Bracey, asked to see her.

She proved to be a pleasant-faced woman, with greying hair and
the usual air of competent assurance of the trained nurse.

She answered Roger's questions readily, with a marked Scottish
accent. There were only two periods during which the bottle had been
out of her observation: during her hour off duty in the afternoon,
when she had gone for a short walk, and while Bracey was with his
wife. 'As if anyone would think o' that puir mon daeing any such
thing. A fine mess the pollis have made.'

'They seem to think he may have been carrying on with some other
woman?' suggested Roger.

'Blether! I ken his kind. It's one woman and one only for that sort.
Ay, it's grand husbands they make.'

'Then what do you think, nurse?'

There, the nurse admitted, he had her. She did not know what to
think. It was mystery to her. She seemed doubtful about the idea of

an accident in the surgery; Mrs Bracey's symptoms, she pointed out, would surely have been much more pronounced had arsenic been present in the medicine from the beginning.

'Then you do think it was murder,' Roger persisted.

'Ay,' replied the nurse gloomily. 'I fear it must have been. Though who could have wanted to murder that puir lamb?'

'And if it is murder, and Mr Bracey didn't do it, the whole thing boils down to the time while you were out for your walk. Someone must have got into the room then, while Mrs Bracey presumably was asleep, and put the arsenic in the medicine-bottle. I must see the servants.'

Roger saw the servants, but they could not help him. The butler had been on duty all the afternoon, and had let not a single person into the house. There had been two callers, a Mrs Ayres and a Miss Jamieson, to ask after Mrs Bracey, but neither of them had come in. Was there any other way into the house? Well, there were the French windows in the drawing-room opening on to the garden. It was just possible, the butler admitted, that someone might have reached them unseen, got inside the house that way, and crept up unobserved to Mrs Bracey's room.

'Having already watched the nurse leave,' Roger added. 'But it would be a great risk.'

'A very great risk, sir. The person would have to cross the hall and go up the stairs, which as you see are under observation from here right up to the landing, and I was in and out of the hall all the afternoon.'

'And yet I don't see how else it would have been done,' Roger said. He had already dismissed the idea that the crime had been committed by someone of the household; apart from any motive, he was satisfied that not one of them was capable of such a thing; it was an outside, not an inside job. 'Well, I suppose I'd better have a word with Mrs Ayres and Miss Jamieson. They might have seen someone. Can you give me their addresses?'

He set off for the interviews.

Mrs Ayres, an elderly lady with a very precise manner, was anxious to help but unable to do so. She had seen no one, she had noticed nothing unusual, she had just left her flowers and gone.

Without very much hope Roger set out to interview Miss Jamieson. He finally ran her to earth at the local tennis club, and had to wait till she finished a set. She was a large, well-muscled lady and hit a shrewd ball, and Roger was not unthankful to sit in a deck-chair for ten minutes and watch her.

On hearing his name and business she exclaimed loudly that precisely the same idea had occurred to herself, as it would have to the police if they had not all been congenital idiots from the Chief Constable downwards. But alas, there was no evidence that she could produce to support the theory.

'But it was a woman, Mr Sheringham,' she boomed, mopping her red forehead. 'Take it from me. The idea of Tom Bracey's so absurd we needn't even consider it. No, it was some woman who fancied she had a grudge against poor Cynthia.'

'Arsenic's certainly a woman's weapon,' agreed Roger, who had already reached the same conclusion.

'What I say exactly,' Miss Jamieson said, nodding violently. 'But it's no use asking me who it could have been, because I've racked my brains and racked 'em and I can't think.'

'I thought of asking Miss Berry if she could suggest anyone who might have had a grudge against Mrs Bracey.'

'Yes, I should do that. Angela would know if anyone did.'

'By the way,' said Roger, 'what time was it that you called at Silverdene?'

'I couldn't say to the minute, but not later than ten past three, because I was playing here by a quarter-past, I know.'

Roger had an idea. 'Could you possibly remember who among Mrs Bracey's friends was here when you arrived, Miss Jamieson? You must have reached Silverdene only just after the nurse went out, you see; so that anyone who was here before you, and who remained here till four, has a complete alibi for that hour.'

Miss Jamieson screwed up her eyes and managed to produce five names, of which only that of Angela Berry was known to Roger. He wrote them carefully down, feeling that he had established something at last, however negative. Angela Berry, too, had stayed at the tennis club till nearly dinner-time, so she at all events was barred.

Roger's next call was on Dr Reid, whom he was lucky to find at home. The doctor was indignant over the verdict at the inquest, and entirely in agreement with Roger's theories. Mrs Bracey's death was plain murder: the nurse was out of the question; someone must have gone into the house during the fatal hour. But he could not even suggest whom.

'Yes, a nice mess those fools of jurymen have got me into,' were his last words. 'I've had the police round at the surgery half-a-dozen times, weighing my stock of arsenic, and comparing it with my poison-book.'

'I suppose it tallies?' Roger asked perfunctorily.

'No, it doesn't,' the doctor chuckled. 'I've actually got more arsenic than my records show, which seems to worry them.'

'But how could that happen?'

'Well, obviously I must have bought an ounce once and forgotten to enter it up. As I told them, it's at least eight years since I gave up making my own pills, and I can't profess to remember what happened eight years ago.'

'And the jar hasn't been touched since?'

'It hasn't.'

As he left Dr Reid's house and walked down Marston High Street in search of that of Dr and Miss Berry, Roger found himself more at sea than ever. That he was on the right track, he felt sure; but it seemed a track impossible to retrace. Still, one could only go on trying.

Dr Berry was out, and the maid seemed very doubtful whether it was possible to see Miss Berry.

Roger produced a card and scribbled a line on it. 'Take her this,' he said, 'and tell her it's very urgent.'

The maid returned with the information that Miss Berry would see him.

Angela Berry must have been a plain woman at the best of times; at present her eyes were red-rimmed with crying, and her face ravaged. Her voice was uncertain as she asked her visitor to be seated.

Roger came to the point at once. 'I'm sorry to worry you, Miss Berry, but it is literally a case of life and death.' He explained briefly his position and ideas, and asked her whether she could name anyone who might have a grudge against Mrs Bracey.

Miss Berry hesitated. 'N-no. No, I can't.'

'Quite sure?'

'Quite,' she said more firmly.

'That's a pity. Well, can you suggest anyone with some other motive for eliminating her? You think Bracey is speaking the truth when he says there was no other woman? He's not shielding anyone? Forgive me; I must speak plainly.'

'Certainly not,' Miss Berry answered, with a touch of indignation that seemed a little out of place. 'Mr Bracey never . . . there is no question of such a thing. Mr Bracey is a very honourable man.'

'I see. Then you can suggest nothing at all? Not even a line along which I might make enquiries? I understand you were Mrs Bracey's closest friend. Is there nothing at all you can tell me that might help?

It's no time for secrets, you know.'

'No, nothing at all, I'm afraid,' said Mrs Berry. She looked at Roger with eyes that slowly widened. 'Mr Sheringham, he's not in — in *danger*, is he?'

Roger returned her look. He was not satisfied. The woman's manner struck him as just a little evasive. I believe she does know something, he thought, or imagines she does; something discreditable to the wife, I fancy; there was a touch of reserve; but she won't bring it out unless she's frightened; I must frighten her.

'Yes,' he said slowly. 'Mr Bracey is undoubtedly in the gravest danger.'

'Oh!' It was a little cry. She clasped her hands on her breast. 'Mr Sheringham, I *know* he didn't do it. He couldn't do such a thing. He's the most upright of men. It's terrible, I — isn't there anything I can do? Shall I go to the police and tell them it *was* an accident — that I was handing the jars to Dr Reid, and must have given him that jar as well as the others? I will if you think it would do any good. I'd do anything. It's too terrible.'

'But Dr Reid has sworn you weren't in the surgery.'

'No, I wasn't. But I might be able to persuade him to say that he said that to shield me.'

'That might lay you open to a charge of manslaughter,' Roger said slowly.

She brushed it aside with scorn. 'What does that matter? Anything's better than that Tom — Mr Bracey should be punished for something he didn't do.' She buried her face in her hands. 'He — they were my best friends. My only real friends in Marston.'

Roger leaned forward. 'Miss Berry,' he said distinctly, 'who did put that arsenic in the medicine-bottle?'

She dropped her hands abruptly, staring at him. 'Wh-what did you say?' she asked shakily.

'You think you know, don't you? Please tell me. It's a better way surely of clearing Mr Bracey by finding the real criminal than by your accusing yourself of all sorts of things you didn't do. Whom have you got in mind?'

She shook her head. 'You're mistaken, Mr Sheringham. I haven't anyone in mind. I — I only wish I had.'

Roger stared at her, puzzled. It was true that she was on the verge of hysterics, but even that could not account for the contradictory impression she gave. In spite of the firmness with which she uttered them Roger felt sure that her last words were a lie; she did suspect someone. Then if she were so anxious to clear Bracey, why not give the name?

Hurriedly Roger tried to find a set of circumstances to account for this reluctance. Was it possible that she had been lying all through — lying when she said that Bracey was an honourable man and there was no other woman? Was it possible that there *was* another woman and that Mrs Bracey had confided as much to her friend, that Miss Berry knew who this woman was and suspected her, but that she would not name her, thinking that this should be Bracey's decision and he must be the judge of whether he was to shoulder the responsibility or not? Such a theory postulated a guilty knowledge on the part of Bracey, but that was not impossible.

In any case Roger himself was bound by no such considerations, though acting as he was on behalf of Bracey it was not easy to know quite what to do. However, this was only theory. The first thing was to find out the truth; one could decide after that what to do with it.

'Miss Berry,' he said meaningly, 'are you sure you have told me all you wish to tell me?'

She started, and seemed to hesitate for a moment. 'Yes,' she answered, but in a not very certain voice. 'Yes.'

'I'd like to remind you that Mr Bracey is in grave danger.'

'He can't be!' she cried, with sudden passion. 'It's too preposterous. The police themselves will see that in a day or two. They'll release him. Of course they will. I mean, they *must*.'

She believes it too, Roger thought, marking the conviction in her voice. No, I can't frighten her; she's one of the ostrich type; she believes what she wants to believe, and that's all there is to it.

'May I see the surgery?' he asked.

Miss Berry took him through the hall and down a dark passage.

Roger inspected the business-like surgery with care. At his request Miss Berry pointed out to him the arsenic jar. It was on the top shelf and certainly above the jar of magnesium carbonate, but it was smaller and by no means so directly above the other as the evidence at the inquest had suggested. Even without the presence of magnesia in the medicine, it would have been an almost inconceivable mistake that one jar should have been taken down for the other. On asking, he learned that the relative positions of the jars had not been changed. Any lingering doubts about the possibility of an accident were dispelled.

Roger took Miss Berry back to the drawing-room, assuring her that he could see himself out.

The front door leading on to the small front garden was already ajar. As Roger pushed it wider he jumped for his life, for a loud explosion right in his ear nearly blew the hat off his head.

In the garden outside a small boy mocked him ecstatically.

'You jumped! I saw you. I made you jump. Sux!'

Roger regarded the revolting child coldly. The urchin appeared to be about ten years old, and he was excessively dirty even for that.

'Did you make that bang?' he asked.

'It was a booby-trap,' replied the small boy with pride. 'I knew you'd have to come out when you'd finished with Aunt Angela, so I put up a booby-trap for you. When you opened the door it went off. And you jumped like anything. Sux!'

'I have a way of dealing with unpleasant children who set booby-traps,' said Roger, and grasped the infant by the shoulder. 'Is there a nice thick stick anywhere around?'

'What for?'

'Because I'm going to beat you.'

'You're not,' asserted the child with confidence. 'No one beats me, not ever. Mummy doesn't let them. Uncle Robert wanted to beat me when I stayed here last year, but Aunt Angela wouldn't let him. When I go to school I'm going to one of those where they don't punish you. Mummy says so. She says it's bad for children to be punished. But I shall punish my children when I'm grown up. I shall punish them like billy-o.'

At that moment the agitated housemaid arrived round the corner of the house and relieved Roger of his charge. She was apologetic.

'Did he set a trap for you, sir? I'm ever so sorry. He's always doing it. Regular little demon, he is. Seems to like making people jump just for the fun of it.'

'I don't,' said the child indignantly. 'I do it because I'm going to be a doctor like Uncle Robert, and I have to begin studying their ractions.'

'A lot you know about such things, I'm sure.'

'I do. I know everything. If you jump far enough when a bang goes off, it's a raction, and you have to be cut open for it. You don't know anything, Effie.'

'It's thankful we'll all be when he's gone, sir,' confided the maid to Roger. 'He's a handful. Why only this morning I caught him in the surgery again. He'd got ever so many bottles down and was pretending to make up the medicines. What the doctor would say, I don't know.'

'I wasn't pretending,' shouted the outraged urchin. 'I was making up real medicine. Doctors have to know about medicines, don't they? And I can go in the surgery whenever I like. Aunt Angela said I can. So sux.'

'Well, my prescription,' said Roger to the housemaid, who really was a charmingly pretty girl, 'is six across the hinder parts with the whippiest switch you can find. Good-bye.'

He went on his way.

As he walked down the road, busy with his thoughts, he became aware that someone was asking him respectfully if he was Mr Sheringham, and admitted as much.

'Been looking everywhere for you, sir. Mr Dane, him as is butler at Silverdene, said for me to come and find you.'

'Yes?'

'I'm the gardener, sir, and Mr Dane was talking to me after you'd gone, and I told him I was working all that afternoon when the mistresses died, bedding out the asters. He thought you'd be interested to know.'

'It sounds most interesting; though I can't say asters have ever been favourites of mine. Is that all?'

'Well, Mr Dane thought you'd like to know, seeing you'd spoken to him about the drawing-room windows.'

'Oh!' Roger's expression changed. 'Where were you working then?'

'Why, in the bed up against the house there, just outside the drawing-room.'

'Were you there from three to four?'

'I was there from two till five, sir. I had to clear it a bit before I could get the plants in.'

'Hell!' said Roger.

The whole basis of all his theorising had gone at a blow.

He turned on his tracks and made for the High Street again and the office of the solicitor, his mind working furiously. As he reached the threshold he shrugged his shoulders and said aloud: 'Well, that *must* be the truth, then.'

He asked to see the head of the firm again.

The little elderly solicitor looked up with a wry smile. 'Well, Mr Sheringham? Have you solved our mystery yet?'

'Yes,' said Roger, and dropped into a chair.

'What's that? You have, eh? Bless my soul!' He adjusted his gold-rimmed glasses and peered at Roger dubiously.

Roger crossed his legs and gazed with apparently absorbed interest at the toe of his swinging foot. 'I have, yes. I must have, because it's the only possible explanation. But I've had to readjust my ideas rather considerably.' He recounted the gist of his interviews, and the theory he had based upon them.

'Assuming murder, you see, and taking for granted that the bottle, which had not passed out of Dr Reid's hands from the time it was filled until it was given to the boy to deliver, was uncontaminated when it reached the sick-room, and relying on my own judgment that none of the inmates of the house was guilty, I was left with only one possible inference — that the arsenic was inserted during the nurse's absence from three till four by someone from outside entering the house through the French windows in the drawing-room, the only apparently unguarded way in. But now we have the gardener's evidence that no one could have entered that way, and so we have to start again from the beginning.'

'Yes, yes,' nodded the other. 'I quite see that.'

'So having already proved that only during that period and in that way could the arsenic have been put into the bottle after it arrived at the house, we are obviously forced to the conclusion that it was *not* put in after it arrived at the house. In other words, it was already there.'

'God bless my soul! Then Dr Reid *did* . . .'

'On the other hand we have Dr Reid's positive assurance that he didn't and couldn't have: which I accept. Therefore it was introduced not by Dr Reid but by somebody else.'

'But I understand that the police are convinced the arsenic must have been inserted after the medicine reached the house, because the first two doses produced no symptoms of poisoning.'

'I think we can explain that. No, the real point of the case seems to me the fact that the medicine contained all the proper ingredients, plus the arsenic. You may say that this proves that the arsenic must have been inserted later, but does it?'

'You don't mean . . . that arsenic was already in the bottle before Dr Reid made the medicine up at all?'

Roger smiled. 'Well, isn't that feasible?'

'It's . . . just possible,' hesitated the solicitor. 'But hardly feasible, is it?'

'That depends upon who might have left the arsenic there.'

'But surely,' the solicitor objected, 'no one would be so criminally careless?'

'That again depends.' Roger thought for a moment. 'As to the first two doses not producing symptoms, a very simple explanation would be that the nurse didn't shake the bottle. Arsenic isn't readily soluble in water, and there couldn't have been a great deal in the medicine. It's a heavy powder, and it sank to the bottom, leaving only enough at the top of the bottle to produce mild discomfort. For the third dose the nurse obviously did shake the bottle.'

'Yes, yes,' approved the little solicitor. 'That is a sound point, without doubt. Perhaps the nurse may remember.'

'She may, but I doubt it.'

'But who put the arsenic in the bottle? That is our real puzzle after all.'

'I think,' said Roger, choosing his words, 'that I know who caused the arsenic to be put into the bottle. And how it was done. But I can't prove it. At this stage the responsible person would certainly deny it. I think . . . yes, I think I'll take a chance. May I borrow your telephone?'

He ruffled the pages of the local directory, and called a number.

'Marston 693? I want to speak to Miss Berry, please. It's urgent. Please tell her it's Mr Sheringham.' He waited.

'But what are you going to do?' asked the solicitor.

'Prove my case,' said Roger shortly. 'It's the only possible way. — Hullo! Yes? Is that Miss Berry? Listen, Miss Berry, please. You remember telling me that you'd do anything to clear Mr Bracey? Well I'm ringing up to advise you what you can do. Just write out the truth, the whole truth, and nothing but the truth, and post it to the police. Yes, I think you understand. I mean, how the arsenic got into the medicine. No, I know exactly; and in two hours' time I'm going to give my knowledge to the police. Not for two hours, I undertake. Let me show you that I really do know by telling you this: the mag. carb. pond. jar was washed out and refilled from the stock cupboard, to make sure that no traces remained. Isn't that so? I'm sure you understand. Put it all in your letter to the police, every detail. Otherwise Bracey will hang. Good-bye.'

He hung up the receiver.

'What is all this, Mr Sheringham? What is all this?'

Roger looked at him. 'Did you know that Miss Berry is hopelessly in love with Bracey?' he said abruptly. 'She is. And she's just the sort of person to believe just what she would like to believe. In this case she found no difficulty in believing that if Bracey hadn't a wife already, he would marry her. So that's why she took advantage of Mrs Bracey's gastro-enteritis to slip a couple of pinches of arsenic into the top of the mag. carb. pond. jar. The powders are much alike, you see, and so are the symptoms. She saw from the prescription book that there was no other medicine that morning requiring mag. carb. pond.; so if she emptied the jar as soon as Dr Reid had gone out, washed it clean, and refilled it, she would run no risk of poisoning anyone else. Ingenious, wasn't it?'

'Well, upon my word . . . but what did she say? What did she say?'

'Nothing. But I think she'll do it.'

'But you shouldn't have warned her,' squeaked the little solicitor. 'It was most improper. You should have laid the theory before the proper authorities. I don't know what to do at all.'

'Why, let her have her chance. If she doesn't take it, that's her affair. But let her have it. Though she's not really a very nice person. She had a second line of defence all prepared in the shape of a loathly nephew, whom she's obviously been encouraging to go into the surgery and play with the drugs. Very cunning. Too cunning. But let her have her chance.'

'Her chance? I don't understand. What chance?'

'I notice,' said Roger drily, 'that contrary to all the rules Dr Reid doesn't keep his poisons under lock and key.'

MIRIAM ALLEN de FORD

Homecoming

MIRIAM ALLEN de FORD *(1888 — 1975) wrote fantasy and crime fiction, and an excellent true-crime collection called* Murderers Sane and Mad. *'Homecoming' is a moving and simultaneously sickening account of the lynching in 1933 of J. M. Holmes and Thomas Thurmond for the murder of Brooke Hart in San José, California. This case also provided the basis of Fritz Lang's first film in America,* Fury *(1935).*

'Effen we don't git a hitch soon,' said Rilla, shifting her feet, 'I'm goin' to walk. My back's killin' me, standin' here like this.'

'I kain't walk, and that's flat.' Adoniram sprawled against the sign that said 'San Sebastian, 12 miles.' 'These shoes is all wore out, and they kain't walk no twelve miles. Gee, I wisht we had the flivver yet.'

'Well, we ain't,' answered Rilla briefly. She dived into the paper shopping-bag and brought out a crumpled blue handkerchief to wipe her face, sweating under the afternoon sun. She unbuttoned the old grey coat with its tan patches and its scabby fur collar that tickled her neck. Another car appeared over the top of the curve. Both of them stepped forward, arms out, thumbs rigidly upward.

Miraculously, the car stopped. It was a flivver, but a bright new one, with only a young man in the driver's seat. He grinned broadly at sight of them.

Rilla ignored the grin.

'Take us to San Sebastian, Mister?' she asked ingratiatingly. She smiled, showing the place in front where three teeth were missing.

The young man looked dubious. He started to shake his head, and against her will tears came into Rilla's eyes. He flushed uncomfortably and opened the door. With the other hand, surreptitiously, he pushed a newspaper over the shiny leather of the seat beside him.

'Well, all right,' he muttered ungraciously. 'Hop in.' Rilla clambered in by his side, while Adoniram, with the two bags, scrambled into the back seat. The young man frowned, swore quietly to himself, and started the car again.

'I'll set by you, so's we can talk,' said Rilla cordially. 'It's mighty nice of you, Mister, to take us along thataway. Niram and me was jest about walked out.'

Her flat drawl amused the driver. He edged a bit away from her, but glanced with a twinkle in his eye at the tall, lean woman with frizzy reddish hair showing under a man's cap.

'And where down south do *you* come from?' he inquired in a tone of patronising friendliness.

Rilla beamed. 'How'd you know that?' she exclaimed. 'We come from Geo'gie, but we been out here most a year now.'

'We come out in our flivver,' volunteered Adoniram from the rear seat, 'but it was plumb busted goin' across the desert, and we sold it for five dollars to a man in Arizony. Sence then we been hitch-hikin'.'

The driver twisted his head a little to catch a glimpse in the mirror of the queer-looking young man in overalls and an army coat. He wondered how old the boy was — his face seemed childish, yet his upper lip and chin were covered with soft, sparse black hairs, a first beard which had never known a razor.

'That your son?' he asked the woman beside him. Adoniram snickered and Rilla flushed.

'Niram and me's man and wife,' she said curtly.

'Oh, say, excuse me. Of course you are — I didn't get a good look,' mumbled the driver confusedly.

'I ain't but two years olde'n him, and he ain't but twenty-two. I been through a lot of hard work and a lot of hard weather, Mister, and I've bore three babies and had 'em die on me. That ain't no beauty treatment.'

'What mought your name and business be, Mister?' Adoniram interrupted. 'Ourn is Sprague, and we been workin' in the fruit. We don't rightly know what to call you.'

'Calvert's my name.'

'Calvert? There was some Calverts in the next county to us, wasn't there Rilla?'

'Sure; old Dud Calvert was the one married Ariana Blake and had all them ijjit kids, wasn't it?'

Their host did not look pleased. He changed the subject quickly.

'So you've been picking fruit, eh? See anything of the strike?'

'We was in it; we lived two months in a camp at Marshallville. We was in the fight they had at Varian, too; Niram, he got knocked down but he wasn't shot or hurt none. The ranch we was on, they were

all white — we don't aim to work with niggers or Greasers ever —
but they joined right in, and we went with 'em. Seems like it didn't
do no good, though, having white folks in it; they lost out jest the
same. The man that got killed was a Greaser, anyway, and that's one
blessin'. But it was jest as near as anything Niram and me wasn't
took to the jailhouse the night the deppities come and raided the camp.
We lit out the back way, across the tracks, and got a freight car out,
or we'd be settin' there now, sure as shootin'. I seen plenty of this
strikin' back home, when we was workin' in the mills after we left
the farm, and I don't hold with it — it don't do no good, with a lot
of furriners mixin' in — but this time it seemed like we was in it before
we knowed it.'

'You said it.' Calvert's voice warmed from patronage to
companionship. 'If the workingmen wouldn't want to hog the whole
works, they wouldn't need no strikes. Now, take me — I'm working
for a collection agency, see? Believe me, I know what it is to be out
of a job. There was nearly a year I thought I'd go crazy, with my
wife home to her mother's and the baby coming and everything.
What'd be the sense of me going out on strike just when I've got a
lousy job and am beginning to pay the bills and all? That's what I
say: treat the bosses decent and they'll treat you decent. Why, I bet
you folks had to leave home and come way out here on account of
a strike or something, with them Communists and all getting you into
it and leaving you holding the bag. Huh?'

'We left home on account of a lynchin' ', Adoniram proffered.
'They strung up a nigger and they was lookin' for me, sayin' I was
in on it.'

'Shet your mouth, you Niram,' snapped Rilla, turning to glare at
him. But Calvert only looked interested.

'A lynching, eh?' he said. 'Is that why you're going to San
Sebastian?'

'No – what do you mean? We're aimin' to git us a job in the spinich
or lettuce.'

'Gee, don't you ever read the papers? Don't you know what's going
on up there?'

'I ain't much for readin',' said the woman briefly, and her husband
giggled.

'Rilla, she kain't read,' he laughed meanly, 'only short words and
such. I kin, but I ain't seen no paper sence the Lord knows when.
What's goin' on?'

'Boy! There's going to be plenty doing in that town today!' With involuntary eagerness Calvert stepped up the speed to the limit, as a sign flashed by, 'San Sebastian, four miles.' 'Was I tickled when the boss told me maybe I'd better work San Sebastian today! He ain't going to get many collections made there, I'll tell him that in advance — I'm going to be plenty busy, and so is everybody in town.

'Why, it's this here Phillips kidnapping — you heard about that, didn't you? This rich boy Phillips that was kidnapped and murdered and they caught the fellow that done it, and he confessed? They got him in jail now, waiting the trial, and this morning they found the kid's body. This guy Slater had slugged him and dropped him overboard into the bay, and they been hunting ever since for his body. There was two fellows fishing hauled it out early this morning, and they're bringing it back to San Sebastian. I heard about it this morning over the radio while I was eating my breakfast. If that don't mean trouble for Friend Slater, then I ain't heard nothing talked about in San Sebastian the past week. I says to the wife this morning when I left, 'Expect me back when you see me, honey. I'm going to be busy today, and I bet I don't mean maybe.''

'You mean they're goin' to string this feller up?' Rilla gazed wide-eyed at the driver.

'I ain't sayin' one way or the other; all I say is, there's going to be plenty doing and I'm going to be there to see the fun. Want I should set you down where you'll be handy for the show? They got this guy in jail right in the centre of town.'

'A feller like that, they'd ought to boil him in oil!' Adoniram's voice cracked in his excitement. 'Is he a nigger — say, is he a nigger?'

'No, he ain't — he ain't even a foreigner or nothing — boy that grew up right there in town. Went to school with the Phillips kid's brother, even — that's how it was so easy to kidnap him, somebody told me. Funny how a guy that might be somebody you'd know yourself could turn out so mean, isn't it? Just plain, original sin — that's what the preacher said about it last Sunday in church, and I guess he's just about right.

'Well, here we are, folks. You never been here before? That there's the county courthouse, and across the alley is the jail where they got Slater. That building going up, the other side of the park, is the new postoffice. Want me to let you off here? Gee, there's a crowd in front of that jail already. See 'em?'

'Let us off by that there hot-dog place, Mister. We ain't et sence sun-up.' Adoniram's voice quivered with agitation and his pointed nose sniffed the air like a hound's. He handed both the bags to Rilla and she saddled herself with them with an air of accustomedness. Calvert gazed curiously at them as they climbed awkwardly out of the car. They started off without a word, and then Rilla stopped and came back to him.

'Thank you kindly, Mister,' she said. 'I take it right kind of you to give us a lift thataway.'

'Oh, that's all right.' Calvert flushed, caught in wiping off the seat with the crumpled newspaper. 'I'll be seeing you, I guess. I gotta make a bluff, anyway, at calling on some of these accounts, then I'll park the old flivver and come back to see the fun. There's going to be some, all right.'

He drove off, and the Spragues, unconscious of the glances that followed them, entered the little restaurant, dumped their bags by the counter, and gave themselves to the solemn business of gulping down hamburger sandwiches and coffee. At last they wiped their mouths with the backs of their hands. Rilla reached down in her coat-pocket for the leather purse in which their funds were kept, and they sauntered forth with the bright eyes of children in the lobby of a theatre. The lunch-counter man called them back; what about those bags, he said.

Rilla smiled engagingly through the gap in her upper jaw. The restaurant man, who had been suppressing giggles for ten minutes, was caught unawares. Embarrassed, he agreed to keep the bags back of the counter until they found a room. As soon as they had turned their backs again, he lifted the paper bags gingerly and deposited them in a back room where he kept a litter of out-worn rubbish. Then, before he returned to the counter, he washed his hands carefully at the sink in the kitchen.

'Did you pipe them?' he laughed to the fat man consuming ham and eggs at the end of the counter nearest the window. 'Did you ever see a pair like them?'

'Hill billies,' said the fat man, with his mouth full. Then they both sat looking out of the window at the scene across the little park.

Outside the jail, between the brick building and the grey stone of the courthouse, uniformed men were building a barricade of wood. As they hammered, a score of boys and young fellows crowded against them, calling and hooting. Everybody seemed good-natured, and there was much exchange of wisecracks. The crowd in the park, now increased to a hundred or so, was made up mostly of women and children, with a sprinkling of men. A baby was wailing and its mother jounced it up and down and crooned to it. Small boys chased one another near the barricade and back again. Some of the sightseers had eaten their lunch there, and the grass under the scattered elm trees was littered with scraps of paper.

The Spragues found themselves, irresistibly drawn, at the other side of the park, separated from the group at the growing barricade by the width of a street.

'We'd ought to be gittin' us a room for the night,' Rilla worried, tugging at Adoniram's sleeve. He shook his head impatiently; his nose quivering again like that of a pointer that sniffs prey.

'We'll git one in plenty of time,' he said irritably. 'The man'll keep our stuff till we come for it. I ain't leavin' here right now.'

The clock in the courthouse tower pointed to five. The crowd began to grow as stores and offices let out and the twilight darkened. The barricade had been finished and the sheriff's deputies had returned to the jail, slamming the heavy iron-bolted door behind them. But the group gathered there did not leave; most of them stood craning their necks, trying to locate the window behind which the kidnapper was cowering. One of them threw an experimental rock, which bounced harmlessly off the wall and brought to a downstairs window the head of Sheriff McKesson.

'You boys quit that!' he shouted, his face red. 'Get out, all of you, and go home, or there's going to be trouble.'

The little group of young fellows cat-called answers, and the cry spread to the crowd behind. People scrambled to their feet and surged forwards, some of them hooting in their turn. Rilla looked about and found a vacant spot under an elm. She let herself down heavily and sat resting her back against the tree; she wanted to take off her shoes and ease her tired bare feet, but she was afraid she would not be able to replace them quickly enough if there should be a rush. When she looked up again Adoniram was stepping off the curb, towards the jail.

'You Niram!' she shrilled after him. 'Don't you git yourself in no more trouble, now!'

He waved a hand airily and was lost in the growing crowd at the barricade. Rilla shrugged her coat around her in the twilight chill and fell into a half-doze of weariness. A low, growling chant jerked her eyes open.

The park was full now, though it was growing too dark to count the mob. The lights were on in the street and before the county buildings, and they cast long shadows of trees. The few lamps in the park were lost in the greater radiance of the street lights. It was the crowd in the park that was chanting; the group before the barricade was silent now.

'Phillips! Phillips! Phillips!' the crowd growled rhythmically. Some people were leaving, struggling out to the street, but more were coming. Rilla scrambled to her feet. A woman dragging a little boy by one hand came rushing up the path towards her.

'I heard they were going to bring Guy Phillips' body right here for everybody to look at!' she gasped. 'Is that right? Have they brung it?'

'I ain't seen nothin',' said Rilla, looking around vaguely.

'I heard they was going to bring Slater out and make him look at it. Ain't it terrible?' The woman's eyes glittered.

'I wanna go home! I wanna go home!' the little boy began to wail. His mother slapped him sharply on his cheek. 'Well, you can't' she snapped.

'Phillips! Phillips! Phillips!' chanted the mob in unison. From the jail came no sign of life, no sound.

Suddenly down the street between the park and the jail, from which traffic cops had been shooing away cars for an hour, rolled unimpeded a big limousine. It stopped, the door opened, and a slight, grey-haired man stood on the running-board and raised his arm.

'It's old Phillips — it's Guy Phillips' father!' ran a murmur through the park. There was a sudden silence and the man's voice was heard, trembling at first, then growing in urgency.

'Friends!' he said, 'Friends and neighbours! Two wrongs don't make a right. My boy's gone and nothing can bring him back.' He choked, shook his head, and went on. 'The man who killed him has confessed — he will be tried and convicted and sentenced just as soon as can possibly be done. I ask you to cooperate with the sheriff, to go away quietly. If you mean well by me, please help me to maintain law and order — don't disgrace our city and our state by any rash action!'

The group at the barricade pushed around the auto, jostling one another.

'How much law 'n' orduh did this here Slater give *you*, Mister?' jeered a voice. Rilla recognised it instantly and craned forward, but she could see nothing over the heads of the crowd between.

The father ignored the interruption. He raised his head to speak again, but a tall young man with heavy shoulders stood out in the glare of the headlights and called determinedly, 'It's no use, Mr Phillips — we're not going.'

Phillips turned and looked steadily at him, and the young man advanced farther, laying his hand on the older man's arm.

'We're not going,' he said again firmly. 'You'd better be leaving, Mr Phillips; we don't want you here if any trouble starts.'

'The sheriff — ' Phillips began hesitatingly.

'We'll take care of McKesson,' said the young man, and there was an answering murmur from his companions. The father threw out his arms in a gesture of despair, then climbed feebly back into the car and motioned the chauffeur to leave. As he turned the corner, a few scattered cheers followed him from the park. As if they were a signal, a sudden rain of pebbles and rocks dashed against the jail. There was a tinkle of glass as a window broke.

The sheriff's angry face appeared again, this time with the head of Clancy, his chief deputy, behind it.

'For the last time,' roared McKesson, 'I order you to disperse. If you're not out of here in five minutes, I'm going to use tear gas!'

Nobody moved at the barricade, but the sheriff's words had carried, and there was an uneasy moving in the crowd in which Rilla was wedged. One or two near her squirmed out and began slowly to work their way towards the edge. Before the gaps could close Rilla had found herself at last in the very front line, where she could see and hear everything. She wished she had taken her blue handkerchief from the paper bag at the restaurant; she sniffed, and pushed her scabby fur collar around her face, as if she smelt already the penetrating gas.

A man appeared from the darkness, ran to the barricade, and wormed his way to the young fellow who had ordered Phillips to leave. For a minute they whispered together, then the young man nodded. The newcomer gave a signal, and again a shower of rocks broke against the jail.

Suddenly all the first floor windows on the side facing the street were thrown up sharply, and at each appeared a uniformed man. A pebble, smartly thrown, hit one of them in the chest; he grunted and grabbed at the place. McKesson turned purple with rage.

'All right, boys, let 'em have it!' he yelled. In an instant the air was full of bombs thrown from the windows.

The pungent gas did its work quickly. Choking and coughing, their faces streaming with tears, the group at the barricade retreated first. Then the gas reached the park, and in a panic the mob began to move backwards. Somebody stepped hard on Rilla's right foot; an elbow jabbed at her side. She hid her face in her arm, wiping the tears away, while with the other arm she clung to the nearest elm tree lest she be trampled down. She could see no sign of Adoniram; in fact she could see nothing at all for the blinding tears. By the time she could look around again, the sound of running feet brought her, with a hundred others, back to the curb.

The assailants at the barricade had retreated only as far as the postoffice under construction at the corner. A dozen of them were returning, armed with a long, heavy wooden beam. The noise brought the windows open once more. Another storm of bombs met their advance. But now they were too angry to care. Shaking their heads, wiping off tears with free hands as they ran, they came on relentlessly. There was a splintering of wood as the barricade broke. The crowd in the park, caught by the infection of excitement, dashed after them. A few more bombs hurtled from the windows, and then they were abruptly shut again.

'Come on, fellows!' yelled a voice from the barricade, hoarse from the gas. 'That's all they've got! All together now, before McKesson gets reinforcements!'

'Stand back!' yelled one of the men with the heavy beam. 'Give us room!'

The crowd around him retreated a few steps, and cleared Rilla's view again. She saw Adoniram, his sleeve almost torn from his coat, holding firmly to one end of the beam. There was a deafening thud as it struck the door. The door shook visibly, but remained intact.

'Why don't you shoot McKesson?' called a jeering voice behind Rilla. The crowd took up the cry in derision. They knew McKesson would not shoot. They were his townsmen, they had elected him; he was not going to risk his career for the sake of a rat like Slater. A woman somewhere began screaming hysterically. Somebody else laughed, and would not stop laughing. Suddenly silence fell, as once more the heavy beam shook the door.

The third blow splintered it. With a yell the men dropped the beam and rushed forward. Stumbling over debris, the crowd followed at their backs.

But inside the wooden door stood another door of wire mesh. Behind it McKesson and his deputies could be seen standing. The sheriff made one more appeal.

'Boys,' he pleaded, 'let me do my duty, won't you? Please go away and let me do my duty! I don't want to have to shoot anybody.'

'You ain't goin' to shoot nobody — you taken away your men's guns — I seen you do it.' That was Niram's voice; he was in the front rank, as he had been that time in Georgia. Rilla felt a little shiver of mingled apprehension and pride. The folks back home that called Niram shiftless — they ought to see him now.

'Let me through!' A short stocky fellow who had helped man the beam elbowed his way forward. In his hand showed a big clasp knife, like a sailor's. Willing arms pushed him up to the heavy wire screen. It took only a minute to rip it from top to bottom.

The men surged forward, but the newcomer who had whispered to the broad-shouldered young man blocked the entrance with his arms. He was older than most of them, and, excited as they were, his voice carried authority.

'Ten's all we need,' he ordered. 'There ain't but four deputies here, besides the sheriff. We'll bring Slater out to you, don't you worry. Ten of you men come with me.'

From the scramble ten men at last won their way to the front, Sprague among them. The sheriff, helpless, stood in silence with his men.

'All right, McKesson,' said the leader curtly. 'Show us which is Slater's cell.'

The sheriff shrugged his shoulders in resignation.

'I've done the best I could,' he said. 'Take 'em up, Clancy. And you other men go around and tell the rest of the prisoners not to worry, nothing's going to happen to them. I guess they're plenty scared.'

Through the broken door Rilla, her eyes goggling, could see it all. She saw three of them, led by Clancy, start up the stairs — Adoniram was one of them. She saw McKesson, turning sharply, reach for the phone in the hall. And she saw the broad-shouldered man shoot out his fist and catch the sheriff neatly on the point of the jaw. McKesson slumped in a heap. The watching mob yelled. Their yells became articulate, resolved themselves into a new chant, like the yelp of a pack: 'Slater! Bring out Slater!' It spread beyond the range of hearing of those at the front.

Upstairs there was a noise of scuffling. 'Give me them keys, you double-crosser!' somebody cried. There was a bump. The deputy Clancy, breathing hard, and blood running down his face from a cut on the scalp, half-staggered down the steps and stood against the wall, gazing dumbly at his unconscious chief.

The crowd yelled again.

Then there came a babble, a high hysterical chatter. It was shut off peremptorily by the sound of a blow. Then it began again, and choked into a gurgle.

'Look out below!' called one of the men above. Then three of them appeared, heaving and pulling at something tied by a rope. It was a man, being dragged headfirst down the stairs. At every step his head bumped, and he clawed ineffectually at the treads. His shirt was torn from his body, and one leg of his trousers was ripped and flapped behind him. At the bottom of the flight the men seized him and pulled him upright. His head sagged, but the cheek that showed was bloody, and an eye, gouged from its socket, fell down grotesquely upon it. His dark hair was wet and matted, and his chest pumped in agony as he tried to breathe. The roar of the mob was thunderous.

Rilla stood right by him as he was hustled through the crowd — near enough to rip a button from his tattered shirt, which she grasped tightly in her fist. The leaders were making for a tree in the centre of the park. Already a man stood beside it, throwing over a big limb one end of a coil of new-looking rope. A lamp stood near it, and lighted the spot like a stage. Slater was dumped like a sack of coal at the foot of the tree. Adoniram was the last to let go of him. For a minute the three men stood gasping for breath, the sweat on their faces glimmering in the light.

The oldest of the leaders kicked the recumbent heap.

'Well, you,' he said contemptuously, 'got anything to say before we string you up?'

'He can't talk,' piped a kid's voice. 'He's got a rope around his neck.' A few persons laughed, but silence had fallen upon the crowd as a whole. The man stooped and untied the rope, tugging at the knot. He pulled the wretched creature to a sitting position, and kicked him again.

Slater seemed to gather all his strength into a final effort.

'Don't kill me, boys!' he croaked in a voice so weak that only those as close as Rilla could hear him at all. 'I didn't do it! I — I — ' He stopped.

Rilla felt her heart pound with a sudden urgency. Hardly knowing what she did, she leaned forward and spat full in the bloody face. She straightened up, feeling confused, her head light and giddy. She saw Adoniram, his face white, his eyes shining, holding one shoulder of the doomed man.

Then everything happened at once. The new rope was fastened about Slater's scarred neck; the crowd screamed and howled incoherently; half a dozen men heaved on the rope till it hung over the limb, seven feet from the ground, with Slater dangling from it. Without a word a heavy-set, well-dressed man stepped out from the crowd, deliberately flicked a thumb over a cigarette-lighter until the flame came, and applied it to the edge of the torn trousers. It flared for a minute, them smouldered and smoked. There was no further sound from Slater; he seemed already dead.

The woman Rilla had spoken to before lifted her little boy high above her head.

'Look, Tommy, look!' she commanded. 'There's something you might never see again in all your born days!'

The child, frightened, tried in vain to hide his face in his mother's hair.

Far back in the crowd, a deep, solemn voice kept intoning tirelessly: 'Thou shalt not kill! Vengeance is mine, saith the Lord. Thou shalt not kill!' It made a sort of background for the confused uproar.

A girl in a fur coat, her heavy make-up fantastic in the light, darted out to the feet of the hanging man, and shook her fist at him.

'How do you like it up there, you bastard?' she shrieked. 'How do you like it? *We* like it — oh, you bet, we like it fine!'

Her spike heels beat a tattoo as she danced about the tree. Rilla, watching her feverishly, saw her dash suddenly towards the little knot of men still standing where they had hanged Slater. She saw Niram, a fixed grin distorted his mouth, reach out his arm towards her. Rilla felt herself trembling. But before she could move a muscle, the scene was over. A murmur grew from the farther edge of the mob. Those near the trees stood transfixed, and through the crowd pushed twenty uniformed policemen.

They were the first, outside of traffic cops minding their own business imperviously at the corners, who had been seen near the jail since the crowd had gathered that afternoon.

Now, however, they pushed forward efficiently, swinging their clubs freely. 'Keep moving, keep moving,' they ordered monotonously. The mob disintegrated, all at once broken up into individuals, individuals who edged away from the magnet which had welded them.

Rilla found herself being shoved and herded. People were moving, but as they passed the tree and its burden nearly everyone, whatever his haste or his fear of the threatening club behind him, snatched at some morsel of the prey. By the time Rilla, labouring for breath, her cap jammed over her eyes, had fought her way to the outer edge of the park, across the street from the still-open restaurant, the body of Slater was practically naked, every bit of his clothes seized for souvenirs. Bark had been stripped from the tree; every leaf that grew within reach was gone. The policemen, unable to untie the rope, had cut it off and lowered the corpse to the trampled ground; and as Rilla stood uncertainly, pushing back her cap to peer around for her husband, the undertaker's car sped by her to gather up what was left of a man.

As she waited still, one eye on the restaurant where their bags were held, almost the last of the crowd, a flivver stopped and Calvert, the man who had given them a lift that afternoon, hailed her. It seemed a million years ago.

'Where's your husband?' Calvert called.

'I kain't figger out *where* he is,' Rilla quavered. She was very tired all at once and wanted desperately to find a bed. Her anger at Adoniram, which had shaken her when she saw the look he gave that painted hussy capering before him, suddenly fell and was succeeded by alarm. Had he got in wrong again, the way he did that time back home? 'You think maybe they taken him to the jailhouse?' she asked pitifully.

'Naw, they ain't arresting anybody,' Calvert reassured her. 'They're just clearing the park. You were real near, weren't you? I couldn't get close enough to see any of the fun . . .Look, here comes your man now.'

Adoniram, weaving slightly, had turned the corner. Rilla sniffed; she might have known it.

'Hello, folks.' He waved a hand limply. 'Reckon you worried I got lost, Rilla, huh? One of them fellers I was with, he bought me a drink.'

'*A* drink!' snorted Rilla derisively. But she was too tired to argue. She had the pocketbook, anyway — she felt apprehensively to be sure it was safe. Calvert was lamenting his bad luck again. 'Me, I didn't even get a souvenir to take home to the wife — that's how close *I* got!'

The liquor had made Adoniram generous.

'Here,' he said, reaching into his coat. It had only one sleeve now; the other had finally been torn off completely. From an inner pocket he brought a shred of cloth. 'This here's off his pants,' he explained. 'You can have it. I got a piece of the rope, too.'

'I got a button off his shirt,' said Rilla proudly. All at once she felt amiable and sleepy. She plucked at Adoniram's one sleeve. 'Come on, Niram,' she urged, 'the man over there'll be closin' up, and we gotta git our things. It's gittin' late, and we ain't got us a room yet to stay in.'

'Jest a minute, woman, jest a minute.' Adoniram was deep in conversation with Calvert. 'And when we got up there, this feller he showed us the cell, but he wouldn't give us the key — no, sir, he plumb wouldn't. So one of the fellers, he slugged him and taken his keys away from him. And d'you know where this feller Slater was hidin?' You'd never think in a million years. He was hangin' by his hands 'way up on the gratin' of his winder; like as if we couldn't see him there! You can bet we pulled him down in a right smart hurry. I got holt of his leg, and — '

Calvert was listening, all agog, but now he suddenly glanced at the courthouse clock.

'Jesus!' he said. 'I gotta be on my way. My wife'll have the cops out looking for me. So long! Ask the guy in the hot-dog place for a rooming-house — he'll show you one. Well, good luck, folks! Some day, wasn't it?'

He was off, leaving them alone on the deserted street. Adoniram yawned.

'Come on, Rilla,' he ordered. 'I'm hungrier'n I am sleepy. Less git us another hamburger, 'n' then we kin find us a bed. That feller, he sure told the truth. Ain't this been a day for your life, though? You know, I kinda like this town; I reckon we'll stay here a while. What say?'

'It's sure got up-and-standin' people in it,' Rilla agreed, as they moved towards the restaurant. 'It sure makes me feel plumb like home.'

HARLAN ELLISON

The Whimper of Whipped Dogs

HARLAN ELLISON *(born 1934) is best known as a hard-hitting and brilliant writer of horror/fantasy/crime/science fiction — he defies categorisation. "'The Whimper of Whipped Dogs" is based on the murder of Kitty Genovese,' he writes. 'The case is now so famous, it's obsessed me . . . Woman terrified to death in the streets of New York's Kew Gardens section while thirty-eight people watched from their window, heard her screams for help, did nothing . . . It took the rapist killer over half an hour to slice her up as she dragged herself around almost a full city block. They could have saved her. They didn't. I was never satisfied with the intellectual theories about why no one aided her . . . It was the kind of situation that could only be explained in terms of magic realism, fantasy.' The story was awarded an 'Edgar' by the Mystery Writers of America as the best crime story of the year, and it provides a stunningly powerful climax to this collection.*

On the night after the day she had stained the louvred window shutters of her new apartment on East 52nd Street, Beth saw a woman slowly and hideously knifed to death in the courtyard of her building. She was one of twenty-six witnesses to the ghoulish scene, and, like them, she did nothing to stop it.

She saw it all, every moment of it, without break and with no impediment to her view. Quite madly, the thought crossed her mind as she watched in horrified fascination, that she had the sort of marvelous line of observation Napoleon had sought when he caused to have constructed at the *Comédie-Francaise* theatres, a curtained box at the rear, so he could watch the audience as well as the stage. The night was clear, the moon was full, she had just turned off the 11.30 movie on Channel 2 after the second commercial break, realising she had already seen Robert Taylor in *Westward the Women*, and had disliked it the first time; and the apartment was quite dark.

She went to the window, to raise it six inches for the night's sleep, and she saw the woman stumble into the courtyard. She was sliding along the wall, clutching her left arm with her right hand. Con Ed had installed mercury-vapor lamps on the poles; there had been sixteen assaults in seven months; the courtyard was illuminated with a chill purple glow that made the blood streaming down the woman's left arm look black and shiny. Beth saw every detail with utter clarity, as though magnified a thousand power under a microscope, solarized as if it had been a television commercial.

The woman threw back her head, as if she were trying to scream, but there was no sound. Only the traffic on First Avenue, late cabs foraging for singles paired for the night at Maxwell's Plum and Friday's and Adam's Apple. But that was over there, beyond. Where *she* was, down there seven floors below, in the courtyard, everything seemed silently suspended in an invisible force-field.

Beth stood in the darkness of her apartment, and realised she had raised the window completely. A tiny balcony lay just over the low sill; now not even glass separated her from the sight; just the wrought-iron balcony railing and seven floors to the courtyard below.

The woman staggered away from the wall, her head still thrown back, and Beth could see she was in her mid-thirties, with dark hair cut in a shag; it was impossible to tell if she was pretty: terror had contorted her features and her mouth was a twisted black slash, opened but emitting no sound. Cords stood out in her neck. She had lost one shoe, and her steps were uneven, threatening to dump her to the pavement.

The man came around the corner of the building, into the courtyard. The knife he held was enormous – or perhaps it only seemed so: Beth remembered a bone-handled fish knife her father had used one summer at the lake in Maine: it folded back on itself and locked, revealing eight inches of serrated blade. The knife in the hand of the dark man in the courtyard seemed to be similar.

The woman saw him and tried to run, but he leaped across the distance between them and grabbed her by the hair and pulled her head back as though he would slash her throat in the next reaper-motion.

Then the woman screamed.

The sound skirled up into the courtyard like bats trapped in an echo chamber, unable to find a way out, driven mad. It went on and on and on . . .

The man struggled with her and she drove her elbows into his sides and he tried to protect himself, spinning her around by her hair, the terrible scream going up and up and never stopping. She came loose and he was left with a fistful of hair torn out by the roots. As she spun out he slashed straight across and opened her up just below the breasts. Blood sprayed through her clothing and the man was soaked; it seemed to drive him even more berserk. He went at her again, as she tried to hold herself together, the blood pouring down over her arms.

She tried to run, teetered against the wall, slid sidewise, and the man struck the brick surface. She was away, stumbling over a flower bed, falling, getting to her knees as he threw himself on her again. The knife came up in a flashing arc that illuminated the blade strangely with purple light. And still she screamed.

Lights came on in dozens of apartments and people appeared at windows.

He drove the knife to the hilt into her back, high on the right shoulder. He used both hands.

Beth caught it all in jagged flashes — the man, the woman, the knife, the blood, the expressions on the faces of those watching from the windows. Then lights clicked off in the windows, but they still stood there, watching.

She wanted to yell, to scream, 'What are you doing to that woman?' But her throat was frozen, two iron hands that had been immersed in dry ice for ten thousand years clamped around her neck. She could feel the blade sliding into her own body.

Somehow — it seemed impossible but there it was down there, happening somehow — the woman struggled erect and *pulled* herself off the knife. Three steps, she took three steps and fell into the flower bed again. The man was howling now, like a great beast, the sounds inarticulate, bubbling up from his stomach. He fell on her and the knife went up and came down, then again, and again, and finally it was all a blur of motion, and her scream of lunatic bats went on till it faded off and was gone.

Beth stood in the darkness, trembling and crying, the sight filling her eyes with horror. And when she could no longer bear to look at what he was doing down there to the unmoving piece of meat over which he worked, she looked up and around at the windows of darkness where the others still stood — even as she stood — and somehow she could see their faces, bruise-purple with the dim light from the mercury lamps, and there was a universal sameness to their expressions. The women stood with their nails biting into the upper arms of their men, their tongues edging from the corners of their mouths; the men were wild-eyed and smiling. They all looked as though they were at cock fights. Breathing deeply. Drawing some sustenance from the grisly scene below. An exhalation of sound, deep, deep, as though from caverns beneath the earth. Flesh pale and moist.

And it was then that she realised the courtyard had grown foggy, as though mist off the East River had rolled up 52nd Street in a veil that would obscure the details of what the knife and the man were still doing . . . endlessly doing it . . . long after there was any joy in it . . . still doing it . . . again and again . . .

But the fog was unnatural, thick and grey and filled with tiny scintillas of light. She stared at it, rising up in the empty space of the courtyard. Bach in the cathedral, stardust in a vacuum chamber.

Beth saw eyes.

There, up there, at the ninth floor and higher, two great eyes as surely as night and the moon, there were *eyes*. And — a face? Was that a face, could she be sure, was she imagining it . . . a face? In the roiling vapors of chill fog something lived, something brooding and patient and utterly malevolent had been summoned up to witness what was happening down there in the flower bed. Beth tried to look away, but could not. The eyes, those primal burning eyes, filled with abysmal antiquity yet frighteningly bright and anxious like the eyes of a child; eyes filled with tomb depths, ancient and new, chasm-filled, burning, gigantic and deep as an abyss, holding her, compelling her. The shadow play was being staged not only for the tenants in their windows, watching and drinking of the scene, but for some *other*. Not on frigid tundra or waste moors, not in subterranean caverns or on some faraway world circling a dying sun, but here, in the city, here the eyes of that *other* watched.

Shaking with the effort, Beth wrenched her eyes from those burning depths up there beyond the ninth floor, only to see again the horror that had brought that *other*. And she was struck for the first time by the awfulness of what she was witnessing, she was released from the immobility that had held her like a coelacanth in shale, she was filled with the blood thunder pounding against the membranes: she had *stood* there! She had done nothing, nothing! A woman had been butchered and she had said nothing, done nothing. Tears had been useless, tremblings had been pointless, she *had done nothing*!

Then she heard hysterical sounds midway between laughter and giggling, and as she stared up into that great face rising in the fog and chimneysmoke of the night, she heard *herself* making those deranged gibbon noises and from the man below a pathetic, trapped sound, like the whimper of whipped dogs.

She was staring up into that face again. She hadn't wanted to see it again — ever. But she was locked with those smoldering eyes, overcome with the feeling that they were childlike, though she *knew* they were incalculably ancient.

Then the butcher below did an unspeakable thing and Beth reeled with dizziness and caught the edge of the window before she could tumble out onto the balcony; she steadied herself and fought for breath.

She felt herself being looked at, and for a long moment of frozen terror she feared she might have caught the attention of that face up there in the fog. She clung to the window, feeling everything growing faraway and dim, and stared straight across the court. She *was* being watched. Intently. By the young man in the seventh-floor window across from her own apartment. Steadily, he was looking at her. Through the strange fog with its burning eyes feasting on the sight below, he was staring at her.

As she felt herself blacking out, in the moment before unconsciousness the thought flickered and fled that there was something terribly familiar about his face.

It rained the next day. East 52nd Street was slick and shining with oil rainbows. The rain washed the dog turds into the gutters and nudged them down and down to the catch-basin openings. People bent against the slanting rain, hidden beneath umbrellas, looking like enormous, scurrying black mushrooms. Beth went out to get the newspapers after the police had come and gone.

The news reports dwelled with loving emphasis on the twenty-six tenants of the building who had watched in cold interest as Leona Ciarelli, 37, of 455 Fort Washington Avenue, Manhattan, had been systematically stabbed to death by Burton H. Wells, 41, an unemployed electrician, who had subsequently been shot to death by two off-duty police officers when he burst into Michael's Pub on 55th street, covered with blood and brandishing a knife that authorities later identified as the murder weapon.

She had thrown up twice that day. Her stomach seemed incapable of retaining anything solid, and the taste of bile lay along the back of her tongue. She could not blot the scenes of the night before from her mind; she re-ran them again and again, every movement of that reaper arm playing over and over as though on a short loop of memory. The woman's head thrown back for silent screams. The blood. Those eyes in the fog.

She was drawn again and again to the window, to stare down into the courtyard and the street. She tried to superimpose over the bleak Manhattan concrete the view from her window in Swann House at Bennington: the little yard and another white, frame dormitory; the fantastic apple trees; and from the other window the rolling hills and gorgeous Vermont countryside; her memory skittered through the change of seasons. But there was always concrete and the rain-slick streets; the rain on the pavement was black and shiny as blood.

She tried to work, rolling up the tambour closure of the old rolltop desk she had bought on Lexington Avenue and hunching over the graph sheets of choreographer's charts. But Labanotation was merely a Jackson Pollock jumble of arcane hieroglyphics to her today, instead of the careful representation of eurhythmics she had studied four years to perfect. And before that, Farmington.

The phone rang. It was the secretary from the Taylor Dance Company, asking when she would be free. She had to beg off. She looked at her hand, lying on the graph sheets of figures Laban had devised, and she saw her fingers trembling. She had to beg off. Then she called Guzman at the Downtown Ballet Company, to tell him she would be late with the charts.

'My God, lady, I have ten dancers sitting in a rehearsal hall getting their leotards sweaty! What do you expect me to do?'

She explained what had happened the night before. And as she told him, she realised the newspapers had been justified in holding that tone against the twenty-six witnesses to the death of Leona Ciarelli. Paschal Guzman listened, and when he spoke again, his voice was several octaves lower, and he spoke more slowly. He said he understood and she could take a little longer to prepare the charts. But there was a distance in his voice, and he hung up while she was thanking him.

She dressed in an argyle sweater vest in shades of dark purple, and a pair of fitted khaki gabardine trousers. She had to go out, to walk around. To do what? To think about other things. As she pulled on the Fred Braun chunky heels, she idly wondered if that heavy silver bracelet was still in the window of Georg Jensen's. In the elevator, the young man from the window across the courtyard stared at her. Beth felt her body begin to tremble again. She went deep into the corner of the box when he entered behind her.

Between the fifth and fourth floor, he hit the *off* switch and the elevator jerked to a halt.

Beth stared at him and he smiled innocently.

'Hi. My name's Gleeson, Ray Gleeson, I'm in 714.'

She wanted to demand he turn the elevator back on, by what right did he pre*sume* to do such a thing, what did he mean by this, turn it on at once or suffer the consequences. That was what she *wanted* to do. Instead, from the same place she had heard the gibbering laughter the night before, she heard her voice, much smaller and much less possessed than she had trained it to be, saying, 'Beth O'Neill, I live in 701.'

The thing about it was, was that *the elevator was stopped*. And she was frightened. But he leaned against the panelled wall, very well dressed, shoes polished, hair combed and probably blown dry with a hand drier, and he *talked* to her as if they were across a table at L'Argenteuil. 'You just moved in, huh?'

'About two months ago.'

'Where did you go to school? Bennington or Sarah Lawrence?'

'Bennington. How did you know?'

He laughed, and it was a nice laugh. 'I'm an editor at a religious book publisher; every year we get half a dozen Bennington, Sarah Lawrence, Smith girls. They come hopping in like grasshoppers, ready to revolutionise the publishing industry.'

'What's wrong with that? You sound like you don't care for them.'

'Oh, I *love* them, they're marvelous. They think they know how to write better than the authors we publish. Had one darlin' little item who was given galleys of three books to proof, and she rewrote all three. I think she's working as a table-swabber in Horn & Hardart's now.'

She didn't reply to that. She would have pegged him as an anti-feminist, ordinarily, if it had been anyone else speaking. But the eyes. There was something terribly familiar about his face. She was enjoying the conversation; she rather liked him.

'What's the nearest big city to Bennington?'

'Albany, New York. About sixty miles.'

'How long does it take to drive here?'

'From Bennington? About an hour and a half.'

'Must be a nice drive, that Vermont country, really pretty. They went coed, I understand. How's that working out?'

'I don't know, really.'

'You don't know?'

'It happened around the time I was graduating.'

'What did you major in?'

'I was a dance major, specialising in Labanotation. That's the way you write choreography.'

'It's all electives, I gather. You don't have to take anything required, like sciences, for example.' He didn't change his tone as he said, 'That was a terrible thing last night. I saw you watching. I guess a lot of us were watching. It was a really terrible thing.'

She nodded dumbly. Fear came back.

'I understand the cops got him. Some nut, they don't even know why he killed her, or why he went charging into that bar. It was really an awful thing. I'd very much like to have dinner with you one night soon, if you're not attached.'

'That would be all right.'

'Maybe Wednesday. There's an Argentinian place I know. You might like it.'

'That would be all right.'

'Why don't you turn on the elevator, and we can go,' he said, and smiled again. She did it, wondering why he had stopped the elevator in the first place.

On her third date with him, they had their first fight. It was at a party thrown by a director of television commercials. He lived on the ninth floor of their building. He had just done a series of spots for *Sesame Street* (the letters 'U' for Underpass, 'T' for Tunnel, lower-case 'b' for boats, 'c' for cars; the numbers 1 to 20; the words *light* and *dark*) and was celebrating his move from the arena of commercial tawdriness (and its attendant $75,000 a year) to the sweet fields of educational programming (and its accompanying descent into low-pay respectability). There was a logic in his joy Beth could quite understand, and when she talked with him about it, in a far corner of the kitchen, his arguments didn't seem to parse. But he seemed happy, and his girlfriend, a long-legged ex-model from Philadelphia, continued to drift to him and away from him, like some exquisite undersea plant, touching his hair and kissing his neck, murmuring words of pride and barely submerged sexuality. Beth found it bewildering, though the celebrants were all bright and lively.

In the living room, Ray was sitting on the arm of the sofa, hustling a stewardess named Luanne. Beth could tell he was hustling; he was trying to look casual. When he *wasn't* hustling, he was always intense, about everything. She decided to ignore it, and wandered around the apartment, sipping at a Tanqueray and tonic.

There were framed prints of abstract shapes clipped from a calendar printed in Germany. They were in metal Bonniers frames.

In the dining room a huge door from a demolished building somewhere in the city had been handsomely stripped, teaked and refinished. It was now the dinner table.

A Lightolier fixture attached to the wall over the bed swung out, levered up and down, tipped, and its burnished globe-head revolved a full three hundred and sixty degrees.

She was standing in the bedroom, looking out the window, when she realised *this* had been one of the rooms in which light had gone on, gone off; one of the rooms that had contained a silent watcher at the death of Leona Ciarelli.

When she returned to the living room, she looked around more carefully. With only three or four exceptions — the stewardess, a young married couple from the second floor, a stockbroker from Hemphill, Noyes — *everyone* at the party had been a witness to the slaying.

'I'd like to go,' she told him.

'Why, aren't you having a good time?' asked the stewardess, a mocking smile crossing her perfect little face.

'Like all Bennington ladies,' Ray said, answering for Beth, 'she is enjoying herself most by not enjoying herself at all. It's a trait of the anal retentive. Being here in someone else's apartment, she can't empty ashtrays or rewind the toilet paper roll so it doesn't hand a tongue, and being tightassed, her nature demands we go.

'All right, Beth, let's say our goodbyes and take off. The Phantom Rectum strikes again.'

She slapped him and the stewardess's eyes widened. But the smile remained frozen where it had appeared.

He grabbed her wrist before she could do it again. 'Garbanzo beans, baby,' he said, holding her wrist tighter than necessary.

They went back to her apartment, and after sparring silently with kitchen cabinet doors slammed and the television being tuned too loud, they got to her bed, and he tried to perpetuate the metaphor by fucking her in the ass. He had her on elbows and knees before she realised what he was doing; she struggled to turn over and he rode her bucking and tossing without a sound. And when it was clear to him that she would never permit it, he grabbed her breast from underneath and squeezed so hard she howled in pain. He dumped her on her back, rubbed himself between her legs a dozen times, and came on her stomach.

Beth lay with her eyes closed and an arm thrown across her face.

She wanted to cry, but found she could not. Ray lay on her and said nothing. She wanted to rush to the bathroom and shower, but he did not move, till long after his semen had dried on their bodies.

'Who did you date at college?' he asked.

'I didn't date anyone very much.' Sullen.

'No heavy makeouts with wealthy lads from Williams and Dartmouth . . . no Amherst intellectuals begging you to save them from creeping faggotry by permitting them to stick their carrots in your sticky little slit?'

'Stop it!'

'Come on, baby, it couldn't all have been knee socks and little round circle-pins. You don't expect me to believe you didn't get a little mouthful of cock from time to time. It's only, what? about fifteen miles to Williamstown? I'm sure the Williams werewolves were burning the highway to your cunt on weekends; you can level with old Uncle Ray . . .'

'*Why are you like this?!*' She started to move, to get away from him, and he grabbed her by the shoulder, forced her to lie down again. Then he rose up over her and said, 'I'm like this because I'm a New Yorker, baby. Because I live in this fucking city every day. Because I have to play patty-cake with the ministers and other sanctified holy-joe assholes who want their goodness and lightness tracts published by the Blessed Sacrament Publishing and Storm Window Company of 277 Park Avenue, when what I *really* want to do is toss the stupid psalm-suckers out the thirty-seventh-floor window and listen to them quote chapter-and-worse all the way down. Because I've lived in this great big snapping dog of a city all my life and I'm mad as a mudfly, for chrissakes!'

She lay unable to move, breathing shallowly, filled with a sudden pity and affection for him. His face was white and strained, and she knew he was saying things to her that only a bit too much Almadén and exact timing would have let him say.

'What do you expect from me,' he said, his voice softer now, but no less intense, 'do you expect kindness and gentility and understanding and a hand on *your* hand when the smog burns your eyes? I can't do it, I haven't got it. No one has it in this cesspool of a city. Look around you; what do you think is happening here? They take rats and they put them in boxes and when there are too many of them, some of the little fuckers go out of their minds and start knawing the rest to death. *It ain't no different here, baby!* It's rat time for everybody in this madhouse. You can't expect to jam as many people into this stone thing as we do, with buses and taxis and dogs shitting themselves scrawny and noise night and day and no money and not enough places to live and no place to go to have a decent think . . . you can't do it without making the time right for some godforsaken other kind of thing to be born! You can't hate everyone around you, and kick every beggar and nigger and *mestizo* shithead, you can't have cabbies stealing from you and taking tips they don't deserve, and then cursing you, you can't walk in the soot till your collar turns black, and your body stinks with the smell of flaking brick and decaying brains, you can't do it without calling up some kind of awful –'

He stopped.

His face bore the expression of a man who has just received brutal word of the death of a loved one. He suddenly lay down, rolled over, and turned off.

She lay beside him, trembling, trying desperately to remember where she had seen his face before.

He didn't call her again, after the night of the party. And when they met in the hall, he pointedly turned away, as though he had given her some obscure chance and she refused to take it. Beth thought she understood: though Ray Gleeson had not been her first affair, he had been the first to reject her so completely. The first to put her not only out of his bed and his life, but even out of his world. It was as though she were invisible, not even beneath contempt, simply not there.

She busied herself with other things.

She took on three new charting jobs for Guzman and a new group that had formed on Staten Island, of all places. She worked furiously and they gave her new assignments; they even paid her.

She tried to decorate the apartment with a less precise touch. Huge poster blowups of Merce Cunningham and Martha Graham replaced the Brueghel prints that had reminded her of the view looking down the hill towards Williams. The tiny balcony outside her window, the balcony she had steadfastly refused to stand upon since that night of the slaughter, the night of the fog with eyes, that balcony she swept and set about with little flower boxes in which she planted geraniums, petunias, dwarf zinnias, and other hardy perennials. Then, closing the window, she went to give herself, to involve herself in this city to which she had brought her ordered life.

And the city responded to her overtures:

Seeing off an old friend from Bennington, at Kennedy International, she stopped at the terminal coffee shop to have a sandwich. The counter — like a moat — surrounded a center service island that had huge advertising cubes rising above it on burnished poles. The cubes proclaimed the delights of Fun City. *New York Is a Summer Festival*, they said, and *Joseph Papp Presents Shakespeare in Central Park* and *Visit the Bronx Zoo* and *You'll Adore Our Contentious but Lovable Cabbies*. The food emerged from a window far down the service area and moved slowly on a conveyor belt through the hordes of screaming waitresses who slathered the counter with redolent washcloths. The lunchroom had all the charm and dignity of a steel-rolling mill, and approximately the same noise level. Beth ordered a cheeseburger that cost a dollar and a quarter, and a glass of milk.

When it came, it was cold, the cheese unmelted, and the patty of meat resembling nothing so much as a dirty scouring pad. The bun was cold and untoasted. There was no lettuce under the patty.

Beth managed to catch the waitress's eye. The girl approached with an annoyed look. 'Please toast the bun and may I have a piece of lettuce?' Beth said.

'We dun' do that,' the waitress said, turned half away as though she would walk in a moment.

'You don't do what?'

'We dun' toass the bun here.'

'Yes, but I *want* the bun toasted,' Beth said firmly.

'An' you got to pay for extra lettuce.'

'If I was asking for *extra* lettuce,' Beth said, getting annoyed. 'I would pay for it, but since there's *no* lettuce here I don't think I should be charged extra for the first piece.'

'We dun' do that.'

The waitress started to walk away. 'Hold it,' Beth said, raising her voice just enough so the assembly-line eaters on either side stared at her. 'You mean to tell me I have to pay a dollar and a quarter and I can't get a piece of lettuce or even get the bun toasted?'

'Ef you dun' like it . . .'

'Take it back.'

'You gotta pay for it, you order it.'

'I said take it back, I don't want the fucking thing!'

The waitress scratched it off the check. The milk cost 27¢ and tasted going-sour. It was the first time in her life that Beth had said *that* word aloud.

At the cashier's stand, Beth said to the sweating man with the felt-tip pens in his shirt pocket, 'Just out of curiosity, are you interested in complaints?'

'No!' he said, snarling, quite literally snarling. He did not look up as he punched out 73¢ and it came rolling down the chute.

The city responded to her overtures:

It was raining again. She was trying to cross Second Avenue, with the light. She stepped off the curb and a car came sliding through the red and splashed her. 'Hey!' she yelled.

'Eat shit, sister!' the driver yelled back, turning the corner.

Her boots, her legs and her overcoat were splattered with mud. She stood trembling on the curb.

The city responded to her overtures:

She emerged from the building at One Astor Place with her briefcase full of Laban charts; she was adjusting her rain scarf about her head. A well-dressed man with an attaché case thrust the handle of his umbrella up between her legs from the rear. She gasped and dropped her case.

The city responded and responded and responded.

Her overtures altered quickly.

The old drunk with the stippled cheeks extended his hand and mumbled words. She cursed him and walked on up Broadway past the beaver film houses.

She crossed against the lights on Park Avenue, making hackies slam their brakes to avoid hitting her; she used *that* word frequently now.

When she found herself having a drink with a man who had elbowed up beside her in the singles' bar, she felt faint and knew she should go home.

But Vermont was so far away.

Nights later. She had come home from the Lincoln Center ballet, and gone straight to bed. Lying half-asleep in her bedroom, she heard an alien sound. One room away, in the living room, in the dark, there was a sound. She slipped out of bed and went to the door between the rooms. She fumbled silently for the switch on the lamp just inside the living room, and found it and clicked it on. A black man in a leather car coat was trying to get *out* of the apartment. In that first flash of light filling the room she noticed the television set beside him on the floor as he struggled with the door, she noticed the police lock and bar had been broken in a new and clever manner *New York Magazine* had not yet reported in a feature article on apartment ripoffs, she noticed that he had got his feet tangled in the telephone cord that she had requested be extra-long so she could carry the instrument into the bathroom, I don't want to miss any business calls when the shower is running; she noticed all things in perspective and one thing with sharpest clarity: the expression on the burglar's face.

There was something familiar in that expression.

He almost had the door open, but now he closed it, and slipped the police lock. He took a step towards her.

Beth went back, into the darkened bedroom.

The city responded to her overtures.

She backed against the wall at the head of the bed. Her hand fumbled in the shadows for the telephone. His shape filled the doorway, light, all light behind him.

In silhouette it should have not been possible to tell, but somehow she knew he was wearing gloves and the only marks he would leave would be deep bruises, very blue, almost black, with the tinge under them of blood that had been stopped in its course.

He came for her, arms hanging casually at his sides. She tried to climb over the bed, and he grabbed her from behind, ripping her nightgown. Then he had a hand around her neck and he pulled her backward. She fell off the bed, landed at his feet and his hold was broken. She scuttled across the floor and for a moment she had the respite to feel terror. She was going to die, and she was frightened.

He trapped her in the corner between the closet and the bureau and kicked her. His foot caught her in the thigh as she folded tighter, smaller, drawing her legs up. She was cold.

Then he reached down with both hands and pulled her erect by her hair. He slammed her head against the wall. Everything slid up in her sight as though running off the edge of the world. He slammed her head against the wall again, and she felt something go soft over her right ear.

When he tried to slam her a third time she reached out blindly for his face and ripped down with her nails. He howled in pain and she hurled herself forward, arm wrapping themselves around his waist. He stumbled backwards and in a tangle of thrashing arms and legs they fell out onto the little balcony.

Beth landed on the bottom, feeling the window boxes jammed up against her spine and legs. She fought to get to her feet, and her nails hooked into his shirt under the open jacket, ripping. Then she was on her feet again and they struggled silently.

He whirled her around, bent her backwards across the wrought-iron railing. Her face was turned outward. *They were standing in their windows, watching.*

Through the fog she could see them watching. Through the fog she recognized their expressions. Through the fog she heard them breathing in unison, bellows breathing of expectation and wonder. Through the fog.

And the black man punched her in the throat. She gagged and started to black out and could not draw air into her lungs. Back, back, he bent her further back and she was looking up, straight up, towards the ninth floor and higher . . .

Up there: eyes.

The words Ray Gleeson had said in a moment filled with what he had become, with the utter hopelessness and finality of the choice the city had forced on him, the words came back. *You can't live in this city and survive unless you have protection . . . you can't live this way, like rats driven mad, without making the time right for some god-forsaken other kind of thing to be born . . . you can't do it without calling up some kind of awful . . .*

God! A new God, an ancient God come again with the eyes and hunger of a child, a deranged blood God of fog and street violence. A God who needed worshippers and offered the choices of death as a victim or life as an eternal witness to the deaths of *other* chosen victims. A God to fit the times, a God of streets and people.

She tried to shriek, to appeal to Ray, to the director in the bedroom window of his ninth-floor apartment with his long-legged Philadelphia model beside him and his fingers inside her as they worshipped in their holiest of ways, to the others who had been at the party that had been Ray's offer of a chance to join their congregation. She wanted to be saved from having to make that choice.

But the black man had punched her in the throat, and now his hands were on her, one on her chest, the other in her face, the smell of leather filling her where the nausea could not. And she understood Ray had *cared*, had wanted her to take the chance offered; but she had come from a world of little white dormitories and Vermont countryside; it was not a real world. *This* was the real world and up there was the God who ruled this world, and she had rejected him, had said no to one of his priests and servitors. *Save me! Don't make me do it!*

She knew she had to call out, to make appeal, to try and win the approbation of that God. *I can't . . . save me!*

She struggled and made terrible little mewing sounds trying to summon the words to cry out, and suddenly she crossed a line, and screamed up into the echoing courtyard with a voice Leona Ciarelli had never known enough to use.

'Him! Take him! Not me! I'm yours, I love you, I'm yours! Take him, not me, please not me, take him, take him, I'm yours!'

And the black man was suddenly lifted away, wrenched off her, and off the balcony, whirled straight up into the fog-thick air in the courtyard, as Beth sank to her knees on the ruined flower boxes.

She was half conscious, and could not be sure she saw it just that way, but up he went, end over end, whirling and spinning like a charred leaf.

And the form took firmer shape. Enormous paws with claws and shapes that no animal she had ever seen had ever possessed, and the burglar, black, poor, terrified, whimpering like a whipped dog, was stripped of his flesh. His body was opened with a thin incision, and there was a rush as all the blood poured from him like a sudden cloudburst, and yet he was still alive, twitching with the involuntary horror of a frog's leg shocked with an electric current. Twitched, and twitched again as he was torn piece by piece to shreds. Pieces of flesh and bone and half a face with an eye blinking furiously, cascaded down past Beth, and hit the cement below with sodden thuds. And still he was alive, as his organs were squeezed and musculature and bile and shit and skin were rubbed, sandpapered together and let fall. It went on and on, as the death of Leona Ciarelli had gone on and on, and she understood with the blood-knowledge of survivors *at any cost* that the reason the witnesses to the death of Leona Ciarelli had done nothing was not that they had been frozen with horror, that they didn't want to get involved, or that they were inured to death by years of television slaughter.

They were worshippers at a black mass the city had demanded be staged; not once, but a thousand times a day in this insane asylum of steel and stone.

Now she was on her feet, standing half-naked in her ripped nightgown, her hands tightening on the wrought-iron railing, begging to see more, to drink deeper.

Now she was one of them, as the pieces of the night's sacrifice fell past her, bleeding and screaming.

Tomorrow the police would come again, and they would question her, and she would say how terrible it had been, that burglar, and how she had fought, afraid he would rape her and kill her, and how he had fallen, and she had no idea how he had been so hideously mangled and ripped apart, but a seven-storey fall, after all . . .

Tomorrow she would not have to worry about walking in the streets, because no harm could come to her. Tomorrow she could even remove the police lock. Nothing in the city could do her any further evil, because she had made the only choice. She was now a dweller in the city, now wholly and richly a part of it. Now she was taken to the bosom of her God.

She felt Ray beside her, standing beside her, holding her, protecting her, his hand on her naked backside, and she watched the fog swirl up and fill the courtyard, fill the city, fill her eyes and her soul and her heart with its power. As Ray's naked body pressed tightly inside her, she drank deeply of the night, knowing whatever voices she heard from this moment forward, they would be the voices not of whipped dogs, but those of strong, meat-eating beasts.

At last she was unafraid, and it was so good, so very good *not* to be afraid.

When inward life dries up, when feeling decreases and apathy increases, when one cannot effect or even genuinely touch another person, violence flares up as a daimonic necessity for contact, a mad drive forcing touch in the most direct way possible.
— *Rollo May,*
LOVE AND WILL

EPILOGUE

JOHN DICKSON CARR

The Black Cabinet

JOHN DICKSON CARR *(1906 – 77), creator of the redoubtable Dr Fell and expert on locked-room mysteries, contributes the tail-piece, a historical extravaganza that gives the book its name and is based on . . . well, that is revealed in the very last line, and we'll say only that it brings the collection neatly full-circle.*

As the Emperor's closed carriage swung towards the private entrance to the Opera, with the gentlemen's carriages ahead and the white horse of the Imperial Guard clattering behind, three bombs were thrown from the direction of the Opera steps.

And, only a minute before, a small nine-year-old girl in the crowd had been almost mutinous.

She was too grown-up, Nina thought, to be lifted up in *maman*'s arms as though she were four years old or even six. True, the fusty-smelling coats and tall hats of the men, even the bonnets and crinolines of the women, made so high a black hedge that Nina could see little except the gas jets illuminating the facade of the Opera and the bright lamps of the Parisian street. But it was warm down here: warm, at least, for a night in mid January of 1858.

Then up Nina went, on the arm of *maman*. Already they could hear in the distance the measured applause — the slow, steady clap-clap of hands, as at a play — and a ragged cheer as the procession approached.

But Nina did not even know what it was, or why they were here.

'Mother, I . . .' she began in French.

Manan's bonnet, lined with ruffles, was so long-sided that Nina could not see her mother's face until it was turned around. Then *maman*'s dark Italian eyes, always so kindly, took on a glassy bulging blare of hatred and triumph as she pressed her lips against Nina's long curls; bright brown curls, like the hair of Nina's American father.

'Look well!' whispered the handsome Signora Maddelena Bennett, in the Italian language. 'At last you will see the death of the devil.'

And Nina understood. She too hated, as she had been taught to hate, without knowing why. She had been schooled not to sob or tremble. Yet tears welled up in her eyes, because Nina was sick with fear. In one of those carriages must be Napoleon the Third, Emperor of the French.

Clop-clop, clop-clop moved the horses; slowly, but ever nearer the carpet of white sand spread in front and at the side of the Opera. Then, suddenly, Signora Bennett's whole expression changed. She had never dreamed that the murderers — Orsini and his conspirators — would hold their hands so long, or might throw bombs from the very side or the steps of the Opera itself.

'No!' she shrieked aloud.

Holding the child closely, Signora Bennett flung the side of her pelisse over Nina's head and dropped down into the half-frozen mud among the spectators. Just as she fell, a black object flew over the heads of the crowd, high-sailing against the gas lamps.

Through a crack between the fur pelisse and *maman*'s fashionable deep-bosomed gown with the steel buttons, Nina saw the edge of a white flash. Though they were protected, the first explosion seemed to crush rather than crash, driving steel needles through her eardrums. There were two more explosions, at seconds' intervals. But the street went dark at the first crash, blinding the gas lamps, setting the air a-sing with flying glass from lamps or windows. Nina's scream was lost amid other screams.

Afterwards the small girl felt nothing.

A curtain of nightmare, now called shock, wrapped soothingly round Nina's mind and nerves. She looked without surprise, or with very little surprise, at anything she saw. Though her mother, also unhurt, still crouched and breathed heavily, Nina stood up on shaky legs.

Most of the black hedge of tall shiny hats had fallen away. It lay motionless, or tried to crawl across bloodied white sand. And, as Nina turned sideways, she saw the Emperor's state coach near the foot of the steps.

'Sire! Sire!' she heard military voices shouting, amid other shouts. And, above it, the bellow of a military policeman: 'Sire!'

The great closed carriage was at a standstill. Stabbed with blast and steel splinters and needles of glass, it had toppled partly towards Nina but remained intact except for its windows. Also, by some miracle, one great gold-bound carriage lantern was still burning on this side.

Before the officers of the Emperor's bodyguard could reach the handle of the coach door, the door opened. There emerged a stately-looking man, plump rather than stout, who jumped to the coach step and thence to the ground.

The carriage lamp gleamed on gold epaulets against a blue coat, and white trousers. His (apparently) steady hand was just putting back on his head the overdecorated cocked hat he wore fore-and-aft. Nina knew, if only from pictures, that he was the Emperor. Though he might be sallow-faced and growing puffy under the eyes, yet between his heavy black moustaches and fox-brush of imperial beard there appeared the edge of a cool smile.

'He is not hurt, the Emperor! Louis Napoleon is unhurt!'

'Long live the Emperor!'

Gravely the sallow-faced man handed down from the carriage a pretty, bad-tempered lady, her countenance as white as her long pearl ear-rings; she must be the Empress Eugénie. Officers, their uniform coats torn and their faces slashed, whipped out sabres in salute.

'Long live the Empress!'

'And the Emperor! And the Emperor!'

A thick, low rattle of drums ran urgently along the line. Foot-soldiers, dark silhouettes, flowed across and stood up at present-arms, so that the Emperor might not see fallen men with half faces or women carrying bomb splinters where they might have carried children. Around that wrecked carriage, with its two dead horses, lay one hundred and fifty persons, dead or wounded.

The Emperor smiled broadly, concealing agitation.

For the first time genuine hatred, a hatred of what she saw for herself, entered into Nina Bennett and never left her. It made her small body squirm, choking back her voice. It may have been due partly to the teaching of her mother's friends of Young Italy, of the *Carbonari* who derisively called Napoleon the Third 'the sick parrot' when they did not call him the devil. But now it was Nina's own hatred.

She could not have explained what had happened, even now. Though she had heard something of bombs, she did not even think of bombs — or of the men who had thrown them. Nina felt only that a white lightning bolt had struck down beside her, hurting, *hurting* these people and perhaps even making them die as her own father had died a year ago in Naples.

Yet the yellow-faced Emperor, with his black moustaches and imperial, had taken no scathe. He stood there and (to Nina) smiled hatefully. He had caused this. It was his fault. His!

Instinctively, amid the reek and the drum-beating, Nina cried out in English, the language her father had taught her, and which she spoke far better than French or even Italian.

'Sick parrot!' the small lungs screeched, the words lost. 'Devil! Usurper!'

And then her mother enfolded her, feeling over her for wounds and whispering furiously.

'Be silent, my child! Not another word, I tell thee!'

Gathering up Nina under her fur pelisse, and adding indignity to hysteria, *maman* fought and butted her way out of the crowd with such fury that suspicious eyes turned. Up in front of them loomed a military policeman, his immense cocked hat worn sideways.

'The child!' cried Signora Bennett, clutching Nina with true stage effect, and tragically raised dark eyes to a dark muffled sky. 'The child,' she lied, 'is injured!'

'Pass, madame,' gruffly, 'Regret.'

Though the distance was not great, it took them almost an hour in the crowds to reach their fine furnished lodgings in the rue de Rivoli. There waited Aunt Maria, also Italian and *maman*'s maid-companion, fiercely twisting the point of a knife into a rosewood table as she awaited news. Afterwards Nina could remember little except a bumping of portmanteaux and a horrible seasickness.

For Signora Bennett, Nina, and Aunt Maria left Paris next day. They had long been safe in England when two of the bomb-assassins — Orsini and Pieri — dropped on the plank and looked out through the everlasting window of the guillotine.

And that had been just over ten years ago.

So reflected Miss Nina Bennett, at the very mature age of nineteen, on the warm evening early in July, which was the third evening after her return to Paris. Nobody could have denied that she was beautiful. But all those years in England had made her even more reserved than the English, with a horror of elaborate gestures like those of her late mother.

Though the sky was still bright over the place de la Concorde, Nina Bennett had told Aunt Maria to close the heavy striped curtains on the windows. Aunt Maria was very fat now. She had a faint moustache of vertical hairs, like a tiny portcullis between nose and mouth. As she waddled over to scrape shut the curtains and waddled back to her chair, wrath exuded from her like a bad perfume.

Nina sat at the dressing-table before a mirror edged in gold leaf.

Two gas jets, one in the wall on either side of the mirror, set up yellow flames in flattish glass dishes. They shone on Nina's pink-and-white complexion, her dark-blue eyes, her bright brown hair parted in the middle and drawn across the ears to a soft, heavy pad along the nape of the neck. The evening gown of that year was cut just an inch and a half below each shoulder, curving down in lace across the breast; and Nina's gown was so dark a red that it seemed black except when the gaslight rippled or flashed.

Yet her intense composure gave Nina's beauty a chilly quality like marble. She sat motionless, unsmiling, her arms stretched out and hands lightly crossed on the dressing-table.

'No,' she thought, 'I am not unattractive.' The thought, or so she imagined, gave her neither pleasure nor displeasure.

At her left on the dressing-table stood a great bouquet of yellow roses in a glass vase of water. Nina Bennett had bought them herself, as a part of her plan of death. In the dressing-table drawer lay the weapon of death.

'I have no heroics,' she thought, looking at the reflection of her blue eyes. 'I do not think of myself as Joan of Arc or Charlotte Corday. Though I may be insane, I do not believe so. But I will kill this puffball Emperor, who still mysteriously reigns over the French. I will kill him. I will kill him.'

Her intensity was so great that she breathed faster, and faint colour tinged her pink-and-white face. Suddenly, out of the darkling background in the mirror, she saw fat Aunt Maria, with grey-streaked hair and fishbone moustache, writhing and flapping with anger.

Aunt Maria's hoarse, harsh voice spoke in Italian.

'Now I wonder,' sneered Aunt Maria, 'why you must close the curtains, and dare not look on the beauty of Paris.'

Nina hesitated before she replied, moistening her lips. Despite her flawless English speech and her tolerable French, she had half-forgotten her mother's Italian and must grope for it.

'You are at liberty,' she said, 'to wonder what you like.'

Again Aunt Maria slapped the chair-arms and writhed, almost in tears. Never in her life could Nina believe that these gesticulations were real, as they were, and not mere theatricalism. Intensely she disliked them.

'Out there,' panted Aunt Maria, 'is the city of light, the city of pleasure. And who made it so? It was your loathed Louis Napoleon and Baron Haussmann, planning their wide boulevards and their lamps and greenery. If we now have the Wood of Boulogne, it is because Louis Napoleon loves trees.'

Nina raised her brown eyebrows so slightly that they hardly seemed to move.

'Do you tell *me*,' she asked, 'the history of the sick parrot?'

The gas jets whistled thinly, in a shadowy room with black satin wall panels figured in gold. Gracefully, with a studied grace, Nina Bennett rose from the dressing-table, and turned around. The monstrous crinolines of the past decade had dwindled into smaller, more manageable hoop-skirts which rustled with petticoats at each step. Glints of crimson darted along Nina's dark, close-fitting gown.

'Have you forgotten, Maria?' she asked, in a passionately repressed voice. 'In these rooms, these very rooms, where we lived ten years ago? How you took a great knife, and stabbed a dozen times into the top of a rosewood table, when you heard Orsini had failed? Can you deny it?'

'Ah, blood of the Madonna!'

'Can you deny it?'

'I was younger; I was foolish!' The harsh voice rose in pleading. 'See, now! This Emperor, in his youth, worshipped the memory of his uncle, the war-lord, the first Napoleon. The first Napoleon they exiled . . .'

'Yes,' agreed Nina, 'and kings crept out again to feel the sun.'

Aunt Maria was galvanised. 'That is a noble line; that is a heart-shaking line!'

'It is the late Mrs Browning's. A trifle. No matter.'

'Well! This young man — yes, yes, it is the way of all young men! — was also a republican; a lover of liberty; a member of the *Carbonari* itself. Once he promised us a united Italy. But he wavered, and more than a few of us tried to kill him. He wavers always! I say it! But has he not done much in these past few years to redeem his promise? Body of Bacchus! Has he not!'

Though Nina was not tall, she stood high above Maria in the chair and looked down at her indifferently. Nina's white shoulders rose very slightly in the dark-red gown.

'Ah, God, your mother has taught you well!' cried Aunt Maria. 'Too well!' She hesitated. 'And yet when she died six months ago, it did not seem to me that you were much affected.'

'I did not weep or tear my hair, if that is what you mean.'

'Unnatural! Pah, I spit! What do you care for Italy?'

'A little, perhaps. But I am an American, as was my father before me.'

'So I have heard you say.'

'And so I mean!' Nina drew a deep breath; the gown seemed to be constricting her heart as well as her flesh. 'My father was of what they call New England, in the state of Massachusetts. His money, though my mother sneered, has kept us above poverty all these years.' Her tone changed. 'Poor Maria; do the closed curtains stifle you?'

Whereupon Nina, with the same grace in managing her hoop-skirt, went to the left-hand window and threw back the curtains. The fustiness of the room, the fustiness of the curtains, for some reason reminded her of men's greatcoats; Nina shivered without knowing why. Then she opened the curtains of the other window.

Outside, to the little wrought-iron balcony above the rue de Rivoli, was fastened a flagstaff at an oblique angle. From it floated the beloved flag, the flag of the Union, the stars and stripes little more than three years triumphant in bitter war.

'Now what patriotism,' jeered Aunt Maria, 'for a country you have never seen!'

'It is more than that,' said Nina, wanting to laugh. 'In a sense it protects us. Have you not heard . . .?'

'Speak!'

'This is our Day of Independence, the Fourth of July.'

'Mad! Mad! Mad!'

'I think not. His Majesty Napoleon the Third made a futile, stupid attempt to establish an empire in Mexico. That did not please the States of America.' Nina lifted her exquisite hands and dropped them. 'But the traditional friendship of France and America has been renewed. This evening, less than an hour from now, your hypocritical Emperor drives in state to the Opera, for a French-American ball, with ceremonies. As his carriage crosses the place de la Concorde into the rue Royale . . .'

Aunt Maria heaved her laundry-bag shape up out of the chair.

'Blood of the Madonna!' she screamed. 'You do not mean this madwoman's gamble for tonight?'

'Oh, but I do.' And for the first time Nina Bennett smiled.

There was silence, while Nina stood with her back to the window, with the soft and magical sky glow competing with these harsh-singing gaslights. And Nina was uneasy.

She had expected Aunt Maria to stamp, to howl, even possibly to shout from the window for help. But the ageing woman only fell back into the chair, not speaking. Tears flowed out of her eyes, tears running down grotesquely past her nose, and the hair-spikes of her moustache. Nina Bennett spoke sharply.

'Come, Aunt Maria. This is ridiculous! Why should you weep?'

'Because you are beautiful,' Aunt Maria said simply.

There was silence.

'Well! I — I thank you, Maria. Still . . .!'

'Oh, your plan is good.' Aunt Maria turned her streaming eyes towards the great bouquet of yellow roses on the dressing-table, and the drawer which held the weapon. 'No doubt you will kill him, my dear. Then you will go to the guillotine, in bare feet and with a black veil over your head, because to kill the Emperor is an act of parricide. You will have had no life, none! No laughter. No affection. No love of men.'

Nina's face had gone white. For some reason she retorted cruelly.

'And your own vast experience of love, dear Maria . . .?'

'That too is ridiculous, eh? Oho, that is comic; yes? This to you!' Aunt Maria made the gesture. 'For I have known love more than you think! And the good strong passion, and the heartache too. But *you* will not know it. You are poisoned; your veins are poisoned. If an honest lover bit your arm until the blood flowed, he would die. Ah, behold! You shrink in disgust like a cold Englishwoman!'

'No, good Maria. And Englishwomen are not cold, save perhaps in public. It is as stupid a legend as the legend that they are all fair-haired.'

'Listen!' blurted Maria, dabbing at her eyes. 'Do you know who poisoned you?'

'If you please, Maria . . .!'

'It was your own mother. Yes! Do you think she knew no man except your father? Body of Venus, she had enough lovers to fill a prison! I startled you? But, because she must dedicate you to her "cause" of murder, she would turn you against men. How long she spoke to you, when you were thirteen or fourteen, in the accursed great cold house in London! Have I not seen you rush out of the drawing-room, crimson-faced, and your sainted mother laughing secretly?'

'I — I have thought of love,' she said calmly. 'I would love well, perhaps, if I did not hate. And now, Maria, it is time to fetch my jewel box; and set out my hat and cloak.'

Aunt Maria paid no attention.

There was a wild shining of inspiration in her eyes, as though at last she had seen some way to turn this inflexible girl from a mad course. But the time was going, the time was going!

'Come, a test!' panted Aunt Maria. 'Are you in truth as poisoned as I said?'

'Did you hear my command, Maria?'

'No! Listen! You remember three nights ago, the evening of the first day we came to Paris? How we returned from our walk, and the young man met you in the courtyard? Well, I saw your eyes kindle!' Aunt Maria cackled with mirth. 'You an American? You are a Latin of the Latins! And this young man: was he French — or Italian?'

Nina Bennett grew rigid.

'You have strange fancies,' she said. 'I cannot remember this at all.'

But she did remember it. As Nina turned around briefly to look out of the long window, where a faint breeze rippled the vivid colours of the stars and stripes, that whole brief scene was re-created in every detail.

As the courtesy-aunt said, it had been at about this time on the evening of July second. Aunt Maria had marched beside Nina as they returned from their walk. Even in this modern age, the most emancipated American or English girl would not have gone through such tree-bewitched streets, full of summer's breath and mirrors a-wink cafés, without a formidable chaperone.

The house in which they had taken furnished lodgings was unlike most of those in the same street. It was of an older day, patterned after a nobleman's *hôtel*. Through a smaller door in high-arched wooden doors you passed through a cool tunnel smelling of old stone, with the *concierge*'s lodge on the right. Then you entered into a green courtyard; it had galleries built around on three sides, and stone balustrades carved with faces. An outside staircase led up to each gallery. In the middle of the green, scented turf was a dead fountain.

As Aunt Maria creaked up the staircase, Nina followed her. Vaguely Nina had noticed a young man standing a little distance away, smoking a cigar and leaning on a gold-headed stick. But she paid little attention. In both hands, if only for practice's sake, she carried a large bouquet of red roses in which was hidden a small but heavy object, and two fingers of her right hand held the chains of her reticule. Though strung-up and alert, Nina was very tired.

Perhaps that was why the accident happened. When she had gone six steps behind Aunt Maria, Nina's reticule — a heavy, flower-painted handbag — slipped through her fingers, bounced down the steps, and landed on the lowermost one.

'Ah, so-and-so!' exclaimed Aunt Maria, and wheeled around her moustache.

There was a flick in the air as the dark-complexioned young man flung away his cigar. He had suffered some injury to his left leg. But, so deft was his use of the stick, that he scarcely seemed to limp when he made haste. In an instant he was at the foot of the staircase.

The cane was laid down. With his left hand he swept off his high, glossy hair, and his right scooped up the reticule. His eyes strayed to Nina's ringless left hand.

'If you will permit me, mademoiselle . . .!' he said.

The man, whether French or Italian, had a fine resonant voice, fashioning each French syllable clearly. His dark hair, parted on one side, was so thick that it rose up on the other side of the parting. A heavy moustache followed the line of his delicate upper lip. His sombre dark clothes, though carelessly worn, were of fine quality.

Nina Bennett, who had turned around, looked down the stairs straight into his eyes. Nina, in a dress of dark purple taffeta and a boat-shaped hat with a flat plume, would have denied coldly that she was a romantic.

'But perhaps he is undeniably handsome,' she was thinking, and without oiliness or exaggeration. He had endured great suffering, by the whiteness of his face and the little grey in his hair. And yet his mockery of eye, as though he knew too much of women . . .!

Abruptly Nina straightened up.

'I thank . . .' she began coldly; and then the worst happened.

Nina, still holding the bouquet of red roses, either by accident or nervousness, jerked her left wrist against the stair-balustrade. The roses seemed to spill apart. Out of their stems leaped a derringer, short of barrel but large of bore. It banged on the step, and clattered down to the lowermost one. Though it was loaded with wad, powder, and heavy ball, it did not explode; there was no percussion-cap on the firing-nipple.

Nina stood rigid with horror, like Aunt Maria. For a moment, in that shadowy green courtyard under the light of a pink sunset, it was as silent as though they stood in the Forest of Marly.

The young man looked strangely at the pistol, and suddenly jumped back as though he feared it might go still go off. Then he smiled. After a swift glance at the lodge of the *concierge*, he dropped the reticule on top of the derringer, concealing it. He picked up both, advanced up the stairs, and gravely handed the fallen objects to Nina.

'Permit me, mademoiselle, to return your reticule and your — your protection against footpads. If I might suggest . . .'

'I thank you, monsieur. But it is not necessary to suggest.'

'Alas, I have already done so,' he said, and again looked her in the eyes. His French voice both pointed the double meaning, yet smilingly robbed the words of offence. Pressing the brim of his hat against the black broadcloth over his heart, he bowed slightly. 'Until a re-meeting, mademoiselle!'

'Until a re-. . . .' said Nina, and stopped. She had not meant to speak at all.

Whirling around her skirts, the roses and pistol and reticule like a mortifying weight in her arms, Nina marched up the stairs after Aunt Maria.

And this was the brief scene which returned in every detail to Nina Bennett, in the dark old room with the gas jets, during the moment when she looked out of the long window over the rue de Rivoli. She had only to concentrate, and it was gone forever. But she felt the pressure of Aunt Maria's eyes, wet and crafty, boring into her back; and anger rose again.

Turning around, Nina took four steps and stood over Aunt Maria in the chair.

'Why do you remind me of this?' Nina asked.

'Oh, then we *were* smitten!'

'Hardly.' The voice was dry. But when Nina opened her blue eyes wide, Maria shrank back because they were maniacal and terrifying. 'Do you imagine that some sordid affair of love would keep me back from the only cause I have for living?'

'This "cause"!' sneered Aunt Maria. 'I tell you, it is a cold warming-pan for a long night, instead of a husband. Away with it! With your looks and your money: body of Bacchus, you might wed any man you chose.' Abruptly, amid her tears, the fat woman began to cackle again with laughter. 'But not the young Italian of the courtyard, poor Nina! No, no! Not that one!'

'And why not?' demanded Nina.

'Listen, my child. Pay heed to an old conspirator like me! For I have seen them all. I know the ingratiating air, the cringing approach, the mark of the almost-gentleman.'

'How dare you!' Nina amazed herself by crying out. Then she controlled her voice. 'You will allow me, please, to pass my own judgement on a gentleman.'

'Oh, then we were not smitten! Oh, no!' cackled Aunt Maria. Then her laughter died. 'Shall I tell you what this young man really is?'

'Well?'

'He is what the French call a *mouchard*. A police spy.'

'You lie!' A pause. 'In any event,' Nina added casually, 'it is of no importance. Since you disobey my order to fetch my hat and cloak and jewel box . . .'

'No, no, I will find them!' said Aunt Maria, and surged up out of the chair.

On creaking slippers she wheezed across to an immense dark wardrobe beside the door and opposite the windows. Opening one door of the wardrobe, she plucked out a waist-length cape of rich material in stripes of silver and wine-red.

'Well!' snorted Aunt Maria, examining the cape and giving no sign of furious thought. 'You will go to kill the Emperor. I have promised not to interfere; good, I keep my promise! But it will be sad for you, hot-blood, when they arrest you — as they will, mark it! — before you have fired the shot.'

Nina's gaze had gone to the grandfather clock, near the alcove which housed the big curtained bed. The time — the time was running out. True, she still had many minutes. But there would be a crowd. She must be in place, the exact spot she had chosen, long before the Imperial procession went past.

Now the meaning of Maria's words stabbed into her brain for the first time.

'What did you say, fuss-budget?'

'Enough,' muttered the fat woman darkly. 'I said enough!'

'Come, good Maria. Is this another of your childish tricks to divert me?'

'Childish!' cried Aunt Maria, now in a real temper. 'Was I your mother's companion for twenty years, or was I not? Do I know every dog's-tail of plotting, or do I not?'

'Of old and clumsy plotting, yes. But my device . . .'

'Faugh!' snorted Aunt Maria, past patience. 'How do you think Louis Napoleon keeps so quiet his bright city, his toy? Ask the Prefect of Police, M. Pietri — yes, I said Pietri, not Pieri — but above all ask M. Lagrange, the chief of the political police! They buy more spies than the sandgrains at Dieppe! By my immortal soul, Lagrange will stir up a riot for the very joy of showing how quickly he can suppress it!'

Aunt Maria shook the cape. With her own version of a haughty shrug, she reached again into the wardrobe and drew out a very wide-brimmed velvet hat of the same dark red as Nina's gown.

'You don't believe an old woman, eh?' she taunted. 'Good! For

I have finished with you. But this I swear on the Cross: you have been betrayed.'

'Lies and lies and lies! Betrayed by whom?'

'Why, by your young man down in the courtyard.'

She was going dangerously far, to judge by Nina's eyes and breathing.

'Little stupid!' she continued to taunt. 'Did you not observe how he started and jumped, when the pistol fell at his feet? He thought there might be a bullet for *him*. Did you not see how he looked with quickness towards the lodge of the *concierge*, who was watching? The *concierge*, who feeds the police with a spoon! You a plotter, when you gave your true name of Bennett? Pah! The name of your mother is a very passport to the Prefecture!'

Now Aunt Maria did not actually believe one word of what she had said about the young man. In fact, three nights ago she had scarcely noticed him except as a possible moustache-twisting sinner of the boulevards. But these ideas foamed into her brain; she could not stop; she must speak faster and faster.

For it seemed to her that there was a hesitation in Nina's eyes . . .

Nina moved slowly to the side of the dressing-table, still looking steadily at the other woman. Gaslight burnished the wings of Nina's soft brown hair. With her left hand she pulled open the drawer of the dressing-table, in which the derringer pistol lay fully loaded, and with a percussion-cap resting under the light pressure of its hammer.

'What do you do?' Aunt Maria screamed out. Then, abruptly glancing at the door and holding up cape and hat as though to call for silence, she added: 'Listen!'

Outside the door, the only door in the room, was a drawing-room with a polished hardwood floor unmuffled by any carpet. There was a sound. Both women heard the soft thump of the cane as the visitor slid forward a lame leg; then silence; then again the bump of the cane. Someone was slowly but steadily approaching the bedroom door. Both women knew who it was.

'My God!' thought the staggered Aunt Maria. 'He really *is* a *mouchard* after all!'

A fist, not loudly, but firmly and with authority, knocked at the bedroom door.

Aunt Maria, terrified, backed away towards the bed alcove and held up cape and hat as though they might shield her.

If there had ever been any uncertainty in Nina's face, it was gone now. Her cold movements were swift but unhurried. From the vase she whipped the bouquet of yellow roses, squeezing the water from the stems and wrapping them in heavy tissue paper from the drawer. Gripping the stems in her left hand, she plucked out the pistol. There was a soft click as she drew back the hammer. She made an opening in the roses, hiding the derringer so that nothing should catch in the hammer when she snatched it out.

They would still be time to reload if she must dispose of an intruder first.

'Enter!' Nina calmly called in French. It was the language they spoke afterwards.

Their visitor, the man of the courtyard, came in and closed the door behind him. He was in full evening-dress, partly covered by his ankle-length black cloak, which yet showed his white frilled shirtfront and a carelessly tied stock. In one white-gloved hand he held his hat, in the other his gold-headed stick.

Again Nina noted the delicacy of his white, handsome face, in contrast to the heavy, dark hair and moustache. Even his figure was somewhat slight, though well-made. 'For this intrusion,' he said in his fine voice, 'I deeply apologise to mademoiselle; and, understood,' bowing towards Aunt Maria, 'to madame.'

'Your best apology lies behind you.' She nodded towards the door.

'Unfortunately, no.' The stranger, at leisure, put down his hat and stick on a table at the left of the door. His dark eyes, with that odd life-in-death quality, grew strong with a fierce sincerity; and so did his voice. 'For I presume to have an interest in you, mademoiselle.'

'Who are you? What do you want?'

The stranger leaned his back against the door, seeming to lounge rather than lean, in a devil-may-care swagger which to Nina seemed vaguely familiar.

'Let us say that I am detective Lecoq, in the admirable police-romances of M. Gaboriau. Lecoq is a real person, remember, as was the character D'Artagnan. Well! I am Lecoq.'

Nina breathed a little faster. Her finger tightened round the trigger of the pistol.

'How did you enter by a locked front door?'

'Believe me, I have passed through more difficult doors than that. Stop!' His white-gloved hand went up to forestall her, and he smiled. 'Let us suppose (I say merely let us suppose!) that Mademoiselle Nina Bennett had intent to kill the Emperor of the French. I who speak to you, I also live in this house. I can put questions to a *concierge*.'

'Did I not tell you?' screamed Aunt Maria, hiding her face behind cape and hat.

Neither of them looked at her.

'To any reader of the French journals, the name of your mother is well known. The nationality of your father,' and he nodded towards the flag outside the window, his nostrils thin and bitter, 'you too obviously display. However! If it be your intent to kill the Emperor, where would you go? Assuredly not far from here, or you would have been gone now.'

('If you must kill this sly one here, Aunt Maria thought wildly, 'kill him now! Shoot!')

'I think,' continued the stranger, 'you have chosen the corner of the rue de Royale and the rue de Rivoli. Every journal in Paris will have told you, with exactness, the route and time of the procession. It is summer; there will be an open carriage, low-built. The Emperor, a fact well known, sits always on the right-hand side facing forward, the Empress on the left.

'How lovely . . .' His strong voice shook; he checked himself. 'How innocent you will look, in your finery and jewels, chattering English and deliberately bad French, on the kerbstone! The military, even the military police, will only smile when you walk out slowly towards the slow-moving carriage, and speak English as you offer — is it not so? — the bouquet of roses to the Empress Eugénie of Montijo.'

('I was mad, I was mad!' mentally moaned Aunt Maria. 'Let him take the damned pistol from her now!')

'Holding the bouquet in your left hand,' he went on quietly, 'you must lean partly across His Majesty. With your right hand you will take out an old-style single-shot pistol, and fire it at the Emperor's head so closely that you cannot miss. Have I, M. Lecoq, correctly deduced your plan?'

Nina Bennett cast a swift glance at the clock.

Time, time, time! A while ago, when she had looked out of the window, far up to the right there had been a red sky over Neuilly beyond the top of the Champs Élysées. Now the whole sky was tinged with pink amid white and pale blue. It brightened the gaslights in that black-silk-panelled room, which might have been a symbol of espionage since the days of Savary and Napoleon the First.

'Are you the only one,' Nina asked levelly, 'who knows of this — plan?'

'The only one, mademoiselle.'

With a steady hand Nina took the derringer from among the roses, moving aside the yellow bouquet. It is a sober fact that the young man did not even notice it.

'And now,' he said in that hypnotic voice, 'I must tell you of my interest in you. It is very easy.' He straightened up, his face whiter, and clenched his gloved fists. 'You are Venus in the body of Diana; you are Galatea not yet kissed to true life. You are — I will not say the most beautiful woman I have ever met — but the most maddening and stimulating.' Cynicism showed in his eyes. 'And I have known so many women.'

'How modest you are!' Nina cried furiously.

'I state a fact. But I tell you one of the reasons, my love, why I will not permit you to go from this room for at least half an hour.'

Again Nina started, almost dropping the pistol.

From the street below, and from the open spaces beyond, there were cries and shouts. She heard the confused running of feet, seeming to come from every direction at once, which can conjure up a Paris crowd in one finger-snap. Very faintly, in the distance, she also heard the slow clop-clop of many horses in procession.

According to every newspaper, the procession to the Opera would be headed by the Imperial Band. The instruments of the band were clear rather than brassy; already they had begun with the swinging tune '*Partant pour la Syrie*', which was the official song of Napoleon the Third.

> Setting out for Syria
> Young and brave Dunois . . .

There was still time. Nina Bennett's hand was as steady as a statue's.

'You call yourself a detective, M. Lecoq. But you are only a police spy. Now stand away from that door!'

'No, my dear,' smiled the other, and folded his arms lazily.

'I will count to three . . .'

'Count to five thousand; I would hear your voice. What matter if you kill me? Most people,' and his dark eyes seemed to wander out to the boulevards, 'think me already dead. Put your hand in mine; let fools flourish pistols or knives.'

'One!' said Nina, and thought she meant it.

The clip-clop of the procession, though still not loud, was drawing nearer. What sent a shiver through Nina's body was the tune into which the band changed, in honour of the French-American ball at the Opera. There were no words. There were only dreams and memories. Slow, sombre, the great battle-hymn, rolled out.

Mine eyes have seen the glory of the coming of the Lord, He is trampling out the vintage where the grapes of wrath are stored . . .

'In a moment,' continued the visitor, unhearing, 'I will come and take that pistol from you. It does not become you. But first hear what I would have to say.' His tone changed fiercely. 'This political assassination is more than wrong. It changes nothing. It is the act of an idiot. If I could make you understand . . .'

Abruptly he paused.

He, too, had heard the music, clear in the hush of evening. His face darkened. Had Aunt Maria been watching, she would have seen in his eyes the same maniacal glitter as in those of Nina Bennett. And he spoke the only words which could have ended his life.

'By God!' he snarled. 'You might have been a human being, without your mother and your damned Yankee father!'

Nina pulled the trigger, firing straight for his heart at less than ten feet's distance. The percussion-cap flared into the bang of the explosion, amid heavy smoke. The stranger flung back against the door, still stood upright and emerged through smoke.

She had missed the heart. But the pistol-ball, smashing ribs on the right side of the chest, had torn open his right lung. And Nina knew that never, never in her life, could she have fired at the Emperor unless he had first uttered some maddening insult.

'I thank you, my dear,' gravely said the stranger, pressing his reddening fingers to his chest, and white-faced at his own choked breathing. 'Now be quick! Put that derringer into my hand; and I shall have time to say I did it myself.'

Then another realisation struck Nina.

'You've been speaking in English!' she cried in that language. 'Ever since you said "damned Yankee". Are you English?'

'I am an American, my dear,' he answered, drawing himself up and swallowing blood. 'And at least no one can call me a police spy. My name,' he added casually, 'is John Wilkes Booth.'

Notes and Acknowledgements

This collection owes a debt to James Sandoe's *Murder: Plain and Fanciful* (details below), which contains an invaluable listing of tales and plays based on real crimes from Poe's 'The Mystery of Marie Roget' (too long and too familiar for inclusion here) up to the 1940s.

'The Trailor Murder Mystery' by Abraham Lincoln, from *The Whig* (Quincey, Illinois: April 15, 1846).

'J. Habakuk Jephson's Statement' by Arthur Conan Doyle, first published in *The Cornhill Magazine* (London: January, 1884).

'The Fall River Axe Murders' by Angela Carter, from *Black Venus* (first published by Chatto & Windus, the Hogarth Press; Picador edition published 1986 by Pan Books Ltd); copyright © 1984 by Angela Carter.

'A Retrieved Information' by O. Henry, first published 1903.

'The Gioconda Smile' by Aldous Huxley, from *Mortal Coils* London: Chatto & Windus, 1922); copyright © 1922 by Aldous Huxley; reprinted by permission of the publishers.

'They Bite' by Anthony Boucher, from *The Compleat Weerewolf*, reprinted by permission of Curtis Brown, NY; copyright © 1943 by Anthony Boucher, renewed 1971.

'The Greeting' by Sir Osbert Sitwell, from *Triple Fugue* (1924); copyright © 1924 by Sir Osbert Sitwell; reprinted by permission of William Morris Agency, Inc.

'Milady Bigamy' by Lillian de la Torre, first published in *Ellery Queen's Mystery Magazine*; collected in *The Return of Dr. Sam: Johnson, Detector*; copyright © 1975 by Lillian de la Torre.

'The Bathroom' by Peter Lovesey, first published in *Winter's Crimes 5*; collected in *Butchers, and Other Stories of Crime* (London: Macmillan, 1985); copyright © 1973 by Peter Lovesey, reprinted by permission of the author and Curtis Brown/John Farquharson Ltd.

'The Crocodile Dressing-Case' by Roy Vickers, from *Ellery Queen's*

Mystery Magazine; copyright © 1953 by Roy Vickers; reprinted by permission of John Cushman Associates Ltd.

'The Wrong Jar' by Anthony Berkeley; copyright © 1929 By A. B. Cox; reprinted by permission of the Society of Authors.

'Homecoming' by Miriam Allen de Ford, from James Sandoe (ed.): *Murder: Plain and Fanciful* (New York: Sheridan House, 1948); copyright © 1935 by Miriam Allen de Ford.

'The Whimper of Whipped Dogs' by Harlan Ellison, first published in Thomas M. Disch (ed.): *Bad Moon Rising*; copyright © 1973 by Harlan Ellison. Reprinted by arrangement with, and by permission of, the Author and the Author's agent, Richard Curtis Associates, Inc., New York. All rights reserved. This preferred text from *The Essential Ellison* (1987).

'The Black Cabinet' by John Dickson Carr, first published in Hugh Pentecost (ed.): *The Cream of the Crime*; copyright © 1962 by Clarice M. Carr; reprinted by permission of David Higham Associates Ltd.

While every effort has been made to trace authors and copyright-holders, in some cases this has proved impossible. The publishers would be glad to hear from any such parties so that omissions can be rectified in future editions of the book.